SCRIBE OF DESTINY

SCRIBE OF DESTINY

PAUL BARRETT
STEVE MURPHY

Charlotte, NC

FALSTAFF
BOOKS
WWW.FALSTAFFBOOKS.COM

1

As I stared at the words written on the cheap pulpreed parchment, I knew Fate was prepared to yank my prosaic life out of my control and leave me flopping like a fish on a ship's deck. I didn't know how, but I knew, sure as my name was Briar, son of Patch the Tailor, and my profession was second-rank scrivener for the Holy Church of Ubel the Benevolent. The change would be the kind that caused nightmares of epic proportions to those involved. Songs would be sung and sagas written about this history-altering event—the type of saga where the hero rarely survived.

I gazed upon my usually precise penmanship, spoiled by my shaking hand, and prepared for death by shearing scythe or lightning bolt. I wondered if it would hurt. My life, which I'd had for fifteen uneventful years, didn't so much pass before my eyes as whiz along, not even stopping to offer condolences.

Sweat beaded on my forehead and gathered at the nape of my neck, despite the coolness of the chamber, deep in the church's storerooms where the Archbishop had called this secret meeting in the pre-dawn hours.

I didn't want my life to change. It wasn't much of a life, but it was the only one I had. It contained many things I enjoyed: Working in the church. Painting landscapes of the beach. Eating. Breathing. These freshly scribed words threatened to destroy that last activity. Which, by definition, would eliminate the others.

I again studied the words, all thoughts of breakfast gone. The text seemed to laugh at me like a maniacal goblin. *Emergency Meeting of the Holy Church of Ubel the Benevolent. First Order of Business: Archbishop Deacon declares Ubel the Benevolent insane.*

As you read this, I've no doubt your eyes widened at the implications. But I picture you sitting by a well-tended hearth, perhaps in a goose-down chair, while the servants fix a dinner of mutton and peas, in a time when the gods behave, and all is mostly right with our world.

Imagine seeing such words for the first time by dim lantern light in a frigid stone chamber that reeked of fish because of the storeroom next door, in a time when Gods were known to occasionally smite followers who displeased them.

Imagine being the one to have to write such words down.

Insane. The word echoed through my brain. Was such a thing even possible? How did a god go insane? What were the repercussions? I couldn't answer the first question, but I suspected the answer to the second was "severe."

I set the quill back in my inkpot and had to be careful not to knock it over. My hand shook like I'd caught the fen jitters, a sickness indigenous to our swamp that makes people dance, shake, and run naked through town screaming insults. It's not deadly, but it's good for a laugh.

I wasn't laughing now. As I pulled my eyes from those deadly words with the same effort reserved for prying clams open with bare fingers, I noticed that no one else seemed amused.

But they also didn't seem particularly surprised. True, they had stopped eating the breakfast of bacon, eggs, and toasted cheese bread thoughtfully provided to everyone but me. They stared at the Archbishop with an expression I had not seen in my whole time as church scribe: interest.

I turned my attention to His Grace, who stood at a lectern to my left, dressed in full ceremonial robes. Their colors of cream, gold, and ostentatious felt out of place in this brown and gray stone room. A miter, stitched with gold thread in a pattern mimicking the sun's rays, sat atop his head.

They look like stunned gophers, the lot of them, the Archbishop thought.

I coughed into my hand to hide my shock and amusement. My jerking knee hit the desk, setting the brass inkpot dancing with a tinny clatter. The quill flipped onto the desk and spattered ink on my hand.

At this point, I should mention that, while I'm not a mind reader, I can occasionally read minds. That is to say, random thoughts come to me unbidden, and I'm sensitive to emotions at all times. I couldn't look at you and tell you your name or the ages of your children, or even where you misplaced your favorite pair of riding gloves. But if you stared at me and thought, exasperated, *I wish this adolescent prat would get on with the story*, I would probably catch an echo of it in my head and give you a dirty look. At that point, you would wonder if I could read minds. I would then get on with the story.

The thoughts mostly come from people I've spent a lot of time with, such as the Archbishop. The strength of the thinker's emotional and mental faculties has as much to do with it as anything; although not the most intellectually adroit, His Grace has strong feelings.

He favored my klutziness with a pasty frown. Seeing me wipe my hand across my blue scribe's robe, smearing it with black squid ink, he shook his head and returned his attention to the assembly of six, two of the town's leaders and four clergymen. One offered a polite cough and another a poorly muffled belch.

"What? No indignation?" the Archbishop said, his voice the sound of a dull blade run across a whetstone wrapped in cheesecloth. "No cries of heresy? No mutterings of blasphemy?"

Brother Elder, the youngest priest on the island, stood. "Of course not. We're none of us the Paladin Lucifer."

The remark brought general laughter from the assembly, and even the Archbishop offered a papery smile.

Brother Elder returned the grin, brushing brown hair from his eyes. He wore his cut somewhat longer than strictly allowed in an attempt to hide his boyishly round face. He abetted this effort by growing a beard, which resembled a fuzzy, tread-worn carpet. I got along well enough with Brother Elder, but I was one of the few who seemed to like him. Most ignored him, many of the other priests laughed at him, and the Archbishop loathed him.

The assembly's reaction to Elder's comment confirmed my suspicion that Lucifer had been left off the invitation list to this gathering. Highly respected for his puissance, the Grand Commander of the Holy Order of Ubel's Paladins could be unyielding in his views, and his devotion to our deity had the intensity of mental instability.

The Archbishop straightened from his hunched position, emboldened by the lack of outrage from the gathering. He scratched at his thin cheek and continued speaking. "I bring it to your attention to see what you think. So, now that it has been brought to your attention, what do you think?"

Brother Sistar stood up, the motion causing the few wisps of his thin hair to float above his head like errant spider webs. Brother Sistar was head priest and still did the twice-weekly services, although he had a habit of giving sermons so boring *he* fell asleep in the middle. His frail voice spoke out, the words pouring like watery mud. "I would like to make a motion that Ubel the Benevolent is insane."

Brother Krius pulled his rotund self into a standing position. "I second that motion."

"Very well, we have a motion," the Archbishop announced. "All in favor."

"Hold on," Mayor Barkar said, his jowls shaking with each word. "Don't you think we should discuss this for a moment?"

"If you wish," his Grace said. You didn't have to read emotions to sense his annoyance as he placed his spindly hand on the lectern's edges, leaned over it, and looked down on the seated Mayor. "You have the floor, your Honor. What do you have to say?" This last was not so much a question as an accusation.

Mayor Barkar looked around at the others, his dumpling face ripe with uncertainty. He hemmed. He hawed. He looked to Vektor, the brawny head of the town guard, for support, but found none forthcoming. The Mayor, known for festival day speeches that lasted an hour at minimum, had nothing to say.

"We are waiting," the Archbishop said, leaning further over the lectern, a fancy-dress spider poised to devour anything that might slip from the Mayor's mouth.

"Well," Barkar finally said, and I knew the Archbishop had won. "I guess I don't really have anything, not being a priest." He grabbed his pipe with a meaty, shaking hand and stuck it in his mouth.

"Very good." The Archbishop straightened and let the tension in the room relax. I released my breath, unaware I had been holding it while waiting for the mayor to speak.

But Brother Elder was not so easily cowed. "Personally, I'd like to know what proof you have."

"Proof? I'm the Archbishop."

4

"That's a compelling argument against the intelligence of your superiors, but I don't think you can blame your promotions on Ubel's lunacy."

As I've mentioned, I like Brother Elder. But it's not without reason that others despise him.

The Archbishop's gritted teeth shredded the words as he spoke. "There have been signs and omens."

Elder pressed on. "What kind of omens?"

"Ominous ones. Last week, the sun disappeared in the middle of the day."

"It's called an eclipse. Happens every few years."

"I saw Mother Talis dancing in the street and speaking in strange languages."

"*That* happens every few weeks. Mother Talis has a fondness for unripe mushrooms."

The Archbishop didn't speak for a moment, and a distinct discomfort emanated from him, mixed with, of all things, embarrassment. He glared at Elder. "If you wish to survive in this profession, you must learn to take the word of your superiors on faith."

He pulled the miter off his head, sat it on the floor, and then began to remove his robe.

"Your Grace, what are you doing?" Brother Sistar wheezed.

"What does it look like?" came the muffled voice from somewhere within the robe's folds. The cloth plummeted to the floor, where it landed with a proud thump and left the archbishop in his undergarments. I looked away in embarrassment and dismay at seeing one so holy in such a state. I wondered if I would have to wash my eyeballs to cleanse myself of such a blasphemous act.

I heard the gentle sound of cloth being pulled around wooden buttons as I looked at the others looking at the Archbishop. *Sweet Ubel, please don't let him go naked*, I pleaded, feeling ill at the thought of seeing that wasted body without clothes.

I almost turned my head at the gasps and expressions of horror that blossomed on the six faces gathered at the table. *He's gone the full road*, I thought as I kept my eyes fixed on the wisps of Brother Krius's hair that stood straight up as if shocked.

"Scribe," the Archbishop said, and I winced because I knew what was coming. "Look at me. You must write what all have witnessed, so there can be no doubt."

I turned as slowly as possible, terrified of what I would see. My eyes eventually reached the Archbishop. He hadn't stripped, only undone and lowered his shirt to show his chest; saggy, old, and lacking muscle. Avoiding physical labor whenever possible, I was weaker than a rabbit, but I could have taken His Grace three out of three.

Across that pale, withered flesh, angry welts stood out, forming words in deep red. *He's driving me insane. Please help. Ubel.*

Silence held in the chamber for several seconds as everyone digested what they saw. My pen scratching across the paper sounded like the roar of waves in that still chamber. I looked back up to the flabbergasted faces, and the Archbishop spoke.

"As I said before, all in favor of the motion that Ubel is insane."

A chorus of "ayes" sounded through the room.

"All opposed."

No one spoke.

"Very well. Let it be written that Ubel the Benevolent is insane."

I couldn't help myself. With a nervous glance at the ceiling, I said, "Excuse me, your Grace, but if Ubel really is insane, do you think it's a good idea to let him know that we know?"

"Silence, scrivener!" The Archbishop said with more whetstone and less cheesecloth in his voice. He always called me scrivener or scribe. I don't think he ever bothered to learn my real name. "Your job is to write and not speak, so write."

"Besides," Brother Elder said, offering what he thought was a friendly grin. "Ubel already knows that we know, so if he wants to fry us for it, he'll be doing it soon enough."

I felt faint. My hand trembled as I wrote. It was bad enough to have written the possibility. To write the certainty was a wax stamp on the letter of my fate—a letter I didn't want to read.

Motion carried: Ubel the Benevolent declared insane by the Church of Ubel the Benevolent. I looked up from the parchment and once again waited for rats to rush in and consume me, or some other equally unpleasant fate.

The Archbishop locked eyes with each member of the gathering as he spoke. "So, now that we agree Ubel has, to put it nicely, fallen off his cloud, the question is, what should we do about it?"

The gathering glanced around at each other, faces blank, mouths muttering. Finally, Brother Friar raised his hand. Middle-aged, with unkempt black hair, Brother Friar looked as if he hadn't eaten a complete meal in ten years. If scarecrows could talk, they would have made fun of him.

"Yes, Brother Friar, you have a suggestion?"

"Yes. We could sign up with a different god. I've heard about this new one in the East that used to be a carp—"

"No, we are not going to join a new god. Remember the Fate of the Kruetons."

I shuddered as I recalled the ancient tales of the Kruetons, desert nomads who worshiped Sal'lad the Vengeful. One day, the leader of the Kruetons, driven to madness by living on nothing but camel meat, camel milk, and loaves of sand-baked bread, declared that Sal'lad would no longer be worshiped since he brought nothing but calamity. Sal'lad, heartily offended at these remarks, quickly showed the Kruetons the true meaning of affliction and turned every one of them into an upright piece of hardtack.

Having ruminated, Brother Friar said, "Well, the first idea is never the best." He sat back down.

Brother Elder spoke up. "Who's driving him insane?"

"What?" the Archbishop said.

"The missive scrawled into your skin said, 'He's driving me insane.' So, who is 'he?' We need to find that out, and then we can figure out what to do about it."

I admired Brother Elder's confidence that we could do *anything* against whatever could perturb a deity.

"Of course, we do," the Archbishop growled, as it was the most obvious thing. His bitter disappointment at not thinking of it first washed over me. "And how do you propose we do that?"

"Simple. We send someone to the Oracle at Hiephi and ask her."

The Archbishop frowned, his wrinkles deepening. "Are you suggesting we take a religious matter to a *witch*? What sort of man of the cloth are you?"

"That is a good idea," Brother Sistar said. "The Hiephic Oracle is rumored to receive visions from all five major gods and a good portion of the two hundred and fifty-five minor spirits."

The Archbishop's smile fell like a dropped mug as the others muttered agreement. After a brief pause, Sistar said, "I motion that we send someone to the Oracle at Hiephi to discover the cause of Ubel's insanity and, if possible, the cure."

"I second the motion," Elder said.

"All in favor," the Archbishop said with a distinct lack of enthusiasm.

Ayes sounded from around the table.

7

"All opposed."

Silence.

"Fine. Write it down."

I thought about correcting the Archbishop's lack of formal protocol, but the man's deadly gaze cooled my impetuous nature. I wrote down the motion.

"So then," the Archbishop said. "Who should we send on this perilous quest?"

Brother Elder spoke up again. "Who better to go on a quest to cure an insane god than an insane Paladin? I recommend we send Lucifer."

"Yes, Lucifer is an excellent choice," the Archbishop said. "But he will need someone to guide him spiritually on this arduous task. Someone who will look after his well-being and assure everything goes well." The Archbishop turned and looked down at me. He gave me the same smile I imagine a rat must see before a snake eats it. "Someone like...you."

2

I reacted to this startling statement with the obvious question. "Me? What do you mean me? I don't know..." I stopped. Everyone stared at me, including the Archbishop, who swiveled his small head on his short neck to regard me down his nose. I was confused. How could he have gone from staring at me and then not and then back at me so quickly that he didn't give himself whiplash?

The Archbishop blinked. "What?"

I blinked and swallowed. "What?"

"Explain your outburst, scribe." Only now did I realize the previous voice sounded nothing like the Archbishop's. I thought back on the words it said, "Someone like you." The voice sounded kind, almost fatherly, even as its words made me want to hide in a hole.

"My pardon, your Grace. For a moment, I thought you spoke to me."

"Great Ubel, why would I do that unless absolutely necessary? May we continue?"

"Yes, your Grace." I stared back down at my parchment. I needed to note the name of Lucifer's escort, but I had no idea who the Archbishop had named.

A strident voice filled in the blank. "I really don't think I'm the right person," Elder said. His boyish face looked like he had been informed he would be flung off a cliff at sundown. "I have nowhere near the experience for a mission like this."

"Perhaps not," the Archbishop said. "But I feel you have the right attitude." *A piss poor one,* the Archbishop thought, *which needs to be somewhere other than here.*

Of course, I sensed Elder's real reason. He was terrified of having to spend time with Lucifer. Having some experience of the Paladin through my brother Raith's squiring, I couldn't blame the priest.

"Look," Elder continued, "any other brother here would be more than-"

His Grace had heard enough. "In the name of our father Ubel, I hereby invoke the Mandate of Silence."

"B-" Elder got no further before the Archbishop held out a bony finger and waved it at him like the Specter of Death. An unnatural hush fell over the room as if even the air paid heed to that gaunt digit.

"Now," said the Archbishop, "let us offer thanks to Brother Elder, who has so graciously offered to accompany the most worthy Lucifer on this perilous, possibly even suicidal, but nonetheless glorious quest to restore our great Ubel to his rightful mind. May the winds guide their sails, and the ground lead their steps to the great Oracle of Hiephi, and may she actually have something useful to say, so their arduous trek is not a complete waste of time and money."

He went on, each sentence more disheartening than the one preceding it. By the time the Archbishop finished his pep talk, Elder's task seemed tantamount to lifting the world with his pinkie.

"So, farewell," the Archbishop concluded, offering a toothy smile to Elder. "Meeting adjourned."

Since he had not revoked the Mandate, no one spoke as they shuffled their chairs back and left the chamber. Elder stormed out after offering the Archbishop as grim a stare as his cherubic face could manage; if looks could kill, his Grace would have suffered a mild headache.

After everyone left, the Archbishop looked at me and gave a start. "You're still here?"

I nodded.

"The Mandate is over," he snapped, "now that the child priest has left."

I had nothing to say except questions that would only get me reprimanded.

Something must have shown on my face because the Archbishop saw it despite the dim light. He sighed. "You do not agree with the Church's decision regarding our most benevolent Ubel."

"That is not my place to say," I offered, eyes down.

"No, it isn't. But this once, you may speak your mind."

I could have dropped into a faint right there. A higher clergyman allowing a lowly scribe to offer an opinion? Maybe Ubel *had* gone insane.

Still gazing at my parchment, I said, "It's only that...well...do you think...I don't know......that Lucifer can really, you know...cure him?" Speech patterns like this are why I'm a scribe and not an orator.

"I don't know," the Archbishop said, his voice turning soggy at the statement's gravity. "But he must try, and, much as I dislike the Oracle, she may be the best chance at an answer."

Something wore on my mind. At the risk of a tongue-lashing, I said, "When you first declared Ubel...well, you know, and I wrote the words, I had a strange feeling, like a great change was coming to me, a change that would alter the world as we know it." I realized how arrogant I sounded. The creator of us all had slipped his oarlocks, and all I could think was that I could change the world. How could I even consider the possibility?

The Archbishop favored me with a frown that gathered wrinkles on his chin like ripples on a lake. "Have you had these thoughts often?" I waited for *silly little boy* to follow in his thoughts, but all I sensed was contemplation, as if my words had merit.

"No, just this once. It wasn't a thought so much as...as..."

"An intuition? As if Ubel spoke to your heart?"

"More like whatever part of your body instills sheer panic, but yes, it was almost as if Ubel spoke to me."

"Interesting."

"Of course, I also thought you told me I had to accompany Lucifer. That's why I spoke out of turn. Maybe I need to lie down until the hallucinations pass."

The Archbishop said nothing, only stared at me, thin finger tapping his weak chin. Most of the time, I would rather not hear what other people think, especially about me. It tends to shatter your belief in others when they say, "my, what an interesting painting," while thinking *I've seen things from the back end of my cows that look better.* For once, I wished I could consciously probe into the Archbishop's mind, but he either had no strong thoughts on the subject, or they had somehow been closed off to me.

After a few seconds, his hand dropped to the side, and his brown eyes glittered in the candlelight. He appeared to have decided, but I wasn't going to learn what it was, at least not right away. "Go scribe the meeting, and then you may take the rest of the day for yourself. You will have no other duties."

I goggled as the Archbishop tottered his way toward the exit. Allowed to express my thoughts and given a reprieve from chores, all in one day? Something had definitely gone askew.

I SPENT the rest of the morning re-scribing the meeting to special archival vellum using sea squid ink. The pulpreed got tossed into a pile where it would be used later to start fires or line the cages of the Archbishop's bird collection.

By the time I finished and filed the minutes in the proper place, it was nearing time for the noon meal. My stomach, having been denied break-fast, contemplated the benefits of self-consumption. I didn't usually take so long to scribe, but I ruined four vellum sheets. Despite the Archbish-op's calm certainty, every time I got to the word *insane*, my hand would twitch and knock over the ink. Something about writing it on vellum, to be preserved for the ages, made it seem all the more real. I don't know which I found more frightening: that Ubel might actually be insane or that he might be angered at me for inscribing it in official Church documents.

Finished, I washed my hands, despairing after the fifth time of getting all the black stains out. I removed my blue scribe's robe and revealed my usual lump of dirt attire: a brown twill shirt, canvas pants, and knee-high boots. I hated brown, but my parents still purchased my clothing since I made precious little coin as a scribe. All I earned was being stashed away for the day when I would go to Kale University in the northeastern prov-ince of Conticut.

My stomach gurgled, so I headed up the stairs and went to the kitchen. I found the Church cook, Gerda, a giantess with wiry black hair that could flay your skin off if you drew too close. My food request met with the sour grunt that passed for communication from her, but she threw two pieces of dark bread on a chipped plate, slathered a stew of fish and vegetables over them, and shoved the mess toward me. I grabbed it and retreated to the dining hall, cavernously empty since the bell for the noon meal had not rung. The stew was lukewarm, and only copious quantities of pepper gave it any semblance of edibility, but I was too hungry to care.

I had eaten worse, and in this very hall. I was never required to take an Oath of Mealtime Suffering, but considering what the priests ate daily, I assumed they did.

The food satisfied my hunger, if not my taste buds. Finished, I decided to hunt down Raith and tell him about the day's strange happenings.

I pushed open the thick wooden side door of the church and stepped outside. Bright sun glared down on me, so I squinted as I started across the expanse of my hometown.

What to say about glorious Frostishak? I could tell you it's a gleaming jewel in the southern continent. I could say it's a shining example of culture, industry, and commerce that reigns as the envy of the known world.

I could say these things, but they would be lies.

Frostishak is a pile of lumber and mud with delusions of grandeur perched atop a high spot surrounded by swamp. The town's only reason for existing is that it sits athwart the only deepwater harbor on an otherwise inhospitable shore. According to the histories, it took about a hundred ships dashing themselves against rocks and reefs before the royal frigate *Lucke Shak* chanced upon the hidden harbor. A sudden storm caught the frigate unawares. Captain Rubus Frost, caught between being battered to pieces by wind and water or dashed to splinters against the rocky shore, opted for the more expedient death and headed for the coast. When the *Shak* beached against sand instead of breaking over rock, the captain realized he had miraculously chanced upon the one spot where a ship could safely dock. Overcome with wonder, some say shock, he promptly fainted.

When he awoke, the storm had ended, and the crew sang his praises for guiding them to safety against the odds. Thrilled to have survived, Frost stumbled down the ship's gangplank and fell to the sand. He declared that a fair city would be built on the very spot, a hub of commerce from north to south, a gateway to the inner realms of this mysterious new continent. The ship's priest, Brother Traumer, convinced that mighty Ubel had saved the ship and led them to this fertile land, promised to build a glorious church in Ubel's most holy name. From this sacred edifice, Ubel's teachings would flow to the unwashed masses sure to teem to this thriving port.

Two hundred years later, both dreams had failed to come true.

I FOUND Raith at the center of town, in front of the five ramshackle wooden stalls that pass for a market. I had tried home first, expecting him to be there eating lunch. My mother said he had already been there, choked down some food, and had left for the market. My mother didn't say "choke," but I knew from experience. I love my mother, but the less said about her cooking, the better. The only thing she had over Gerda was a more pleasant personality.

I was drenched in sweat by the time I reached Raith, thanks to the sweltering miasma that passed for air in Frostishak. Those early shipwreck victims had discovered their paradise surrounded by a swamp on three sides. It's not really dangerous, but it's damned uncomfortable. A breeze often blew in from the ocean, but it never reached beyond the dock warehouses, beaten into submission by the marsh-generated humidity. Dampness was a constant companion, but this time of year was always the worst; summer heat joined to make a walk across town akin to swimming in tepid soup.

Raith stood before a fruit vendor, placing strawberry melons into a burlap bag. Such items are a luxury since they are imported from Skaldor on the mainland. He wore his apprentice clothing, a white tunic and gold pants demarcated by a bright red belt. He looked like a festival ornament.

Although our mother swore Raith and I had the same father, our disparate looks gave us thoughts to the contrary. And we weren't the only ones. There were whispers in the town, rumors that Raith ignored, my mother and father denied, and I lashed out against.

Raith was pale and flabby, with hair the color—and sometimes consistency—of mud. His eyes, a light azure shade, seemed owlish in his long, pinched face. They constantly watered, just as his nose always ran. Raith perpetually looked like he was either on the verge of crying or had just finished. Light brown freckles covered his plump body in random patches. He reminded me of a diseased peach or a banana two days over-ripe. At five-foot-two, he stood two inches shorter than me, despite being two years my senior.

By contrast, my wheat-colored hair was a few shades lighter than my tanned skin. I had gray eyes that, when they looked back at me from a reflective surface, showed a lean body resting under a puckish face with high cheeks and a thin mouth.

Neither of us bore facial hair, but poor Raith bore no hair in any place that marked a man, and his voice still rang like a tenor who's been slammed below the belt by a heavy mallet. It seemed manhood had simply decided to give him a pass.

Raith and I were alike in one respect: we both had nothing resembling a muscular physique. Hence, a tongue-lashing was the most abuse I could offer my tormentors. Even then, I had to be careful not to push too far, lest I get Raith in trouble. He had taken any number of beatings on my behalf when my mouth got the better of me. He always threatened to let the tormentors "mud stomp my ass" to teach me a lesson, but as yet, he hadn't done it. I think he felt responsible, as the older brother. I could never figure out why he didn't just run when I did.

"What are you doing?" I asked.

Raith turned to me with his owlish eyes. "What does it look like I'm doing?" Thankfully, my mental abilities had never extended to my family, but I didn't need them to tell me he wasn't happy.

"It looks like you're planning to start your own melon festival. Why are you buying so many?"

"Lucifer wants them. There was a page looking for you earlier."

Raith had been apprenticed to Lucifer for two months. I knew his apprenticeship encompassed several menial duties, but I didn't realize it included buying the Paladin's groceries. "A page. What for?"

"Said the Archbishop wanted to see you."

"I just spent an hour with the Archbishop. What does he want now?"

Raith shrugged and stuffed another melon in the bag.

"Which page was it?"

"That one," he said, pointing over my shoulder.

I turned to see a small form striding toward me like a terrier called to dinner. I never liked pages; they have a pride of station far above their efficacy. They always looked down at other servants, as if running through town fetching food and delivering pieces of parchment they couldn't read were less crappy duties than those given to others. This particular page, ten years old with spiky black hair and squinty eyes, was the Archbishop's personal servant and the worst of the lot. I suppose I knew his name once, but I always thought of him as Crow, or, if I was feeling particularly nasty, Crowshit.

He paused to regain his breath, and I noticed the sweat on his forehead. "I've been looking everywhere for you. Where have you been?"

"Maybe you should have tried the church. I do work there on occasion."

His lip curled up as if he had stepped in something best not described. "The Archbishop wants to see you."

"Why?"

"Does it matter?"

It didn't, and it irritated me that I had no comeback for the little prat. "Very well," I sighed. So much for my day of no duties. I should have known it was too good to be true.

"Does it displease you to see the Archbishop?" The curl turned into a snide smile, and I could feel his eagerness to report some indiscretion on my part to his master.

"No, just you." I turned back to Raith. "Are you back to the training ground?"

"In a bit. I have to make one more stop. See you later."

"So, what's with all the melons?"

"Today, please," Crow said, arms crossed, foot tapping.

"Piss off, you runt." That's what I wanted to say, but such rudeness would have been just the sort of thing to make the snit happy. So instead, I said, "Lead the way."

He turned on his heel and walked across the town center, so he didn't see the strangling motions I made behind his back.

We passed through the busiest part of town, which is like saying we walked through the brightest part of a cave. A few people nodded politely, but most just ignored us. Even the others my age paid me no attention. I tended not to cultivate friends. Another side effect of my chronic empathy. As soon as I became close to someone, I learned their inner thoughts. Even if it isn't about me, I found most people's way of thinking too disturbing to handle for long. So, I kept to myself, did my paintings, and scribed. I knew someday I'd make an excellent hermit.

Crow and I returned to the church in silence. *The little imp must be tired from hunting me down*, I thought. He was usually a rolling commentary on the superiority of pages, especially clerical pages, who, he claimed, served not only nobility but the representatives of holy Ubel himself. In a moment of weakness, I once tried to explain to Crow that church clergy were not necessarily—in fact, were rarely—nobles. Crow had favored me with a look that said he believed that no more than he would accept a trout could walk. When I offered to read documents to him that explained this, I might as well have suggested he peel his skin and make rope from it. After that, I gave up trying to teach any page anything.

Once we left the market square, the church loomed before us in all its ugliness. The cathedral of the ages Brother Traumer envisioned upon his arrival never came to pass. Still, he did manage to get an architectural monstrosity designed by a madman and built by a drunkard. It was the largest building in town and the only one made entirely of jade stone dredged from the ocean bed on either side of the harbor. Its pale baby puke color was the least of its offenses. Spires pointed off at odd angles, walls weren't straight, and the belfry looked in constant danger of toppling and crushing the rest of the building. It took five years to build but probably should have been given five more to be done correctly. If this was the best we had to offer our god, no wonder he left his cookies on the plate.

Crow pushed open the small wooden side door where the servants entered. "This is for pages only," he said. "Don't make a habit of coming in this way."

I had used this entrance since my apprenticeship started nine months ago, and Crow had often seen me. Not for the first time, I wondered if he had been dropped on his head as a babe.

"You can follow me since I'm sure you've never been to the Archbishop's chamber before."

I kept silent and imagined the numerous ways Crow could be made to suffer without actual physical harm. I once caught Keller and Triff, two eleven-year-old kitchen boys, pissing into a soup kettle. They weren't much better than the pages, but I knew they had no love for Crow and his ilk. Maybe I could convince them to make a special meal for the spike-haired twit.

Thus, I kept myself amused as we walked through the crooked halls and up the slanted stone stairways until we reached the Archbishop's chamber. Crow knocked on the stout door.

"Enter."

Crow pushed open the door and walked in before me. Protocol dictated that I, as the guest, should have been allowed first entrance—just another petty slight. I was going to have to invent an outstanding payback. Crow had to know it would come. He didn't serve the Archbishop at all times, and when he was off-duty, he was fair game.

The chamber was large and well decorated, with straight walls covered in soft sheer curtains and tapestries, most depicting saints martyred in gruesome ways while serving Ubel. A four-poster occupied one corner, wrapped in dark blankets. A stout wooden desk sat in the room's center, clean except for a single sheet of parchment upon which the Archbishop scribbled with a quill. Light streamed in from an open window, aided by large oil lanterns that gave off the salty scent of whale.

As I looked about the room, a strange sense of unreality walked over me, a collision of what was with what used to be. For the briefest moment, I felt like a piece of taffy tugged on by two ravenous children, each wanting the lion's share of my mind. This chamber was how the rest of the cathedral should be but wasn't. Or was the cathedral right and the chamber wrong? It gave me an instant headache.

"Are you okay?" the Archbishop asked in his dull, grating voice. "You look as if you've seen a ghost."

"Ghosts don't exist," I said reflexively.

"Don't they?" the Archbishop said with an amused smile. He looked at Crow, who stood beside the large desk, and his smile faltered. "Why are you still here?"

"I await your Grace's pleasure."

"Well, his Grace's pleasure would have been to have breakfast ready before he left home this morning, but since you were nowhere to be found, his pleasure now is that you depart since nothing here concerns you."

Crow's face fell as if the Archbishop slapped him. Which he had, in a way. Only great effort kept me from cheering. Crow glared at me. I offered a smile and a dismissive wave of my hand. We both knew I had won this round.

"As your Grace wishes." He bowed and left, closing the door harder than strictly necessary.

The Archbishop eyed me for a moment, as a butcher might study a choice cut of meat. I shifted on my feet and stared at the rug-covered floor, unable to meet the man's gaze. Today was the most direct contact I'd had with him my whole time in the Church since I usually worked with the priests or the archivist.

He cleared his throat, and I looked up to find him folding the parchment. He grabbed a small taper, dripped wax onto the fold, and pressed a ring into the wax. "Have you had any more strange feelings since I saw you last?"

You mean other than the feeling this room exists in someplace outside the rest of the building, I wanted to say. I still could get no sense of what the Archbishop thought of my earlier peculiar behavior and didn't want to push things. But I couldn't outright lie either. "Just a headache," I said.

The Archbishop held up two pieces of parchment, one large and square, the other small and rectangular. "I want you to deliver these to Elder. This one," he indicated the smaller one, "he is to read." He waved the larger one. "This he is to deliver to the Holy Unseen."

He gave me another grin, the kind you offered to people at funerals. "I understand from the priests that you are a good scribe. It will serve you well. Now take these."

Puzzled at his strange comments, I walked over and took the parchments. As I touched them, I caught the thought *nice working with you* and felt the kind of sizzling jolt you might get from a torch smashed across your forehead. I looked at the documents as the Archbishop stepped back. These documents were another piece of the life-shift puzzle that had begun to assemble this morning. I couldn't make out exactly what would happen, but I felt the answer was close.

Had I known how close, I would have burned the parchments, scattered the ashes, and moved to the swamp for the rest of my life.

3

I walked past the brownstone wall surrounding the Paladin's training ground and stepped through the gate in time to watch a mass of pulpy red goo land at my feet with a wet smack.

Great Ubel, somebody's been killed, I thought as my stomach lurched, eager to evict the recently-consumed fish stew. I kept the food down by sheer force of will; I had no desire to taste it again.

THWACK!

The sound drew my attention from the bloody chunk of I had no idea what—or who—lying at my feet.

"Take that, you sacrilegious villain," Lucifer cried as he swung his sword, and something set atop a five-foot-tall post fell to his wrath.

Great relief washed over me when I saw it wasn't a person, only a strawberry melon. I had mistaken its pulpy red interior for a bloody head. My stomach relaxed.

"And that, you blasphemous cur." With a mushy thwack, the paladin's two-handed sword, Heathensmasher, sent another gourd to an early grave.

Raith stood nearby; melon pulp dotted his white squire's tabard and pale face, although it was difficult to discern the pulp from his freckles. He stared at his master with a look of almost pure disgust.

Lucifer was the paragon men aspired to be and women desired to love.

He stood six-foot-two and weighed at least eighteen stone, every pebble of it rippling, densely packed muscle, the kind produced by good breeding and years of intensive training. His hair, clipped to just above his collar, was a rich chocolate brown, with hints of yellow that shone like glints of gold through a miser's fingers. His face was chiseled stone turned to flesh, with a firm cleft chin and cheekbones on which one could set ale mugs. His emerald green eyes could be either friendly or intimidating at the flick of a lid.

As the last melon fell to his fearsome attack, he turned to Raith and said, "More heretics, squire," in a voice deep as the ocean and friendly as a two-week-old puppy.

Raith hated him.

But my poor brother also wanted to emulate him. The only way to do that was to be his squire, so he left a comfortable life as a librarian's apprentice to haul melons and clean juice-coated swords and armor.

"Of course, Sire," Raith said.

As Raith gathered more sacrificial fruits from the burlap sack resting on the table, I walked toward him, stepping around the various splatters covering the dusty ground. Raith noticed me. "Greetings, good Briar," he said, his high voice taking on the formal tones required in Lucifer's presence. "Do you have a message for my esteemed master?"

I suppressed a smile. In our private conversations, Raith called Lucifer anything but "esteemed."

"No," I answered. "The Archbishop gave me the day off."

Lucifer offered me a suspicious stare, and I could sense him trying to ascertain if I was lying. Lucifer loved to catch those under him in venial sins. "A day off from duties? Has the Archbishop gone mad?"

"Not him," I offered and said nothing more. I wasn't going to be the one to break the news to Lucifer, especially while he was holding a long piece of sharp metal.

"These are the last melons, Sire," Raith said as he set up the hapless gourds on their posts.

Lucifer's face turned dark. "The last? But I have yet to practice with my mace and my long knife. You must go purchase more."

"I tried. The fruit vendor said we've bought our allotment for the month."

"Allotment?" Lucifer asked. His high brow furrowed in puzzlement. "Explain this new concept."

Raith sighed. Physically perfect Lucifer might be, but not the brightest candle in the chandelier. "An allotment means he only has to sell us a fixed amount. He can then sell the rest to other customers."

Lucifer's eyes narrowed as he glared down at Raith. "What sort of blasphemy is this? The Church demands he sell us the melons we want."

"No," Raith said, and we both stepped back. When Lucifer was disputed, he became irate. When he became irate, he had a disconcerting habit of swinging weapons in random directions. We probably weren't in danger, but neither of us wanted to be looking down from Godshome realizing our mistake.

Out of immediate threat range, Raith continued. "The Church of Ubel demands the merchants sell to us at a discounted price, but all the members of the Merchant's Guild belong to the Church of Parsimony, God of Money. The Parsimonites decided the Paladins were cutting into their profit too much, so they have given a set number of melons we can buy a month."

"And what number has this blasphemous lot set?"

Raith stepped back further and put himself behind a wooden post. As an extra precaution, I put myself behind Raith. "Thirty," Raith answered.

"Thirty?" Lucifer roared, and *Heathensmasher* flailed wildly about. "That is outrageous. Do they not realize they risk offending Ubel, the only True God? This miserly god they worship is a false religion."

"I tried telling them that, but they said they preferred their false bankrolls to Ubel's true insolvency."

"Those heathens! Would that mighty Ubel the Benevolent give me leave, I would take Heathensmasher to the Merchant's Square and show them the error of their ways." For emphasis, Lucifer swiped at the recently placed melon, which fell neatly in two.

I briefly considered explaining "benevolent" to him.

"I'm sorry. Is this a bad time?"

Startled by the unexpected voice, Lucifer swung around, his two-handed weapon poised to strike. "Are you a merchant?"

Elder stood at the gate. Wiping the flung melon pulp off his face and sighing, he looked first at Lucifer and then at us. Raith stepped from behind the pole, and I followed. I sensed Elder's surprise at seeing me, but he said nothing. Instead, he offered Raith a quizzical look, hoping to get some clue about Lucifer's question. Raith shrugged.

Elder looked at Lucifer, who still had his sword poised, ready to dispatch this sacrilegious shopkeeper if necessary. "No, I am not a merchant, good Lucifer. I am Brother Elder, a priest."

"Of whom?"

Elder rolled his eyes. "Of Ubel the Benevolent. Don't you recognize the emblem?" He pointed to the shoulder of his blue robe, where two open palms underneath a yellow sun had been embroidered.

"Forgive me, Holy Brother," Lucifer said, sheathing his sword into the scabbard on his back and bowing. "I have just heard distressing news from my squire, and it has addled my wits."

"That's your excuse for now," Elder muttered. In a louder voice, he said, "And what is this distressing news, Sir Lucifer? Should the Church be concerned, or can the Most Holy Order of Paladins handle it?"

"The Merchants' Guild, all worshipers of the infidel God Parsimony, has decreed the Brotherhood may only purchase thirty melons a month for sword practice."

"Well, then," Elder said, his too handsome face breaking into a grin. "I have news that will make you, the Merchant's Guild, and helpless melons everywhere very happy. Your sword may soon be put to better use."

"Someone is to supply us with heathens?" Lucifer asked, his eyes brightening.

"Not exactly, but there may be heathens along the way."

"Are we going somewhere?"

"Yes. You and I are going on a journey for the Church."

"A journey? Is this a quest to rid some remote corner of the world of heathens and evil influence?"

"Not exactly."

"Has a demonic portal appeared, and we must slay the hellspawn that spew forth in untold numbers?"

"No, and you're not even close."

"Save a town from a vile baron?"

"Sounds fun, but no."

"Rescue a damsel from a dragon?"

"Uh-uh."

"Free religious prisoners?"

"Nope."

"Well, blast it, don't keep me guessing, good priest. What is this perilous quest?"

"Well...I'm not exactly sure the best way to explain it. It's rather delicate because..."

I had no intention of being the first to say anything. To this day, I have no idea why I spoke up. Even as the words poured from my mouth,

I kicked myself for being six kinds of an idiot. All I could guess—and later events backed my theory—is that some other force worked through me.

At least that's what I tell myself when the injuries flare up.

"Ubel has gone insane, and you have to find out why."

"What?" Lucifer said, his eyes wide with shock.

"What?" Raith echoed, his pudgy face also stunned.

Elder said nothing, but he gave me the same dire glare he offered the Archbishop earlier. It had no effect on me either, but the gravity of what I had uttered almost did his work for him. This wasn't the kind of message one delivered to a Paladin, and I had no idea what Lucifer's views might be on the whole "killing the bearer of bad news" concept.

"That's considerably less tactful than I would have put it," Elder said, giving equal attention to Lucifer and me. "But the big-mouthed scribe is correct. The Church has determined Ubel is insane, and you and I have been chosen to go to the Oracle of Hiephi and find out why. You because of your fine skills and piety, and I because of a bitter old man's petty revenge. Why are you pulling your sword back out?"

"I'd suggest getting behind a pole," Raith offered as he took his own advice. I remained rooted, hoping my anonymity would shield me from my big mouth.

"Tell me," Lucifer said in a voice only slightly less threatening than the finely crafted, Dwarven-smithed, five-and-a-half-foot piece of steel he held inches from Elder's throat. "Exactly how did the Church come to this conclusion?"

"We discussed it with two town council members and put it to a vote," Elder told him, trying to ignore his imminent decapitation.

"And since when did the Church become a democracy?"

Raith spoke up from behind the pole. "It's always been a democracy, Sire. Ubel the Benevolent declared it so during the Time of Troubled Waters. The Council votes on the upper clergymen's edicts and allows a vote in proceedings to a secular minority, except in the case of—"

"Silence, bookworm," Lucifer bellowed even as he lowered his sword. "You babble more useless trivia than any ten squires. How did you learn so much being a mere librarian's apprentice?"

I looked back at Raith. I couldn't read his thoughts, but his perplexed stare said it all.

"Well, I'm glad that ended without violence," Elder said, wiping the sweat from his face, where it had pooled in the spaces left by his beard.

"You know, threatening a member of the Church is a severe offense, especially for a Paladin."

"How long have you been a priest, Brother Elder?"

"Six months, ever since the old priest, Brother Young, went to live with Ubel."

"My good priest, I have been a Paladin for twenty years, almost as long as you have been alive, and head of this Order for ten. All I have heard from your mouth so far is blasphemy. I could strike you dead for a heretic now, and the Church would say nothing."

Raith spoke up again. "Actually, according to the Articles of-"

"-this Brotherhood, a squire can be severely flogged for failing to fully support his Paladin."

Raith considered a moment. "Well, you got me on that one."

"So, priest, if you really are a priest and not an impostor sent by the Merchant's Guild to further destroy my melonic privileges, explain to me why the Church decided Ubel is...as you say he is."

"Without getting too graphic, the Archbishop spelled it out pretty well for us."

"I see," Lucifer said, though he obviously didn't. "But it seems to me consulting with the Oracle is blasphemy."

"Perhaps, but the Church has ordered it. To defy Church orders is heresy, and if I know anything, it's that Lucifer Memnoch, a.k.a. Lucifer the Pious, would never disobey directives of the Church."

Lucifer stood a little taller. "What you say is true. I will follow the will of the Church, though I agree with it not."

"That's a good fellow. Look at the bright side. There may be a chance to smash a few heathens. And when we get back, I'll look into correcting this distressing melon business."

"You are a good man," Lucifer said.

As Lucifer returned Heathensmasher to his broad back, I felt the strange taffy-pulling sensation again and squinted at the sharp pain in my head. I caught movement out of the corner of my eye. I looked to see a two-headed rat snatch a piece of melon and run across the training yard, where it was pounced upon by a black cat. In a blink, the cat lashed out with a forked tongue, wrapped it around both of the rat's necks, and broke them. "Ominous signs," I muttered in amazement.

"What did you say?" Lucifer asked.

I looked up to find Lucifer studying me, his emerald eyes as hard as their name stone, his sword only half in its scabbard. I had unwittingly drawn his attention back to me. I swallowed and said, "The Archbishop said there are ominous signs."

"And you have seen these signs?"

I read the intention in his question as clearly as you can read these words. A cloud of despair formed over me as Fate laughed its ass off. I wanted to say no, to pretend I had seen nothing unusual, to return to the church and be a scribe, but I could not lie. I was trapped like a collected bug, squirming on the dual pins of my big mouth and my vows. To lie would be to condemn myself to hell. To be honest would be to sentence myself to time with Lucifer. I wondered which would be worse.

Like a man pronouncing his own death sentence, I said, "Yes, I've seen them."

I swear I felt an actual *click* as my life fell into its new course.

"Then you will come along on our journey and point these signs out to me, so I will know the Church's pronouncement is true, and not some clever ruse of Parsimony's followers."

Maybe if I pointed out a sign now, I wouldn't have to leave. But of course, the cat had already run off with its meal. I considered arguing that the Archbishop wouldn't want to lose his favorite scribe, but we were a silver a dozen, literally.

The Archbishop! I remembered the parchments he gave me, forgotten when I saw the splatter of dead melon. I pulled the missives out and handed them to Elder, indicating the smaller one. "You're supposed to read that one." This was my chance at a reprieve. Maybe the Archbishop really did want me to stay here. That was the life shift I'd sensed—a promotion within the Church.

It was a nice thought, but even as Elder broke the wax seal, I knew there was no chance in Ubel's sweet playground it was true. I was doomed. I looked at Lucifer, who stared at me expectantly. "Do I have to go?"

The Paladin nodded. "Come, Raith, we must prepare. We leave..." he looked at Elder. "When do we leave?"

"First thing tomorrow morning," he said as he read the letter.

"First thing tomorrow morning." With that, Lucifer strode from the training yard toward his quarters.

Raith began gathering up Lucifer's equipment, but I barely saw him. My world was spinning, the rug had been pulled from under my feet, and any number of other disorientation clichés assailed my stunned brain. I was going to have to leave the comfort of home, step foot outside the walls of Frostishak, and journey to strange places, possibly never to return.

My breath hitched and before I could stop myself, I threw up. As I suspected, the fish stew tasted no better the second time.

"Are you okay, Briar?" Raith asked as he threw a mace onto his equipment wagon.

"No, I'm not okay," I shouted. "You may want to go on bloody stupid adventures and follow that pious clod around killing people and curing psychopathic deities, but I don't. I'm perfectly happy here, scribing and eating and...well, staying alive." I looked at Elder. "What does the letter say? I'm supposed to stay here and help the Archbishop, right?"

Elder shook his head. "Quite the opposite. The Archbishop says the success of our mission may depend on you."

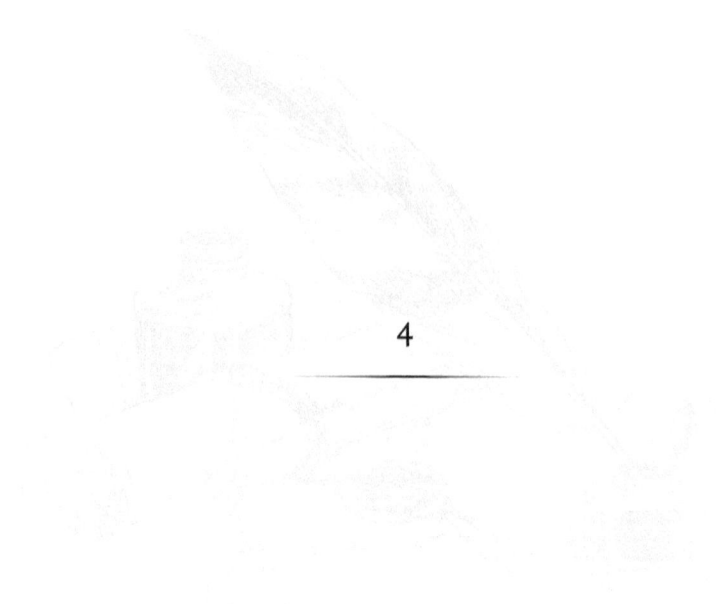

4

Though my eyes were closed, I heard Raith moving around the room, pulling on his clothes. "Briar, it's time to get up," he said. His voice sounded as miserable as I felt. Neither of us slept, instead lying in our shared bed and discussing the coming adventure—or crisis, as I saw it. Raith confessed a strange mixture of excitement and fear. He would miss our parents, but not having to get beaten up for me was certainly an added bonus. He saw this as his chance to prove he could be more than a librarian. He would do Lucifer proud, no matter how difficult it proved. He would grow tall and strong under his master's exemplary tutelage. His growth would come upon him, and he would return to Frostishak a strong man, and perhaps a hero.

Such are the delusions we allow ourselves in the middle of the night.

I, on the other hand, was utterly terrified. I didn't want to leave home, I had no desire to be a hero, and manhood could stay away as long as it wanted. The added pressure put on by the Archbishop's message—and I still hated him for making me deliver my own doom—only made things worse. I said very little, afraid my voice would shake and I would cry even more than I already had. Just knowing I would have to board a ship made me queasy. My stomach lurched if I stood near the docks. Frostishak wasn't much, but it was familiar, and that was enough for me.

Hoping Raith would go away, I rolled over and pulled the goose feather blanket over my head. It didn't work.

"Come on, Briar, get up."

Raith yanked the covers off the bed, and the chill air slapped me, sending a wave of goosebumps across my unclad body. I shivered as I jumped from the bed and scrambled for my clothes. "Ubel's Jewels, what is your problem?" I shouted.

Raith let out a low whistle. "For a church scribe, you've got a dirty mouth."

"Only when I'm damn near frozen by some pillock pulling blankets off me. Why is it so cold? And dark?" I added as I realized I could barely see Raith in the dim room, and what I could see came from a strange pale blue light shining through our bedroom window. It looked suspiciously like—

"Is that moonlight? Is it still night? Did you wake me up before dawn?"

"It's close enough. I need to go and get Lucifer's things ready."

"Fine, go," I said, dancing from foot to foot as I shivered in the frigid room. Why was it so cold? "I don't have to do anything but get dressed. Mother can wake me up later."

"No," Raith said, frowning. "We need to leave before mother rises. She's upset enough as it is, thanks to you."

I couldn't argue his point. When we told mother about the church's decision, you would have thought we said the world had split open and swallowed us. She wailed, tore at her clothes, and threatened to give the Archbishop a tongue-lashing that would burn the ears of the five great gods. I prodded her along, offering to take her directly to his Grace's bedchamber. But Raith and Father stepped in, calming her down and explaining she could not countermand the Church's will.

"Sure you can," I had said. "The deacons do it all the time."

Father had given me his scowling glare. His dark blue eyes gleamed as if to say, *I know you're not my son, no matter what your mother says.* A thrashing usually followed that expression, so I withdrew, making no further protests. Father and Raith finally convinced Mother that we had to go, so I spent the rest of the evening miserable. Mother tried to make my favorite foods for dinner: basil-stuffed swamp leaves and garlic-seared salmon. She failed miserably, but it didn't matter because I barely tasted anything.

"Fine," I growled, pulling on my undergarments and brown pants. "Why is it so cold?" I repeated. We never worried much about cold, even in a house as drafty as ours. Mornings tended to coolness, noticeable

29

mainly as a clamminess that replaced the usual swelter, but cold was unheard of this time of year.

"I hadn't really noticed," Raith said with a shrug.

"How could you not-" I stopped, staring at the dim light on his face. Moonlight, to be sure, but something was wrong with it, a quality to the scant glow I never noticed before. I felt the odd reality taffy pull again, like seeing a mirror that suddenly shifts, throwing off your perception. That was the third time it had happened, and it was beginning to annoy me. Both intrigued and worried, I walked to our window and looked outside.

"Raith, please tell me that isn't what I think it is."

Raith stepped up beside me and flinched when he saw what I saw. "Blessed Ubel, how is that possible?"

"Insane Ubel, that's how it's possible," I offered.

Snow often came to Frostishak in the dead of winter, when the swamp froze into one giant patch of dingy green ice. In the middle of summer, it was rare enough to be considered a miracle.

Or, as I saw it, a dire omen.

"No school today," I said reflexively, forgetting in my astonishment that our schoolmaster left during the summer months to train at Kale— the same place I planned to someday go, providing I survived this fiasco.

"Really?" Raith said, cocking his head at me. "Snow coats the ground, and all you do is jest about it."

"No, I can also say I'm even *less* inclined to leave here and go on some half-assed trek across the world, and I didn't think that was possible. Couldn't the snow have at least waited until we were out to sea?"

"Guess we had best dress warm," Raith said.

We finished dressing, and Raith threw the burlap sack with our extra clothes over his shoulder. And by extra clothes, I mean another set of dull brown for me, and Raith's squire's outfit, which he would have to don at some point.

As we stepped outside, it turned out our attire was nowhere near warm enough for the strange chill that had descended upon our town, so we quietly slipped back inside and threw on a second layer. Raith pulled on the leather gloves he used for fighting practice. But I previously had no need for such items and had to content myself with a pair of socks pulled over my hands.

It seemed a cruel joke that we had to again enter the house where I so wanted to stay. As we added clothing, movement in my parents' room told me they were awake. Every part of me burned to run in and grab hold of my mother and not let go until they said I could stay at home or they dragged me, kicking, screaming, and still clutching my mother, to the docks.

But I knew any opposition was doomed to failure. My desire to not further upset my mother outweighed my selfishness. I prayed they would come out any moment and say it was all a big mistake, but their door remained shut, and the noise ceased.

"Let's get out of here," I said. We finished dressing and slipped out again. I had to fight back tears. I think Raith did, too, but it was impossible to tell with his constantly watery eyes.

Two layers seemed to do the trick, although my nose and ears turned frigid and the strange white vapor coming from my mouth made me wonder if my insides were freezing. The extra clothing made for awkward walking through the four inches of snow, and I fell twice.

We reached the cathedral stables to find Elder and Lucifer already there. Lucifer had on his shining plate mail but no helmet. A red riding cloak hung on his shoulders. Elder wore a fur-lined leather coat and a white cape. Ivory rabbit fur peeked out of his brown leggings. They both looked the picture of warmth, not the shivering bundle of frozen parts that I felt.

Lucifer sat astride his charger, Justice, a robust and solid animal with a rich brown coat and white socks. Elder was tightening the cinch on his horse's saddle and was a bit rougher than necessary, judging by the animal's whinny of protest. Testing the saddle's tightness, he glared at Lucifer.

Sensing the tension, I put out a hand and stopped Raith.

"Now," Elder said as he pulled himself onto his mount. "I just want to make sure before we set out. You do understand that one minute after midnight is *not* the same thing as 'first thing in the morning'"

"I already said I was sorry," Lucifer muttered, unlike his usual demeanor.

"And I accept. I would like to go through this trip able to sleep until somewhere close to dawn every day, barring unforeseen attacks by marauding heathens and such."

"Yes, you will. I…"

"I mean, after all, a tent is much less private than, say, a person's bedroom, so anyone who would burst into a bedroom at midnight is much more likely to barge into a tent."

"Don't labor the point. I understood you the first time."

"Okay," Elder said, letting the issue go with the reluctance of a dog leaving off a new strip of chew leather. "As long as we got that straightened out."

I cleared my throat to attract their attention. Both men turned toward us.

"You're late, squire," Lucifer said. "You still need to pack the mule and your own mount, plus whatever mount the scribe needs." Lucifer glanced at the sky, which had begun to show signs of lightening. "You have a quarter of an hour."

"I don't ride," I said as Raith moved off with shuffling feet and a glum face.

"Yes, you do," Lucifer said, as if the mere utterance of the words would give me the necessary skill.

"I should help Raith." I started toward the stable.

"No, you shouldn't." Lucifer's words stopped me as cold as if he had struck me. I tried to sense the reason behind the denial but got nothing. I could only assume it was punishment for Raith's tardiness.

So we waited, none of us speaking as we listened to the noise of Raith packing, along with his muttering, which didn't sound at all friendly.

Having had so little sleep, I knew I should be tired, but the chill had snapped away all fatigue. I looked at the ground. The snow had been trampled, turning it a slimy brown. "I don't suppose you noticed the snow," I said, kicking at the almond-colored sludge.

"Of course, we noticed," Elder said. "Although I don't recall seeing it at midnight," he added with a smoldering stare at Lucifer.

The Paladin chose to ignore the comment. "Is this one of the subtle signs you spoke of?"

Subtle? I suppose it was to Lucifer, whose idea of subtlety was beating you into conversion to Ubel instead of sending you to discuss it face-to-face.

"I would think so," I said. I suddenly saw my chance to escape. In a firmer voice, I added, "Yes, it is definitely a sign. The world is on its way to the end. Ubel has gone...well, you know. You have seen the signs for yourself. You don't need me to come along."

"But we do," Lucifer said, implacable as an undertow. "We will need someone to scribe our grand quest and enter it in the official Church archives."

"And the Archbishop's message said you must," Elder added as if he thought I could forget.

"But I'm useless," I protested and meant it. Other than writing and painting marginal seascapes, there wasn't anything I could do with skill.

"You will come." Lucifer's green eyes took on a glazed, starry look I had seen before in other clergymen, usually right before they made some dire pronouncement or issued a Holy Edict; it was the gaze of the zealot.

"Ubel spoke to me last night as I meditated," Lucifer's voice was deep with the rapture of the memory. "He said you must come along. You will be needed ere the end to set things aright."

Me? Set things aright? If Ubel required that for healing, the world was doomed. "Well, Ubel isn't exactly himself right now, so anything he says is suspect. He probably meant, 'Whatever you do, for my sake, leave the scribe at home. He'll only screw things up.'"

The world did its little niggling jump thing again, and something hummed in my head.

No, a voice said, but it wasn't Lucifer. It had Lucifer's mellow deepness but was ten times more fatherly and lacked the implied air of superiority. *You must follow my priest and protector. Only you can save me.*

I glanced around for the source of the voice, thinking to spot some heretofore unseen priest or deacon. No one I actually knew in the Church sounded this kind. Then I recognized it as the voice that spoke to me the previous day in the meeting chamber.

I am speaking to you in your head. You must follow.

Great. As if sensing other people's thoughts wasn't bad enough, now I had voices telling me to do the exact opposite of what I wanted to do.

You must come, the voice said again, only there was a note of pleading this time. *Tell my protector-*

Who are you thinking to? A dark voice asked, evil in its petulance.

No one. I was just stretching my mind.

You're trying to talk to that silly prophetess again, aren't you?

Of course not, not after what you did last time. The fatherly voice sounded scared, and I caught the briefest glimpse of horrible torture and immense pain, which thankfully disappeared before I saw or heard too much.

My relief was short-lived. The petulant voice spoke again, and this time a vision formed with it.

In the Archbishop's sermons, he often spoke about the face of evil, and I had never really been able to get a clear image.

I can now say the face of evil is covered with pimples and belongs to a blond-haired teenager with bloodshot blue eyes, a flaxen-colored unibrow, and a permanently fixed sneer of arrogance.

I don't know who you are, this scowling adolescent thought, *but you need to GO AWAY.*

On these last words, his eyes pulsed a bright red—one of the two primary colors of evil—and searing pain flashed across my brain.

The vision disappeared, and I stumbled backward until my back slammed into one of the stable's wooden walls.

"Are you okay?" Raith asked as he came out of the barn, followed by two ponies and a pack mule.

"No matter how many times you ask me that, as long as I'm being forced to go on this 'quest,' the answer is no. I don't want to leave, and I will continue to not want to leave for as long as I'm gone. I'm scared, I'm cold, and I want to be at home." I realized I was shouting. "You hear that, you evil freak," I yelled, staring up at the sky since I couldn't look into my head. "I *want* to stay away."

Raith studied me as if concerned for my sanity, a look I doubtless would have given me too. "I meant, are you physically okay? Your nose is bleeding."

So it was, as a quick touch to my face revealed by turning a large patch of my gray woolen sock dark red. Wool was expensive; I could already picture the browbeating I would get from my parents for ruining such a costly item. These thoughts disappeared as a pounding in my head replaced them, and pretty much anything else.

"Ahhh," I screamed, or something like it, as I dropped to the ground and put my hands against my ears, hoping to strangle the drummer inside my brain.

Enough. The sentiment was faint through the cloud of pain, but Lucifer's irritation followed on the thought's tail, and its force cut through the miasma as his sword cut through melons. I opened my eyes, which had closed on their own accord, to find Lucifer had dismounted and now strode toward me, his face grim and agate eyes set with purpose.

He knelt beside me. "You whine like a child, even though you look more like a man than your brother." He pulled his metal gauntlets off and reached out with his large hands. Callused palms covered my vision, and the scent of horse and oil filled my nose. "By the will of Ubel the Benevolent, be healed of this affliction."

I had heard that Paladins with enough faith could heal the sick, but I never believed it, just as I never thought people could use magic. That is, magic beyond the "pick which cup the ball is in" variety. As Lucifer spoke, I realized, through my throbbing dizziness, that he thought he was one of these miracle workers.

I'm not sure what I expected. Perhaps a dazzling burst of white light, an overwhelming feeling of calm, and a cessation of all worries as my hurts mended and my troubles dissolved away.

That would have been nice.

Instead, I saw a pinprick of blue light and felt a strange sensation of wet packing in my nose, as if someone had taken wads of seaweed and stuffed it into my nostrils. It continued upward, tendrils of this invisible kelp filling my head, threatening to overtake and become my brain.

Through the pressure, I noticed the pain had disappeared. The seaweed smothered the drummer. Pulling off my ruined socks, I felt my nose with a bare hand; the bleeding had not stopped but slowed to a trickle that would soon cease on its own.

The strange healing pressure disappeared, leaving me clear-headed yet dizzy.

That's the best I can do now, the paternal voice from earlier said as I pressed the socks against my dribbling nose. *Tell the protector there will be no more until I am found. I-*

The voice broke off, and I shuddered, suspecting the cause of the abrupt departure. The Pubescent Evil One had returned.

Hoping that sinister, pocked face wouldn't reappear and do more damage, I looked at Lucifer. He stared at his hands with an expression I'm sure hadn't crossed his square-jawed face since birth: doubt.

"You are not fully healed," he said when he noticed my gaze. "I have somehow failed mighty Ubel. I must atone."

"No," I said, my voice nasal and weak. "I don't think you've failed. Ubel told me that was the best he could do. He also said he would be able to do no more until he was found."

"Ubel spoke to you?" Lucifer's expression went as flat as his voice.

"Well, yes...I mean...sort of..." I was hesitating again, a sign of my sudden discomfort. "I mean...we didn't have a conversation...really...he just told me things."

"And you heard his voice? His actual voice?"

"I...well, I guess. He sounded very fatherly," I offered, hoping it would help.

It didn't.

Lucifer stood and returned to Justice as if he had a board strapped to his back, or perhaps in a more awkward spot. He mounted and inspected me from astride his eighteen hands high charger. Despite the sneering uncertainty on his face—or perhaps because of it—he looked like the Paladin of Paladins. The sun even broke through the clouds at that moment, but the effect wasn't quite there since the beam landed ten feet to Lucifer's right.

"I have been a Paladin for twenty years," Lucifer said. "I have spoken thousands of times to Ubel. He has often guided my heart. But never once has he blessed me with the sound of his voice. Now, in this darkest hour," the sun disappeared behind the clouds, making the Paladin's words much more dramatic than they deserved, "why does Ubel reject me and choose a…a *scribe* to receive his blessed benevolence?"

"I don't think he chose me so much as saw me as a last resort. Besides, I thought you said Ubel spoke to you last night and said I had to come along."

"He speaks to my heart, not to my head."

Probably because there's not enough there for things to snag on. This came from Elder, although I don't believe I could have thought it any better.

"If it's any consolation," I said, "he spoke to my head but not my heart, which really isn't into this whole endeavor."

"Silence," Lucifer thundered. "You will not speak such blasphemy. Ubel has chosen you, and he is never wrong, so your heart will follow what the divine one decrees." He paused a moment, and his face turned hopeful, like a child seeking presents on Giftfest morning. "Did he at least say something about me?"

I wanted more than anything to be able to lie at that moment. I wanted to say, "Yes, he spoke of you as his bravest and most loyal knight. Only you are fit for this quest and are the chosen one to save the world." I wanted to say that, but the words hung in my throat. My Vow and conscience conspired to silence me like a rag jammed in my mouth. Ubel had called Lucifer "the protector," but I didn't see the point of mentioning it; it seemed nothing more than a divine version of the Archbishop calling me "the scribe."

What I managed to get out was, "He was probably going to, but I think he ran out of time. He seems to be in great danger."

I then explained everything to them, trying in vain to keep the shudder from my voice when I talked about the evil one. The only thing I kept to myself was the mental "gift" that probably allowed me access to Ubel's thoughts. When you tell people you can sense emotions, they have two reactions: they either look at you like you've lost a few fish from your net, or they avoid you and make gestures to ward off evil whenever you come near. I wanted to sidestep such unpleasantness, so I kept it to myself. Not for the first time, I was glad the Church had no Vow of Full Disclosure.

My explanation seemed to mollify Lucifer, even as it turned my thoughts gloomy. Any last chance of remaining in Frostishak had now deserted me. I suspected Lucifer saw me as a new way to communicate with Ubel and would always want me near him. I didn't know whether to cry or vomit.

His following words confirmed my suspicion. "Since Ubel has chosen you as his instrument of salvation, you must lead us to him. I will swear to protect you with my life, so I may redeem my failure and return to Ubel's good graces. You will also record the tale of our glorious undertaking."

I sighed. Lucifer was determined to play the martyr, but that's what fanatics do. I looked at Elder, who had been strangely quiet during this whole thing, and saw his round face suppressing a smirk even as I sensed his amusement. What he found humorous about any of this, I could not fathom. Ludicrous, maybe, but not comical.

Lucifer continued. "We shall waste no time in our quest. Take that pony beside your brother. What is the beast's name, Squire?"

Raith looked at the small, bay-colored animal and shrugged. "Pony number two."

It was my turn to keep from laughing as Lucifer frowned. Raith had never bothered to give his pony a name and simply called it Pony. "That seems a bit cumbersome. How about I call him Number Two."

"I suggest you give him a proper name," Lucifer said.

I thought about it a moment. Lucifer was most likely going to be controlling my destiny for some time, whether I wanted him to or not. But in this instance, he had no control over me. "Number Two it is," I said, offering Lucifer a wide grin.

Lucifer's square jaw clenched as his frown deepened, but he said nothing. I had won this round.

My amusement lasted until I realized two things: it was probably the only round I would win, and I was about to put precious parts of my body in harm's way. More than once, Raith complained about soreness in his unmentionables after a day's riding. I thought about reiterating my lack of riding ability, but such complaints would fall on deaf ears. I slipped the socks back on my hands, wincing as the chilled blood touched my bare skin, and walked to the miniature horse.

"Nice horse," I said, putting a gloved hand on its neck and quickly pulling away as the creature turned his large head toward me. "Do they bite?" I asked Raith.

"Only if you're a carrot or a sugar cube."

"How do I get on?"

Following Raith's instruction, I managed to pull myself onto the beast after several false starts. The amusement from Elder and derision from Lucifer didn't help things, but I did my best to ignore them since I couldn't tell them to stop thinking such thoughts.

Once I sat reasonably straight on the creature, Lucifer clacked his heels against Justice. The large charger led the way, his massive hooves throwing out clods of snow. I belatedly wished I had asked Ubel the meaning of the unseasonable weather.

Had I been able to get an answer, it would have saved me a lot of pain since instead of whining to not go, I would have flat refused to budge.

"When we get on board ship," Lucifer said over his shoulder. "I will expect you to brush Justice, clean his hooves, and shine his teeth, since you didn't see fit to get up early enough to do it this morning."

"Of course," Raith said, not entirely successful at keeping his voice neutral. He disliked Justice almost as much as he did Lucifer. The creature was the equine equivalent of his rider, all rippling muscle and superior attitude. Even at a walk, the horse threw up its legs as if to say he was the only horse who knew how to do it properly.

Raith told me it didn't help that Pony had developed an annoying crush on Justice, which caused it to snuggle close whenever possible and make goo-goo eyes and strange sighing sounds at Justice. I suppose it wouldn't have bothered Raith if Pony had been a mare.

We left the stables, Lucifer in the lead and myself in the rear, with Elder and Raith abreast between us. Luckily for me, Number Two seemed willing to follow without guidance, so I held the reins loosely and did my best to remain in a position that would avoid permanent damage to my testicles.

As we started down the snow-covered main road, a breeze blew off the swamp, dry and cold. Two words I never expected to connect with our environment, and certainly not in tandem. I shivered as I glanced around at the buildings of clapboard and mud and wondered if this would be the last time I ever saw them.

"I would have thought there would be people from the Church to see us off."

Elder snorted. "Before His Grace's sunrise meeting yesterday, I don't think most Church elders even knew the crack of dawn existed."

Lucifer frowned but kept silent.

As we moved down the road, other signs of life began to appear in the town. The smell of bread wafted gently through the air, doing a reasonably good job of hiding the odor of recently dumped chamber pots. In the pathetic Merchant's Square, the tradesmen began setting up, opening stalls, and placing their wares in gaudy but thoroughly unappealing displays. I caught snatches of conversation, and it all centered, not surprisingly, on the strange snowfall and what it meant. Everyone seemed to have a theory, but most were way off the mark.

Lucifer took every chance to snarl at any nearby merchants, most of whom just favored him with a blank stare. As they neared the fruit stand, Lucifer's hand drifted toward Heathensmasher.

"Let it go," Elder said. "I promise you can deal with them when we get back."

Lucifer seemed to consider it a moment, then said, "Very well."

"I don't suppose we could get a little breakfast while we're here?" Raith asked, and I suddenly realized I was also hungry. We had left the house, twice, without bothering to grab anything to eat, not even a slab of bread or an apple.

"I will not give these heathens good coin for their tainted wares," Lucifer said in a voice loud enough to draw several stares and a few mutters. "But you may obtain a small loaf at the alehouse next to the east gate."

"East gate alehouse," Elder said, his voice full of surprise. "That's a thousand feet out of our way to the docks. Why exactly are we stopping there?"

"Because it also serves as the local Paladin chapterhouse," Lucifer explained.

"Oh. Did you forget something?"

"Yes. My chapter."

Elder halted dead in his tracks, and I fell and landed face down in the snow as Number Two, paying no attention, slammed into the ass end of Raith's stopped Pony. "Did you say your chapter?" Elder asked, paying no attention to my fall.

"Yes."

"As in, you're going to bring them on this journey?"

"Yes."

As I stood, noting with dismay that my shirt was now as ruined as my socks, an overwhelming wave of dizziness washed over me, as waves will. I wondered if the fall had hurt me, and I checked my nose for a renewal of bleeding. Dry. I looked at the others to mention my sudden vertigo when the sight of Elder's pale face told me the dizziness was not mine but his. "Are you sure that's absolutely necessary?" he asked Lucifer.

"Of course," Lucifer stated. "It is my duty to protect members of the church, and that's you and the Holy Seer." He stared at me as he said this last, and I wondered how I had transformed from a lowly scribe hardly worth consideration to a Holy Seer in less than two minutes. It must have been his way of dealing with the disappointment of not having Ubel speak to him. As far as I was concerned, he could have it.

"Besides," Lucifer continued in his implacable way, "You said there might be a chance to smash some heathens, and it would hardly be sporting of me to keep all the smashing to myself."

"Of course," Elder said, with nowhere near the Paladin's enthusiasm. "Then let's get them."

"Are you hurt?" Lucifer said to me, finally noticing my mud-and-melted-snow coated clothing and face.

"I'm physically okay." I wiped my face with my bloody socks. I refused to say I was fine, which described exactly what I wasn't.

"Here," Raith said, offering me a clean towel from his saddlebag. "You look like you just ran through a slaughterhouse."

"Thanks." I took the proffered towel and continued wiping my face. It possessed an unpleasant tang of lemon and horse. I rubbed it between my fingers and found it slightly oily. Great, I was wiping my face with a cleaning rag.

I pulled it away once my face felt dry and saw what Raith meant. Pink colored the rag, the mixture of sock blood and face water. I handed the cloth back and re-mounted, only needing two attempts.

We journeyed down the road, heading for the east gate. Clouds covered the sky above. The day seemed to be getting colder as it got lighter, a direct contradiction to how days usually went.

I prodded Number Two, and he begrudgingly, as if I were asking him to leap a mile-wide canyon, sidled up to Elder's gold-colored horse. "Brother Elder, may I speak with you?"

He looked at me for a moment, surprised at my request. "Certainly."

I moved closer, Number Two cooperating for the moment, although I was sure he would turn on me at some point. "I really will be useless on this journey," I said. "And I have it on good authority that I'm not really wanted," I added, remembering the strong request that I remain behind by whoever had Ubel imprisoned. If he was strong enough to take on a God, I didn't figure I would present much of a challenge. "Don't you think you could talk Lucifer into leaving me behind?"

Elder gave me a look that made me wonder why I even asked. "Do *you* think I could talk him out of it?"

"I don't guess so," I sighed. Lest you get the impression I'm slow on the uptake, I knew intellectually that I would have to go, but that wouldn't stop me from trying to weasel out of it at every opportunity. After all, a condemned criminal knows he's going to hang, but he still struggles walking up the gallows stairs.

I asked Elder my second question. "Why don't you want Lucifer's chapter to join us?"

He gave me the same discouraging expression, and I made a mental note to think twice before asking him anything else. "You've seen how Lucifer acts?"

I nodded.

"Imagine that times twenty."

I quivered at the thought, and I suspect I turned pale. "They can't all be as bad as him," I said, demanding with my tone that the statement be true.

"Taken individually, probably not. But together," Elder shook his head, at a loss for words. "This is the sort of task that gets you sainthood,"

"If you survive," I said.

"I could have done without that addendum."

Further conversation ceased as we left the heart of town, such as it was, behind, and I had no noise to cover my whining. Lucifer glanced back at me but offered nothing. I offered the same in return. I vowed that the less I said, the better.

If only I could have remembered that promise in the days to come.

5

By the time we reached the alehouse, maybe a quarter-mile away, the chill air had numbed my damp hands and uncovered face. None of my companions seemed uncomfortable, and I envied their dry, weather-appropriate clothing.

We arrived at the alehouse to find twenty armored and stamping horses, twenty nickering and whinnying ponies, and twenty shivering and muttering squires but no paladins. Lucifer frowned. "Raith, go inside and see what is keeping our brethren." He trotted over to speak with the squires, all of whom sprang to attention and did their best to stop their teeth from chattering.

As he slipped off his horse, Raith muttered under his breath to me. "Bet you a gold piece to a goblin's ear it's hangovers."

Elder heard it and frowned as Raith walked away and entered the alehouse, a squat wooden building painted pale gray. It had all the charm of a cauliflower stalk. "For a squire, your brother doesn't seem very deferential to the Brotherhood."

I looked askance at Elder. "You don't exactly think they're the fish gills yourself."

"True, but I'm a priest, and the Paladins work for me, so I can think what I want about them. Privilege of being the boss."

"I never considered hypocrisy as a fringe benefit," I said. "Maybe I should become a priest."

Elder turned his frown on me, so I moved to a different subject, cursing my mouth less than ten minutes after vowing to quit over-working it. "Raith became a squire because he has delusions of becoming a Paladin, though I don't know why."

Elder nodded. "He does seem a bit..." He suddenly realized he was talking to the brother of the subject under discussion. "Well, he's a little..."

"Pudgy and weak," I offered.

"I wouldn't have put it quite that bluntly."

"I say what I think, usually a half-second before thinking it. It's a common failing in my family, although Raith hides it better."

"Well, if anyone can teach your brother the proper way to be a Paladin, it will be Lucifer."

I couldn't help myself. "Are you kidding? Lucifer's random, dangerous, the wrong side of stupid, and psychotically devout."

Elder smiled. "Like I said..."

Lucifer returned to us. "The squires know nothing, only that they arrived here to find none of the chapter outside, so they have been waiting here."

"Didn't anyone go inside to ask?" I said.

"Of course not," Lucifer said as if the idea were akin to a priest walking into a bordello.

"Squires are not allowed in chapterhouses without permission from their knights," Elder explained, anticipating the "why not" moments before it left my lips.

I found that restriction stupid in so many ways. I didn't bother to ask the fidgeting and obviously irritated Lucifer why he didn't go in to see what was keeping Raith. He probably needed permission from the Archbishop.

Elder wasn't as shy. "Should we go see what's keeping them?"

"No, they are most likely making last-minute preparations, though the squires seem to have everything handled."

No sooner had Lucifer spoken than the Paladins began exiting the building. More than half of them looked like twice-baked death, and each had a suit of blue-tinted plate mail on his body and a brown mug in his hand.

"HERE THEY ARE, MY LIEGE!" Raith yelled from the back of the group. He gave me a grin and a wink as several of the men grabbed their heads. I caught a wave of dismay from the squires, who didn't like to see their masters treated in such a manner. I would have to warn Raith not to rile them. They all appeared several years younger but many pounds more muscular than him. They also outnumbered him twenty to one.

"For a former librarian's apprentice, your squire has a very loud mouth," a Paladin with a silver circle etched on his breastplate said.

"Sorry, Sergeant Glawen, I'll be quieter!" Raith said directly in the man's ear as he walked by.

Glawen winced and quickly took a drink from the mug. "Hair of the orc," he muttered.

"What is the meaning of this, Sergeant?" Lucifer asked, his voice booming over the group.

"Ubel's benevolence was overflowing last night, my lord, and we perhaps partook more than we should have."

"We shall discuss it later," Lucifer threatened, his agate eyes boring down on the sergeant. "MOUNT UP!" Two of the Paladins fell down at the thundered command.

Their squires helped them up, and all the Paladins straggled to their horses. After several aborted attempts and even more draughts from their mugs, the Paladins were soon on their horses. The squires, being younger and sober, mounted their ponies with ease.

Lucifer looked at the assembled group. His expression revealed his displeasure as he studied the men, many swaying in their saddles and a few nodding toward sleep or insensibility. I thought the whole thing a tad ostentatious. Was it absolutely necessary to take forty people with us?

As it later turned out, it was. I shiver now even as I shivered then. Now it's with the knowledge of what happened, then it was a sense of what was going to happen. I make no claims to predicting the future, but something told me many of those men would never see Frostishak again.

"They shouldn't go," I said.

Lucifer either didn't hear or chose to ignore me. He looked at the sky and smiled. "This unnaturally cold weather seems to have made most of you sick. I suggest all you men put on your helmets, so you may sweat away your chill." His tone made it anything but a suggestion.

There was a great deal of groaning, but each Paladin did as he was told.

"Okay, let's move out."

"They shouldn't go," I said louder.

"What do you mean we shouldn't go," Sergeant Glawen growled through his helmet. "Who are you?"

"He is a prop-"

"No one," I said, interrupting Lucifer at great peril. It was bad enough he thought me some sort of prophet. I didn't need the rest of them looking to me for divine guidance or laughing at me. "I'm just a scribe for the Church."

"A scribe?" Glawen scoffed. "Then you should stick to writing and not speaking."

"Excellent advice," I said, wondering how many times I would hear that tidbit of wisdom. The sergeant's attitude cleared matters up for me. The fate of these men was not my concern. They chose to be Paladins; they could live, or not, with the consequences.

And I could hope the dread in the pit of my stomach was indigestion.

We left the alehouse—which seemed a stupid place to house alcoholic Paladins—and went back through town, a huge progression marching over the snow-covered streets toward the docks. Children had come out to play in the unexpected weather, flinging dirty snowballs at each other and giggling.

Elder, Raith, and I rode at the rear of the progression. Elder looked at Raith. "I had some bad thoughts about you earlier. I think I owe you an apology."

"No," Raith said, giving the priest a watery-eyed grin. "You owe me a goblin's ear."

6

D uring the half-mile trek to the docks, the clouds dispersed. The bitter cold still dominated, but the bright sunlight at least gave the illusion of warmth. I could almost feel my hands again.

Another thing I could feel was every step of the pony, which simulated someone rhythmically slamming a cloth-wrapped hammer against my crotch. I shifted, and I squirmed. I tried every way I could to ease the discomfort, but it was a hopeless cause. I had to assume people who rode horses for any time gave up all possibilities of fathering children.

We reached the docks, which announced themselves with a stench that could kill small animals. It was a particularly unique aroma, combining fish, rotting seaweed, saltwater, and the peculiar odor of slaving dockworkers who never met a tub of water they could abide. Fortunately for us, it was early enough that the pall had not gained full strength.

The most amazing thing was that so much smell came from three berths and two warehouses. As I've mentioned, Frostishak is not a major trading center.

"There is our ship," Lucifer said. He pointed to a pile of nailed and tarred boards that could only be called a ship because it had sails and somehow managed to stay afloat. I was no expert on water vessels, but I've seen pieces of driftwood that looked more seaworthy. The hull consisted of so many wood colors it looked like a floating patchwork quilt. The sails didn't seem much better, multi-colored, tattered, the ropes holding them in place spliced with various knots. The figurehead had probably been a beautiful woman at one time, but the beauty had been so chipped away, charred, and covered in bird droppings that it more resembled a sea hag or pissed-off fishwife. Painted on the side was the vessel's name: DIRE CONSEQUENCES.

That did nothing for my confidence.

Elder seemed to have the same assessment. "That's the best you could do?"

Lucifer looked embarrassed, an emotion that seemed to cause him physical pain. "On such short notice, yes."

"What about one of the merchant cutters?" Elder asked, pointing to the sleek, glimmering vessels nestled beside the floating pile of cobbled debris we prepared to board. I noticed one of them was named HONEYDEW.

"I would rather swim than deal with the likes of them."

Elder sighed. "I knew I should have made the arrangements. Well, it can't be helped now. Let's get on board."

As we rode the short remaining distance to the ship's gangplank, I watched it drift up and down in the bay's gentle swell, and my stomach churned. I looked at Raith's back to keep myself steady, but he chose that moment to step onto the quay; Pony's weight set the dock to moving, which made Raith jiggle up and down. My stomach lurched.

I knew it was going to happen, but there was nothing I could do to stop it. As soon as my stupid miniature horse stepped onto the floating wooden planks, I threw up. The violent motion made the docks rock even more, so when I finished the first time, I threw up again. And again.

By the third time, there wasn't much left, and although the dock still swayed, my body at least seemed disinclined to continue the food ejection process. My stomach gave a few half-hearted quivers before coming to rest. The upheaval had dots dancing in front of my eyes, and I gripped tighter to the saddle pommel to keep from falling into the water. I had no idea how I managed to stay on the horse during my stomach's party. I heard laughter coming from the vague direction of the ship. As I sat back and wiped my mouth, I blinked to chase away the motes. My vision cleared, and I saw the laughter's source.

Standing at the top of the gangplank stood the ugliest and filthiest man I had ever seen. His clothing, black pantaloons and a red shirt with bloused sleeves, was so bedraggled as to be little more than threads held together by dirt, which covered his body in copious quantities. Long hair straggled from under a faded blue tri-corner hat with one corner missing, chopped off by a sword from the looks of it. His hair was the color of a rusted bucket, as was his scraggly, unkempt beard.

What few teeth he had left were capped in gold that had gone an orange hue of no metal known to man. A gray feathered bird, its quills mangy and tattered, sat on his shoulder. It must have been missing its right eye since a round piece of black cloth covered it, held on by colored bits of string knotted together and tied off around the creature's head. The man stopped laughing long enough to speak, his voice the bray of a donkey with a sore throat. "Most people usually wait until they're on the boat to heave their guts."

"And most people can't grow plants on their bodies," I spat back, wishing for a swig of water.

"What does he mean by that, Cap'n?"

I wondered who he was talking to since no one else stood nearby, when the bird squawked and spoke. "He means you're filthy. Brawk! And he's right. Brawk! How someone who works around water all the time can end up looking like a walking mushroom farm is beyond me."

I stared at the creature, flabbergasted. Except for the strange squawks, the creature's voice was pleasant, something you would hear coming out of a professional bard, not a one-eyed bird. I wasn't the only one stunned by this. Elder's cherubic face gaped with slack-jawed astonishment, and Raith's owlish eyes blinked in amazement. Most of the squires seemed puzzled, and I have no idea what the Paladins thought since their expressions were the blank faceplates of their helmets.

Only Lucifer seemed unfazed. "Greetings, Captain Shivers," he said with a nod of his head.

"Brawk. Correction, good Paladin. Timbers. Captain Paulie Timbers." He indicated the man on whose shoulder he sat with a light tap of his beak on the man's hat. "He's Shivers, me Timbers. Brawk!"

"My apologies," Lucifer said. "I sometimes have trouble with names."

"It's true," Raith said. "I've been his squire for six months, and he still doesn't know mine."

"Of course I do," Lucifer said smoothly without turning away from the ship. "Your name is Squire Who Will Be Grooming the Other Paladins' Horses Tonight."

Raith frowned, and I felt rather than heard titters from the other squires.

"Permission to come aboard, Captain."

"Brawk. Permission granted, good Paladin."

Lucifer spun about on Justice and looked at his chapter. "ALL ABOARD!"

Several Paladins swayed, but none of them fell off their horses. Apparently, the brief trek in their helmets had returned them to a semblance of sobriety. I did notice several had large drops of sweat standing on the shoulder pieces of their armor.

The embarkation took some time. Lucifer supervised, since he insisted on being the last man on the ship. I'd like to think it had something to do with knightly chivalry, but I suspect it was to make sure I didn't bolt.

First, all the Paladins had to dismount. Gravity helped, but it gave too much assistance to a few of the more inebriated, and their squires had to assist them in standing. With a disgusted look, Elder boarded during the chaos.

Once the Paladins boarded, sweating and huffing under their helmets, the squires led the horses up the gangplank. Many of the animals seemed reluctant to board—a feeling I shared—but with persistent tugging and a few choice words that drew reprimanding looks from Lucifer, the stubborn equines were soon aboard. Justice, of course, practically led Raith up in his eagerness to do his master's bidding. Pony followed without urging, nipping lovingly at the larger horse's tail.

Shivers wasn't the only one amused by my dockside performance. By the time I boarded, next to last, with Lucifer all but pushing Number Two up the gangplank, most of the crew had heard about my weak stomach and gathered on deck to see me, pointing and giggling. The crew was surprisingly young, many not much older than me and several a few years younger. Things seemed a little more promising; I had no friends in Frostishak, and this appeared a prime opportunity to make some. I hadn't made a good first impression, but I could overcome that with charm and intelligence.

Shivers ended that fantasy. "All hands, welcome aboard Pukeboy."

The crew roared with laughter, the youngest snickering the loudest. My face grew hot, and the sour taste of embarrassment overrode the bile flavor in my mouth. I considered diving over the side and praying for a quick death: broken neck on the dock or smashed between the pilings and the ship; either would work.

Just when I thought things couldn't get worse, Lucifer spoke. "Silence, blasphemous heathens," he thundered. The entire deck hushed. Even the lapping of water against the hull grew quieter, and the gulls cawed softer. I didn't dare interrupt the Paladin in front of this many strangers, so I was helpless to stop what I knew was coming. "This is Briar, son of Patch the Tailor, and he is a holy prophet blessed by visions from Ubel. None of you are fit to mock him. You will treat him with due respect, or you will feel the wrath of the Church."

I wanted to hide my head in my hands, bury myself beneath the piles of rope stacked on the deck, or continue with my first plan of leaping. I scanned the crew and saw in their weathered faces a range of expressions: disbelief, disgust, hatred. Everything but respect. Any chance of finding a friend had been irrevocably destroyed by Shivers and Lucifer. I had to salvage the situation and make sure I avoided regular ass beatings. "That's right," I shouted. "I am beloved of Ubel, and should any harm come to me, there will be such woe upon my assailant as to make grown men weep. Ubel will strike a curse that your grandchildren will feel."

I thought it sounded pretty good, and so patently untrue I wasn't really surprised when a massive gust of wind whistled through the rigging and set the boat rocking. The sudden motion caught me unaware and slammed me against the deck railing. I came back with my nose bleeding for the second time that day. But this time, I knew it was bleeding because eye-watering pain followed it.

I heard the crew start up again, but their merriment was cut short by a loud "Brawk!"

"All hands pay heed to the captain," Shivers brayed.

"All right, you scurvy sons-of-bitches," Timbers bellowed in a surprisingly big sound from such a small animal, "this is a ship's crew, not a comedy troupe. Brawk! We have the honor of having Lucifer and his cadre of Paladins aboard our ship, and his guests are to be treated like you would treat your own mother." Captain Timbers paused and flapped his wings, fluttering Shivers's rusty hair and sending a few feathers wafting into the air. "Brawk, make that better than your own mothers. I know what bastards some of you are. Brawk! In fact, treat them like you would if mistreating them got you five lashes and two days in the crow's nest."

That sobered the crew considerably. A few cast evil glances my way when they felt their one-eyed captain wasn't looking.

"First mate Shivers."

"Aye, Captain," Shivers said, turning his head to stare at Timbers.

"Brawk! Give the orders." He flew off with another flap of wings and disappeared into the hold.

Shivers watched until Timbers disappeared and then faced the crew. "All right, you heard the captain. Our guests are to be treated with respect. But it's time to shove off, so run 'em over if they get in your way."

With that, he began to shout out a litany of indecipherable commands. These screams sent the crew into a frenzy of movement. I soon found all my attention fixed on avoiding getting trampled by people or struck by swinging ropes and unfolding canvas. I knew several of the crew went out of their way to try and hit me, but I somehow managed to dodge everyone. Raith wasn't so lucky. When Lucifer saw his squire go down, he took two strides and, with one swing of a meaty fist, sent Raith's assailant to the deck, where he lay stunned.

My respect for Lucifer rose a notch; he had protected his squire.

It immediately fell again when he reached down with that same large hand, pulled Raith to his feet, and said, "Find out what that man was doing. As punishment for being in his way, you will do his job."

I soon saw Raith heading up a mast, followed by two laughing boys.

After about a half-hour of this organized chaos, the ship lurched away from the dock. That first jerking lunge sent me to the rail and my head over the side. Thus, I started the journey to the northern continent of Skaldor with an empty stomach, which I kept for the majority of the voyage.

7

D uring the next ten days, my misery, like human stupidity, knew no bounds. I had often heard ships were damp, smelly, cramped things, not fit for civilized people. Whoever said such a thing wins the Grandmaster of Understatement award. I began to look back with great fondness on the time when I shared bed space with no one but Raith. Even though only half of those on board slept at any one time, that still left me surrounded by no less than six other people. We slept head to foot, packed tighter than pickled fish. Most people aren't aware that sailors rarely wear shoes onboard a ship. This allows their carbuncled and calloused feet to pick up the odors of salt, tar, bilge water, and guano, an olfactory delicacy I experienced every night when the twin midshipmen, Salic and Silix, crunched in next to me. Though only twelve, they had the feet of men who had spent the last twenty years stomping on glass.

When I did manage to ignore the smells and snores and get to sleep, visions plagued me. I knew they were visions and not regular nightmares because the strange sensation of reality being torn apart like a rag doll in the hands of a spoiled brat always started them. Fuzzy and fragmented, they all had the same theme. The pockmarked leer of the Evil One looking down on the kind face of Ubel. I sensed torture and pain. They spoke in a language I didn't understand, but it became apparent the Evil One was asking questions Ubel refused to answer. These disturbing premonitions often woke me and I would invariably find a foot belonging to Salic or Silix's—sometimes both—splayed across my chest.

I fared better during the day, but not much. The ocean is never still, and it has a disconcerting habit of shifting just as you've grown accustomed to a particular level of movement. These unexpected changes always sent me to the railing, where the musical laughter of nearby crewmen sound accompanied my retching. And by musical, I mean loud and obnoxious. But only if the captain wasn't nearby.

It also didn't take me long to discover that life aboard a ship, if you're not involved in keeping the vessel afloat and moving, is monotony personified. My daily bouts of puking were punctuated by strings of boredom so intense that smashing my head against the mainmast began to form a valid entertainment option. Everyone else had something to do. The Paladins and squires, including Raith, kept busy with training, daily prayers, and tending the horses. One small grace was that I didn't have to deal with those lumbering creatures, who smelt marginally better than the sailors, but made up for it by producing unbelievable amounts of manure. Despite daily shoveling, the stench lingered and mingled with the other scents trapped below deck to create an almost visible vileness. I was thankful the sailors took nature calls outside, although my embarrassment at trying to hang over the deck when my needs called was its own little slice of hell.

Elder found himself attached as the crew's spiritual adviser and confidant. They had been without a priest since their last one, no doubt distraught at the workload, killed himself. Elder spoke to me a few times during his brief moments when some sailor wasn't taking him aside to ask for advice or forgiveness; he often looked ready to cry at the weight being thrown upon him. I could sense his stress and a certain amount of disgust at the proclivities of the shipmates forced upon him. I knew he longed to share the burden with me, but I didn't encourage it. Before he could really start to unload, he was called away for another consultation.

So everyone, for good or bad, stayed active. I had nothing but my scribing gear. My first and only attempt to make notes about our journey ended with half a page of illegible gibberish and me in my accustomed position over the rail. Writing and waves don't mix.

On the vomit scale, Raith fared better than I did. After being sick the first day, he acquired his "sea legs," managing said feat even quicker than his master, which made him immensely proud. He began to befriend several of the younger crew. They spent their moments of leisure time exchanging stories of squiring and sailing: one sea yarn for one account of horse grooming or melon gathering. On the boredom exchange, I think the seamen came out worse.

"They're not so bad," Raith told me halfway through the trip. "You should sit with us sometime."

"That's okay; I wouldn't want to intrude," I said. I had already classed sailors as the seagoing version of pages: unbearable, odious, and thoroughly not worth my time. They probably felt much the same about me. The name Pukeboy had stuck, always spoken in a whisper or simply mimed in my direction. No one ever treated me with outright disrespect, but they never invited me to their evening socials either.

The one bright spot of this blighted voyage was my friendship with Captain Shivers, which started right after my disturbing encounter with Belas. Despite my ostracism by the rest of the crew, Belas approached me the second day, his broad, tanned face offering a friendly, if toothless, smile. Stout and strong, he had the look of a true sailor, weather-beaten but wise in nautical knowledge.

"Pay no attention to the others; they are all rude children," he said, his voice deep and hoarse, no doubt from a lifetime of shouting over wind and water. "I am Belas. What's your name again?"

"Briar," I blurted, thunderstruck that someone actually wanted to know.

His smile grew broader, revealing his dark gums. "Stick with me, Briar, and I will teach you the sailing life."

The only thing I really wanted to know about the sailing life was when this trip would end, but I could hardly turn down this single overture of friendship from a crew member. Things went well for the first two days, and I learned a great deal about nautical terminology. I once knew the difference between a mizzenmast and a topmast, a mainstay and a backstay, and why a forecastle is pronounced as if several of its consonants have gone missing, but I've long since forgotten such trivial things. I found the knowledge boring then, and unimportant now. It wasn't the learning I craved but the companionship.

That companionship ended the day he said he wanted to show me some things below deck. I had no desire to see the bilge pumps or cargo holds, which were about the only areas below I hadn't seen, but I still felt honored by his friendship. I followed him as he walked back to the cargo hold, wondering exactly how many different names a box could have. He slipped behind a crate and pulled me with him. A strange glint came into

SCRIBE OF DESTINY

his gray eyes, only slightly less distracting than the glint on the dagger he pulled from behind his back. "Ublek sends his love. And a wish for you to rot in hell."

If he had stopped with the first statement, I wouldn't be telling anyone my story. But he got talkative, giving the shock enough time to wear off. He thrust the knife toward me, his face a mask of snarling hate. I side-stepped. The blade snagged my shirt, ripping it, and sliced along my ribs. Had I not moved, I'd be staring at the hilt sticking out of my chest.

Purely on instinct, because I was in no way trained to fight, I lashed out with a kick and caught him square in the spot that makes every male wince. He doubled over; the knife fell from his hand. I stared a moment at the shining metal triangle of the weapon, one edge wet with my blood. Feeling queasiness that had nothing to do with the ship's swaying, I ran up the steps—which for some stupid reason sailors call a ladder—and onto the deck. This time I didn't even reach the rail. Bile spilled onto the boards and splattered my shoes. Hands on my knees, head down, I waited for more, hoping my sudden shivering would subside.

A piping voice, one of the older midshipmen, said, "Look, Pukeboy's gone and fouled the deck again. What an albatross."

I had often heard the expression "something in him just snapped," usually in reference to Lucifer, but this was the first time I ever experienced it. I think the betrayal by Belas did it; I saw him as a friend, and he saw me as a target of opportunity. That's the kind of thing that can push you off the emotional cliff. I stood up with my hands clenched and saw the leering face of the midshipman ten feet away, but it wasn't *his* face. It was the face of every crewmember that teased me and ignored me. It was the face of Belas, who deceived me. It was everything I hated about this whole "adventure."

I leaped at the midshipman, my arms flailing as I prepared to beat him senseless.

He never stood a chance. From the first jab to the last uppercut, there was never a possibility he could do anything but pound me into fishcakes.

I woke up when the water, warm and salty, splashed me in the face. My eyes opened to stare directly into the sun. I slammed them shut, wincing at the fierce pain, and turned my head to the side so I could open them again without going blind—assuming I wasn't already too late.

It took a moment for the dancing dots to clear my vision; when they did, they were replaced by what appeared to be every crew member looking down at my supine body, a body that felt three kinds of swollen

55

and innumerable varieties of pain. Foremost in my vision was Timbers, who looked down at me and nodded—in approval of my beating or the fact I had regained consciousness, I wasn't sure. The midshipman, who now looked like a dark-haired, tanned teen and not some hideous amalgam of my hatreds, stood beside first mate Shivers. He didn't seem to be gloating and, if anything, looked perplexed at what had just happened. Raith stood beside him, his left eye swelling, and one of the other squires with a hand on his shoulder. Once again, he had tried to defend me.

"Sorry," I mumbled to the midshipman and Raith. The word bounced through my hurting head like a gong.

"Can you stand up?" Shivers asked, his braying voice shredding my brain.

"I don't know."

"What transpires here?"

I groaned. There was no way to keep Lucifer from finding out; the ship just wasn't that big. The crew stood aside as the Paladin shoved his way through, followed by a black-haired squire, who had no doubt run to get his Commander when he saw Raith fighting. Elder trailed close behind. When they saw me, Lucifer's face grew stern, the squire flinched, and Elder looked faint, which gave me a good indication of how bad I appeared.

"Are you okay, Scribe?"

"Briar," I muttered, irritation momentarily overriding my pain. I sat up, and the pain reasserted itself.

"What?"

"His name is Briar," Elder said, his face turning red. "Do you hear that?" He raised his voice so all could hear him. "Briar. Not Scribe, not Pukeboy. And out of everyone on this ship, he's about the only one who isn't sick in mind and body. Now, what in Ubel's holy name happened to him?"

There was a moment of stunned silence as the crew took in the sight of the formerly mild priest, shaking and flush, screaming at them and calling them names. I sensed a slight twinge of irritation from Lucifer at what he felt was Elder's attempt to usurp authority.

During the pause, when the creaks of the ship and slosh of waves were the only noise, Raith helped me stand, an exercise that felt akin to climbing stairs with my nose. I still shook with the knowledge of near death.

"Well, answer me," Elder shouted when no one spoke. "What happened?"

"He started it," the midshipman said.

"Is this true?" Lucifer said. I guess he had let Elder lead long enough and wanted to take back over.

"It depends on your definition of started," I managed to get out. In my mind, Belas had started it two days ago when he befriended me on false pretenses. The midshipman just happened to be in the way when it turned ugly.

Lucifer clarified things for me. "Who threw the first punch?"

I looked at the deck. "That would be me."

I felt Lucifer's surprise and could picture the astonishment on his square face without looking at him. He wasn't sure what shocked him more: that I could throw a punch or that I *would*. I sensed a slight increase in respect from him and decided to keep it to myself that I hadn't thrown the punch so much as gently tossed it.

He looked at Raith. "And you got involved?"

"He's my brother," Raith's watery eyes dared Lucifer to reprimand him.

Lucifer nodded. "Admirable, but we'll discuss this further later." He turned back to me. Respect or not, he couldn't let such behavior from one of his own—or so he considered me—go unpunished. "This is unacceptable," he said, pitching his voice to boom over the deck so all could hear. "You will be confined to your space for-"

"Brawk! I don't think that will be necessary."

All eyes turned to the wheelhouse, where the captain sat on the railing, his gray plumage especially drab in the sun beating down on the deck. When he had everyone's attention, he tucked his head under his wing a moment and scratched with his sharp black beak.

"Captain Timbers," Lucifer began. "I can-"

The captain's head whipped out from under his wing, and he gave Lucifer as menacing a glare as a one-eyed bird can. It must have been enough, for the Paladin fell silent. The captain returned to his grooming for a few seconds and then gazed at Lucifer.

"Brawk, I don't believe punishment will be necessary, good Paladin. These matters are easily forgiven." Even after so many days, I had trouble rectifying the plump bird with the soft voice.

"But the Sc—Briar and my squire have committed assault against one of your men."

The captain looked from me to Raith to the midshipman, and his head cocked in what I took for amusement. "Then I think they have been well punished for their indiscretion." He fixed his one eye on the midshipman. "Brawk! Midshipman Samaan, do you wish to see these two punished?"

"No, sir," Samaan said, and I sensed he honestly didn't, and his answer wasn't just to appease the captain's wishes. I offered a tentative smile; he frowned, but there was no real animosity behind it.

"So, there you are, Paladin Lucifer. If young Samaan wanted your men disciplined, we would do so without hesitation. Since he doesn't, there is no need."

Lucifer nodded. "I see your crewman has the benevolence of Ubel about him. If he forgives them, then so do I."

"However," Timbers said with his single eye cocked at me, "I would like to know what brought about this behavior. Boredom?"

I gazed around the deck at the faces regarding me and spotted Belas standing amongst the crew as if nothing had happened. My stomach clenched as I pointed toward the would-be assassin. "He tried to kill me." Every sailor stepped aside as if I were accusing them. All except Belas, who stared with wide, innocent eyes.

"That's a lie," he said. "I barely know you, boy."

"Then how did I get this?" I held my torn, bloody shirt away from my side.

"Ships are dangerous places."

"Brawk! Mr. Belas, so far, the only thing I know is a lie, is you. You've been around this lad the past two days."

"I never, Captain."

"It's a small ship."

Belas paused, and I could all but hear him trying to figure out the next excuse.

"Brawk. Mr. Shivers, if you would."

Shivers stormed across the deck, moving faster than a man his bulk should have been able. The crew scattered like birds fleeing a dog. With a toothless yelp, Belas turned to run. I don't know where he thought he would go.

Shivers reached him, grabbed him by his collar, and lifted his dagger like a pickpocket taking a pouch.

I was lucky Belas wasn't the sharpest nail. Not only had he kept the dagger, he hadn't even cleaned it. My blood still clung to the edge. I wavered, things going gray for a moment. If I hadn't moved…

All the old sailor's bravado disappeared. "I had no choice, Captain. I had—"

"Mr. Shivers?"

"Aye, Captain."

"Toss him over the side."

Before Belas could react, Shivers grabbed him by the collar and rope belt and took four quick steps. Easily as I might fling a piece of toast, he slung the screaming man over the railing.

I stood there stunned, as were my companions. I had expected Belas to be punished—wanted him to be punished—but this? I shivered.

"The sea is harsh but fair," Captain Timbers intoned. The crew repeated the phrase.

Lucifer didn't speak for a moment, staring at the railing where Belas had gone overboard. Then he nodded to the captain. "I trust you know your affairs better than I." His agate eyes fell on me. "Are you okay?"

Of course, I wasn't, but a nod was the easiest thing, so I gave a spastic jerk of my head, wiping at my eyes. I didn't trust myself to speak yet.

"Brawk!" Timbers said, and I damn near jumped over the side myself. That made me think of Belas, and I wanted to scream. "Everyone back to work. I'm fairly certain there are sails needing mending and ropes needing splicing. Brawk! Any man who feels the desire to be idle can get a pry and work on scraping barnacles."

The deck burst into a flurry of movement, and sailors disappeared into their work.

Captain Timbers looked at me. "Would you join me?"

I nodded and walked up the short ladder, stumbling as dizziness hit me. My body hurt in several places, and my emotions were as bruised as the rest of me. At that moment, I believed the aches would be with me forever. I stopped beside the captain and looked at the deck below. Elder walked away with a dazed expression not much different from his typical look. Lucifer returned to practicing with the Paladins. The squires stood nearby, doing their best to keep sails between themselves and the sun while also being ready to do their masters' bidding at a moment's notice. Had no one else just seen a man get thrown over the side like a bucket of swill?

Up until now, I had never heard the captain do anything but shout, so it surprised me when he said, in a quiet voice, "What happened?"

That surprised me. The captain had sent a man to his death without knowing all the facts. I shivered at the cruelty but told him the whole story.

The captain nodded when I finished my tale. "Who is Ublek?"

"I have no idea. I thought maybe he was another sailor."

A feather floated to the deck as Captain Timbers shook his head. "Not on this ship."

I considered events for a moment as I stared at the sea, which had calmed. Or I had gotten used to it. Some of the turmoil was beginning to roll away from me. A man was dead or on his way to dying, but I didn't kill him. Still hard to swallow, but not impossible. "I know Belas tried to kill me. And he betrayed my trust." That hurt almost as much as the attempted murder. "But his punishment seemed a bit..." I paused, trying to think of a word that wouldn't offend the captain.

"Excessive," he offered.

I nodded.

Timbers fluttered his wings in such a way that I knew he was offering a shrug. "We had an agreement when he came on board, and he didn't keep up his end of the bargain, so I kept up mine."

I wanted to ask about the agreement but figured I wouldn't get an answer. I had a pretty good idea anyway. "But why even have him on board if you know what he was like?"

"Because he was a good sailor, and I believe people should get second chances. What you start as isn't what you have to stay."

I felt a rushing wave of sadness, tinged with outrage, boiling off his avian body, and I suddenly understood. "You weren't always a parrot, were you?" I blurted out but still managed to keep my voice low, so the whole ship didn't hear.

"Macaw, actually," he corrected. "And no, I haven't always been like this."

"You've been cursed," I whispered. I had read about curses in the Church library. They were the province of witches and warlocks, who handed them out like candy at a spring festival. According to the church's books, all you had to do to receive a hex from such spiritually wrecked practitioners of the black arts was look at them the wrong way. Suddenly my encounter with Belas seemed trivial. I had come out of it unscathed, if even more wary of friendship now.

"You don't have to whisper; the whole crew knows."

"How did it happen? What terrible sorcerer did it to you?" I prepared myself for a great story of some seafaring adventure gone horribly wrong —a lost battle with a coven, perhaps.

"As for how and why that is my business and no others'. As for who, it was the Oracle at Hiephi. The very person you and your companions are going to see, I believe."

That gave me a moment's pause. "I thought the Oracle was benevolent."

"I suggest we discuss something else," Captain Timbers said.

I took the hint. "How did you get started as a sailor?"

"I was born in the Opripeligo. My options were sailor, singer, talent manager, or pirate. I wasn't ruthless enough for the last two, and I couldn't carry a tune."

"The Opripeligo?" I asked. "Which island? Diva?"

"Worse. Brawk! Aria, which is the fart from Diva's ass."

The shock must have been mapped across my face. The captain looked at me with his good eye and let out a squawking laugh. "I forget you work in a church. Brawk! I should think you would be beyond such language bothering you, having been on the ship as long as you have."

It was true almost every other word out of the sailors' mouths was profanity or blasphemy. It didn't bother me, and I had picked up several colorful phrases I hoped to eventually use. But I suspected Elder's wan look and stress came from his shipmates' language as much as their confessions. Lucifer seemed strangely oblivious to it, but I would bet good silver he kept tabs in some way.

"The language didn't bother me," I assured the captain. "It just surprised me to hear you so emotional about something."

"I have powerful emotions, but the only way of expressing them is by either going 'brawk!' which I do enough involuntarily, or flapping my wings and jumping around, which makes me shed and tends to upset the crew. Brawk! So, I've learned to keep them in check, but you struck a sore spot."

I leaned against the railing. "You hated it that much?"

"Obviously, you've never been there, or you wouldn't have to ask."

"It can't be as bad as Frostishak."

"Brawk!" Captain Timbers jumped up and down and flapped his wings, flinging dust and bits of feather into my eyes. Some of the nearby crew stopped their work and looked our way, most favoring me with glares of contempt. Nice to see things were back to normal.

I smelt Shivers before I heard him come up behind us. Six days at sea had made him dirtier and more odoriferous, an accomplishment I thought impossible when we first boarded. I turned to find him snarling at me. "Is everything okay, captain? Do you want me to have Pu- Briar removed?"

"That's okay, Shivers. I was demonstrating why I don't become agitated. Carry on."

"Aye, Captain." He glanced at me, irritation pouring off him. It amazed me how he could hold such a grudge over one insult.

After Shivers walked away, I turned back to find the Captain staring ahead, looking over the relatively calm ocean. Wondering if I was about to be dismissed again, I said, "I'm sorry, but all I've ever known is Frostishak. Perhaps Aria is worse." I paused a moment and took the plunge. "Would you be willing to tell me why?"

"No. I've done my best to forget it since I left all those years ago, but trust me, Frostishak is a paradise compared to Aria. I couldn't wait to be gone from there."

I felt a sudden affinity with the captain. I didn't think anyone could hate his home as much as I did, but here he was. Not only that, he dared to get away and look for something better, whereas I only had the will to gripe. Even now, having gotten out, I wanted nothing more than to be off the ship and back home.

Sometimes I didn't understand myself.

I kept silent and waited for the captain to continue at his own pace. He stared over the glassy sea a moment, his one eye getting as much of a far-away look as a solid black orb can. I sensed his troubled thoughts as he fought to push down the memories my questions tried to dredge up, and guilt gnawed at my heart. First the Oracle and now this. I much prefer to anger someone than hurt them.

Thinking he wouldn't speak further, I prepared to dismiss myself. Then his head gave a twitch as if he were physically pulling himself back to the present. His eye pinned me, and I dropped any thought of leaving.

"I took work on a ship as soon as I turned eleven," he said, "which is the age of apprenticeship in the Opripelago. I joined the *Slippery Slope* and started as a ball monkey."

I tried to keep from giggling, but I wasn't that mature yet.

"Brawk! A stupid name," Captain Timbers muttered as I quickly removed my smirk, "but a demanding job. A ball monkey is in charge of loading a ship's slings, and shot can weigh as much as three stone, depending on the sling. Some slings require two monkeys to arm them."

"If it's so tough, why don't they use grown men?"

"Because most ships have their slings in the hold, hidden from view and somewhat protected from enemy fire. Brawk! As I'm sure you've noticed, the below decks is not the roomiest of areas. Children are the only ones small enough to squeeze into the load spaces. However, I was the monkey of a scattersling, a smaller piece of machinery located on the fore or aft quarterdeck. You load the basket with pebble-sized beads of iron, which is fired to clear the deck of crew."

I shuddered as I considered the sight of hundreds of black pebbles flung toward flesh at high speed, shredding skin and breaking bones. I had never seen a sling fired, but one look at the four the *Consequences* possessed, their wash basket-sized buckets and stretched leather straps as thick as my arm, told me they held the power to kill with ease.

The captain noticed my eyes wander to the bow sling. "That's a round-sling," he informed me. "The *Consequences* has two roundslings and two chainslings. Brawk! The roundslings hold, as you might guess, rounded stones, all at least two-stone in weight. They're used to punch holes in a hull, preferably below the waterline. Chainslings hold three-foot lengths of iron chain which are used to shred rigging and sails."

"You don't have any scatterslings?"

The tremor of revulsion I felt and saw run through the captain confirmed the truth of my earlier vision of that weapon's destructiveness. "Brawk! I refuse to use such things against other people again. I swore if I ever gained captaincy of my own vessel, scatterslings wouldn't be allowed."

"How come your slings aren't below decks?"

"They were added as an afterthought. The ship was originally a tender. It traveled as part of a fleet and carried supplies and food for the larger vessels. By tradition, tender vessels were never attacked; since either side could use the supplies, it made sense to leave them intact. If you won the battle, the tender was a great prize. But during the Skaldor-Estin War, the Prelacy changed the rules. They made any ship fair game, so all the tenders were armed as best as possible. We still lost several, but they could at least offer resistance. The *Consequences* has three ships to her credit, although she's almost been sunk at least ten times."

That explained the patchwork look of the ship's hull. I almost asked the captain why he didn't try to find patch wood that was at least close to the same color. Instead, I stared out at the empty ocean and said, "How come you don't travel in a group now? Isn't it unsafe to travel alone?"

"Not really. Since the war ended, the Prelacy stays on their side of the line, except for the trading vessels, which are lightly armed and don't bother anyone."

"What about pirates?"

Captain Timbers let out a parroty cackle. "Skaldor patrols are the best on the ocean, and the pirates know it. There hasn't been a pirate attack in these waters for three years."

"Captain," a voice shouted from the crow's nest. "Pirates, dead ahead."

Gee, what a surprise.

8

Captain Timbers and First Mate Shivers shouted orders as the pirate ships moved in, one on either side of the *Consequences*. Again, people ran to and fro. The air filled with the creaking of ropes and clatter of stones as sailors hoisted sails and loaded the slings. The smell of sweat floated in like rancid butter. I wondered if any of these men had ever seen battle. I planted myself on the main deck, back pressed to the wall just below the wheelhouse, which I had discovered was the best place to avoid being trampled.

All the Paladins, including Lucifer, ran below deck, followed by Raith and the other squires. They apparently planned to hide until the fight was over.

That seemed like a good idea. I was about to join them when the *Consequences's* chipped, guano-coated figurehead let out a wail, high-pitched and ululating, that bolted me to the deck and set my neck hairs dancing as if they wanted to seek refuge in my navel. A trick of sunlight made the hag move before my eyes.

"The figurehead's come to life," I screamed.

A passing sailor heard me and gave a grin, exposing enough gold to make a Dwarf faint. "No, that's just the shark chase whistle. Scares the sharks away for miles around."

Since I'd been on board, I hadn't seen a shark, and I spent so much time at the rail that all the porpoises following us had first names. "Why would there be sharks?"

"Because there's going to be blood." His grin grew more expansive for a moment, and then he dashed off to do something sailorish.

I felt faint, a feeling that grew as I saw Salic and Silix slinging sand onto the deck. "What's that for?" I asked, sure I didn't want to hear the answer.

I was right. "To soak up the blood," they said in unison. Their young, round faces weren't smiling; they looked terrified as me.

I glanced over at the single rowboat, its seaworthiness suspect at best but certainly better than the *Consequences's* would soon be. The twins noticed, looked in the same direction, looked at each other, and looked back at me, terror changing to conspiratorial glee. I smiled back at them.

We had gone three steps toward the boat when a cacophony of clanking metal reverberated from below and marched onto the deck in the form of twenty fully armored Paladins. Lucifer led the way. Elder walked beside him—the priest's look of exasperation aged his boyish features. "I still think this is a stupid idea. Even you have to see that."

"We must protect the ship."

"I agree, but how are you going to do that standing on the ocean floor encased in metal?"

Lucifer turned, his plate mail clinking, and glared at Elder. "You seem to underestimate the abilities of my men."

"Their abilities? Not at all. But I do wonder about their sobriety."

The Paladin appeared ready to reach out and do something not very Paladin-like to the nattering Elder. Instead, he paused, took a deep breath, and said, "I appreciate your concern, but I will lead my men. I suggest you pray to Ubel to give us help against these wretched pirates." He scanned the deck. I knew who he was searching for and sought a place to hide.

"Briar," Lucifer said when he spotted me. "Will you speak with Ubel and ask him to use his holy benevolence to smite these foul pirates?"

I once again wondered about Lucifer's concept of benevolence. "I can't speak to him. Remember, I can only hear him." And if you didn't count the nightly visions, I hadn't heard from him since that one time in Frostishak. Not exactly what I'd consider constant communion.

"Of course, but perhaps you could still invoke him to aid us. Speak to the sky and call his name. I'm sure he'll listen to you since you are his favorite."

Lucifer wasn't going to let it go. I wondered how offended the sailors would be if I started shouting Ubel's name aboard their ship. Most sailors worship Titanicus, the God of Water and Things That Sink. I sighed. The crew disliked me already, so I didn't have much to lose on that score. Much as I hated to admit it, Lucifer was correct in one respect: Ubel and I had some sort of connection. I didn't think the Evil One would let Ubel answer, but it couldn't hurt to try.

Boy, how naïve.

I looked to the sky and held my hands out. "Holy—

"Holy shit, what is that?" Shivers shouted.

I turned and looked, and work faltered as every other head on deck did the same. Though still a half-mile away, the pirate ships appeared sleek, ominous, and monochromatic, everything the *Consequences* wasn't. Their mainsails, black and crisp and flying a flag with skull and crossbones writ large across them, riffled in the wind blowing at the ship's stern. Men milled about the decks, tough and seasoned-looking, and I'd have wagered not one of them under thirty years of age. Glints of silvery light revealed the sabers in their hands, glittering weapons that would soon be soaked in red.

But frightening as the sight was, it was nothing compared to what had elicited Shivers's outburst.

Thick clouds the color of clotted milk formed over the pirate ships, expanding through the clear sky like taupe ink poured onto paper. They soon met between the vessel and melded into one cloud. Orange light flickered within, dancing with the chaotic rhythm of flames.

"Holy Ubel has sent fire clouds to smite our enemies," Lucifer shouted.

It was a nice thought, but I knew better; I think most of the crew did too.

The clouds turned gray and then black, as if the dancing light inside burned them. They kept pace with the pirate ships, which came on much faster now. Everyone seemed to hold their breath.

"Brawk! Forward sling, aim left. We'll try and take the bigger one first. Turn two points to starboard."

I guess the captain saw some difference between the vessels. They both looked the same to me: large, deadly, and closing much too quickly. I pondered the irony of dying on the sea, a place I had spent my life avoiding, and found myself not amused.

The clouds went beyond black, into a shade of darkness so intense it hurt to see. The orange light grew brighter and more rapid. As the wind blew into my face, I caught a smell that reminded me of charred meat.

A splash drew my attention to the port rail. I saw Salac and Silix disappearing over the side toward the lifeboat, which no longer sat in its cradle. The little bastards had deserted without me, and after I gave them the idea.

I wasn't the only one who noticed. Other sailors ran to the rail.

"Brawk! Stand your ground, men," the Captain shouted, but not before two men had gone overboard. I saw three others who I felt seriously considering it.

"The next man who even thinks about abandoning ship gets a bolt in his stomach," Shivers bellowed, aiming a loaded crossbow toward the men by the rail. The other sailors muttered and turned away, returning to their positions.

The pirates were less than a quarter-mile away. I could hear them cheering and waving their sabers, the fiery orange glow from within the clouds dancing on the blades. Onboard the *Consequences*, everyone waited, holding clubs and short swords distributed by the midshipmen. A few of the sailors had managed to slip on leather jerkins. Lucifer spread his Paladins amongst the sailors. Their bright swords and gleaming armor, the crest of blue hands beneath a yellow sun standing out in defiance of the pirates' leering skull, seemed to give the sailors hope, despite the obvious stupidity of wearing fifty pounds of metal on the open sea.

My position put me far enough from the railing to avoid Shivers's wrath but close enough to see the rowboat as it labored away from the ship, the two adult sailors working the oars while the twins sat in the stern area, their relief noticeable even from this distance.

"Bastards," I shouted. "I hope you all drown." I truly didn't wish them harm, but my fear bubbled out as anger at their quick thinking. I didn't hate them; I just envied them.

A sound rumbled out of the clouds, like thunder only deeper, with a high crackling noise beneath. The din grew, and the orange light flickered faster as if the cloud's grumbling agitated it. The crackling turned into a hiss, a portion of the cloud parted, and with a whip-crack sound, a ball of flame erupted from the opening. The size was impossible to judge, but *massive* pretty much covers it. We all watched, helpless, as the flaming sphere flew with unbelievable speed toward the rowboat.

"Look-" was all I managed to get out before it struck the boat, sheared it in half, and set it aflame. The ball hit the water and sent liquid and steam up in a geyser. The heat incinerated all four of the boat's passengers before they could even scream.

I wanted to feel horror at the senseless death. I wanted to be sickened by the hideous manner of their demise. I wanted to experience the sadness of no longer having the twins and their gnarled feet around me at night.

All I felt was relief that I hadn't been on the boat.

Even that emotion was short-lived as another crack issued from the cloud.

"They're heading this way," Shivers shouted. Unnecessarily, since everybody could see two balls hurling toward the ship. They weren't as large or fast as the first one, but they struck the sails, which immediately burst into flames. This spread to the ropes, which went up like pitch-soaked candle wicks. Within thirty seconds, every piece of flammable cloth or hemp was ash floating to the deck, leaving the mainmast standing like a tree stripped of its leaves. We had no means of moving. The only fortunate turn was that the flames had been so aggressive in their consumption that the deck had not heated up enough to catch. The sailor in the crow's nest—the man who first spotted the pirates—had not been so lucky.

Another crack, another ball of flame. Although no bigger than a melon, I couldn't help but notice it headed straight for me. I stood frozen as I watched my death fly toward me.

I felt a twinge in my head and a feeling of *reaching*, as if something tried to escape my body. I figured it was my soul, a backpack on its meta-physical shoulders, heading for the next life. The feeling retracted, coming back toward me, and I heard a startled yelp. With a clanging of metal, the Paladin nearest me leaped through the air. The sight of his flying body broke my paralysis, and I dropped to the deck as he and the fireball met. His steel-clad form did nothing to slow the flaming orb's momentum. Heat and the stench of burning metal and skin hit as he soared over me, slammed into the deck rail, shattered it, and flew another thirty feet before splashing into the water and sending up a plume of steam.

I hadn't even recovered when I again felt the reaching sensation at almost the same time I heard the whip crack. Another unsuspecting Paladin tossed himself before a flaming ball of death, with the expected results.

"Stop it," I said, beginning to suspect the source of the Paladins' lemming-like behavior. I wanted to be no one's pawn, not even a god's—

especially not a god who would so casually toss away his most devout followers.

I'm trying *to stop it,* Ubel said, confirming my suspicion. *Give me control of your mind, or you and* everyone *on the ship will surely die.*

That changed my perspective. Better a live pawn than a chunk of charred meat. "Go ahead."

A white light took over my brain.

I CAME to staring at a clear sky. At least it would have been clear if it weren't for the cluster of faces gaping down at me from all sides. Captain Timbers sat on his first mate's shoulder, his face showing the only expression a bird's face can: blank. But the others ranged from mild concern to downright worry. I had grown so used to contempt and irritation from my shipmates that *I* became worried.

"Am I dying?" I croaked as nails danced on my head, and a gong sounded a constant note in my ears.

"He's awake," Raith shouted, his voice a hammer pushing the nails through my head and out the back.

"Obviously," Elder said. He spoke softer, but it still rattled my sensitive skull.

Lucifer, no longer in his armor, knelt and blocked the other faces as he stared into my eyes. "How do you feel?"

What a stupid question, I thought. Or at least I thought I thought it, but the hardening of Lucifer's green eyes and firming of his square jaw told me I had, in fact, spoken aloud.

"I'm sorry," I said. "I feel like a sheet that's been pounded on rocks and run through a drying press."

"You still use ten words when one will do, so I think you'll survive," Lucifer informed me, leaning back on his knees. Given my present condition, that didn't provide as much comfort as he wanted it to.

"Here's some water," Raith said, kneeling with a tin cup. I could smell the oak and tar of the cask the water came from, but as Raith poured it into my mouth, thirst drove out any other concerns. I gulped down two cupfuls. As I drank, I felt drops strike my chest. I smelled salt. I searched for the source and saw water dripping off the sleeve of Raith's squire's tunic, now more of an off-white after six days on the ship. It was only then that I noticed he was soaking wet, the water beading in his hair, making it look more like mud than usual. A glance at the people around me revealed all of them, except the captain, were in the same condition.

"Did everyone go swimming?" I asked when I finished drinking.

"After a fashion," Raith said, sitting the cup on the deck. "You blew everybody into the water."

"I did what?"

"What's the last thing you remember?" Elder asked, kneeling beside Raith. I was beginning to feel like an altar.

"I remember fireballs and two of the Paladins getting hit, me telling Ubel to stop, and him telling me to let him take over or we would all die. I told him to go ahead, and that's when it goes blank."

Murmurs rose among the crew within earshot, which I think was most of them. I heard the words "blessed" and "savior" thrown in there; I assumed people were offering prayers to Ubel.

Lucifer again had that strange look of awe mixed with envy. I found the expression terribly disconcerting.

"The pirate ships were closing in on us," Elder said. "Two more fireballs aimed for you, and you avoided them. They struck the ship and caught it on fire." He pointed at what I assumed were the spots where the flames struck, but I couldn't see them in my current position, and when I tried to crane my neck to look, someone stuck several invisible jellyfish along my spine. I groaned.

"Don't try to move," Lucifer said. He didn't have to tell me twice.

Elder continued his tale. "You suddenly started glowing white. You ran up to the wheel deck, shouted 'Enough,' and held out your hands. A wave of white light rushed across the deck and toward the pirate ships. Everyone went over the side, knocked over by the light. When I got back on deck, the clouds and pirate ship were gone."

"You didn't see what happened to them?"

Elder shook his head. "I fell off near the bow, so I didn't see anything."

"I did," Raith said, his voice shaking. I had often seen Raith afraid, usually right before a punch meant for me hit him in the face. But when I stared at him, I saw something I never expected in his owlish blue eyes: fear of me.

"The wave of light hit the ships and the cloud, and it was like those battles between the gods we used to read about before great Ubel forced them into a truce. Fire rained down from the clouds, and water rose up from the ocean. They met on the decks of the pirate ships and fought."

There were more murmurs around the deck, whether of agreement or incredulity, I couldn't tell.

But I knew what I thought. "What do you mean 'fought?'" The last thing I needed was rock-steady Raith turning as bizarre as his mentor.

"Just what I said. The fire and water struck each other and moved around the deck like they were alive. They fought, and whenever they touched a pirate, he instantly burst into flames or drowned. Some did both. More and more fire and water joined the battle. But then, more white light appeared between the ships, and then—" he stopped for a moment as if even he couldn't believe the next thing he was about to say. "Then you were standing in the light, floating between the ships."

"What?" I jerked, trying to sit up, but the jellyfish were back, and my legs twitched as I groaned again.

"I said don't try to move," Lucifer said. I guess he did have to tell me twice.

"You were floating in between the ships. You held up your hands, said, 'cease this attack.' Then white light flew from your hands, and it got so bright I had to look away. When I looked back, everything was gone. I climbed back on deck, and you were laying here."

"That's impossible," I said, but only because I wanted it to be impossible. After all, if a god can create a world, how little effort would it take to marionette me and destroy two ships and a cloud?

"Brawk! Impossible or not, the boy speaks the truth. I also saw it."

"And I saw it," another voice said.

Soon there was a chorus of assent, with those who saw the event relaying it to those floundering in the wrong part of the ocean. The details were different, but they were all variations of Raith's tale.

The thought of people in the ocean clicked something in my still throbbing head. I looked at the armorless Lucifer. "Where are the rest of your men?"

He glanced over at Elder, his face a mix of chagrin and pain. "It turns out Brother Elder was correct. We should not have been wearing our armor on the ship. I was the only one who managed to doff mine and return to the surface."

BECAUSE OF MY INFIRM CONDITION, the crew put me in the relative comfort of the ship's doctor's cabin and laid me on an actual bed with sheets. The room stank of herbs and strange unguents, but the comfort of a pillow and mattress made such things bearable. I had seen the doctor, an aged man with bad eyes and shaking hands, perform his brand of healing, and was thankful I would not require his services. Had I gone in with a cut, I might have emerged missing a hand.

I spent the day drifting in and out of sleep, completely unaware of my surroundings and too exhausted to summon the energy to vomit. It was the best day I spent aboard ship.

By the next day, though, I had recovered well enough to return to the deck, where things went on as normal, with one very irritating difference: instead of hatred and indifference, the crew now treated me like a living holy icon. They nodded with respect when they drew near. My name had changed from Pukeboy to Most Esteemed, as in "thank you for saving our lives, Most Esteemed servant of Ubel," or "would you care for more tea, Most Esteemed savior?" None of them would still speak to me as an equal because I had gone from barely worth their contempt to a higher station they could not hope to obtain. Mingled with the respect, I sensed a good measure of fear. They were afraid if they displeased me, I would institute a holy zap and turn them into chutney. I'm sure many of them recalled their past transgressions against me and hoped my memory wasn't as good as theirs. I was still being ostracized, only now for a different reason.

Between being bowed to or offered tea and food, I looked over the purple ocean and considered the previous day's events. Spares had replaced the lost sails, and we were moving again. I no longer felt seasick, so at least one good thing had come from my holy experience, but the cost of my cure seemed much too high.

The only ones who didn't offer me praise were the squires. They were now bereft of their livelihood and the possibility of becoming Paladins. By Church law, any squire who let their Paladin die forfeit any chance at knighthood. An idiotic law since a Paladin's job was to try and get themselves killed in service to the Church. The squires moped about in a mob, a score of lost, wretched souls. When they saw me, which was often on the small vessel, their faces turned dark, their eyes glinted with malice, and I sensed my death in twenty different ways. Only Raith didn't offer me such hatred, but he was my brother and still had his master. Apparently, his association with me had lost him the friendship of the squires.

"Of course, I didn't have much of their friendship to begin with," he told me, joining me briefly in my solitary watch, "but now they positively hate me."

"Don't they understand it's not your fault?" I asked. "Ubel's jewels, it's not even my fault."

Raith reflexively glanced skyward at my blasphemy, but I didn't much care. Ubel had become personal with me whether I wanted it or not, so I felt I had the right to swear at him a little. "They know that," Raith told me, "but it doesn't make them feel any better."

It didn't really make me feel any better about it, either. Twenty men dead because of me. Never mind that if Ubel hadn't interceded through me, over a hundred would be gone, including me. It still didn't seem right.

I glanced to the forecastle and spotted Lucifer speaking to Brother Elder. "I should talk to Lucifer about it."

"Not yet," Raith warned me. "I'm afraid he might forget his Paladin's vows."

I sighed. Lucifer never thought much of me, and now he was torn between hatred and envy. These two emotions were dangerous enough alone. I looked at Raith. The wind blowing across the ocean made his eyes waterier than usual. At least, I assumed it was the wind. "So, what do you think of our grand adventure now?"

He didn't answer. After a few moments, he wiped his eyes and walked away.

Left alone again, I considered yesterday's attack, looking beyond the events to the reasons. One of my duties as scribe had been to learn a code often used in messages between clerics, where they would scribble special characters in the spaces between sentences. Combined with certain words within the document, these symbols would offer the true meaning of the message with no fear of being discovered should a layperson gain possession of the note. Being isolated on an island in peacetime, there had been little need to use the code, but I had learned it anyway. So now, as I did with the Church documents, I tried to look between the lines to discover the attack's real purpose.

As it turned out, there wasn't much between the lines. The attack, first and foremost, was against me; the lifeboat's destruction was a bonus. The eradication of said lifeboat indicated an intelligent force behind the cloud. If that force meant to destroy the ship, there were far better targets than me. I wasn't even standing near anything necessary to the vessel's func-tioning, but two fireballs were aimed directly toward me, only to be deflected by two men who had the misfortune of being pious and armored.

I was willing to bet the malevolence behind that cloud had a spotted face and greasy blond hair. The Evil One wanted me dead for some reason. By communicating with me, Ubel had gained me the enmity of a being almost beyond my comprehension.

I suddenly felt an illness that had nothing to do with the ship's motion.

9

After ten interminable days, I heard the cry I wanted to hear nine days earlier. The beautiful three-word sentence drifted down from the newly-built crow's nest. "Captain, land ahead."

Had I any agility whatsoever, I would have somersaulted or, at the least, managed a cartwheel of joy. As it was, I contented myself with a slight jump of elation.

"Brawk! All right, men, let's make preparations for docking. Taverns are waiting."

An enthusiastic uproar launched from the crew, and the flurry of motion that preceded our departure from Frostishak began again, as confusing and random as the first time. The only thing my days at sea had given me was the hope that they would be my last, not counting my trip back home, which I already dreaded. That assumed I survived to make it back home, but I didn't want to think about that.

In order to be out of the way and as close as possible to the approaching land, I took position near the still dispirited-looking figure-head. Since the battle two days ago, she had made no other sound, but I'm sure if she did, it would be a request to somehow end her misery, or at least scrape the bird crap off her.

With excitement I hadn't felt since...well, since ever, I watched the land draw closer. What I first thought were strange hills, tall and almost perfectly square, covered the town; as we drew closer, I realized they weren't hills; they were buildings!

It boggles the mind is a cliché only to those who haven't had their mind boggled, but the port town of Pelican jiggled my young brain almost out of its moorings. To describe it as large was akin to calling Lucifer pious: far too easy and wholly inadequate. With so much to take in, I could only absorb it in chunks, like a swamp rat breaking apart a *larkus* leaf. Buildings, all at least twenty feet tall and made of gray stone, stretched as far as I could see from left to right, packed so tight and in such a slapdash manner that I couldn't see how far from shore they extended. For all I knew, they stretched to the mountains I could barely make out in the distance.

The buildings registered first, being the most obvious. As we drew closer, I took notice of the multitude of ships resting in the docks, all of them well-tended and gleaming with polished wood of a single color. Figureheads, painted in bright hues and devoid of bird droppings, festooned the bows of all but the smallest ships. Compared to the magnificent vessels lining the numerous docks, the *Consequences* looked like the floating rat barge it truly was.

Other details jumped forward. The docks teemed with people moving about in various indecipherable errands. It was the chaos aboard the *Consequences* magnified a thousandfold. Their clothing rivaled their actions for the ability to invoke utter madness, so outlandish and varied were the colors and styles. I saw everything from plain-colored tunics and pants for the dockworkers to expensive, multi-hued frocks with feathered hats for the women. I found it odd that nobility would be found among the docks. Even in a pitiful village like Frostishak, there was a hierarchy, mainly because the clerics decreed it, but here it seemed the rich mingled with the common man. This novel idea made me think I might like this town. Of course, after our harrowing sea journey, I'd be happy landing among a mound of fire ants.

The smells hit me last. I hadn't noticed them before because the wind blew at my back, chasing away all but the saltwater tang, which went unnoticed after two days aboard ship. But as we closed on the docks, the wind shifted slightly and the odors slapped me. It reminded me of potpourri only because it was a mixture of smells. But potpourri is pleasant, whereas this was the olfactory equivalent of a kick in the head. The pungency of fish took me back for a moment to the meeting that started all this, but it didn't last long. Other odors, even more noisome, blended to create a stench that made the acrimony of the Neverending Swamp as agreeable as a bouquet of spring flowers. Pitch was certainly one of the ingredients, hot and redolent, ready for application to ship seams. Animal excrement joined the fray. Other scents, unknown to my sheltered existence but offensive nonetheless, filled in the gaps of this effluvious nightmare. And the reek of tanning leather topped everything like a sprig of rotten parsley on a moldy dinner.

As we drew close to our berth, I realized something askew in my earlier perception. I had thought the townspeople were dwarfed by the buildings. Now I realized the structures were average-sized, but most of Pelican's citizens were dwarves.

I had only heard about dwarves since none were brave or stupid enough to venture to our swamp-laden shores. Most people had a low opinion of them, describing them as taciturn and ugly. I thought they couldn't be all that bad; surely my fellow townsmen were just provincial.

As it turned out, they were being kind and limiting themselves to the dwarves' better qualities.

"What a right piece of crap!" spoke a gruff voice from the docks. I glanced over the rail to see a squat figure with red hair and a beard covering half his face staring up at the *Consequences*. Although I agreed with his sentiment, it seemed beyond impolite to state it aloud.

"Just as well," said another red-headed figure. "Being crap looks like the only thing keeping it afloat."

Both wore identical outfits: gray tunics and pants, tiny black skullcaps that did little to contain their frizzled fiery hair, and black boots that would have reached mid-calf on me but rode up to the Dwarves' knees. They could have been brothers. The only difference I could see was that the second dwarf had a large rune tattooed on his forehead, the black ink standing out through his red hair.

"Guess we best tie this crap bastard up and hope it doesn't sink and take the dock with it," Mr. Tattoo said. He put stubby fingers into his beard, in the approximate position where a mouth would be. A moment later, an ear-splitting whistle burst from him. Several dark-brown beetles emerged from his beard and dropped to the dock, where they lay still, stunned or dead.

A dozen dwarves sauntered from a ramshackle shed, emerging like the beetles and not moving much faster. They all wore the same clothing, and had blazing crimson hair and thick beards. I had read about doppel-gangers and wondered if I saw the results of some strange magic.

The crew of the *Consequences* tossed large lines of rope over the rails. The ends, knotted into loops, landed on the docks with dull thuds. As the three lines came to rest, the dwarves split into foursomes and crept toward the separate lines, moving like molasses over ice.

They finally reached the ropes just as the ship bumped into the front of the dock. Fortunately, there was a thick cushion of burlap to absorb the shock, else either the boat or the pier would have been holed.

The crew broke into more activity behind me, presumably preparing to depart. I continued watching the dwarves, fascinated that any still-breathing creature could move so slowly. One picked up the rope and tied it around the mooring post while the other three stood and watched. The tattooed dwarf, who I guessed was this group's leader, sauntered toward the gangplank that our crew lowered toward the dock. The plank hit the dock and teetered near the edge, riding up and down with the water's swell.

First Mate Shivers looked down at the dwarf. "Could you grab that and secure it?"

"Hell, no," the Dwarf yelled back, putting squat hands on his thick hips. "Do you see this tattoo?" He flipped his hair back, briefly revealing more of the rune before the tonsorial mass reclaimed his forehead. I recognized it from my studies as the Skaldorian equivalent of the letter S.

"Yeah, I see it," Shivers yelled back. "I got a few tattoos myself, including this one of lips on my ass you can kiss if you'd like, but what's that got to do with grabbing the plank?"

A flutter of wings announced the arrival of Captain Timbers. He landed on the rail next to me. "Brawk! I'll handle this, Shivers. Make sure the cargo is unlimbered."

"Aye, Captain." Shivers offered a last glance at the dwarf, who glared back with eyes of granite, both in color and hardness. I could sense the first mate's urge to spit at the hairy creature below, but he reigned in his anger and redirected it toward the crew. "Come on, you slugs. Get below decks and untie the swag."

The captain looked down at the truculent dwarf. "Brawk! Good stew-ard, could you see fit to ask your crew to secure our gangplank?"

I guess the S on his forehead stood for steward, but I had no idea what that meant.

"I don't take orders from no bird," the steward declared, but I could sense his confusion. This bird talked unlike any other bird in his experience. Which is to say, it talked.

"Be that as it may, I am the captain of this ship, and if you wish to receive your fee, I will need my gangplank secured. Or do I have to take matters up with the Dockmaster?"

The steward's eyes turned from granite to limestone. "That won't be necessary, sir. I'll get my crew on it when they're done tying off the ship."

As usual, I couldn't help myself. "You've got nine men standing around doing nothing. Get a couple of them to grab the plank."

Granite was back. "They're not 'doing nothing;' they're back-up." The steward stormed off, moving at a slow walk, the fastest I had seen any of them move.

Captain Timbers looked at me. "Brawk! First time to a dwarf city?"

"First time to any city."

"The dwarves have a different way of doing things. They have three speeds: slow, slower, and dead. It is best not to get them riled up, or the second speed is the best you'll get from them."

I nodded. "Then why not get someone else to work the docks?"

The captain let out a series of choking squawks, his avian way of laughing. "Because you would end up with a shut-down city, that's why."

"I don't understand."

The captain fluttered closer and spoke in the softest voice possible. I sensed his fear that the dwarves attaching the ropes might hear him. It seemed a misplaced worry; they looked somnambulant at best. "The Dwarf Guilds control Pelican. Nothing gets done without their approval, and they have set rules for how things are accomplished. We will not be here long, so my advice would be to keep your mouth shut, as hard as that may be, and let me handle things."

I felt stung by the captain's words. I had considered him a friend, and here he thought of me as nothing more than a child who couldn't stay quiet when necessary. Little matter that he was correct; one never likes to have their faults spoken openly.

"I'll keep that in mind," I said, trying to hide the pain of the rebuke by turning to stare again at the dwarves. They had finally completed mooring the ship. Two groups of four moved away, and the third group shuffled to the gangplank, which had already more or less settled on its own. Still, they grabbed a nearby set of clamps and secured the plank to the dock.

The captain sensed he had offended me but wasn't sure how. "I must attend to the crew."

I grunted at him, and he flew off, leaving me to study the strange city until Raith wandered over. "What's the matter?" I asked. "Doesn't Lucifer need you to help pull his head out of his ass or something?"

"What's wrong with you now?"

"What isn't?" I answered.

Raith chose to ignore my sour mood; he had experienced it so often it no longer fazed him. "It's quite a sight, isn't it?"

I gazed at him and saw a sparkle of excitement in his wide eyes, like glimmers of quartz shining through mud. He was enjoying this madness. "More like quite a stench. Did you know dwarves control the whole city?"

"Yes, Brother Elder told me. He used to live here."

"Really?"

"Yeah, spent his teenage years as an acolyte in the main church until he refused the join the Acolytes' Guild."

"The Acolytes have a guild?"

Raith picked at a large splinter on the rail. "In this city and in Katbreth, up North. Doesn't seem quite right, does it?"

As far as I was concerned, the church was already overly organized. Anything that attempted to make it more organized was one step away from pure evil. Having come face to face with pure evil did nothing to change my opinion. "Doesn't seem right at all."

"Elder said not to mention it to Lucifer. He would probably not approve and might cause some problems."

I frowned as a golden opportunity passed me by. Had I not felt so guilty about unintentionally killing Lucifer's chapter, I would have knocked Raith over in my haste to share the news. As it was, I just nodded and said, "I'll keep it to myself."

The dwarves finished their work on the gangplank and slithered away, all without a word. I became convinced that not only were they doppelgangers, but also zombies.

Raith and I watched the bustle of the city, the unintelligible nattering of people performing incomprehensible business. The stench grew less noticeable, and it amazed me how quickly I could adapt to such unpleasantness. Still, growing up around the swamps in Frostishak gave me plenty of practice. In the summer, the wetlands emitted an odor all to themselves.

I began to discern a pattern in the clothing; the colors and style marked a person's guild membership. Four seemed to be a magical number among these guilds since that was the minimum number of people I saw performing any task, no matter how simple or easily accomplished. The sole exception was three young dwarves I saw on three separate occasions—their youth denoted solely by the lack of scraggle in their beards and a more pronounced stubbiness to their legs—running through the docks, wearing bright red and orange loincloths and nothing else. They looked like their privates were on fire. They ran like it, too, but each carried a rolled parchment, so I assumed they were part of a messenger guild.

Fascinating as the city was, it dawned on me after about a half-hour that we should be leaving the ship. I thought that with the gangplank secure, the unloading would begin, but apparently not.

The crewmembers wandered back up from below decks empty-handed. They kept a respectful distance—one of the few advantages to being considered a savior—but no one moved to disembark.

"What are we waiting for?" I asked Raith.

Raith shrugged and scanned the deck. I followed his eyes as he spotted Elder near the stern, his arms waving in agitation as he spoke to Lucifer. Despite his obvious irritation, Elder kept his voice low enough that nothing came across but murmurs. They were too far away for me to pick up any sense of their thoughts. Lucifer looked adamant in the manner only Lucifer could manage. The twenty squires, all missing a Paladin, stood behind Lucifer, their expressions between low anxiety and outright apprehension.

"Shouldn't you be over there with Lucifer?"

Raith snorted, an oddly agreeable noise coming from his pinched face. "He has more squires than he knows what to do with, most of them better suited to the responsibilities and *all* of them better suited to kissing his backside."

I smiled. This was the brother I remembered from before his apprenticeship, the one I liked. "Nice to see he didn't completely shrivel your jewels."

As Elder finished his impassioned, if quiet, oration by dropping his hands to his sides, Lucifer spoke back, his voice loud and commanding, not caring who heard. "I will wait a bit, but beyond the Church and her holy representatives, no one commands a Paladin what he can and can't do."

Elder's shoulders slumped even as he threw up his hands in defeat.

Lucifer turned to walk away, and the squires followed on his heels like a pack of swamp dogs tailing their mother.

"Brother Elder," Raith said, "may we speak with you?"

Elder looked at us, turned, and watched the retreating Lucifer as he disappeared below decks, twenty obsequious heads descending with him in an orderly formation. Once they disappeared, he turned his attention back to us.

"I wonder if they wipe for him," I said as we waited for Elder. Raith didn't answer, but his widened, owlish eyes and slack jaw told me Lucifer still had some sway over him. I'd have to work on that.

Elder drew closer, head down, muttering what could only be imprecations toward Lucifer. When he glanced up and realized we were watching him, he stopped, cleared his throat, and walked with better posture, his yellow robe blowing from his self-generated breeze. His beard had grown longer but still had spots where hair refused to appear. His face had also become more angular, so he looked much older than when we left Frostishak. The dark circles under his eyes didn't help. He resembled a dangerous beggar more than a priest. I was astounded a person could change so much in so little time. I looked closer at Raith to see if the journey had wrought any metamorphosis on him.

It had. He seemed less doughy; the constant training and moving about on the ship had affected his physique. His tunic didn't cling quite so tight around his middle, and I could see his cheekbones. His hair still resembled mud, but in a strange way, it went well with the deep red of his sunburned face.

The journey had done little to me that I could tell except make me skinnier from lack of being able to keep any food down and even less inclined to accept anyone's friendship

"Yes?" he asked once he reached us.

"What's wrong with my master?"

"What isn't," Elder muttered. I smiled at the repetition of my own phrase while Raith, as expected, did the opposite. Elder continued. "I had to explain to him that we can't debark until the cargo has been unloaded; he didn't seem to appreciate it."

"Why can't we?" I asked.

"Guild rules. No one can leave the ship until all cargo is unloaded. Cargo first, then passengers. Lucifer said it was a stupid rule, and Paladins could do what they wish."

I wasn't sure about the Paladins doing what they wished, but I agreed it was a stupid rule. I wasn't sure what disturbed me more: the rule, or my accord with Lucifer's assessment.

Raith, as was his wont, tried to consider the optimistic view. "Well, I'm sure it won't take that long."

From my brief observation of the dwarves, I knew better than ever to consider such a statement valid. Elder turned his round face to Raith and said, "You've never been here, have you?"

WE ARRIVED in port about an hour after the sun came up. We were finally allowed to disembark as it started behind the city's taller buildings.

The longest time involved waiting for the Stevedores' Guild to show up, which they finally did about an hour after lunchtime, dressed in deep blue tunics and pants, hands covered by brown leather gloves, and heads topped with green helmets.

The captain and crew appeared used to this sort of thing, but Lucifer was fuming. He could have occupied himself if he had some Paladins to train, but I had taken care of that, leaving him with nothing but twenty brown-nosing squires. More than once during our interminable wait, he made to move down the gangplank, but Shivers or Timbers stopped him by appealing to his good nature and reminding him the ship could lose its docking privileges. And more than once, as the sun parboiled my brain, I considered spilling the Acolytes' Guild story to Lucifer and goading him into stepping off. But my conscience, uncharacteristically overactive, stopped me.

The steward, his forehead emblazoned with an S tattoo like the previous guild's leader, stepped up to the edge of the gangplank. Shivers walked down, the captain perched on his shoulder, and stopped at the plank's edge. They spoke together, the dwarf's gruff voice and the captain's squawk making a strange musical point and counterpoint. I couldn't understand a lot of what they said, but they seemed to be negotiating. Words like *percentage*, *guild minimum*, and *pension* got thrown around a lot. Lucifer stood at the top of the plank glaring at the Dwarf, his Paladin chivalry fighting against his desire to walk down and strangle the red-headed runt.

"You know—" I started, but a sharp pain in my foot stopped me.

"Ouch," I said as Raith drew his heel back from where it had stomped on my toes.

"Can't you for once just stay quiet? I knew I shouldn't have told you."

I didn't know what he was talking about for a second. Then I realized I was preparing to tell Lucifer about the Acolyte's Guild to get him riled enough to start trouble. I hadn't been aware I was about to do it. Did I really have so little control over my own actions?

I heard an odd, familiar laugh at the back of my mind, and the pimply face of the Evil One danced for a moment across my vision. I shivered as I considered the implications if he were somehow inside my mind and trying to control me. But that couldn't be the case. In the brief time I had watched Ubel and the other struggle, I had felt the Evil One's great power. If he wanted to control me, there would be no "trying" involved.

After about five minutes of discussion, Shivers and the steward shook hands while the captain said, "Brawk! Agreed." They walked back up the plank as the dwarf turned and shouted orders in Dwarvish, a language that sounds like rocks being turned to dust by a large file, to his twenty blue-suited men.

When the captain and Shivers reached the deck, the captain said, "Brawk! Begin unloading, men."

For the next several hours, I, along with Raith, Elder, Lucifer, and the twenty goslings, stood by feeling useless while the crew, using a bewildering array of ropes and pulleys, hauled cargo from the hold and lowered it to the dock. There, the dwarves took over, moving like arthritic snails as they loaded the crates onto wagons and drove them toward the nearby warehouses. I watched all of ten minutes before I wanted to pull my face off in frustration at the whole process.

With little else to do, I moved away from the others, sat down on the deck, and pulled out my scrivener tools to make some notes about my journey.

Naturally, that's when Elder decided he wanted to talk to me.

I watched as he walked my way, a "let's talk seriously" look on his face. He crossed his legs and lowered himself beside me, so I set aside my parchment and pen and waited.

He stared at me a moment, cleared his throat, and asked, "Are you okay?"

I didn't know how many ways I could say no before he would understand I was anything but. Then I realized maybe he was asking something else but didn't know how. I glanced around to make sure no one could hear us. Lucifer paced back and forth on the deck, smacking his hands together, no doubt wishing he had a dwarf's head in each one. The goslings, Raith included, followed his movement as if their heads were attached to his shoulders. The deckhands were too busy to pay attention to anything other than boxes and ropes.

I looked back at Elder. He seemed genuinely concerned, but perhaps he was just seeking a confession that didn't involve whiskey bottles or carnal relations with farm animals.

"I'm scared," I said, surprised at how good it felt to be admitting it to someone. "I think Ubel may be in real trouble, and I don't know what someone like Lucifer is supposed to be able to do about it. He's just so...so..."

"Stupid and arrogant," Elder said.

"Well, yeah, that's what I wanted to say, but I was trying to be polite."

"Don't, or I won't know who you are. He is both of those, but he's also an excellent fighter and feels a great duty to protect you." He gave me a shrewd look, lips pursed. "And I don't think Lucifer is the one Ubel is counting on."

"Well, he's wing-tying the wrong griffon if he's counting on me. I'm a writer, not a fighter. What can I do?"

"Based on what happened the other day, a lot when you put your mind to it."

"You mean when *he* puts my mind to it. I have enough problems when it's just me in control; I don't need any help. And what if..." I trailed off, unwilling to even consider that Pimple, as I had named the evil face, could treat me like a puppet as easily as Ubel. "Why did he pick me anyway? He should have chosen Lucifer. He may be stupid, but he's strong and can kill things."

"The same can be said of a brick, but maybe Ubel wants someone who can think for himself, who will know what to do when the time is right."

"The only thing I want to do is go home, and the right time is now."

Elder gave me a friendly pat on the back. He spoke in the tone of voice one uses to calm excitable puppies, but his words left me cold. "Well, that's not going to happen, so you might as well grow up and accept it. For what it's worth, if Ubel believes in you, so do I."

He stood up and left me there to ponder his words. I realized he was right. I had been nothing but a whiny brat this whole time. I needed to grow a pair, man up, prove my mettle, and a whole host of other coming-of-age metaphors. This was my chance to prove I was more than Briar the

Scribe. I had some strange, unknowable power. I had a god relying on me to save him. I had total strangers looking to me for guidance. I could be Briar the Hero, Briar the Savior. I could prove to my father that I would be more than, in his words, a sack of turnips. Elder spoke a truth that went straight to my gut. It was time for me to be a man.

I ran to the railing and threw up.

10

Finally, the dwarves hauled the last piece of cargo away, and we could depart the ship. By tradition, the crew members not commanded to remain behind for dock watch left first. Captain Timbers sat on Shivers's shoulder, while the first mate handed the crew silver and copper coins. As the men passed me, the emotions of how they intended to spend their money turned me into a beet of embarrassment. They planned some things I didn't think were legal in civilized society. But all of them gave me a friendly smile as they left, and a few touched me on the shoulder, muttering "for luck." With all of the death surrounding me, that seemed strange, until I realized I had been lucky...for them.

As the last crewman left, Lucifer stepped up and said, "I shall go next to ensure the way is safe for Ubel's holy prophet." It sounded nice, but the Paladin just wanted to disembark as much as I did, and my newfound status made me a convenient excuse. The goslings followed, their equine charges in tow. Things proceeded smoothly. The horses seemed much less reluctant to leave than they had to board, but it still took a half-hour of excruciating time. I just knew, having traveled successfully for ten days, something was going to sink the ship in my last minutes. A burning rock or some other projectile sent by Pimple would slam into the craft and take me down in flames. I wanted to run screaming down the gangplank but couldn't with horses occupying the entire area. I settled for bouncing from foot to foot.

"Brawk, go to the other side and pee if you can't wait," Timbers said as he landed on my shoulder.

"I'm fine, just ready to get off this damn ship. No offense meant."

"Brawk. None taken. Some people aren't cut out for the sea."

"I'm not cut out for travel, period."

Raith went last, pulling Justice along. Pony followed, giving playful nips at the larger horse's tail. Raith looked at me and rolled his eyes. Pony Two came behind, having no choice since he was tethered to his namesake.

Finally, I could depart. Only the fear of falling kept me from dashing down the gangplank like a gazelle hunted by a lion. I reached the dock and almost dropped down to kiss it in thankfulness for my safe arrival. One look at the dark, glistening boards changed my mind—I feared my lips might stick.

I arrived just as Lucifer had arranged horses and squires to his liking. Raith handed me the reins to Two while Lucifer stopped a passing dwarf in an orange and yellow tunic. He looked like all the others, except maybe a bit shorter. I began to consider my doppelganger theory as an actual possibility. "Excuse me, good sir, is there a chapterhouse of Ubel in this city?"

"Of course."

"Can you tell me where it is?"

"Of course not. You have to get directions from the Directors' Guild."

"Where can I find someone from the Directors' Guild?"

I mouthed the words a half-second before the Dwarf said them.

"You'll have to ask someone from the Directors' Guild."

Luther's face darkened. "What? I have to ask someone from the Direc-tor's Guild how to find someone from the Director's Guild."

"Exactly. But do me a favor and don't tell anyone I told you. I could get in trouble with the Information Guild if they found out I stepped over the line. Have a good day."

The Dwarf walked away. Lucifer's hands went toward Heathens-masher. Captain Timbers took off from my shoulders so hard it pushed me back a few steps. I teetered at the edge of the dock, windmilling my arms to avoid falling in. A wash of water shifted the dock upward and pushed me away from the edge, where I stood with my heart beating like a drummer playing ramming speed.

"That was lucky," Elder, who witnessed the incident, said.

Timbers landed on Lucifer's hands and pecked at them with his large beak, stopping the Paladin from drawing his giant sword.

A splash in the water made me look back. I wish I hadn't. A dolphin floated near the ship. Its skin gleamed black, and its eyes glowed red, two features not generally associated with the docile mammals. It also had a severed arm in its bottle-nosed mouth. When it saw it had my attention, it spat out the arm, winked at me, and hissed.

Sheer force of will kept me from peeing in my pants. "Look," I shouted at the dolphin. "I don't want this any more than you do. I've gotten your message, so you can stop with the omens and threats."

"Who or what are you talking to?" Elder asked. I turned to him, and he appeared ready to either run or call for men to tie me up in sheets. I looked back at the water. No great surprise, the dolphin was gone, replaced by a piece of floating driftwood that vaguely resembled an arm. Who or what indeed? I wondered, not for the first time, if my brain was going the way of overripe cheese. Maybe empaths were prone to delusions. Maybe I had even deluded myself into thinking I was an empath.

But I knew better. My visitations by Ubel and Pimple were real enough, and threescore people witnessed my destruction of two pirate ships. No, my mind was fine. It was the gods that had slipped their tethers.

"That piece of driftwood," I answered. "It has a bad attitude." I turned away, ignoring the wave of concern coming from Elder. Like me, he wondered if my mind was something to be sliced and placed on crackers.

Captain Timbers had apparently calmed Lucifer down and explained how things worked in this strange city. The Paladin didn't look happy as he turned to us, his entourage, and said, "We must seek a Dwarf dressed in black and white, with a red floppy hat. This will be a member of the Director's Guild, and they can point us to the chapterhouse. Two silver fillets to the first free squire to spot one."

The squires scattered like grain seeds in a windstorm, leaving us and the horses standing on the dock. Raith remained beside his master, his eyes downcast at his ineligibility to win the money.

"Brawk! I could have told you where to find one. I've been to this city more times than I can count."

"It's one way to finally be rid of the little brats," I said.

"That wasn't what I intended," Lucifer said, favoring me with one of his familiar dark glares.

"What did you expect?" Elder said. "That's more money than most of them will see in a year. Now we're going to have to wait an hour, and we'll end up with twenty guides."

He was wrong; we only ended up with nineteen. One of the boys slid on a pile of sewage within a bowshot of leaving and hurt his ankle, so he hobbled back and had to wait with us. Lucifer gave him a lecture about safety and a copper urchin—I have no idea where they came up with these coins' names—as a consolation prize.

But in everything else, Elder proved correct. An hour later, nineteen squires returned, each towing a dwarf wearing a black tabard over a white vest and black pantaloons. On each head sat a red hat that hung long on one side, as if it had not been put on straight and was prepared to leap away at the slightest provocation.

It took another half hour to get everything straightened out. It was impossible to say which boy found their quarry first, so Lucifer was obliged to pay all of them. Many of the boys had gotten lost on their search and had to be led back to the docks, so the directors demanded payment for those services, along with something called a "premium" because they didn't get paid in advance. We didn't need all nineteen guides, so Lucifer had to dismiss eighteen of them, but he had to pay them a "minimum" simply because they showed up. By the time the whole mess got sorted out, Lucifer's coin pouch had shrunk like cold water hit it.

"I bet that'll teach him to think before he opens his big mouth," I whispered to Raith and Elder.

"So says the pot about the kettle," Elder observed.

"And I doubt it," Raith offered.

Lucifer got things whittled down to one director, a dwarf who had a fire-red beard that hung almost to his feet and wore a round piece of glass over one eye. His voice was even harsher than most dwarves, which is to say, listening to him made my ears want to mutate into eyes.

"Otto at your serfice. Ver do you vant to go?"

"What?" Lucifer said, his broad face scrunched in concentration.

"Ver do you vant to go. In vhat direction?"

"You're not from around here, are you?"

"Nah, I am frum the vest."

Lucifer shook his head. "No, I don't need a vest; I need directions."

Otto shook his head, making his beard waggle like some strange red snake. "No, no, the vest." He pulled the glass piece from his eye and used it to point as he spoke. "Norf, souf, east, vest." He remained facing that direction. "I am from the vest, past the Commody Mountains."

Lucifer still looked troubled. "You wear a vest when you go to the commode in the mountains?"

Only Lucifer would hire a worker he couldn't understand. I couldn't take it any longer. "He said he comes from the west, past the Carmody Mountains."

"Yah, that's vhat I say." He offered me a friendly smile and placed the glass back against his eye. I was adding to my list of skills. First prophet, now interpreter.

Comprehension finally smacked Lucifer, a rare occurrence. "I see." He looked at Otto and started speaking loud and slow. "Which...Way...To... The...Chapterhouse?"

Otto looked at me. "Vhy he speak that vay? Ist he haf the damaged brain?"

I hate when I get offered such temptations, but I successfully resisted. Instead of answering Otto, I looked at Lucifer. "He's foreign, not deaf or stupid."

"Well, Holy Seer, since Ubel has blessed you with the ability to speak his language, ask him which way to the chapterhouse."

The water suddenly seemed appealing, death dolphin or not. I looked at Otto and rolled my eyes. "Which way to the chapterhouse for Paladins of Ubel?"

"Vhich von? Norf, souf, east or vest?"

It would be too much of a strain on Lucifer to consider four options. "Whichever one is closest."

"How about the one that resides within the High Cathedral?" Elder asked.

Lucifer looked surprised. "You understand this fellow's language too?"

"Enough to get by," Elder answered with a straight face.

"Der High Cavedral?" the dwarf looked at me for confirmation.

"Yes."

"Follow me."

"Hey," Lucifer said. "I understood that. He said 'follow me'. I'll have the knack of this in no time."

"We're going to the chapterhouse to drop off the squires, right?" Elder asked, the desperation almost leaking out his ears.

"Of course."

"Good." Elder's sense of relief almost knocked me over.

But Lucifer wasn't finished. "And replace them with twenty new Paladins who can travel with us."

"Well," Elder said, trying to soothe his disappointment, "maybe at least these will be sober."

We set off down the street, a parade of horses and people following a dwarf. I imagined us as quite an unusual sight, but no one in the city paid us the slightest bit of attention.

Captain Timbers took off from Lucifer's shoulder and came back to land on mine. "Brawk. I had to get away from Lucifer in case stupidity is contagious."

"My brother thinks it has to do with the size of your muscles. Why aren't you staying at the ship?"

"Because I'm going to travel with you to see the Oracle. It's high time I got this mess between us straightened out. You don't mind, do you?"

"Not at all," I said. "Just don't poop on my shoulder."

As we traveled the streets, I tried to take in everything and failed miserably. Every building was made of stone, something I had never imagined. And not just gray stone, but stone painted in colors to rival the Dwarves' attire. Taken by itself, each building was hard on the eyes. Yet the structures somehow managed to blend together in a way that was thoroughly disturbing, if not downright nauseating.

And people. More people than I imagined existed in the world, all crowded together so that they could barely walk without stepping on each other. A few people *did* step on my feet, although they certainly gave Lucifer a lot of room. I wondered if I should start wearing armor and a two-handed sword.

Dwarves dominated the streets and shops, dressed in the clothing that denoted their guild. It was like walking through a madman's rainbow. Although they were the largest population, they were far from the only race represented in this metropolitan stew. Humans were present, as were elves. Gnomes seemed to make up a small portion of the city, and halflings flitted about, usually trailing a food-filled burlap bag. I had only read about these other species before. To finally see them in person was depressingly uninteresting. They all looked like extra-tall or extra-short humans, some with pointed ears, others with slanted eyes or reddish complexions. I'm not sure what I expected, but nothing I saw matched anything I imagined. For some reason, it all made me incredibly homesick.

As the sun settled on the horizon, we reached the High Cathedral, a structure impressive in its tackiness even amongst the cornucopia of chintz surrounding it. The building stood at least fifty feet tall, with towers at each corner that doubled that. It was painted a blinding gold, except for the mortar between the bricks, which glowed red as blood. Standing out in bas relief on one tower was a sword and on the other a shield, both painted bilgewater gray. The two back towers had nothing on them I could see, but they were at least two hundred feet away. I had thought our cathedral in Frostishak was big, but this building could have engulfed the whole village. The wooden double doors, ten feet high, were painted hunter green. I have no idea why, since that color isn't and never has been associated with Ubel. Hazards of going with the lowest bidder was my only guess.

"Here is der High Cavedral. That vill be von silfer piece."

"One silver," I told Lucifer before he could even ask.

Lucifer fished the coin out of his purse and handed it over. "Thank... you," he shouted.

"You...velcome...moron," Otto shouted back, pocketing the silver piece and leaving.

Lucifer watched the retreating dwarf. "Odd fellow. Wonder why he yelled at me."

"What now?" Elder asked.

"Now, the squires wait out here while we go inside and rest and get some food."

"That doesn't seem hardly fair," Raith said, then looked at Lucifer with instant regret on his face.

"Don't worry. You'll be able to eat as soon as you've brushed, bathed, dried, and then brushed again Justice, Pony, and Number Two."

"All three?"

"Yes."

I stepped up. "That's okay, I can take care of my own horse."

"Me too," Elder said, although without as much enthusiasm as I faked.

"Nonsense," Lucifer said. "You are a priest, and you a Holy Seer. Young Raith should feel honored to attend to your mounts." The Paladin looked at Raith with his dark eyebrows lowered. "Shouldn't he?"

"Well, he *should*," Raith said.

"Excellent," Lucifer said, missing the implication as much as I missed home. "You other squires, attend to your horses. I will send the stable master out directly to escort you to the stables. Once your horses are attended to, we will see to having meals for you. Then we must figure out what to do with you."

"Sending us home would be a good start," one of them, a black-haired boy with a crooked nose, muttered quietly enough that I heard it, but Lucifer didn't.

"If they do, let me know so I can stow away," I said.

"Sure," he answered in a tone that convinced me he would do nothing of the sort. Probably still mad I had killed his master. Since that particular problem was nowhere in the vicinity of my fault, I had forgiven myself while we waited to debark. Apparently, the squires didn't see it that way.

Lucifer gave three solid knocks to the door, knocks that echoed back with dull booms. A minute passed before the door creaked open to reveal a man who looked a hundred if he was a day. He had a thin face with a pointed chin and wrinkles that were probably older than Lucifer. Any semblance of hair had long ago given up and turned to wisps of fine white straw. His eyes leaked like a badly sealed pipe, and he stood hunched as if a stone the size of a horse rested on his back. His clothing, tan pants and shirt with a yellow tabard, hung like his skin, wrinkled and baggy.

"May I help you?" he asked in a raspy voice.

"I am Lucif-"

"Speak up, youngster. My ears aren't what they used to be."

"I AM LUCIF-"

"About half that if you please. I'm hard of hearing, not stone deaf."

"I am Lucif- is that good?"

"Perfect."

"I am Lucifer of Frostishak, Grand Commander of the Most Sacred Brotherhood of the Holy Paladins of Ubel, Southern Chapter. I am on a divine quest and require assistance."

"Well, come on in. Someone is waiting for you."

"Really?"

We were all surprised by that announcement. Had word of arrival somehow reached here before us? Considering how long we had been delayed, it was possible. Despite myself, I was curious.

"Follow me." The old man turned and hobbled across the large, candlestick-laden foyer. We followed, although I had to resist the urge to pick him up and carry him so we could move faster.

We passed the narthex and entered the nave, a region as impressive as it was gauche. Bright orange candles, hundreds of them in shiny gold holders, lined the walls on either side and gave the chamber a cloying jasmine smell. They threatened to bring the whole building down in flames as they burned only a few feet under the tapestries of Ubel's miracles that competed for wall space. These squares of cloth were covered in eye-destroying primary colors and most of them looked as if a child with shaky hands and lousy vision had sewn them. We had similar items back home, though none quite as large. It fell upon members of the clergy to create these iconic textiles. Judging by their quality, artistic talent and religious fervor were bitter enemies.

Larger and, thankfully better designed, were the giant blue and yellow banners that hung above the gilt-colored pews. The banners bore the sigil of Ubel set above another symbol, different on each standard. Chapter emblems was my guess, a theory borne out by Lucifer's outraged voice.

"Why does my chapter flag hang at the rear instead of its accustomed place above the chancel?"

Our guide's rheumy eyes relayed his confusion. "Accustomed? Why it hasn't been there since..." It must have dawned on him precisely who asked. He offered an apologetic smile. "I'm sure one of the cardinals has an explanation."

"Yes, an explanation will be forthcoming," Lucifer grumbled.

Our guide quickened his pace to that of a lethargic turtle, no doubt wanting to avoid any more questions from Lucifer. We reached the chancel. The podium was bright blue with a yellow sun painted on the front.

The old man held his hands above his head, fingers spread out like the sun's rays, and wiggled them while he said, "Bless us, Ubel, to know your benevolence and share in your wisdom."

Each of us followed suit in the ritual prayer. I had always thought it a rather stupid practice and wondered how Ubel felt about it. I made a mental note to ask him if I ever heard from him again.

The guide turned left and we continued our painful trek until he reached an opening in the wall. We left the nave behind and stepped into a side hall. It was large and ostentatious, much like I expected. Suits of armor stood on either side, and tapestries depicting noble-faced paladins in heroic poses hung from the walls. The arrogance floating through the room made me want to sneeze.

A hundred agonizing feet later, the old man finally reached a dark wooden door. Muffled laughter came from the other side.

"There you go, young man. You'll have to open it. I can't quite manage it these days."

I assumed he was talking to me since I was the youngest person present, so I forged ahead.

"I'll get it, Holy Seer," Lucifer said.

"I think I can handle this one," I said. Pushing on the latch, I shoved open the door. Laughter and merriment rolled over us like water, followed by the heady smell of ale and mead. Eighteen familiar faces looked our way.

"Hello, Commander Lucifer," Sergeant Glawen said, holding a tankard. "Hope you don't mind; we went ahead and started the celebration without you."

All the Paladins I had knocked off the ship were standing or sitting in that cozy room, all drunk off their asses.

11

Pole-axed steer came to mind as I saw Lucifer's stunned expression, a countenance and sentiment mirrored by Elder, Raith, Timbers, the squires, and most likely myself. I had the shock. I can only assume I had the moon-calf stare. I couldn't have been more surprised if Ubel himself stood there with a mug. Considering recent events, I would have been less surprised.

"By what great blessings of Ubel do you come to be here and alive?" Lucifer asked, crossing his arms above his head in a sign of praise.

"Mermaids," Glawen said, staggering toward Lucifer.

"Mermaids?" Lucifer asked.

"Mermaids. Daughters of Titanicus. What—" here he paused to belch and take another swig of ale. "Whatever you want to call them. They had been following the ship. They do that, you know." He looked at Captain Timbers. "Did you know that?"

"Brawk, I had heard such a thing, but never having seen them, I thought they were a myth."

"No, they're real, all right. And *very* friendly, if you know what I mean."

I did, even without his lecherous smirk, or as lecherous as possible with his head bobbing and his eyes glazed as pound cake. Obviously, Lucifer caught the meaning, too, since his firm jaw tightened and his agate eyes appeared ready to drill holes through Glawen. "Continue your story, sergeant."

The tone reached through Glawen's stupor. He tried to straighten himself, and his broad face became less deviant. "Well, Commander, they saw us fall in and watched us sink toward the bottom, what with having all the armor on."

I told you, you pious idiot. This thought came from Elder, strong enough that I had to check to make sure he hadn't said it aloud.

"So, they followed us down. I thought sure we were goners and that they were Ubel's angels sent to take us to heaven, even though I wasn't sure why they would have fins and such, seeing as you'd think they could just float through the water. I held my breath as long as I could. When I was just about to open my mouth, which would surely have been the death of me, the mermaids said something I didn't understand and suddenly we could all breathe. They took us to their home where they—"

He stopped, no doubt remembering whom he spoke to. "Where they were...very hospitable. They asked what we were doing so far from land, and we explained we were traveling with you but didn't rightly know why. They asked if it had anything to do with Ubel's disappearing. I told them I didn't know Ubel *had* disappeared. Has he?"

"He's been kidnapped," I answered. "Kidnapped and held somewhere by an evil teenager."

I thought it sounded stupid when I said it. Still, Glawen didn't laugh at me, only stared with his frosted cake eyes for several seconds and then took another drink.

Lucifer had a somewhat different reaction. He looked at me. "Why did you not tell me this before?"

"Would it have changed anything?"

I thought Lucifer was going to hit me or cry. Maybe both. "Of course, it would. Instead of wasting our time traveling here, we could have gone directly to where Ubel is being held and rescue him."

Now I wanted to cry. I wasn't sure which inanity to address first. I opened my mouth and closed it a few times, like a gasping fish.

Elder stepped up and helped me, forever winning my gratitude. "Briar, do you know where Ubel is being held?"

"No."

"But you must," Lucifer insisted. "He speaks to you as his Holy Seer. Surely, he told you all."

"I've already told you he speaks to me as his last resort, and he hasn't been able to say anything about his location. I'm not even sure *he* knows where he is."

"But Ubel knows everything," Lucifer said, and a chorus of drunken affirmations rumbled from the room.

It had been several hours since I inadvertently said or did something horribly stupid, so clearly, it was time. "Well, he obviously doesn't, or he would have known enough to not get kidnapped."

Silence filled the room, and I swear I felt the temperature decrease. I gazed around at a plethora of faces with expressions ranging from hostile to murderous. Elder nodded thoughtfully, and Captain Timbers's face looked affable, but it always looked affable.

I noticed Lucifer's hand had drifted toward his back and the hilt that rested there. A glance at the ceiling gave dismaying confirmation that he had plenty of room to wield Heathensmasher.

"I spoke in haste," I said, hoping haste described the speed at which my brain would come up with a way to keep me breathing. "Obviously Ubel...well, knows everything because he's Ubel...the...the supreme God, most holy of the five." Inspiration struck, which can happen when you're close to death. "Which means he knew he would be kidnapped and let it happen anyway."

Lucifer's hand rested on Heathensmasher's pommel. But he hadn't drawn it—a good sign. "Why?"

I wasn't ready for a follow-up question. "Because...because..."

"Because he wants to test us, to see if we are capable of serving him," Elder said, stepping next to me. I could have kissed him.

Lucifer looked uncertain—still a disturbing expression on his solid face. Then the uncertainty changed to hurt, which I found more disconcerting. Never in my life did I expect to see a Paladin pout. "I have served him for over twenty years. Surely, he knows I am capable."

"I'm sure he does," Elder countered. "But what about the rest of us?"

"Have you been backsliding?"

"Not me," Elder stepped back, eyes wide because Lucifer's hand had drifted back to the sword. I think it was a reflex action, and he wouldn't actually have drawn it on the cleric.

Although to this day, I'm not sure about that.

"When he said us, I don't think he meant 'us,'" I pointed to Elder and then myself. I lowered my voice, so hopefully only Lucifer could hear me. "Perhaps he meant them." I nodded my head in the direction of the lubricated Paladins. By saying perhaps, I kept my statement from being a lie and more in the realm of stretching things to save my ass.

Of course, since it came from Lucifer's Holy Seer, he took it as gospel. He turned and faced the Paladins. "The Holy Seer has declared that because of your backsliding drunkenness, Ubel has seen fit to be abducted rather than be confronted with your sins. To atone, you must cease this debauchery and continue this quest to find most Holy Ubel and rescue him from the clutches of...of whatever has abducted him."

The wealth of inference he took from my simple, half-hearted accusation astounded me.

"Therefore, I expect all of you to be ready to depart in the morning, at dawn's rise, *sober*. And there will be no more wine until Ubel is found or we die trying." Lucifer turned and stomped out in dramatic righteous anger, leaving us standing there facing the eighteen Paladins.

It took their sodden minds a moment to work out precisely what had happened. The dots finally connected for them, with me at the center. If I thought my earlier blunder had chilled the room, Lucifer's pronouncement of my "declaration" threatened to give me mental frostbite. They stared at me. I stared at them. I could feel their resentment; my empathy almost overloaded with it. There was grumbling, there was muttering, but no one actually spoke.

I jumped when the forgotten old man spoke at my elbow. "Come this way, gentlemen. I'll show you to the guest room."

"I hope it has a strong lock," Elder said.

"So," Elder said, "do you think you'll ever learn to keep your mouth shut?"

Elder, Timbers, and I sat in the common guest room. Other than the six narrow mahogany beds, it looked much like the rest of the chapterhouse, complete with thick carpeting and tapestries of Paladins staring down on us in imperious silence. It was almost like they had taken up the anger of the group we left downstairs.

"When I'm dead, I suppose." Following the glacial old man up the stairs to the room gave me plenty of time to ponder that very question. Almost all my life's miseries had been a result of the disconnection between my mouth and common sense. Even my first word caused problems. Calgin, the prince of Skaldor and nominally our sovereign, had come to Frostishak on a "tour of the colonies" as he called it. Along with the rest of the town, my parents stood in the streets as the prince strolled along, deigning to shake hands with the commoners. When he reached us, my mother held out the drooling eight-month-old me and said, "Please bless my baby, your highness."

The prince touched my forehead, and even though I shouldn't, I still remember the images that crossed my mind. I looked at the prince and uttered my first word.

"Thief."

That got my parents two weeks in the small Frostishak jail, and me labeled as abnormal. Things got stranger when we heard months later that the prince had been sent away to the far north because of raging kleptomania.

People started avoiding me after that and did so for many years. Eventually, the story was forgotten, but it foretold how most of my life would go.

"When you're dead," Elder repeated as if having to remind my wandering mind of what I said. "You're certainly trying to make that happen sooner rather than later, aren't you?"

"No, I'm not. In fact, I've tried at every opportunity to make sure anything else happens. I tried telling you back in Frostishak that I wouldn't be worth anything."

Something knocked against the window. I looked over to see a bird sitting on the sill. It was dark out, and I shouldn't have been able to see the stupid creature, but it was glowing red, like a torch. Both its heads looked at us as it bounced around on its three feet.

"See, this is all I'm good for," I said, walking to the window and pointing at the shimmering avian. "Spotting strange shit like this so I can freak out about it and wonder what I've gotten myself into. Oh yeah, I'm also great at hearing voices of abducted gods and seeing evil, pimply faces in my mind." I pounded on the window. The bird gave a frightened squawk, hissed at me, and took off. Spittle from its hiss struck the window and set off lazy drifts of smoke as it burned holes in the glass. "Oh, that's nice." I looked back at Elder. "See, that's what I'm trying to avoid. I don't want to deal with two-headed birds that spit acid, or black dolphins. Let Lucifer deal with it. That's what he's trained for."

But I need you.

"Great," I shouted. "Ubel's back. Quick, before Pimple shows back up, does anybody want to ask him anything? Someone go get Lucifer so he can ask all his questions. Or better yet, I'll ask one. Why me instead of Lucifer? He's the one with the unswerving faith and ultimate devotion."

He's also the one with the mental acuity of an overripe turnip. He's a wonderful servant, but he's a man of action, not thought. His job is to make sure you live long enough to find me. I fear that will be plenty for him to handle. But to save me, I need someone with your special gifts and brainpower.

"Gifts? What special gifts do I have apart from penetrating cynicism? How am I supposed to save you?"

As for your gifts, you will learn about them as necessary. As for how to save me, I don't know. That's why you have to go to the Oracle.

"But you're the great Ubel. You're supposed to know everything."

Obviously I don't, or I would have known better than to get kidnapped.

Stop talking to him! I caught the barest glimpse of Pimple taking a swing at me, but Ubel pulled himself from my mind before his young tormentor could damage me.

I looked at the other three. Elder wore an expression of stunned disbelief. Timbers wore the expression of a macaw. "Neither of you heard Ubel, did you?"

They shook their heads in unison.

I couldn't stand it. A god admits he's fallible, and I'm the only one who knows it. And I knew it before I even knew I knew it. I started laughing, overcome with hysteria.

I didn't stop laughing until lack of breath made me pass out.

While I was out, I had a vision. The whole thing took place in a white expanse badly in need of some decoration to break up the monotony. Pimple and I stood on either side of Ubel, who towered over us. He was glowing and imperious, as gods should be, instead of begging and pleading, as I had seen him recently. In his hands, he held a globe, at least three feet wide and five tall, which I recognized as a representation of the world. Above Ubel's head sat the other four gods, as if on a panel of judges. Parsimony, God of Thieves, Moneylenders, and Lawyers, sat to the left, twiddling a gold piece through his fingers. Phoebe, blond Goddess of Children and Cute Things, sat beside him with her legs crossed. She wore nothing but a gauzy, almost transparent white robe. A gray kitten and yellow fuzzy duck played in her lap while she fiddled with her braided hair and wore a vacant smile. Horn, God of Marriage, Lust, and Divorce, sat beside Phoebe, staring at nothing but her. He was a large, brown-haired man with a broad chest and a thick beard that did nothing to hide his leering grin. He wore nothing but a loincloth held on by two gold buttons. Titanicus, God of Ships and Things that Sink, sat beside Horn. He had blue skin and stringy green hair. His face constantly moved, going from a grin to a frown and back as if he couldn't decide his mood. He held a model ship in one hand, a giant rock in the other, and wore a gray robe.

Ubel let go of the world, which floated to the ground like a feather and settled. It amazed me how real it looked, with mountains and valleys and oceans that moved. It was nothing like the crude wooden globe in the church back home, which had roughly carved blobs of land surrounded by oceans of chipped blue paint. Many call Ubel the Architect of the World, and I wondered if I was looking at his prototype.

Ubel held out a hand, larger than my head, to me and one to Pimple. Swords appeared, hilts facing us. In Ubel's giant hands, they looked like twigs. Mine was white and glowing, while Pimple's was black and anti-glowing. That is, it seemed to absorb the light around it, which evil artifacts are wont to do. I stared at the ivory sword like it was an albino snake, which it might as well have been for all the experience I've had with either. Pimple held his as if he were born to wield death.

"Take it," Ubel said, shaking the sword like playing fetch with a dog. I took it even though I would have rather eaten glass. If I had to fight Pimple, I knew the outcome would be much like my fight on the ship, except instead of getting a splitting headache, I'd get a split head.

The sword felt much lighter than I expected, no more substantial than the quills I use. I swung it around like I had seen Raith do occasionally, and it moved with ease. For some reason, I felt almost confident.

Sneering in the way evil people do, Pimple also swung his sword. It made a frightening whistle as if it wounded the air. He twirled it around his body and whipped it over his head, an impressive display that drained my confidence like beer from an axe-broached keg. I looked at Ubel. "I hope I turn out to be a better servant than I am a savior."

"Shut up and let's go," Pimple said. "I've got better things to do."

"Then by all means, go do them," I offered, but his better things could apparently wait. He seemed to know as well as I did that this wouldn't take long. He walked toward me, and I stood there with my sword extended. I wasn't going to rush toward him like some heroic idiot. If he wanted to kill me he'd have to make the effort of walking the twenty feet to do so.

The front of the globe suddenly cracked with a thunderous sound and opened like a door, swinging outward toward Pimple. The wicked little twit couldn't stop soon enough, and there was a satisfying thump as the world smacked him in the face. Laughter rang from above. I looked up to find the gods above Ubel chuckling at Pimple's misfortune.

Pimple stumbled back. The back of the globe door blocked my view, but the noise told me he had taken a good whack. Maybe I could catch him while he was stunned and end this quick.

Movement inside the globe caught my attention. It was hollow and dark, but I could make out the form of an old woman as she emerged from the darkness. She wore a shimmering pearl dress that matched her pale complexion, and she appeared as ancient as the mountains. I thought the chapterhouse's chamberlain was old, but he seemed a strapping youth compared to this wizened lady. Still, her green eyes sparkled, and she stepped from the globe with grace and dignity.

"You cannot win this way," she said, her voice dusty as old books in a library.

"I know that," I said, trying to glance over her shoulder to make sure Pimple hadn't recovered and was sneaking up on me. "But I need to convince Ubel."

"Ubel is not himself," she offered with a wave of a hand fragile as scrimshaw. "He is…preoccupied."

"No wonder you have a reputation for being so wise," I said. "I would, too, if I constantly stated the obvious."

Her eyes flashed, and her crevassed face looked strangely childlike as she gave me a petulant frown. "You'd best be nice to me, you little twit. I'm the only one who can tell you how you can win."

I was shocked. Not that she was *the one who could reveal all*; I'd pretty much guessed that was the dream's purpose. What stunned me was that someone so ancient and regal would resort to calling me a twit. "I apologize for my rudeness. It's an unfortunate fact of my existence. Please, oh wise one, tell me what I must do."

"You must come see me at Hiephi."

I waited a few seconds to see if there was more. "That's it?" I finally asked.

"Yes."

"I was already doing that."

"Yes, but you were trying to figure out a way to not do it. Hopefully, I've convinced you otherwise."

"What will I learn if I come to you?"

"You will learn about yourself, for that is the only way to win."

Learn about myself? Boy, that was a great way to not say much. "Teach me about myself now. Then I don't have to come to you."

She looked like I had asked her to remove her clothes, a thought as frightening to me as it would be to her. "I can't do that."

"Why not. This is a dream, and you came to me. So, teach me."

"Can't. Cosmic rules. To gain true knowledge, you must journey to its source, which in this case is me."

"Cosmic rules? What, who, whose stupid idea was that?"

The air temperature dropped around me. And I don't mean figuratively, like when I was in the room with the Paladins. I mean, the air turned colder. And a tremendous pressure bore down on me from above. My ears popped and made a strange crackling sound. The Oracle didn't have to answer my question; she left that to the gods. I gazed up to find them looming over me, every face awash in wounded pride. It's taught in church that the gods are prideful, and I've learned it firsthand. I waited to see which one would smash me under their thumb and wipe me out like the insignificant bug I was.

Phoebe spoke, her voice deep and melodious but with anger seething underneath. "We made the rules, and it is for you humans to abide by them and not question them. Do not ask, only obey." She leaned down so that her face hovered inches from me, even though she had been at least thirty feet away a second ago. "Understand?"

Even I'm not stupid enough to back-talk an angered goddess, especially one ready to chew off my face. "I...I...yes, I understand."

"Good," she said. Suddenly, she hovered way above me again, all smiles and friendship. "Here, have a puppy."

I woke up with a wet face and something cold and rough rubbing against my forehead. Perhaps Phoebe's gift puppy was licking my face. But I opened my eyes to find Raith bent over me with a damp cloth.

He saw I was awake and smiled. "Are you—" he stopped, realizing he was about to ask me what I had told him to stop asking me. "Well, you know."

"Yes, I'm okay. For now. But I'd still be better if I was back across the ocean."

"We all would," Raith said, pulling away the cloth and slapping it into a bowl of water. "But you know, sometimes in life, you have to do things you don't want to do, and whining about it doesn't make it any better. In fact, it usually—"

"Makes it worse," I finished for him.

Raith's watery eyes grew wide, and I feared they might drip on me. "That's right."

"Sorry I've been such a prat. I'll try and do better."

Raith looked up at Elder, who stood nearby with concern wrapped around his round face. "I told you he bumped his head when he fell," Raith said.

"No, I'm fine, really, but I had a dream that, well, explained things to me." I sat up and leaned against one of the beds, catching the smell of damp horse from Raith. "What are you doing in here? I thought you were off grooming horses."

"I was, but Brother Elder summoned me to tend to you. Like it's not bad enough I have to take care of your horse."

"That wasn't my idea. Where's Captain Timbers?"

As if my question had magical summoning powers, the door opened, and the captain floated in on Lucifer's shoulder. The Paladin had removed his armor and now wore a tight blue tunic and a pair of white hose that showed off every dimple and sinew of his legs, and of other areas I didn't really want to see.

"I thought Paladins took a vow of modesty," I muttered to Raith.

"No, you're thinking of monks. Paladins take a vow of vanity."

"They also take a vow of knowing when their squires are spreading impudence. I believe there is still a matter of horse grooming you need to attend to."

"Of course, master," Raith said, rolling his eyes at me. "I assume you're okay to tend to yourself now."

"I think I can manage," I said, taking the cloth.

Once Raith had left, Lucifer pulled up one of the heavy wooden chairs from the dining table and sat in front of me.

"This doesn't look good," I muttered.

"Brother Elder tells me Ubel spoke to you again."

"Brother Elder has a big mouth."

Lucifer frowned, as did Elder. "Brother Elder is a priest. Curb your impudent tongue."

Being commanded was the last thing I was in the mood for. I couldn't do much when a god told me what to do, but I'd be damned if I would take orders from this half-witted sword swinger.

"Or what?" I asked, leaning up toward Lucifer. "You'll make me scrub horses or wipe your ass. I'm not Raith, and I'm not one of your Order's little goslings. I'm a Ho—" I stopped myself. I had almost fallen into believing Lucifer's claims of my being a Holy Seer. "I'm a church scribe, here to record this odious trek, nothing more."

Elder spoke from behind me, his voice harsher than I ever remember it. "And as a member and employee of the Church, you are subject to those of superior rank. I'm sure it will not surprise someone with your intelligence that both Lucifer and I fit that description."

This kid really needs to learn when to keep his mouth shut, Elder added in his thoughts.

I sensed great smugness coming from Lucifer as he sat before me, even though his face remained blocky and neutral.

I realized, with the feeling of a fish who understands the worm he's eaten has something sharp in it, that Elder was right. They owned me as surely as they owned Raith, but they had been lenient. I suspected those days were over.

"Now," Lucifer said, locking those sharp eyes with mine. "Let's try again. Brother Elder tells me you spoke with Ubel."

"Brother Elder is correct."

"What did Ubel say?"

"Word for word?" I hoped he wouldn't ask for that. My eidetic memory would let me, and my stupid Vow of Veracity would force me. I didn't relish the thought of Lucifer's fury when he found out what his patron thought of him.

I was spared. "You can summarize."

"He said he needed me to save him."

"Why you and not me?" Boy, this was really eating away at Lucifer. But I guess if I devoted my life to scribing only to watch someone burn my documents in my face, I'd wonder why too.

"He said you were a man of action, not words. I have special gifts that would be needed."

His brow furrowed, and I felt the idea confused him as much as it did me.

"I don't know, and neither did Ubel," I said in answer to the question Lucifer hadn't asked.

"But Ubel knows—"

"No, he doesn't," I snapped. I may have to obey them, but I couldn't totally give in. "He as much as admitted to me that he is fallible. Why do you think I passed out?" Well, it was indirectly why I passed out.

"Everything you've said is true?"

I've never understood why people ask that question. If I was prone to lying, I certainly wouldn't tell the truth about not telling the truth. "Yes."

Lucifer stared at the floor, and I wondered if he would start crying. I imagine it was a lot for him to take in. Despite his arrogance and hubris, he really was scared and insecure. I sensed it around him, clinging like the smell of rotten cheese. A couple of weeks ago, I would have used that to my advantage, but things had changed. Death could be around any corner, and a confident protector is far better than one who's lost his purpose.

"Ubel also said that your job was to keep me alive long enough to find him, and that task would test you to your full mettle. You are my protector. Ubel needs you to watch over me." I wanted to vomit at the next words, but I forced them out. "I need you to protect me."

Lucifer raised his head, still not convinced. "But if Ubel is fallible, how do I know any of what he says is right?"

Lucifer wasn't bright, but he was strangely perceptive at inconvenient times. "I think this other evil god somehow fooled Ubel."

"But how?"

I didn't know. It wasn't my place to know. Elder, apparently wanting to make up for being a jerk to me a moment ago, spoke up. "Well, if Ubel has a fault, and I'm not saying he does," he hastily added as Lucifer's eyes swung to regard him like a hawk might view a tasty field mouse, "but if he did have *one* flaw, it would be trust. He is a trusting god. So, if another being were to play on that trust, he could easily trick Ubel. After all, I still feel the gods are infallible as far as humans are concerned, but among other gods, they may have the same faults as we do among ourselves."

"That sounds a great deal like blasphemy," Lucifer rumbled.

"Yes," Elder agreed. "But considering the past week's events, it also sounds a great deal like the truth."

"Brawk," Timbers said, scaring the hell out of all of us. Preening his feathers and saying nothing, he had blended into the background, and we had forgotten he was there. "This Pimple Briar speaks of sounds nothing like any of the four other Gods, and I don't think any demigods would have the power to fool Ubel. Brawk."

We all pondered that a moment. I certainly didn't have an answer, and no deities popped into my head, as was their habit of late, to offer one.

Then Elder spoke the ultimate blasphemy. "Maybe Ubel really is insane."

Lucifer stood up with his fists clenched. "I suggest you explain...quickly."

"Now, now," Elder said, backing up toward the door. "You said a vow to not harm clergy members."

"Which is why you still stand."

That seemed to give Elder courage, although if it were me, I still would have put a hand on the door. I could already see where Elder was heading with this, and I knew Lucifer wouldn't approve.

"Perhaps something happened to Ubel, something none of us can comprehend, and somehow his personality split, like a log under an axe."

"You're comparing great Ubel to a piece of wood?"

"Of course not; it was just for purposes of demonstration. I think maybe there are now two personalities to Ubel, a good and an evil."

"But why would his evil half be a teenager that doesn't even look like him," I asked. It didn't make sense.

"He really doesn't look like that; that's only what your mind sees. After all, Ubel is a god and is something we can only see when he wants us to. We know him as the benevolent father, so that is how he looks to you. This Pimple is your own fear given substance. Perhaps there's some other boy you're afraid of?"

In our town? Not likely. It's true, in Frostishak, I had several people happy to beat me up, but they didn't consider me an enemy so much as a target of opportunity. And as long as I had Raith willing to stand up for me, I didn't really fear them. I suppose some of the pages were enemies, especially Crow, but I'd be more frightened by a dust bunny than any of them. Still, there was something about Pimple that looked very familiar.

Lucifer had been strangely silent, considering the subject matter. I waited for the outburst, but he only looked at Elder and said, "I must ponder what you have said. Ubel being divided and warring with himself would explain many things." I caught him throwing a sideways glance at me, and I knew "many things," included why Ubel spoke to me and not him. "I will pray about it."

"To who?" I asked, again allowing my mouth to open when it shouldn't.

But Lucifer either didn't hear me or chose to ignore me. He walked past Elder, who quickly slipped out of the way before the Paladin could change his mind.

Once the door had closed, Elder wiped a bead of sweat from his round face and said, "Well, he took that pretty well, considering the circumstances."

"A little too well," I said. "I'm worried about him."

"Since when do you worry about anybody but yourself?"

"I'm worried about him because it affects me," I corrected since Elder was in the mood to be picky. "He seems to be really anxious about Ubel talking to me and not him. He can have it as far as I'm concerned."

"Yes, you've made that abundantly clear on numerous occasions."

"Then why doesn't he believe it?"

"I don't know," Elder said. "I also don't know how many times I can stick my neck out for you."

"Plenty," I said. "Just ask Raith. But I appreciate it, even if it doesn't always seem like I do."

Elder nodded.

"I just hope the Oracle can tell me something useful like she said she would."

"Like she...never mind, I don't want to know."

"I'm hungry," I said as my stomach rumbled. "You think they have anything in this place besides alcohol?"

12

As it turned out, they had good food and lots of it. Although, after ten days of ship food, a roasted rat would have been a treat. We ate in a large hall with the other Paladins, all of whom sobered up in surprisingly short order. There was a tense moment when I first walked into the hall as every eye turned toward me, and all noise stopped. I stood at the doorway, ready to run if someone so much as dropped a fork. Elder paused beside me, and Timbers shook his wings, sending a few nervous feathers floating to the floor. I mentally chided myself for being such an idiot to forget how things had been left with these twenty armed and dangerous men. It surprised me they hadn't hunted me down in my bedroom. But then, they didn't have to. I was stupid enough to come to them.

Breaths were held, and heartbeats stopped for five agonizing seconds. Then Glawen smiled and waved his large hand in a "come sit" motion. "Come and join us for dinner, Holy Seer."

Relief warred with irritation. They weren't going to kill me, but they had bought into Lucifer's nonsense. I had half a mind to tell them off... and then run.

Glawen shoved at the man next to him. "Chafin, move so the Holy Seer can sit beside me. And fix him a plate of food, as much as he wants. And ale if he wishes."

I realized being a Holy Seer might have some advantages.

I took a seat next to the Sergeant and Chafin sat a plate before me, heaped with colors and smells to turn my mouth into a waterfall. "Look," I said to Glawen as Chafin poured me a large mug of ale, "I'm sorry about the whole knocking you off into the water thing."

"It's fine," Glawen said, accepting a mug from Chafin with a nod of thanks. "You were doing Ubel's work. Besides, the mermaids took proper care of us, if you know what I mean."

I did, and my face could have lit candles. To regain myself I took a gulp of ale. I had never had it before, my parents being temperate and neither I nor Raith having the balls to sneak a drink. I don't know what I expected, but I found the taste quite agreeable, like syrup, only less sticky. It tasted so good that I took another gulp.

"Well, I'm glad you're okay. I felt really bad about what I did." Although right after I said that, I realized I hadn't felt bad about it. It never crossed my mind to feel one way or another about it. Was I really that selfish, that I could send twenty men to death and have no remorse about it? Granted, I hadn't been in charge at the time, but it still seemed wrong to have zero reaction.

Disturbed, I took another drink of ale. "No, I can't lie," I said. "I didn't think about any of you at all. It happened, and apparently, I didn't care that it happened. Ubel certainly picked an insensitive bastard for his Holy Seer, didn't he?"

Glawen gestured at me with his mug. "I think perhaps Ubel made it so you wouldn't feel anything. Imagine how crushed your soul would have been had you really considered what you'd done."

I tried and couldn't, so perhaps he was right. Ubel had numbed me to the idea. But still, I wondered how much of it was my own lack of compassion. I took another drink of ale and noticed my mug had somehow become full again. I hadn't even seen anyone refilling it. "I thought there was supposed to be no more drinking."

"Good Lucifer said no more wine," Glawen explained. "This is ale."

I continued to eat and drink and began to thoroughly enjoy myself. At some point Elder departed with admonitions to drink less, or at least have some water with my ale. Glawen regaled me with tales of their chapter. Lucifer's Louts, as they referred to themselves. We continued to drink long after dinner ended, and I noticed all the other Paladins had taken up mugs. The closest my mug ever came to empty was when, wanting to see how close to empty I could get it, I drank as much in one draught as I could. I heard cheers rising around me and chants of "chug, chug, chug."

Much of the ale splashed around my mouth and onto my shirt, but the liquid finally ended. I sat the mug down and saw it had turned into three mugs. I uncrossed my eyes, and the two phantom tankards merged back into the real one. And it was full again. I looked at Glawen. He seemed unsteady on his feet, but I matched him sway for sway, so it was okay.

He grinned. "I see you have learned the secret of Ubel's bountiful mugs."

"That's great," I said. At least, that's what I meant to say, but it came out as "Thash graith."

Glawen apparently understood me. His grin grew wider. "Aye."

"Dosh Luthifer know bout thish?"

"No," Glawen said. He put a friendly, bulky arm around me. and we both almost fell over. Only a quick hand from me to the table saved us a spill to the floor. "And you have to take the oath as a member of the Brotherhood of Lucifer's Louts to never tell him."

I looked into his brown eyes. Overcome by emotion, I started to cry. "Thank you," I said, or rather blubbered. "I've nefer belonged to anyfhing. I schwear to say nofing, even if he sticks hot pokers under my fin...gernails."

"Here now, lad, stop your tears. Lucifer's Louts don't cry. And Lucifer don't go in for torture so much as chastisement and decapitation, so there's no count in getting overwrought. Ain't that right, gentlemen?"

"Huzzah," they shouted, and two of them fell over stone-cold unconscious.

I don't remember much after that. I know there was singing and maybe even a little dancing. And plenty more drinking. Timbers departed, shaking his head and saying something about "bad as sailors."

Things eventually tapered off, either because people left or passed out. Finally, Glawen said, "Off to bed with you. If I know Lucifer, we'll be leaving early in the morning, and we need to be sober."

Being drunk—or as the common people refer to it—shit-faced, made me bold. "Is Lucifer always such a prig?"

"There's no call for that, my boy. He is a fine commander, if a bit stern and unyielding, and a touch stupid. But a fine commander nonetheless. You'd do best to—"

I never found out what it would be best to do because Glawen stopped with his hand in the air, his eyes crossed, and he toppled over like a felled oak tree.

"I'll do that," I said as if he had imparted the wisdom of the ages to me.

I looked around to discover I was the only one still standing. I guess that meant the celebration was over.

"Good night," I said to Glawen's prostate form. I searched for the door, a task hampered by my vision, which refused to cooperate with the rest of my head. I would turn to look at something, and two seconds later, my sight would catch up and sometimes go past before settling back to where I wanted to look.

Despite my treacherous eyes, I eventually spotted the door. I stumbled over a few bodies on my journey to reach it.

The hallway confused me. I couldn't remember the way to my room and no one conveniently appeared to give me directions. It didn't help that the corridor offered an impressive imitation of a pendulum. I eventually picked a direction simply to get moving and hopefully stop the hall from doing so. It worked to a point, but I still had to shift from left to right and back to stay in the center. It reminded me of being back on the ship. I giggled a lot as I walked.

For once, luck was with me. I was about to give up and head the other way when Raith came out of a door at the end of the hall and walked toward me. He saw me and stopped as if he had caught me stealing the reliquary. "Where have you been?"

I leaned against the wall, hoping my weight would slow down the still-rocking hallway. "Where have you been?" I burbled back.

"Privy," he said.

I suddenly felt tired, and my mouth seemed sticky. "Where's our room?"

"You're leaning against the door."

I looked at the wall and saw it was indeed a door. "Well, that's amazing," I said as if I had discovered a pile of gold in a wheat field.

"Are you drunk?" Raith's voice dripped with scandal.

"Am I?" I saw Raith had turned into twins. "Yes, I suppose I am."

Raith walked over to me. From his crinkled nose and squinted eyes, which suddenly watered more than usual, I gathered I smelled like an upturned keg. "That's horrible."

"Actually, it's quite nice," I countered.

"It won't be if Lucifer finds out. Where did you get ale?"

"From Glawen and Chafin. They're really great guys."

"They'll be really dead guys. If Lucifer asks, you have to say you took it from the cellar. You can't tell him the other Paladins gave it to you."

Despite my condition, I felt insulted. I straightened up to face Raith, felt dizzy, and took to the door again. "I can't do that. I took a Vow of Veracity."

"Then I suggest if you want to keep Glawen and the others out of trouble, you take a Vow of Silence tomorrow."

I made a *phttt* sound, which make me giggle because it tickled my lips. "Lucifer's not going to ask me anything. I won't be drunk tomorrow. He'll never know."

Raith favored me with an expression people usually gave to dumb animals or babies. "Trust me, he'll know."

"WHERE DID YOU GET THE ALE?" Lucifer asked. He hadn't shouted, but it certainly sounded like it as his voice echoed through my throbbing head. Raith was right; Lucifer had almost immediately picked up on my previously inebriated state. I wasn't sure what gave it away: my constant moaning and head holding or that as soon as I sat down to breakfast, I ran off to the privy with cheeks bulged and returned no doubt looking as haggard as a wheat stalk beaten by a flail.

"What do you mean?" I asked.

"YOU ARE HUNGOVER, WHICH MEANS—"

"You don't have to yell."

"I'M NOT YELLING. IN YOUR STATE, IF I YELLED, IT WOULD MOST LIKELY KILL YOU." He paused a moment and lowered his voice to a whisper that, while tolerable, still sounded like a gong ringing beside my ear. "I know you had ale, and a Holy Seer would not have partaken without persuasion. I must know who gave it to you to make sure they are properly punished. Now, who told you to drink?"

I looked around at the Paladins gathered about the tables, eating their breakfast and looking anywhere but at me. How could they possibly eat? Just smelling the food made me want to flee again.

"BRAWK!" Timbers said, and I thought my eyeballs were going to fall out. "Leave the lad be. He is of an age to drink."

"It is not the drinking I mind," Lucifer said, although I felt his displeasure even through my foggy state. "It is the excessiveness."

"Would it help if I said I'll never do it again?" And I meant it. No matter how much fun the night before had been, it wasn't worth the sandpaper tongue, the watery eyes, and the general feeling an ingot must have after a day under the blacksmith's hammer.

"It might, except I have often heard that from my men." He glared around at said men, but they avoided his gaze as assiduously as they did mine.

I played my last gambit; one that I hated myself for doing but that I knew would garner a favorable reaction from Lucifer. "I promise as Ubel's Holy Seer that I will never drink again." I quickly decided to amend it. Even at fifteen, I knew forever was a long time to promise anything. "For as long as we are on this quest and I am in your company."

Lucifer's large forehead crinkled as he considered my vow. He would have preferred a forever promise but suspected he would have to settle. "Very well, we will say no more about it."

He stood and I started to breathe a sigh of relief, but I should have known he wouldn't let it go so easily. He looked around the dining hall. This time he did shout, and I fell off the bench in agony. "SINCE THE HOLY SEER SEES FIT TO PROTECT YOU ALL AS A GROUP, YOU SHALL BE PUNISHED AS A GROUP. IN THE COURTYARD AFTER BREAKFAST. EXPECT A LOT OF PAIN."

Great, I thought as I stared at the stone ceiling. All the progress I made with the men last night destroyed. They were going to hate me again. The ceiling did a little half-spin as if mocking me. Last night when I lay in bed, the room had uprooted and began whirling like parchment caught in a dust devil. It refused to stop until I stuck my foot on the floor and anchored the room. I had woken up—or more accurately, come to—with my foot still on the floor.

"Do you want some help up?" Raith asked.

"I want to get out of here and go back to bed." Breakfast had started an hour after sunup. I went to bed about three hours *before* sunup.

Lucifer stared down at me, disgust and disappointment doled out in equal measure on his broad face. He shook his head once, then turned and walked away. I didn't really care; I was more concerned with what the Paladins planned to do to me after the brutal punishment their master promised to mete out. No doubt they wouldn't do anything except tell their squires, all of whom still hated me, to make my life miserable. More miserable, if that were possible considering how I felt now.

Raith knelt and helped me stand. The room wobbled, and nausea jumped up, but I forced it to pass. I leaned on Raith's shoulder. "Tha—"

"Thank you" was what I meant to say, but the nausea had tricked me. I thought it had passed, but it was waiting to pounce when I opened my mouth. I vomited down the front of Raith's tunic.

"I'm sorry," I said, trying to ignore the laughter around me. All the mirth came from the squires, none from the Paladins. They were so angry they couldn't even find humor in my misery. The next several weeks on the road to the Oracle stretched before me as a path to doom.

"It's okay," Raith said, although I noticed he now looked a touch green himself. "Let's get you back to the room."

It took fifteen minutes, five of which I spent bent over a privy bucket. Another five found me staring at what I thought was a gray sky, but it turned out to be the floor. I rolled over and moaned for Ubel to kill me. At that point in time, Pimple could have shown up and shoved a sword through my head, and I would have thanked him. I eventually reached my bed, slammed my shins into it, screamed, fell over, and passed out.

I CAME to with the hulking forms of Glawen and Chafin standing over me. With a curse at myself for falling asleep and letting down my guard— as if having a guard would have mattered—I scrambled away, confident they had come to kill me in my sleep. Even in my fear, I was flattered they came to do it themselves and hadn't sent their squires. My back slammed against the wall, and the jar to my body started my head pounding again.

"Calm down," Glawen said. "It's okay."

"I'm sure it's okay for you," I said. "You're not the one about to be murdered."

The senior paladins glanced at each other, and I felt the surprise and confusion coming off of them. They looked back at me. "Murdered?" Glawen asked.

Their confusion confused me. Then I remembered they were Paladins, and Paladins of Ubel the Benevolent, no less. "Okay, I'll take the beating like a man."

"I think you have our intentions wrong," Chafin said. "We have come to make sure you were okay. Eleven hours is a long time to be asleep, even for as much as you drank."

Eleven hours? It was impossible to tell in this windowless room, but they had no reason to lie.

"Brawk! How are you feeling?"

In my initial shock, I hadn't noticed Captain Timbers sitting on Glawen's shoulder. You'd think it would be difficult to miss a foot-tall bird, but his gray coloring blended in well with the room's stone walls.

I considered his question and realized, the revitalized headache aside, that I felt much better. Still tired, but nowhere near as ravaged as earlier. "I think I'm going to live," I said. A statement I couldn't have made with any certainty this morning.

"It is past dinner, but we could have the cook bring you something."

My stomach growled, answering for me, but I had other thoughts at the moment. "Aren't you angry with me?"

Again, I sensed surprise, but then Glawen discerned my reason for asking. "Not at all. In fact, me and the boys consider you an honorary Paladin."

So shocked I didn't even consider correcting his lapse in grammar, I said, "But I got all of you in trouble."

"No, you kept two of us from getting in big trouble. You held your peace and stuck with your mates. Teamwork is one of the major tenets of being a true Paladin. Even Lucifer was impressed."

Now I began to think perhaps I was in the middle of an alcohol-inspired dream. "Lucifer?"

Glawen winked at me. "He won't admit it, but he feels that your willingness to stick with us and say nothing, with no regard to what consequences you might suffer, showed you to be of the high character worthy of the Holy Seer."

Consequences? In my bedraggled state this morning, it never occurred to me there might be consequences to myself. Had I realized refusal could result in me suffering, I would have spilled names like a broached keg pours beer. I'd been accused of many things, but having high character wasn't one of them. Quite by accident, I had done the right thing to ingratiate myself to Lucifer and the Paladins.

This meant that, more than ever before, there was no way in hell I would be able to leave before we went to the Oracle. I had to hope that once we reached her, she would prophesy that the world's fate hung on my spelling ability or something equally prosaic. My dream had already shown me I couldn't beat Pimple physically, as if I needed a dream to tell me that. I had to hope there was some other calm, peaceful, or downright sneaky way I could best him.

Maybe I could challenge him to a painting contest.

13

We didn't leave town for two more days. The trek across the mountains required considerable provisions and planning, and the dwarf guilds were apparently not making things easy. I stayed inside to avoid encounters with black-skinned dolphins or two-headed rats, so I only heard about the problems. I often saw Lucifer storm through, muttering to Glawen or some other chapterhouse figure I didn't know. He looked harried and upset, but it kept him away from me.

Raith wasn't so lucky. "He's insufferable," my brother told me while we washed in the squire's bathhouse on our second night there.

"Yes, I know."

"No, you don't. He's even worse than normal."

I tried to imagine that possibility and decided my brain wasn't equipped to handle such disturbing concepts. I lay back and rested my head against the side of the tub. Even though this bathhouse was only for lowly squires, it was an exceptional room, especially for someone used to bathing in a three-foot diameter wooden tub. The room stretched at least twenty feet to a side and the tub, more like a pool, took up a sizable portion of the chamber's center. Four feet deep and filled with warm, sandalwood-scented water that swirled in a gentle circular pattern, the pool was so comfortable that if Raith hadn't been there to talk to me, I could have easily fallen asleep and drowned.

Raith and I were the only ones in the room, the other squires having bathed earlier while Raith groomed Justice, Pony, and Two. I had offered —though not with any real enthusiasm—to tend my animal, but Lucifer would have none of it. He again reminded me the Holy Seer rose above such base tasks. I didn't protest. He seemed to have forgotten entirely about my night of debauchery, which suited me fine.

"I wish I could help," I told Raith, "but I think Lucifer would hang me up somewhere if I approached anything close to work."

"I know you don't really mean it," Raith said as he scrubbed at his mud-colored hair, "but thanks for pretending. It wouldn't be so bad if it weren't for the dwarves. They have so many rules and regulations. Did you know they get a fifteen-minute break every two hours no matter what they're doing? And the Gods forbid you're in their way when the break whistle blows. They almost crushed poor Kerly in a stampede to the teader."

"The what?"

"Teader. It's this cart that rolls up near break times, run by a little gnome-"

"Are there any other kind?" I asked, rubbing soap over my arms.

Raith ignored me. "The dwarves gather around it, and the gnome sells them tea and pastries, and they stand around and drink and smoke their pipes. Then when the whistle blows again, they sort of pack their things away and drift back to their work, which takes another ten minutes. I think that's the part that really drives Lucifer mad."

"Lucifer deserves some uncertainty in his life."

"That's easy for you to say. You're not the one he takes it out on."

Raith ducked his head under the water to rinse the soap from his hair.

The water turned black and grew still. No longer swirling, it settled down to a surface smooth as ice. And damn near as cold. Goosebumps popped up on my arms as I crossed them over my not-quite-as-pudgy-as-before-I-started-this-trip belly. Images appeared in the water, horrific visions of decapitated men, slaughtered animals, and plates filled with cooked cabbage, a vegetable I detested.

This was obviously more of Pimple's doing. "Look, you stupid shit," I shouted at the ceiling, "I'm not the one you need to convince. Send a few of these Lucifer's way, and you might get some results." I knew cussing a god, or whatever Pimple was, wasn't the best move, but I had grown sick of his games. I began to suspect they were the only things he had. For whatever reason, he couldn't do anything to me physically. He could only try to scare me. He was doing a fine job of that, but as I started to assume he was pretty much powerless against me, I became braver.

At this point, it's probably no great surprise to learn I would soon discover my error in such an assumption.

"Did you say something?" Raith asked as he came back above the water. Water that again swirled with warmth, only this time as a result of my plumbing and not theirs.

"Just talking to my evil friend. You know, the one behind this whole fiasco."

Raith gave his own little shiver. "I must confess, it's a touch bothersome when you casually talk about great powers."

I shrugged. "Familiarity breeds contempt."

"I'm done. Are you ready to get out?"

Chilling visions aside, I could have stayed in the water all night, but the bed was just as comfortable. I walked up the stairs that led out of the tub to towel off, and Raith followed.

"Briar, do you think I'll ever become a man?"

"What?" I asked, sounding as stupid as Lucifer. The sudden change in subject threw me.

"I wasn't off cleaning the horses. Well, I was, but I finished an hour ago. I don't like bathing with the others. They make fun of me."

"They're just jealous."

"Of what," Raith asked, pointing at his underdeveloped, hairless body. It was rather sad, and I'm sure it didn't help to see his younger brother two inches taller than him and more hirsute in all the hairy areas, not to mention larger in the naughty parts.

Such things are important to young men.

"You are squire to the greatest—if stupidest—Paladin known. That alone would turn most boys green. But you are also intelligent, caring, and generous. Why wouldn't they be jealous?"

"You sound like someone telling an uncomely lass how charming in personality she is," Raith said as he stared at the floor. "I'm seventeen and still look and sound like a pudgy twelve-year-old."

"Not so pudgy anymore," I offered. "The time on ship took care of that."

"So, I look like a thin twelve-year-old."

I sat on the bench and began dressing. "I wish I knew what to tell you, Raith, but consoling people isn't my strong suit. All I can say is that all boys become men. They have to, don't they?" He didn't respond. "Maybe you should talk to Elder."

He sat on the bench and looked thoughtful for several moments. "Maybe I will. Or maybe the Oracle will have magic that can help me."

"I don't know that Oracles do that sort of thing, but I suppose it can't hurt to ask."

I SPENT most of the next two days in the chapter library to avoid everyone else. The Paladins had befriended me, but the squires saw my lack of duties as a self-proclaimed affront to their efforts. Raith tried to explain that Lucifer wouldn't let me work, but they didn't accept it. After all, they reasoned, why wouldn't Raith cover for me? None of them seemed to notice Raith worked as hard as they did. Probably more, since Lucifer was the most demanding person in the chapterhouse. Not only that, but Raith had to take care of the animal that should have been my responsibility. The squires didn't do anything outright harmful to me, but, Holy Seer or not, they had little use for me. Even worse, they snubbed Raith. He took it in stride, as Raith did most things, but I knew it bothered him. Not because I could read his thoughts, but I had known him long enough to read *him*.

The library lacked anything near the realm of interesting. It had a little more than a hundred books: seventy dealt with some form of chivalry, twenty with the care of horses, armor, or armored horses, and ten concerned themselves with the teachings of Holy Ubel. There were single books on various subjects, all of them sleep-inducing. Why would anyone, let alone a paladin, want to read the history of hammers?

"Gift from a dwarf prince," the librarian answered in response to that question. He was almost as old as the chamberlain who greeted us our first night here. But this man was thin as a stalk of hay and bald as a field in winter. "Dreadful insult if we refused it, even worse if he came back and found it missing."

"Has he ever come back?"

"No, but no sense taking a chance. Besides, it doesn't hurt anything just sitting there."

I couldn't argue with that.

There was one interesting book among the rest. It was a history of the chapter, which had existed for a hundred years, nearly as old as the city. Lucifer became commander ten years ago, and there was nothing else written after that.

"Why does it end here?" I asked the librarian.

"Guess he grew too busy to write."

"Who?"

"Lucifer."

"Lucifer wrote this?" I hefted the not inconsiderable weight of the tome and stared at it as if it might eat my brain. "I didn't think he could read."

"He's changed a lot, our Lucifer." The librarian made a *tsk*—the sound of intrigue and secrets—with his thin lips.

"What do you mean?" I asked. Perhaps a bit too eagerly. The librarian backed away, a reed in motion, and stared at me like I had stared at the book.

"I've said too much."

"You haven't said anything. I'm getting ready to travel with Lucifer for who knows how long into dangerous territory, facing who knows what kind of peril to confront a witch woman and demand answers about an insane god. I think I deserve to know who I'm traveling with." So maybe I laid it on a little thick, but I was curious. And I knew Ubel wasn't insane, but I was pretty damn sure Pimple was.

The man studied me a moment longer, and I waited for him to refuse. But he settled his bony arms on his desk and stared at the ceiling as if he saw what he wanted to say written there. "It happened about seven years ago. He was walking down the second-story hall and hit a spot of grease. Must have spilled off a plate carried by a careless squire. Anyway, Lucifer slipped backward, stumbled over the railing, fell to the lower floor, and struck his head." The man's brown eyes turned wistful as if he were revealing the most divine secret known to mortal man. "Before the accident, he was ever singing, writing, drawing maps, and performing all manner of ambassadorship for the church. Ever since the accident, all that has changed."

I managed a full five seconds of silence before the indignation took over. "That's it? He fell?"

My ire had no noticeable effect on the man's contemplative gaze. "He died in that fall, but Ubel returned him to do unfinished business. He was truly touched by our Holy Father that day."

"The only thing he was touched by was a block of stone," I snapped and left the librarian and his eyes to their melancholy ways.

Had the people here been feeding Lucifer that hog swill, that his accident had been some sort of divine grace? That might explain his jealousy of me. After all, in his mind, he was Ubel's favorite before I came along. I had often wondered if Lucifer had been dropped on his head as a child. Not quite, but close.

It did explain why the leader of the most significant order of Paladins working for the largest church in the known world was wasting away in a crab hole like Frostishak. The church is a harsh mistress—some would say cold bitch—but she is loyal. When Lucifer fell on his head and lost much of his sense, the church elders had a dilemma. They wouldn't remove him from office. That would occur only if he did something insane, like hacking up the congregation. But they couldn't have him representing the church in important matters. He just didn't have the ability to be diplomatic anymore, if he ever had. So, they sent him to what amounted to exile. Probably told him with smiling faces that it was Ubel's will.

I seem to remember that it was my will, but I can't be sure anymore, Ubel thought

"Look, I really don't appreciate you reading my thoughts. I mean, thanks for creating me and everything, but anytime you show up to talk to me, Pimple isn't far behind, and I'm not in the mood to deal with him right now."

He's asleep.

"Gods sleep?"

Of course. And we eat and drink. We're not much different from you, only far more powerful and nigh unto immortal.

"Sure, not much different at all. We're practically brothers."

Interesting.

"What?"

Nothing. What were we talking about?

Great. Ubel was turning as brain-damaged as his most loyal follower. "You thought Lucifer's coming to Frostishak might have been your will."

Yes, I'm almost sure it was. And you might want to quit talking out loud. People are staring.

I looked around. Without realizing it, my walk down the hall had put me near the chapel, where a pair of priests placed candles, and three altar boys cleaned the floors. They had stopped to stare at me. I pointed to my skull. "Ubel's talking to me. Holy Seer and all."

Without a word, they returned to work, staring at anything but me. I continued walking, but I followed Ubel's advice. *Why would you send Lucifer to Frostishak?*

To watch over you, of course.

Why?

Because you're special.

You keep saying that, but what makes me so special?

I can't tell you that.

Why?

Cos-

Never mind, I thought with as much exasperation as one can manage silently. *This Cosmic Law thing is a great catch-all loophole, isn't it?*

It's very rude to interrupt.

I'm a very rude person. I figured you would have known that by now.

I did, but I thought maybe you should know.

A strange void in my brain told me Ubel had left. I didn't know if it was because Pimple had woken up or because Ubel was tired of talking to me. It seemed very rude to tell someone they're rude and then leave without giving them a chance to respond. But what could one expect of gods? Being all-powerful and immortal had to warp your worldview.

My wandering brought me to the dining hall, so with nothing better to do, I grabbed something to eat: a slab of beef, a chunk of cheese, and a scoop of chopped greens. The gods knew I could complain about almost anything, but the chapterhouse food wasn't one of them.

As I ate, I considered Ubel's words. Was I really that rude? I didn't think so, but then parents never think their offspring are ugly either. I knew I was cynical. Growing up with people talking about your parentage behind your back, but just loud enough so you can hear, makes you defensive. I never got along with any people my age and never really wanted to. They all seemed so, well, beneath me, if I'm honest. None of them were as clever or witty as me and certainly didn't have the learning I did. Where they had me was in bullying and gossip, since I was never big enough for the former nor interested in the latter. The only thing that kept me from being stomped regularly was Raith. Despite his small and harmless appearance, he was a wild tiger if anyone threatened me. He lost as many fights as he won, but the bullies eventually grew tired of dealing with him, so they moved on to less protected prey.

The people in Frostishak were provincial, dull, and useless. And as I sat there eating, I realized I missed them all so much that I would have given almost anything to be back in my fetid little swamp town. Even the prospect of seeing Crow didn't dull my desire to return.

I gave up thinking about it. If I was rude, so be it. If dragging me from home against my will and making me traipse across the world was Ubel's way of teaching me politeness, it was doomed to failure.

The following day, we set out for our month-long journey to reach the Oracle.

14

"Wake up, Briar."

"Go away," I muttered, my eyes still closed.

"If you don't get up," Raith said, "I'm going to yank the covers off, and I know how much you hate that."

"Which is exactly why you do it," I said, but I opened my eyes and looked up at him. He already wore his festive squire's uniform and looked ready to take on the day. "What time is it?"

"An hour before sunrise."

"Why in the name of Holy, but insane, Ubel, do you wake me up so early? I'm not a farmer."

"We're leaving," Raith said. "We're off the see the Oracle."

His excitement burned through the fuzz of sleep that surrounded me. I looked at him and found him almost hopping from foot to foot.

"Do you have to pee?"

He knelt down, a broad grin on his doughy face, and almost yelled into mine. "Lucifer has made me head squire."

That woke me up. "He what?"

"Made me head squire. They found Jim, Jack, and George drunk and banished them from the chapter."

"I thought heavy drinking was a pre-requisite."

Raith shrugged. "Maybe for the Paladins, but for the squires, it's forbidden. Glawen was fit to be tied because now he's short two paladins *and* three squires. It will take the church months to requisition replacements."

Our church is an unholy mass of paperwork, hence the need for scribes like me, and nothing can get done without the blessing of at least three priests and the signature of two bishops. That we somehow started on this venture without three copies of a canonical writ was the first clue things had gone horribly wrong.

"I should offer to be his squire," I said, a sure sign I wasn't totally awake yet.

"You can't; you don't have the proper training."

"It can't be that tough; you do it."

Raith's eyes narrowed as his grin dissolved. "That was mean, even for you."

"Sorry," I said and meant it. "I'm not responsible for anything I say before dawn."

"Besides, as head squire, I get to choose who has to fill in for the missing squire, which means someone will be doing duty for two."

Raith's face had taken on a grim look I hadn't seen on him in a long time. "You have someone in mind."

"Yes, and I think he's going to be sorry he upbraided me so much." His eyes caught the lamplight and cast back a wicked gleam. "Yes, he's going to be most sorry."

I smiled. My brother planned to use his position of power to take out petty revenge. It did my heart good to see Lucifer hadn't completely broken him.

We left two hours later, our departure quite different from when we left Frostishak. After a hearty breakfast, the head priest made a benediction, blessing our party with Ubel's good grace. Considering Ubel's current condition, I wasn't sure about the wisdom of such a prayer, but I managed to keep my mouth shut. We then drank a glass of consecrated wine. Again, not sure about the sagacity of such a maneuver, but I let it go. As we left the church, every member of the clergy and several early worshipers cheered us on, wishing us luck and good speed in recovering the item we sought. I got the impression Lucifer hadn't been entirely honest about our mission.

The sun crested the horizon and threw dull orange light over the squat city as we trekked through across town. Uniformed dwarves moved through the streets, heading toward their first break, which they got immediately upon arriving at work.

One advantage of our delay was that I got a new outfit of clothes to replace the horribly beaten one I had before. I had a blue tunic and riding cape, two pairs of gray pants, and a set of soft black leather riding boots and black riding gloves. I was so used to wearing nothing but brown when not scribing that I almost burst into tears the first time I tried the clothes. At least I matched everyone else instead of looking like something they had dragged on the road for miles.

"I feel like I've joined a circus," I told no one in particular. Elder rode to my left and Raith to my right. Captain Timbers sat on my shoulder. I once again rode on the trusty back of Two. Lucifer sat astride Justice, a few feet ahead of us, his back straight and plate armor gleaming in the early sun. Heathensmasher rested across his back, and I have to admit he made a truly imposing figure as he led our caravan through the city.

For caravan it was. In addition to the eighteen Paladins and seventeen squires, we now had five wagons, each pulled by two horses and sporting a driver, and six hay carts pulled by mules. A minstrel, a blacksmith, a cook, and a friar, each riding their own horse, tagged along. I didn't know if we were going to visit the Oracle or build a town around her. We kicked up enough dust to choke a dragon, which was good because we would never hear one coming over the clanking of armor, creaking of wagon wheels, and clop of hooves.

"You have," Brother Elder offered to my comment. "The circus of the church of Ubel."

Lucifer glanced at Elder. "The church is not a circus, Brother Elder. I suggest you refrain from such blasphemy, or there will be punishment."

"What, something worse than this?"

"Much."

Elder went quiet. His dark mood surprised me almost as much as my light-hearted one. Somewhere between waking up and now, I had decided to embrace this adventure and accept it for the once-in-a-lifetime opportunity it was. Some people went from birth to death without leaving their home village. Here I was, at fifteen, traveling across the world. Sure, I had an addled god intruding on my thoughts and a malevolent one trying to kill me, but what fun was life without a little challenge? "What exactly was in that blessed wine?"

"Feeling ready to take on the world, are you?" Elder asked with a smirk. He had shaved the scraggles he tried to pass off as a beard. His lack of facial hair made him look more than ever like a petulant child. He favored Raith more than I did.

"Actually, yes, I am," I said, smiling with giddy delight. Although everyone else looked normal, I could feel the same eagerness radiating from them. Maybe not quite as eager as me, but certainly ready.

Everyone, that is, except for Elder and Lucifer. Elder seemed his usual benign presence, and Lucifer his normal stoic self.

Elder looked at me. "In addition to being blessed, the wine is dosed."

"With what?"

"A secret," Lucifer said, giving Elder a glare that should have melted him on the spot. "Known only to the highest church officials."

"I guess I should be flattered then," Elder said, "because I know, and I never considered myself that high up."

Already elated, I didn't need an argument between Lucifer and Elder to make me happy. I waved a hand toward our entourage. "Truthfully, what is all this?"

"This is a typical church pilgrimage," Elder said. "It's like a picnic, but with fighting and conversions."

I shook my head, making Timbers ruffle his feathers and shuffle to a better position. "Sorry," I told him. I turned my head back to Elder. "I thought it was bad enough with forty people when we left Frostishak. This is just insane."

The boyish priest dropped his voice. "Considering the quest and its leader, that's rather appropriate."

I couldn't argue with that. "What's in all the wagons?"

"One of them has camping gear, tents, pavilions, and such. No sleeping out of doors for this journey. Another has supplies. Food and that sort of thing. The third most likely has armor, weapons, and whatever the blacksmith needs to do his work."

"Is the Oracle likely to go to war with us?"

"I don't think so, but now that Lucifer can have his full retinue back, he isn't going to miss the chance to take it. And just because there's no war doesn't mean there won't be trouble. I seem to recall an incident aboard ship."

"What about the other two wagons?" I asked quickly, abashed.

"One of them probably contains medical supplies. But I confess I have no idea what's in the last wagon.

"Brawk. Tribute."

I hurt my neck trying to look at the captain on my shoulder, so I turned forward and said, "Tribute? For who? We're not passing through any sovereign lands, at least not according to the last map I looked at."

"It's for the Oracle."

"A wagon full of treasure just to answer a couple of questions? Greedy little witch, isn't she?"

"Brawk. Say that when she can hear you; then I'll have someone I can talk with eye-to-eye."

Well, now I knew what the captain had done to warrant his current avian state and shuddered at the implication. How touchy did someone have to be to make you a bird just because you insulted her?

"She's very sensitive," Timbers said as if he'd read my mind.

"Do you think there's any chance in the three hells she'll change you back?"

Timbers shifted on my shoulder. "I can only hope."

Something occurred to me as I looked at the laden carts trundling before us. "Are all these going to be able to make it over the mountains and through the craters?"

"Brawk! Cartographers tend to get carried away. The craters aren't quite as numerous as they appear on our map. And the trolls and dragons on the margins aren't representative of what actually lives there."

"I didn't expect there to be trolls," I said. I was glad about the craters though. On the map, the Craterlands resembled the face of a teenager with a terminal skin condition. They made me think of Pimple, and I shivered despite the good feelings of the wine.

"As for the mountains," Timbers continued, "I don't know. The passes are pretty narrow."

"I doubt they'll make it," Elder said. "Lucifer doesn't think that far ahead."

"What is the matter with you?" I asked, suddenly tired of his doom and gloom and alarmed at how much the wine had changed me. For some reason, I wanted Elder to not be miserable, even though I shouldn't care. I knew it was wrong, but part of me wanted to thank him for bringing me on this fabulous expedition. I wondered how long this false euphoria would last.

"Remember that letter you gave me from the Archbishop?"

I took a wild guess. "Bad news."

"The worst."

"I thought it just told the Holy Unseen what we had decided and gave the Archbishop's reasoning."

"Oh, it had all that," Elder said as he navigated his horse around one pile of manure, only to have the poor thing walk through another. "But it had a little extra the Archbishop threw in."

"Like what?"

"That no matter how much I begged, pleaded, or cajoled, I was not to be released from this journey. The letter said, and I quote, 'Brother Elder has much growing up to do, and this will help him learn his proper place in the church. Either that or it will kill him. In any case, problem solved.'"

My jaw went slack with shock. "The Archbishop said that?"

"I may have added the bit about it killing me, but he might as well have said that. That's probably what he's hoping, cantankerous old bastard."

"How did you find out about it?"

"How do you think I found out about it. While I was in front of the Holy Unseen, I did all three."

"All three what?"

"Begging, pleading, and cajoling. The sot made me do all three before he showed me the letter. I think he enjoyed it."

"What does the Holy Unseen look like?"

"I don't know; I didn't see him."

"But you just said—"

"He sits behind a dark curtain. No one sees him, not even his high attendants."

"Why not?"

"Because they're all blind."

The wine not only made me enthusiastically happy, but it also slowed down my thinking because I only then realized something I should have caught sooner. "Wait a minute, what about all that crap you handed me on the ship about accepting my fate and acting like a man?"

"That was all well and good when I thought I would get to stay behind."

"Does the word hypocrite mean anything to you?"

"I don't know. Does the word annoyingly sarcastic smart-assed twit mean anything to you?"

"That's more than one—" I stopped, realizing what Elder had done. "You really should have had some of the wine."

15

We traveled for several hours. Turning off the main road, we trekked across trackless plains covered in stalks of deep green grass that came up to the horse's knees and gave off a scent of overripe lemons.

The wine's effects wore off after an hour or so. I noticed because the minstrel's singing, which had sounded strong, on-key, and tuneful, suddenly transformed into none of the three. Cries from the swamp creatures around Frostishak had more melody. No one else seemed to notice, so they were either still drugged or tone-deaf. His lute playing was scarcely better, his discordant picking the sound of a chicken being plucked.

To this day, I feel bad that I almost cheered when a rock slammed into his jaw and silenced him.

"We're under attack," one of the knights shouted, unnecessarily, as arrows and stones flew through the air, followed by screams, whinnies, and curses.

"Paladins to the fore," Lucifer roared. Horses began shuffling as the soldiers moved to obey their commanders. The squires, most looking as terrified as I felt, followed their knights. Raith had a grim smile that made me question his sanity.

"Scions of Ublek," a voice yelled from somewhere, "capture the usurper." This was followed by a chorus of voices shouting something nonsensical like "uhuhuhuhuhuhuh."

Men on horses sprouted up from the grass a hundred feet away. I had no idea how they had hidden there, but they continued to appear as if growing from the earth like some demented equine crop. By the time they were done, the riders outnumbered us at least twice. They all wore lacquered black chain mail. Their curved swords gleamed a shade of wicked that made me shiver. Large ebony helms in the shape of a three-eyed jackal covered their heads. They looked ridiculous, which strangely made them even more frightening.

Uncertain of my options and what to do, I chose to panic.

Before I could work myself up to screaming and fleeing, my vision blurred, and everything not in my immediate area went out of focus. Time slowed, noise disappeared. I wondered if this was some after-effect of the wine, much like the pain you feel a day after eating hot peppers that no one ever warns you about. I felt a presence I knew all too well and gritted my teeth.

Pimple appeared before me, still translucent but more solid than ever before. He wore a black tunic and pants, of course. Strange symbols embroidered in red thread covered his pants, and a representation of the three-eyed jackal blazed in red from the tunic. So, these men were his. My ill-considered assumption that he couldn't physically hurt me flashed through my mind. Perhaps *he* couldn't kill me, but the six score of men about to charge us, swords raised, looked more than capable.

Pimple's eyes glittered as he stared at me. "Hope you like my welcoming party." He stomped his foot like a six-year-old throwing a fit. "It's all mine; you get none of it," he screamed. I didn't know what it was, and chances were if it involved Pimple, I didn't want it. But staring at him as he pouted at me, trying to look malevolent but only pulling off an attitude of a spoiled brat, my good sense snapped like a rotten plank. I glared at him, all my anger, fear, and untempered sarcasm boiling out of me.

"Too bad," I snarled in a voice I barely recognized as mine. "Do your worst, you psychotic twerp."

For a moment that might have been an illusion, Pimple appeared uncertain, disbelieving I had grown a pair of stones. Considering our past, I didn't blame him. I couldn't quite believe it either.

But the reservations disappeared, and he gave me a smile to inspire night terrors.

"Nice knowing you," he said, clapped his hands, and disappeared in a burst of thunder.

"Can't return the sentiment," I shouted at the empty air.

Shouts roiled around us, and the mounted riders charged, their horses kicking up enough dust and grass to trigger a thousand allergic reactions.

"Paladins," Lucifer shouted. "Engage." He drew Heathensmasher from his back and held it aloft in both hands. With a whinny that shrilled through the cacophony, Justice launched forward. The sun struck Lucifer, setting his armor aglow, and for the first time, I could see why his men followed him and would die for him.

However, that didn't mean he inspired me. I had no desire to die for him or anyone else. Pimple's disappearance had restored my self-preservation instincts. Amid the clash of swords against armor, thundering hooves, and screaming men, I tried to figure out where I could hide. I saw the blacksmith holding a small hammer and a pair of tongs in one hand. I had no idea what he planned to do with tongs, but I soon found out. As a rider charged him, the horse's head thrust forward, the blacksmith stood his ground. At the last possible moment, before the animal passed him to allow its rider to skewer him, the muscular man shoved the tongs forward, the pincers spread just far enough apart to lodge themselves in the animal's nostrils, which is exactly what they did. The collision jarred the tool from the armorer's grasp. The horse, squealing in surprise, reared up and took the impromptu nose cleaners with him. The shocked rider fell from the horse and slammed onto his back. Before he could recover, the blacksmith ran up on him, and side-swung the hammer at the snout of the jackal helmet. The blow's force tore the helmet from its owner's head and skittered it across the ground. Following through, the hammer arced up in a circle and back down, smashing into the man's face. I had a flashback to the watermelons in Frostishak, and nausea almost brought me to my knees.

That was all I saw clearly before the unwanted emotions of others overwhelmed me. Fear, anger, pain, and confusion. They all slammed into my far too-open mind, paralyzing me. I caught glimpses, a sword thrust here, a burning wagon there, and all overlaid with screams and shouts and dying. Tears ran down my face as I stood amid the chaos.

A hand grabbed my arm and broke through the emotional storm. A three-eyed jackal, still ridiculous and terrifying, glared down at me. The man had his sword aloft, coated with blood and other matter. A growling voice, muffled by the helmet but clear enough, spoke. "Come on, boy. Don't make me hurt you. You're my capture. The master will—"

The man suddenly grew an extra sword-shaped appendage from his chest. It cut his gloating short in a geyser of blood that sailed past me and splattered the grass. The man collapsed, revealing Glawen standing behind him, his armor not gleaming quite so much, dented and gore splattered. He looked at me. "Run, boy. We'll hold as long as we can. Flee!"

I recalled my idea had been similar, if not quite so proactive. Running seemed a much better option than hiding. I picked a direction based on nothing tactical or discernable, heeded Glawen's advice, and ran.

I hadn't gone ten feet when Raith's voice cut through the torrent of battle and froze me.

"Help!"

16

I turned and saw my brother on the ground thirty feet away, a sword in his hand, Lucifer's banner lying on the trampled grass. A blood-stained rip marred the left side of his tunic, and tears streaked trails down his dust-coated face. A soldier menaced him, a smile on his scarred face. I thought about all the times Raith had protected me.

Let me help you, Ubel said, his warmth overflowing me.

That didn't go so well last time, I thought, remembering what had happened on the ship.

The soldier raised his curved sword. Raith brought his weapon up, but the soldier's sword would easily crush my brother's block, and he would die.

"Stop," I screamed as I ran toward the soldier.

The soldier swung his blade.

"No," I shouted. Warmth pulsed through me, and something chased my shout, gushing from my head like an invisible fountain of water. It left me dizzy.

But it didn't affect me nearly as much as it did my brother's would-be killer. The blast struck the man, and he flipped through the air, an unwilling acrobat. And not a graceful one. He landed fifty feet away. On his head. I winced as the resulting crunch reached me across the battlefield.

Raith looked at me, fear in his watery eyes, but he nodded to me in gratitude.

It's your power now, Ubel said, as warmth engulfed me. *Use it.*

What are you doing? Pimple's voice cut the warmth like an icicle, and Ubel disappeared.

But the power remained. I didn't know what it was or how I came to possess it, and I wasn't entirely sure I wanted it. But I looked around at the desperate fight, Lucifer's Paladins besieged, some of the wagons on fire, and Raith standing and heading to protect his master, a man who could end up getting him killed.

Use it, Ubel had said.

"Don't mind if I do," I growled.

I walked toward the fight. One part of my brain screamed at me that I was an idiot. But the part filled with this swirling energy silenced the whiny, bratty part.

Three men surrounded Chafin, the other Paladin who had been kind to me. His armor, like Glawen's, was dented and bloody. He held his own but looked exhausted, his defense crumbling like day-old toasted bread.

"Leave him alone," I said, throwing out my hand at the men. I didn't know if that was necessary, but it seemed more dramatic. I figured if anyone was watching, it might terrify or inspire them, depending on their side in the fight.

The trio sailed through the air, much like their comrade had, in separate directions. One crashed into a burning wagon, which promptly collapsed and buried him in flaming wood and cloth. Another came down, threaded himself onto a companion's raised saber, pinned himself through the abdomen, landed on the soldier holding the weapon, and crashed both of them to the ground. The third fell on top of another wagon. This one wasn't on fire, but it carried the blacksmith's anvil, a fact revealed by the loud clang as the man slammed onto it, wrapped around it, bounced off, and fell to the ground. His breastplate occupied the space that used to be his breast.

I cringed. I hadn't wanted to kill anyone, only to get the men away from Chafin, hopefully scare the rest, and get them fleeing like whipped dogs.

But the fighting continued. The Paladins had made a good show, working toward evening the odds, but I saw several down and many squires too.

I spotted another attacker, advancing on the blacksmith, who defended with his hammer and tongs, recovered from the horse. Just as I saw them, the attacker swung. The blacksmith blocked with the tongs, but the saber swing knocked them out of the way. The blacksmith dodged back, barely missing decapitation. The sword drew a thin line across his neck but not deep enough to do serious injury.

"Go away," I said. I didn't bother with the hand since no one had paid attention the first time. I simply thought the man away, and he sailed through the air.

And went through a horse. He severed the poor creature in half and emerged out the other side, impaled on the animal's ribcage while the beast fell to the ground in two parts.

"Oh, come on," I screamed. "Really?"

That performance got some attention. Several of the attackers stopped and looked at me, which was exactly opposite to the reaction I wanted. An exceptionally tall and fierce-looking man pointed at me. "Seize him."

From there, things got ugly, if you can imagine something uglier than a bifurcated stallion. Men charged me, and I repelled them. And each died in some painful, odd, or humiliating way. Even if I tried, I couldn't have deliberately pushed someone through a wagon wheel and collapsed the wagon on them. But that happened to one of my would-be kidnappers. The power came to me as easily as wetting the bed when I was two. I only had to wish for the person flying, and they did. No muttering incantations, no sacrificing virgins. The power was simply mine, with no effort.

The attackers soon realized things had changed. Pimple had no doubt told them I would be a pushover. He would have usually been right, but not today. Today I was invincible.

Right up to the point when the survivors fled. Raith ran over to me, his face a map of the Kingdom of Astonish. "What did you do?"

"I—" was all I said before the ground smacked me in the face.

I woke up once again with familiar faces surrounding me. This time, instead of dripping with water, most of them had blood, grime, and sweat covering them. Only Elder looked well-off, his garments mussed but bloodless.

You know, I thought to Ubel, even though I had no idea if he could hear me, *giving me power isn't going to help much if I faint every time I use it.*

As I looked at the faces, I noticed they didn't seem quite as concerned as last time. In fact, they mostly looked disturbed and uneasy. Except for Timbers, who, as always, looked like an emotionless bird.

"What's wrong?" I asked as my heart tried to sink through my back and into the ground. "Did I accidentally try to kill all the paladins again?" Unlike when Ubel took me over, I remembered everything that happened this time. At least, I thought I did, but I couldn't be sure.

"No, not the Paladins," Elder said as he licked his quivering lips. He looked pale as if he had eaten rotten apples.

"I have no problem with you killing them," Lucifer said, "for they were surely doing the same to us. But I am disturbed by the viciousness of your attacks."

It hit me like a cold fish in the face. "I didn't mean to do that," I said. "I only wanted them gone."

"You accomplished that," Raith said, his voice barely a whisper.

I sat up, and they all flinched away, taking at least two steps back. "I'm not dangerous," I said, which I guess wasn't wholly accurate. "I'm not *intentionally* dangerous," I amended. "I just pushed the men away. It wasn't my fault they had bad luck."

"How did you do it?" Brother Elder asked.

I looked at Lucifer and didn't want to answer, but I had no choice. I turned to Elder. "Ubel gave me the power."

Predictable as a rooster crow, Lucifer's face went flat, and he stood up. "I shall prepare us to leave. Squire, attend me." He didn't stay to see if my brother followed his order.

"I better go," Raith said.

"Are you okay?" I looked at his bloodied tunic and caught a glimpse of bandaging underneath.

"It was a small slash," Raith said. "The healer took care of it for me." He stared at the ground, and a flush came to his round cheeks. "Thank you for saving me."

"Happy to do it. You're the only brother I have."

He nodded, looked at me, and then stood. I think he had tears again, but as always it was hard to tell.

"Hey," I said. "Tell Lucifer if I could let him have the power, I'd gladly do it. I don't want it."

He smiled. "I'll let you tell him. But I suggest you do it from long range." He turned and walked away.

That left Elder, with Timbers sitting on his shoulder, beside me. The aftermath of the attack was in evidence everywhere. Most of the wagons were destroyed, some by fire, others by my casual flinging of men like toys. I heard moans and smelled the tangy copper scent of blood mixed with charred wood. Here and there, Paladins stood with their squires, but there seemed to be several missing. "How bad is it?"

"Bad," Elder said. "We lost twelve Paladins, eight squires, all but four carts, many of the animals, and the cook."

"Glawen?" I wanted to thank the commander for keeping me alive.

Elder shook his head.

Now tears filled *my* eyes. Glawen had saved my life, and I could not return the favor. Despite the awesome but uncontrollable power at my disposal, I couldn't keep alive the one person who had helped me. Couldn't save the upstanding Paladin who hadn't beaten me to a pulp when I got everyone in trouble. Glawen had been proud of me, unlike his commander.

My sadness changed, the worm of dismay transforming into a butterfly. A dark, vicious butterfly of anger. Fear still dominated my thoughts, and had Pimple kept his attacks confined to me, he would have succeeded in scaring me off. The thwarting of my every attempt to flee this nightmare hadn't made me any less prone to trying. Fate be damned, I would have found a way to ditch this ridiculous "adventure."

But the evil little twit had taken it a step too far. His minions had almost killed my brother. And they *had* killed someone I dared to consider a friend. Even worse, he had made me kill people.

That realization caught me off guard and slammed me with the weight of a war mattock, ready to crush me like I had crushed the soldier under the wagon.

In my anger, I had stood up without realizing it. It only came to my attention as I landed back on my butt under a tide of dizziness.

"Are you okay?" Elder asked.

"Not in the least," I answered. I stood back up, wincing at my sore tailbone, and looked at the sky. "Okay, Pimple, or whatever your name is. I don't know what I've done to piss you off, but if you want a fight, you've got it. You couldn't stop at ominous omens or freakish animals; you had to be a serious prick. Well, you don't scare me. I've got my own power now, and I'm ready for whatever you want to throw at me. You and me, anytime, anywhere. Let's duel, you psychopath."

The words pouring out of my mouth terrified me, but I couldn't stop them. I had power, sure, but no idea how to control it or bring it to bear.

Both times, Ubel had been there to give it to me. What if he didn't show up next time? What if Pimple took up my boast and appeared right now, ready to row? I would die, and that was something I still found highly disagreeable. I needed to stop talking, but the anger boiled through me. I raised my hands and pointed them, shaking, toward the sky. "Come on, you wimp." I tried to think hot thoughts full of fire, ready to blast Pimple if he appeared.

"Are you sure that's wise?" Elder asked, his pale face looking at the sky.

"Absolutely not," I said. His question broke through my trance of angered stupidity. The rage still lingered, but caution intruded back in. I dropped my hands and stared at Elder.

"Maybe," the priest said, "we need to gather everyone up and leave before the insane being with magic powers and an army decides to take you up on your challenge."

"Probably a good idea." I didn't tell him that if Pimple wanted to find us, he could. No sense in anyone else being frightened witless at my rash declarations.

It took several hours, since Lucifer insisted on burying all the dead with full honors and prayers. For once, I couldn't fault his piety. However, he, like everyone else but Raith, Elder, and Timbers, avoided direct eye contact with me. I could still sense fear from the survivors, and I couldn't blame them.

I said my goodbyes to Glawen and stood solemnly as Elder recited over the graves. I wondered if Ubel could actually hear the prayers or if Pimple somehow kept him unaware.

Eventually, our much-reduced company mounted up and left, but we only traveled two miles before it grew too dark to ride, and we had to settle for the night. I think Lucifer just wanted to get everyone away from the scene of the slaughter. Once more, I agreed with him.

The only good thing to come out of the debacle was the minstrel's broken jaw, which kept him from being able to sing.

17

For the next two weeks, we traveled toward the Hiephi Mountains to find the Oracle. The only thing that kept me from dying of boredom was the ever-present tension and fear of another attack from Pimple. It plagued me like a low-grade fever, never debilitating but always there. I had plenty of time to consider my rash challenge, and I pictured him stewing over my insults while he planned his response. It seemed my assumption that he couldn't attack me directly had proved true, but that didn't preclude him digging up another band of mercenaries, or zealots, or whatever he had sent the first time. To my increasingly paranoid mind, every copse of trees became filled with hordes of hired barbarians ready to leap upon us; every hillock hid a hundred mounted riders prepared to die for Pimple.

Except I now knew Pimple's real name, or at least I thought I did. The men who attacked called themselves Scions of Ublek. Pimple didn't look old or virile enough to have fathered a hundred grown men, so I assumed the name was symbolic. But my astounding deductive reasoning led me to believe Pimple was actually Ublek, although Pimple fit him much better.

They had named me usurper. The only thing I had ever usurped was my father's seat at the dinner table, which had the biggest portion of food. My mother was an awful cook, but hunger overrides your common sense when you're a teenager. So, I found Pimple's dislike of me as puzzling as his awareness of me disquieting.

I had other concerns that kept my mind stirring during the butt-numbing hours I spent on Two, who had survived the massacre and still followed Pony around at an apathetic pace. For one thing, I felt abandoned. Raith, Elder, and Timbers spoke to me, but everyone else avoided me like they might spontaneously burst into flames if they came too close. The squires didn't concern me. They hadn't liked me from the beginning and barely tolerated me as the Holy Seer. I returned the animosity, so no significant change there. I hadn't known the surviving civilians before this trek, and we hadn't had time to get to know one another, so nothing different there.

But the rebuff from the Paladins hurt. It seemed to me we had started bonding. Sure, it was a bond of shared misery brought on by a drunken stupor, but I took what I could get. The death of their commander had subdued them to the point that they only got drunk every other night, and even when Lucifer berated them, his heart didn't seem in it.

It wasn't that they hated me, and I sensed they were actually grateful I had saved them. Without me, the fight would have gone to Ublek's forces, with no survivors on our side.

So, they appreciated me, but I had become a dog that might turn on them if they came too close. They had seen me bite their enemies and get a taste of blood. Now they feared I might bite *them*. If I spoke to them, they replied and then slipped away as quickly as they could. I didn't have to be empathic to sense their unease.

I tried to explain to Elder what happened, that I really hadn't wanted things to be so destructive. "I believe you," he said. "I know your temperament wouldn't allow such wanton butchery. If anything, you would tend toward too much leniency."

I suspected he was calling me a wimp, but I didn't care. "Do you think you can convince the others?"

"I can try."

It was the best I could ask.

LUCIFER BECAME MY BIGGEST CONCERN. He not only avoided me but had taken to actively disliking me. Not that he said anything outright, but I saw it in his dark looks and, worse, sensed it roiling off him whenever he chanced near me. Our group was small enough that this happened with more regularity than I liked.

Finally, eight days into our journey, as we moved through rolling foothills, the plains behind us, and the Hiephi Mountains looming ahead of us like the black, jagged teeth of a lamprey luring us in with the light of the Oracle, I decided to confront Lucifer. I wanted to do it sooner, but he still wore Heathensmasher on his back. To his mind, I skirted the fine line between divinity and blasphemy. This discussion would put me on one side or the other. I feared what would happen if I ended up on the wrong part of the divide.

So, we settled for the night, and Lucifer sat in his tent, which rested several yards from the main camp. My tent also did, but only because the squires set it up for me and wouldn't put it any closer. A tent to myself was the only benefit of being a pariah.

Raith stood at the entrance to Lucifer's tent, a large, masculine affair colored in gold and white stripes. It had started out spotless, but travel had soiled the bottom so it looked like a tabard dragged through a mud puddle. A flag with Ubel's symbol, two upturned palms underneath a yellow sun, hung three feet above the tent's peak, strapped on the center pole. Somehow the flag had gotten twisted and wrapped around itself.

I shivered. "Attacking us isn't enough?" I said to Pimple. "You have to offer cheap symbolism too?"

"What?" Raith asked. Like the tent, his clothing had seen better times, but I suspected I didn't resemble a freshwater lily either.

"The flag," I said, pointing at the knotted cloth.

"Oh," Raith said and flushed. "Yeah, I jammed it into the box wet after that rain yesterday and didn't feel like fixing it. Lucifer doesn't seem to care anymore."

That was the most disconcerting statement I had heard Raith make in a while. I could tell from the look in his owly eyes that his master's behavior concerned him too.

"May I see him?" I asked.

"I doubt it, but let me check." Raith pushed the flap aside and stepped in. I caught the smell of goldenrod incense, a scent I had grown to detest working in the church. It was the ordained scent of Ubel, and his priests burned it in forest fire quantities. I sometimes left my work wondering why I didn't blow out pollen when I sneezed.

The flap closed, and I heard a brief exchange of words, although the thick tent fabric didn't allow me to understand them. Raith came back out. "He says he doesn't want to see you right now." Raith pursed his mouth and bit the inside of his cheek. "Or ever, really."

"Great Ubel, what's that?" I said, looking to my left and pointing.

"What?" Raith said, taking a wide-eyed step in the direction I pointed, clearing the tent's entrance.

I stepped passed him and into the tent.

Ideally, I would have had a door to slam and lock. But since I didn't, Raith, cursing, followed me so fast he stepped on my heel and pushed me further into the tent. "Why do I always fall for that?" he muttered. "Come on, Briar."

"No," I said, staring at Lucifer, who had glanced up from his evening meal when I burst into the tent. Three lanterns lit the space, giving it a warm, cheery atmosphere far opposite the gloomy feelings I gathered from its occupant. "We need to talk."

"You forget your place," Lucifer said. "You come into my tent only when invited. Now leave."

"Nice to see you can still talk *at* me, but I'm not leaving. You're going to talk *to* me, and we'll get this straightened out once and for all."

Lucifer stood up. He wasn't wearing his armor or shirt, only a pair of breeches. His armor always made him look big, but I'd forgotten how muscular he was, the kind of muscles that could crush things. Like impertinent scribes. He walked toward me and refreshed my memory on how tall he was too.

"I tried to stop him," Raith said to Lucifer. Then, in my ear, he added, "You're on your own." I felt the wind on my back as he ran from the tent.

Lucifer stood over me, his hands flexing, the sinews in his forearms large as my head. I wanted to gulp, but I didn't. I also wanted to pee my breeches but suspected that would be a dead giveaway to how terrified I was. Instead, I stared back at Lucifer's emerald eyes, which looked at this moment like they could cut me into shark chum. I had faced down Pimple. I had lived with a god in my head. I had powers. I could stand up to a simple Paladin.

What I couldn't stand up to was the slap Lucifer delivered to the side of my face. *That* sent me five feet across the tent, tripping over his cot and landing on my stomach.

"Why did you do that?" I said, rubbing my face. It vied with my hip for most painful.

"I have put up with your rudeness because you are beloved of Ubel for some reason that is lost to me. But I will not be disrespected in front of my squire. It may put ideas in his head."

"He's my brother," I reminded Lucifer.

"And yet he is so much more respectful than you are."

Lucifer had me there. Raith was always the kind one, the one who got along and tried to see the good in people. He obviously saw something to like about Lucifer long before I did. I respected the Paladin, despite his assumption to the contrary. But I wasn't going to let him off easy. I sat up, ensured the exit was where I could reach it quickly, and said, "What exactly have you done to earn my respect?"

His eyes looked even sharper than before. "I am the Grand Commander of the Frostishak Chapter of the Paladins of Ubel," he said with the same pride as he might say he was Ubel himself.

Your mother must be so happy, I thought.

But knowing the circumstances of his ascension to such non-lofty heights, I said, "I respect that position, but what have you done to make me respect *you*? All you've done is force me to come along on a quest I didn't want to follow in the first place, and since then, you've pouted because Ubel likes me better than you. Raith and I never cared which one of us our parents liked better." Although I knew my father cared for Raith more than me.

Lucifer frowned. "And all you have done is whine about how miserable you have been and how much you wish you hadn't been blessed by Ubel's graces."

"That's because I have been miserable. And I do wish I wasn't blessed. And that's nothing I haven't said to Ubel. You're the Paladin; you should be the one with all the powers and Ubel talking to you. I know that and you know that."

"But that is not what great Ubel has chosen," Lucifer said, his voice so sad it almost broke my heart. "Things are totally wrong, and I don't understand it."

And there, I saw the problem clear as spring water. I considered things from Lucifer's point of view, something I had shuddered to do before. But I saw that, hard as it was for me, it had to be even more difficult for him. He had dedicated his life to a god he now thought insane. Ubel wasn't insane, only held captive and made powerless by a psychotic adolescent, but that somehow seemed worse. The events had ripped me from my home, but they had torn out Lucifer's faith, stomped on it, and chopped it into kibble. And being shunned by the god he served probably hadn't done his self-esteem any favors.

I stood and walked toward him, still ready to run in case things went sour. "Look, I'll make you a deal. Pimple messed up when he attacked us. He made me mad, and I *will* make him regret it." I had no idea how, but I decided to retain that privileged information. "I don't know why Ubel chose me. I don't know why any of this is happening. But I do remember Ubel said you were my protector. You've done an…adequate job of that so far." I rubbed my cheek. "Hopefully, the Oracle can sort all this out for us and make us both happy, or at least less miserable."

"What is your deal?"

"What? Oh, deal. Right. I'll do my best not to complain, and you stop treating me like I'm anathema."

The blank stare on Lucifer's face told me I had overreached his intelligence.

"Stop treating me like I'm the enemy. Like I made Ubel choose me to spite you. Trust me, I'm not, and I didn't. But since Ubel has chosen me, I'll do whatever I can to help find him and save him." Plus, I really wanted to give Pimple some payback. Somehow.

Lucifer considered my proposal. He considered it so long that I feared I had somehow damaged him. Finally, he held out the hand that had slapped me. I took it and winced at the bone-crushing force as we shook.

"I have been remiss," Lucifer said. "I see that now. My duty is to serve Ubel, no matter what trials he puts before me. I let pride get the better of me, and I must atone." He knelt before me. "I pledge from here on that I will defend you with my life. My strength is your strength. I will do whatever you command me in Ubel's name, and I will treat you like the Messiah Ubel obviously intends you to be."

Lucifer didn't do anything halfway, and his views flopped more than a beached salmon. In his eyes, I couldn't just be Briar, the unwilling vessel of superhuman powers. I had to be Ubel's Messiah. Never mind that the Tome of Ubel never spoke of any such being.

"That sounds…well…great?" I said. I hesitated, then put my hand on his large head. "Rise, protector. Go forth in peace and know you have my gratitude and my blessing." I had to force myself to keep from giggling at the pretension. Still, it seemed to be precisely what Lucifer needed. He stood, his green eyes misty, and bowed. Zealots require a cause.

"Thank you, Great One." He strolled out of the tent, chin high, chest bare.

Only then did I realize I had sent the Paladin from his own tent. "Lucifer, wait, come back."

IF I THOUGHT HAVING Lucifer ignore and dislike me was terrible, having him on my side was even worse. The rest of the journey, except when I was sleeping or occupied with a call of nature, the Paladin never strayed more than five feet away from me, astride Justice, ensuring I was protected, fed, and generally pampered. No longer was I just the Holy Seer. I earned a promotion to the Great Messiah. The four squires who no longer had knights were made my personal retinue, required to do anything I needed. A nice gesture, but one look at their hatred-filled faces kept me from demanding much of anything. However, Lucifer took up my slack, insisting the squires care for Two, set up my tent next to his, and fetch my meals. I hesitate to this day to think of how much spit I ate with my stew.

So, the days passed, the squires hating me, the Paladins begrudgingly beginning to accept me again, and my three compatriots doing their best to stick by me while avoiding Lucifer as much as possible since he would proselytize about my greatness to any who came near. It got to the point that I got sick of hearing about myself and worried I would never be able to live up to all the great things Lucifer expected me to accomplish.

As we drew closer to the mountains, my fear of reprisals from Pimple increased. The Hiephi Mountains were tall, jagged, black, and full of crevasses, chasms, and other areas suitable for plunging to a hideous death. They might as well have been named the Ambush Cliffs. The first day in, we had to abandon the wagons, and the second day we almost lost a horse and Paladin as the creature made a misstep and nearly plunged into a gaping fissure. I watched a dislodged rock fall until it disappeared into the darkness with no sign of reaching the bottom. I pressed myself against the cliff wall.

"Told you the horses would never make it," Elder said, pressed beside me, face pale.

"Perhaps you should have mentioned it to Lucifer before we got this far."

Like it would have mattered, he thought, his boyish face conveying those exact words as he stared at me.

"The horses will never make it," Lucifer said. "Someone must take them back and wait at the foothills."

"I will," I said, momentarily forgetting my resolve to carry on. At the same time, the hands of my four squires went up so fast I wondered that the motion didn't carry them into the pit.

"No, squires, you must attend the Messiah." They glared at me. I gave a shrug that I hoped conveyed "not my idea" but which they probably saw as, "kneel before me, fools."

In the end, Lucifer sent the friar, who was so rotund he probably would have eventually bounced off the wall and tumbled away, and the minstrel. Despite his broken jaw, he had tried, after a three-day reprieve, to entertain us in the evenings with his singing. He sounded better than he had previously, but the coyotes howling each night spooked the horses.

We continued on foot for another five days. We saw animals, goats and bobcats mainly, thankfully none with more than the requisite number of heads or appendages. It rained and grew cold, but the weather seemed more or less back to normal. Unfortunately, this only made me more paranoid, a state of mind not helped when I saw my squires giggling every time I ate. Lucifer stuck close to me, no doubt waiting for me to make some messianic pronouncements, but the best I could offer was, "looks like it's going to rain today."

Despite my concerns, we proceeded unmolested. Near the end of the twelfth day after entering the mountains, we came up over a ridge and looked down into an obsidian valley that stretched for at least a mile, ringed on all sides by the jagged mountains. The sun had already descended behind the crags but still gave enough light to show the glassy black, fissure-covered valley. A clearly defined saffron-colored path snaked toward the valley's center, as eye-catching as a canary in a cluster of blackbirds and lit at regular intervals by lanterns. At the valley's center, the road ended at a large, unnaturally round hole. A set of stone bleachers, six rows high, flanked the road on either side and sat perhaps thirty feet from the hole. Six black, rectangular monoliths loomed behind the hole, opposite the bleachers. Etched into each monolith were three circles, spaced at even distances, the bottom circle three times as large as the top one. Lanterns lit up the area, throwing circular patches of light about with careless abandon.

"The arena at Hiephi," Elder said, his voice filled with awe. Around me, I could feel similar sentiments from the others. I didn't get it. Someone had painted a yellow line across some volcanic glass and carved a couple of rocks. Not exactly an earth-shaking accomplishment.

Only Lucifer looked displeased, but that didn't surprise me. This whole thing smacked of blasphemy to him. "Let us descend and get this over with."

"Brawk, make sure you stick to the path," Timbers said. "It's sure death if you fall onto the obsidian."

"The Oracle couldn't live in a nice village, could she?" I asked. "A cozy hamlet with trees and an inn?"

Timbers just twitched his head, his way of shrugging. "Brawk. Trust me, this fits her."

"Great," I said. We descended into the valley as night came upon us.

18

We reached the valley bottom and followed the saffron path, which upon closer inspection, proved to be rough cobblestones, different from the obsidian around us. We walked down the trail The arena slowly, all too slowly, drew closer. Despite the danger to my groin, I wished we still had the horses to ride.

Arrha.

I heard the incoherent thought and then felt the hatred behind it. I turned toward the source to see one of my squires, a tall, brown-haired teen, rushing toward me, hands outstretched. He was going to push me off the path. All this time, I worried about Pimple coming after me. It never occurred to me someone within our group would hate me so much. Dislike intensely, sure, but to the point of murder?

He had lost surprise but didn't realize it. He ran toward me. I stepped out of his way, and he rushed right past, his snarl changing to open-mouthed shock.

He tromped off the path and just past the reach of the lantern light before he stopped. He turned around to come back. The obsidian under his feet cracked, and he disappeared through the hole like a stage performer slipping through a trapdoor. We heard his screams and the delicate tinkle of obsidian for fifteen seconds before the shouting stopped short.

Nobody moved, unsure what to do. I turned and stared at the other squires Lucifer assigned to me and saw the same glare of hatred. I hadn't done anything to earn it. I had asked for nothing from them, didn't expect them to care for me, and barely spoke to them.

But as I recalled the days past, I realized they had done everything anyway. My tent was always set up, my food always ready, albeit a bit saltier than it should be. Two was constantly groomed and fed, and numerous other little things never required my attention, like my clothes being cleaned and laid out for me every third day. I hadn't asked for it, but as squires, they did the work anyway. Their hatred wasn't because they had to serve me; it was because I didn't acknowledge them. Even Lucifer, hard as he was on Raith, offered praise when my brother did something well.

And I didn't even know my squires' names.

Lucifer, red-faced, sputtered as he jumped off Justice and stormed toward the three remaining squires. They recoiled in fear and edged back until they ran out of cobblestone and risked death if they took another step. "How dare you try to harm the Messiah," he screamed. "I'll have each of you flogged, I'll—"

"Lucifer," I said. "Shut up."

He wheeled around on me, cheeks flushed, granite jaw clenched. "How dare you tel—"

"I am the Messiah, and I damn well do what I please. You forget yourself."

As if I had pummeled him with a fence post, he fell to his armored knees and cast his gaze to the stones. "Forgive me, Holy One."

I felt like a heel, but it was the only way I could think of to get him to stop. "Forgiven," I said. I walked toward the squires, well aware that should they decide to rush me, I would take a long fall through black rock.

"I'm sorry," I said. "I've been concerned with my own problems. I want to thank each of you for what you've done for me. I understand your hatred, and I've done much to deserve it. I've been a jackass, and I apologize. What are your names?"

They stared at me like I had just told them Lucifer was a woman. Their mouths hung open, and their eyes opened so wide their lids disappeared.

Lucifer looked up at me and then at the squires. "Answer the Messiah," he barked.

The shortest, wiry with blond hair, said, "Rikan."

"Timin," answered the tallest, with black hair and a broken nose.

The last one, somewhere between the others in height, but the oldest based on the shadow of a mustache that matched his brown hair, said "Malian."

I looked at each of them in turn. "Rikan, Timin, Malian, I hereby release you from my service, should you desire to go, but—"

I got no further before Timin turned and ran back up the path, heading toward the valley's upper end, shouting joyously. A big part of me wanted to follow him.

I returned my gaze to the two who remained. "As I was saying, if you stay in my service, I promise to no longer treat you as invisible but to thank you for a job well done, to speak with you and help you if I can, and to remember your names. Do you accept?"

They regarded me for a moment, and I waited to hear their shouts of rage before they shoved me to my death. Instead, they both nodded in turn, and Rikan even smiled.

"Thank you," I said.

And almost simultaneously fell to my knees as a dulcet chime, loud enough to rupture eardrums and possibly blood vessels, rang from the direction of the monoliths. I threw my hands over my ears, as did everyone else except Timbers, who fell from Raith's shoulder and lay on the ground, either stunned or dead. I looked toward the hole as the chime rang again and noticed the circles in the monoliths vibrating. What I had thought was carved into solid rock were actually holes covered in black fabric.

The chime sounded a third time and a man's voice, smooth and deep as the volcanic glass around us, said. "So begins wisdom. Approach and heed the Oracle."

As the echoes from the voice receded, I removed my hands from my ears. They still rang, a solid humming sound, and I wondered that I didn't have blood on my hands. Timbers jumped up, stumbled a moment, and then shook himself, sending mottled feathers drifting in the air. "Brawk! I had forgotten about that."

"How could you forget about something like that?"

He held out his wings and cocked an eye at me. "More drastic things happened."

I nodded as the former man jumped up onto my shoulder. Elder stood at the edge of the path, near where the squire had fallen, his head bowed.

"Offer no prayers for that one," Lucifer said. "He attacked the Messiah.

Ubel will deal with him as necessary, and your benedictions will not change it."

That seemed a harsh sentiment to me, and Ubel didn't actually deal with the dead. That was the province of Titanicus, since death is nothing more than the sinking of life. I decided now wasn't the time to nitpick. Elder waited until Lucifer walked away and offered a quick prayer. I did too, for the unnamed boy who died and for all of us to make it through this insanity.

When everyone more or less recovered, we continued toward the large hole.

"That's one fat bottom bowl," Elder said over his shoulder.

"What?" I asked, confused.

He stopped and waved his hands at the vast pantheon. "Fat bottom bowl," he repeated.

"You mean it's a big-ass arena."

He nodded, "That's what I said." He turned and resumed toward the structure.

I followed, more than ever wanting to go home.

As we drew closer, I heard the unintelligible mix of many voices speaking. The bleachers were canted in a V shape, the point facing us, so I could see the ends as we approached. People sat on the stone seats and talked among themselves as they stared toward the hole in the ground. I had no idea how they could hear after that ear canal-crushing bell. They wore clothing of varying styles and colors, showing a multitude of nations, but they had the same fervent look in their eyes, the zealous look I had seen in Lucifer too many times. These people weren't here just to listen to the Oracle, they were here to worship her.

A path led through the two sets of bleachers, so we walked down it. We had gone no more than ten feet when a towering form stepped from a strategically positioned shadow and startled me, which surprised Timbers.

"Brawk!" the bird cried.

Lucifer had Heathensmasher halfway drawn before the shadow resolved into a tall woman, only half a head shorter than Lucifer. She wore blue linen pants and a yellow tunic. A leather belt with three large pouches hung on her waist. She had black hair pulled into a bun with so much tension it surprised me she could blink. Stern angles engulfed her face, made more severe by the lantern light casting down upon her. The only thing missing was a flash of lightning and a crack of thunder.

"Tickets?" she said, voice sonorous as a church bell.

Lucifer, realizing battle wasn't imminent, released his sword and stepped up. "Tickets?"

"Yes, tickets," the woman repeated. "Do you have them?"

"For what?"

The woman glanced over her shoulder and then back at Lucifer, perhaps thinking he was joking. When he didn't laugh, she said, "For the Oracle."

"No," Lucifer said. "We were not aware we needed tickets to see the Oracle."

"Hmmm." The woman looked thoughtful, distinguishable from her looking scary by her thick eyebrows bunching close enough to join forces. "Not really my problem."

"See here," Lucifer said, putting on his most imperious tone, which I could tell would get him nowhere. "I am with the Church of Ubel, and we have traveled a great distance through much peril to see the Oracle."

As I predicted, the woman appeared thoroughly unimpressed. She waved her large hand at the others sitting in the bleachers. "Yes, and these people all arrived here by magic, with minimal effort."

Scary or not, I liked this woman immediately.

Lucifer tried a different tact. "How do we obtain these tickets?"

"You have to speak to the Ticket Master."

Lucifer's eyes narrowed. "That sounds like a title a self-important merchant might give himself."

"Says the Supreme Commander of the Paladins of the Church of Ubel," I muttered.

"I'll handle this," Elder said, slipping between Lucifer and the woman. He looked like an infant standing between two titans. "Where can we find the Ticket Master?"

"You're looking at her."

"Wouldn't you be a Ticket Mistress?" I asked.

Everyone ignored me, and Elder continued. "We need to buy," he did a quick calculation with the aid of his fingers, looking at the sky, and moving his lips. "Twenty-five."

"Sorry, I can't," the woman said. "We're sold out."

"Uh," Elder said. "Why didn't you say that before?"

She hiked a thumb at Lucifer. "Because he's a jerk."

Elder put a hand against Lucifer's chest to forestall comment, probably the bravest thing the priest had ever done. "You'll get no argument from anyone here," Elder said, "but be that as it may, we really must see the Oracle."

"There's another divining in a month."

"That won't work. The matter is pressing."

"That's what they all say."

I smiled. "I guarantee you I can trump anything they've got."

"Any chance of a private meeting?" Elder continued. "We have the full backing of the Church of Ubel, and we brought a great deal of tribute."

Lucifer ground his teeth so fiercely I feared *mine* might break, but he remained silent.

The woman's caterpillars raised. "What sort of tribute?"

"Gold and jewels and rare perfumes," Elder said. "It, uh, was all lost in a bandit attack, but we can get it replaced."

Her eyebrows crashed back down, threatening to engulf her eyes. "The Oracle doesn't do private consultations."

"Not even with the world's fate in the balance," I said, offering my best innocent look.

Not good enough. The Ticket Master scowled. "Get out of the way. You're holding up the line."

I looked behind our group. "What line?"

"The line of security I'm about to whistle for." She put her fingers to her lips.

Things might have gotten nasty, our journey ending right there, but someone tugged on the woman's tunic. He had approached unnoticed, most likely because he was short and dressed in black from neck to feet. It was a stylish outfit, well cut to his diminutive frame and glistening under the torchlight. The only splash of color was a large ruby on a gold ring he wore on his pinkie finger. His pinched face held a dirt-colored beard and a ruddy complexion. He had no hair on his crimson head and wore round glasses with lenses as black as his clothing. I had no idea how he saw out of them.

The Ticket Master looked down at him and frowned. He beckoned her with a stubby pink finger, and she leaned over, bending herself almost in half to reach his mouth level. He whispered something in her ear. Her frown deepened, but she nodded and stood back up. The short man, whom I realized was a gnome, stared at me and smiled, revealing a diamond in his front tooth. He turned away before I could smile back.

"It seems the Oracle was expecting you."

I couldn't help myself. "Wouldn't be much of an Oracle if she didn't."

The woman's expression went flat. "Gosh, I've never heard that one before." She waved a large arm and a boy, probably the same age as Crow — my nemesis back home in Frostishak, ran over. He wore plain gray pants and a red tabard with a stylized crystal ball. "Take those four," she pointed to me, Lucifer, Elder, and Timbers, "to the VIP section. The rest sit wherever you can."

"Yes, mum," the boy said.

I pointed to Raith. "He comes with us."

She looked ready to argue, then threw up her hands. "Fine, those five."

We followed the boy down the aisle between the bleachers. As we drew closer and closer to the large hole in the ground, I wondered if we had fallen into some trick. VIP was code for something like Vertical Immediate Plunge, a fancy way of saying "throw them down the hole." All our trials would end with us pitched into a chasm, saving Pimple the trouble of doing it himself.

Of course, I was wrong, and I chided my paranoia as we turned right ten feet away from the hole. I tried to look in and saw only black. We stopped at a section of the stone seats cordoned off by gold-colored rope. No one sat in them; I noticed a few people giving them envious stares. I didn't see anything special other than the proximity to the hole, and the cushions that rested on the stone. We would be moderately more comfortable than the people around us, but that didn't warrant the death threat eyes we received as the boy opened the rope to allow us in. We stepped in and seated ourselves. There was easily room for twice our number, so maybe the people hated us because we could raise our elbows without hitting our neighbor in the kidney.

No sooner had we sat than all the torches lighting the area when out as if a giant had blown out all the candles on his birthday cake. The chattering ceased.

A low rumbling started in the monoliths behind the hole. I immediately threw my hands up to my ears, although I didn't think it would do any good this close. I expected I would soon be deaf.

"Ladies and gentlemen," the voice said, loud but not as overwhelming as the bells had been, "boys and girls, humans and demi-humans, welcome to Hiephi."

I removed my hands from my ears as the voice continued. "Are you ready to divine?"

The tumult from the crowd almost flung me into the pit. People screamed, cheered, whistled, and generally acted as if they had lost any sense of decorum. And if *I* think you've lost decorum, you're in trouble.

The voice spoke again. "I can't hear you."

I suspected that was a lie, but the crowd believed every word. They redoubled their frantic cacophony, making so much noise I feared the vibration might break the fragile ground beneath us and send us all to a noisy death.

"Then put your hands together for the Diva of Divination, the Princess of Prognostication, the Sultana of Soothsaying. Here she is, the… Oracle…of…HIEPHI."

I didn't think it possible, but the din grew louder, almost to the point of making me want to pierce my eardrums with a dagger just to enjoy silence. Timbers had put his head under his wing, Elder winced at each wave of noise, and Raith had tears in his eyes. Only Lucifer remained stoic, a frown on his face. A closer study showed me he had stuffed wads of rolled cloth in his ears. And hadn't even offered to share. So much for knightly chivalry.

A groan of machinery echoed from the hole, adding to the aural deluge. Barely discernible over the rest came the hissing and cranking of gears. Shimmering waves drifted from the hole, the kind of thing you see looking across a field on a hot day. A sweet smell, like lemons mixed with cinnamon, followed. The noise slowly died down. I felt lightheaded and noticed a few other people smiling. The grinding sound continued. Despite the darkness, lanterns set at regular intervals along the benches provided enough ambient light that I could see what was happening. A platform of gray rock rose from the hole. A dais sat on the platform, and on the dais sat a chair, its high back facing us, so we couldn't see the occupant. Considering our location, Timbers's earlier comment, and my vision from a few weeks ago, I expected some wizened crone, no doubt missing teeth, hair, or maybe an eye. The platform jolted to a halt with a final hiss and blast of leminnamon scent, with a generous helping of grit. I rubbed my eyes and stared at the chair.

Four attendants stood around the throne, each beside a gold-colored pole. They wore banana-yellow robes that engulfed their bodies like tents, leaving only their blond heads exposed. They appeared so similar I suspected they might be quadruplets.

Nothing happened for a few seconds while the platform settled. Then a chant started, low at first, then growing in intensity.

Or-a-cle. Or-a-cle. Or-a-CLE. OR-A-CLE. It took about a minute to get to the all capital letters, yelling version, and it was quite a thing to see. Or hear, since I couldn't really see the people behind me.

From behind us, a beam of light descended at a diagonal over our heads and landed on the chair. It revealed a crystal ball emblem etched into the chair's back. People shouted in joy as if the dais had begun dispensing gold coins. Then a second light struck from a different angle, and you'd think the gold had turned into platinum. I had never seen this many people this excited about anything. It frightened me, and I could tell Raith wanted to run screaming.

Each attendant grabbed a pole on the base and slowly began to turn it. I wondered why the platform didn't come up with the chair already facing us and decided the occupant must be so hideous she had to be revealed slowly so onlookers could absorb the shock.

The chair spun around, and I saw the Oracle for the first time. The cacophony receded, overtaken by the thudding of my heart.

Instead of the haggard old woman from my dream, I got flowing brown hair that cascaded over the throne and touched the ground. Brilliant eyes, the dark green of overripe limes, a delicate face of high cheekbones, slender nose, full lips as red as cherries, and skin the whiteish color of that rock that begins with an A, the one I can never remember. She wore a dress of pale yellow, several shades lighter than her attendants. It clung to her body in interesting ways. And by interesting, I mean mindnumbingly sensual. Looking at her made me forget all the pain, suffering, and whining I inflicted on others to get here.

She was the most beautiful girl my age I had ever seen.

She stood up from the chair, and the screaming and shouting returned to my attention. Someone near me fainted, but no one seemed to care.

I didn't care either. This vision in saffron strolled across the platform, toward her audience, toward me, and I found myself cheering like the other maddened inmates in this deranged pit. As she walked, the lights followed her, and more lanterns at the foot of the platform came to life, bathing her in yellow light that made her glow like a sunlit porcelain angel. Her eyes locked with mine, their emerald gaze cutting into me. I knew she was there solely for me, even as I also knew every other person in the audience felt she was there solely for them.

Except, as it turned out, I was right. She came to the edge of the platform and looked at me, her gaze intense. I felt heat in my cheeks.

She raised her hands, and the audience grew hushed. My ears rang in the silence.

"The Oracle speaks," the voice boomed from the obelisks, and I winced.

"What's your name?" she asked, her voice so musical I expected a backup choir to harmonize the question.

I pointed at myself like an idiot, as if her direct stare and question weren't confirmation enough of who she spoke to.

"Yes, you."

"Briar," I said, although my tongue wanted to hide down my throat in embarrassment.

"Do you have a question for me?"

My heart stuttered, and my brain sizzled like eggs on a griddle. I wanted nothing more than to impress her with my brilliance, to show I could be the light of her life, that she should run away with me and teach me everything.

But she looked so different from the Oracle in my dream the question that popped out was, "Aren't you a little young to be all-knowing and all-wise?"

The people nearest me let out a collective gasp.

The Oracle's glittering green eyes narrowed, and she glared at me like an ivory cat about to pounce. Timbers's talons pierced my shoulder as his feet clenched.

"Brawk!" he said as softly as his you could make a high-pitched squawk. "I hope you like crackers."

19

As the Oracle stared at me with her narrowed lime eyes, I realized my question had not made a good first impression. No surprise, first impressions aren't my wheelhouse. But I feared this time it might have serious repercussions. I suddenly wanted the crusty old lady from my dream. She might be nowhere near as pretty, but she probably wasn't as prone to rash action. As the Oracle's jade gaze flickered over me, I wondered if my fate, after all the misery, was to wind up the feathered victim of a wise but petulant girl.

But she broke into a huge smile, which lit up her beautiful face and made me dizzy. It also frightened me as much as if she pulled a dagger on me.

As it turned out, she had something far worse in mind. She waved one of her long-fingered hands at me. "Come up here."

"What?"

"Come on up. I'm going to answer your questions." She raised her hands to the audience. "Don't you want to hear his answers?"

The crowd roared. Once again, I wanted to jump into the fragile black glass and plummet to my death. But as I stared at her smiling face, I saw the Oracle's game. I had embarrassed her, so she wanted to return the favor. I could handle that. It beat being turned into a bird.

"Come on," she coaxed. "And bring your friends with you. All of you, come on up. Even the ones who got put in the cheap seats."

That surprised me but also gave me comfort. I might get embarrassed, but at least I wouldn't be alone.

As we left our seats and ascended a set of rickety wooden steps to the platform, it dawned on me she might still transform me. Maybe she needed to be close, or perhaps she wanted to use me as an object lesson to the audience. I stopped, and Raith ran right into me, stumbling me onto the stage. There were titters from the audience as I pulled myself from the near fall with as much dignity as I could muster. I glared back at Raith, and he shrugged his shoulders.

It took a while for everyone to reach the stage, but not as long as it should have. I felt a sudden pang at the people we had lost on this journey. I wanted to make it worth their sacrifice, but things weren't starting out well.

The silent Oracle stared at the audience, who stared back at her, until we stood on stage beside her, like her choir or personal guard. She regarded me with an unreadable expression, then looked at the audience again. "Everyone, say hello to Briar."

The crowd roared a greeting at me, and the sound almost knocked me backward. I assume they said "hello, Briar," but it came across as a distorted wave of indecipherable noise that most closely resembled "her-robrer." I stood rooted, gazing at the mass of people barely visible beyond the lights shining in my face. But I felt them, their numerous emotions roiling over me, cutting into me and paralyzing me with fear. I suddenly longed for the simple terror engendered by Pimple and his fanatics.

The Oracle returned to her chair and sat. She held up her hand, like a queen presiding at court, and the audience, her faithful subjects, quieted again. She turned her gaze on me, pinning me with those twin candles of chartreuse fire under her brows. "Like many of you, Briar has come a long way through many trials to ask me a question. A question so important he risked his life and the life of two score plus other people to arrive here and ask it."

I knew where this was going and felt as small as a termite with a growth deficiency.

The Oracle continued. "Could you repeat the question so everyone could hear it?" She asked casually as if she had asked me to repeat a far less embarrassing question.

"I'd rather not."

"But not everybody could hear you. Go ahead."

"It wasn't the question I came to ask."

164

"But it was the question you did ask, so you're stuck with it. Go ahead."

I fidgeted, I squirmed, I tried to figure out how to swallow my tongue without choking, but to no avail. She had me. As low as I thought I could get away with, I said, "Aren't you a little young to be all-knowing and all-wise?" Through some evil magic, my words came out of the monoliths, echoing past me and ensuring my ignominy reached everyone in the seats. As expected, the audience gasped, and more than a few booed.

The Oracle held up her petite hands, and the audience fell silent. She smiled. "Perhaps I am," she answered, "but—"

"It's just that you looked so different when you came to me in my vision," I blurted out.

She paused and stared at me, eyebrow arched, head tilted. If I didn't know better, I'd think she was confused, but I got no emotions from her. Finally, she shook her head and said, "You shouldn't interrupt. It's very rude, and I expect more courtesy from a god's son."

"I'm sorry, I just...wait, what did you say?"

"I said you're very rude, and I would expect more from the son of a god." She put a long, slender finger against her dimpled chin. "No, I said I would expect more from a god's son." She shrugged. "It's the same thing."

"Brawk!" Timbers said. Something warm and heavy splattered my shoulder as the captain let loose. I would have been annoyed had I not felt like doing the same thing. Murmurs started in the audience as they began to grasp what the Oracle said. More emotions spilled onto me from the crowd: surprise, shock, confusion, disbelief. I latched on to that last one and took it for myself.

"Hold on," I said. "Everyone knows Oracles speak in riddles. This is a riddle, right? A metaphor. 'God's son' means I'm a devout follower of Ubel, so he thinks of me as a son."

The Oracle shook her head again, making her hair ripple-like fine-spun chocolate. "No, I thought I spoke plainly." She took in the crowd. "I did speak plainly, didn't I?"

A massive chorus of assent resounded across us.

She nodded. "You are Briar, son of—"

"Patch the Tailor," I said, desperation in my voice, sweat under my arms. I turned to the crowd, pleading with them. "My mother is Stella the Weaver, and my father is Patch the Tailor." Even as I spoke, I knew it wasn't true. At least the part about my father. The final piece of my shifting life puzzle fell into place. Fate had trapped me like it wanted all along. All Ubel's strange comments and knowing looks, and even the Archbishop's cryptic glances and mumbled questions, now made perfect sense. I was a demigod, and no one had the nerve to tell me except the Oracle.

I couldn't tell you, Ubel thought. *Cos-*

Yeah, I know. Cosmic Loophole. Very convenient.

You've really got to work on your manners.

And you should work on not sleeping with other people's wives, I thought. A rush of anger almost knocked me to my knees, followed by embarrassment.

We'll talk later. Then my father was gone. I felt ill.

"First, you insult me," the Oracle said, bringing me back to the dire situation before me, "and now you interrupt me. Twice. You're probably the rudest person I've ever met. Isn't he rude?"

The crowd booed with great fervor, and several made rude gestures, hostile shadows behind glaring lights.

But none of that mattered because something else I would have never expected affected me. After you've been reprimanded by a god, a god that's your father no less, you would think the same harangue from a girl with a dulcimer voice wouldn't have much effect, but it did. More than Ubel ever could, she made me understand how boorish I was, forced me to recognize my insensitivity, called me to task for being a heel. Basically, she made me feel like a real shit. And she did it in front of at least a thousand people.

But far be it from me to accept that with any sort of grace. "It's also rude to blurt out to someone that they are the son of a god. It's like telling a person their child is ugly or stupid. It's the kind of news you want to break gently, not just toss out like a kettle of rotten fish." My eyes shifted to the audience and then back to her. "It's also something you should do in private."

Her eyes de-narrowed and went back to their pleasing round shape. "You didn't know?"

"What was your first clue? My open-jawed reaction or my insistent denial?"

And she went back to cat eyes. They contracted so tight I was surprised she could still see. The hissing I heard earlier started again, followed by that odd lemon-cinnamon smell. Lightness and pleasantness once again bounded through my brain. I saw the Oracle's attendants shiver, making their yellow robes ripple. The Oracle took a deep breath, and a smile came to the Oracle's face. Her eyes opened again, as glazed as a duck breast prepared for the oven and black as the rock that surrounded us. I heard a deep buzzing sound, like a nation of bees harmonizing.

"What is past is prologue," she almost sang. "All that has happened before is but preparation for what is to occur."

I had no idea what she was talking about. "What are you babbl-" I stopped when Timbers flexed his talons. "Saying?"

"I was saying what is past is prologue."

"Fine, but what does that mean?"

"It means that—oh, where are my manners?" She stood and fluttered over to me. I caught a whiff of flowers from her clothes. I didn't know the smell and didn't care. Her closeness made me palpitate.

"Would you like something to drink or eat?" she asked. "I could have Mathra get something from the concession stand." She pointed to one of the servants. I had no idea how she could tell them apart.

"I think we're fine. Now-"

"Speak for yourself," one of the surviving Paladins said. "After what we've been through, I think we deserve a round of stout and perhaps some liquor." There was a chorus of assent from his companions. There were even a few shouts of agreement from the crowd, the crowd I had somehow forgotten as the Oracle approached me.

I turned to Lucifer, expecting him to shout his people down and berate them. But he stared at me like a child looking at a month-old puppy. Pure adoration radiated from him. As soon as he saw me staring at him, he turned his eyes away.

"Forgive me," he said. "I'm not worthy to look at you."

"You were worthy five minutes ago. Nothing's changed." Of course, it had changed. But like everything else, I wanted this to go away, too.

"You are Ubel's spawn," Lucifer said.

I winced. "Don't put it that way. Makes me sound like a fish."

"We shall call you the Holy Scion."

Holy Scion, the crowd whispered.

"How about you just call me Briar? It's worked for fifteen years."

"As you wish, Holy Briar."

Holy Briar.

I sighed. It was probably the best I was going to get.

"Would you like me to chastise those who spoke out of turn?" Lucifer asked.

"No," I said. "I don't want anybody to change just because of what they've learned about me. I know I'm not going to." Although even as I said it, I wondered how truthful I was. I looked back at the Oracle. She stared at me beautifully and with great patience. "I guess some people are thirsty. Perhaps you can help them."

The Oracle clapped her hands, and the servant named Mathra stepped off the dais and came over to us. "Those who wish to purchase refreshments, follow me." There was a pause as everyone took in the word "purchase," but eventually, people followed her, soon leaving only me, Raith, Lucifer, Elder, and Timbers. Except for Timbers and the giant crowd who watched us as if we were a traveling theater troupe, it was the same group I had started with on this folly. I considered the Oracle's words about the past being prologue and shivered.

"Now then," the Oracle said, "we can attend to other matters. Why are you here?"

"You're the Oracle; you should know already," I blurted out and then wanted to bite off my tongue. If I kept it up, I would soon have the ability to fly and an urge to poop on statues.

The crowd gasped again. Nothing like having live commentary while your world is upended.

I winced, waiting for the magic thunderbolt as the Oracle held up her hand. I wondered if transformation hurt. But then I caught another whiff of the now-familiar vapors that drifted up from under her dais. I also noticed one of the servants stepping on something on the floor repeatedly. Her robe made it hard to see, but I caught the motion. I also noticed the exasperated glare she gave me.

The Oracle turned at the sound and her nostrils flexed. She turned back to me and stared at her hand as if noticing it on the end of her wrist for the first time. She flexed her fingers, giggled, and regarded me. "Fine, if you want to play that way. You're here because you think the father of all the gods has gone insane, and you want to know how to cure him. And Timbers is here because he wants me to change him back into a man. And your brother Raith wants to know if he will ever hit puberty." I turned to Raith, who appeared ready to hang himself with his intestines to escape this humiliation. Elder gave him a sympathetic pat on the shoulder, but Lucifer and Timbers paid no attention. The former still stared at me, and the latter focused on the Oracle.

She had a self-satisfied smirk on her face, which made her still look nothing less than gorgeous. "A hundred percent?" she asked.

I nodded.

She closed her eyes and put her slender, long-fingered hands to either side of her head. She shook as if trying to jar something loose. I saw the servant's foot move again and caught the smell of the vapors. My head danced, and I suddenly wanted a glass of lemonade and a plate of snicker-doodles.

Eyes still closed, she held up her hands. "Listen well!" The crowd hushed. Expectancy hung in the air like a pregnant albatross. "Here are the answers all seek. Ubel isn't insane. He's been kidnapped and cut off from his powers, which is making the world go insane. Timbers, I won't change you back, but there is a way you can change yourself, and Raith, puberty will start for you tonight, brought on by your overweening interest in me. Your voice will start to drop, hair will begin sprouting in odd, and rather disgusting, places, and your testi—"

"I get the idea," Raith said in a strangled voice.

I tried to ignore the stab of jealousy toward my brother. Half-brother, I realized. I was the only one supposed to have feelings toward the magnificent creature in front of us. "How is that possible?" I asked.

The Oracle opened her eyes and looked at me. "It's possible because of chemical changes in the body that occur in adolescents and cause—"

"Not that," I said. "And I apologize for interrupting you again," I added as she glared at me. "I know how puberty happens. I want to know how it's possible for a god to be kidnapped. Who has that kind of power? Surely it wasn't one of the other gods."

"Oh, are you an Oracle too?"

The question threw me. "What? No."

"Then how do you know it wasn't one of the gods?"

"I don't. Was it?"

"No. But you shouldn't be so certain about things you have no way of knowing."

"That wasn't...I wasn't...I didn't..." I wasn't sure why she had me so flustered.

Elder, Ubel bless him, saved me. "Briar wasn't asserting a certainly so much as voicing a profound hope."

I pointed at Elder. "What he said."

"Then your hope has been fulfilled. A god did not kidnap Ubel."

"Then who did?"

"Your half-brother."

Shocked that he had been brought back into the conversation, Raith said, "I didn't."

"Not you, silly," the Oracle said with a giggle that sent odd, pleasant tingles up my spine. "Your other half-brother."

"Other—" It slapped me like a flounder to the face. The bastion of evil trying to kill me, the pasty-faced weasel who had destroyed half of Luther's entourage and forced me to swear vengeance, going against my cowardly self-interest, was a relative.

And I thought I was the one who didn't fit in.

"Pimple," I said. "That figures."

"Pimple?" The Oracle's fragile face bunched up in confusion for a moment, then she smiled again. "Oh, because of the pockmarks on his face. Well, we can't all have baby butt skin."

About this time, the group who had left returned to the stage, towing beers and other, more alcoholic, drinks in hand. I heard several of the Paladins muttering things like "overpriced" and "watered down," but I ignored them. I had more important matters to discuss. "Okay, so Pimple—"

"His name is Ublek."

"Now, who's interrupting?"

"See, not very fun when it happens to you, is it?"

I ignored that too. "Fine, Ublek has kidnapped Ubel. How do we free him? And if you say anything about cosmic loopholes, I'll scream."

"That's not very heroic."

"I never claimed to be a hero."

She nodded, conceding my point. "No cosmic loopholes. After all, you came to me to answer this very question. That was the whole meaning of your quest, wasn't it?"

"It's not my quest," I said, but that was also no longer true. It had become mine, almost accidentally, like a cat that follows you because you drop a piece of cod next to it. I turned and saw everyone staring at me. Lucifer still had the adoration of a lovestruck girl, Elder respected me, and Timbers was mad and confused over why the Oracle wouldn't change him back. After all, she had formed the curse.

The others stood on stage, drinks in hand, awaiting their orders. They could have all left at any time. I thought they stayed because of Lucifer, but it was because of me. I was touched to see that Rikan and Malian had bought an extra drink for me. Malian held it toward me. I nodded, and he came up and handed it to me. The mug had a leather cover over the top with a reed punched through it. Following Malian's example, I put my lips over the reed and drew in the liquid. It tasted of strawberries and understanding. I turned back to the Oracle. "Okay, I guess it is my quest. So, how do I free Ubel?"

Thunder cracked from the monoliths, and the deep male voice that had spoken earlier roared out of them, nearly deafening me for the third time today. "Are you ready for the Grand Pronouncement?"

The momentarily forgotten spectators reasserted themselves with a roar of affirmation.

The lanterns flashed like they were having some sort of epileptic fit, and light of various colors danced across the platform, sweeping back and forth. I had no idea where they came from. The voice spoke again. "I said, are you ready for the Grand Pronouncement?"

The crowd roared with unseemly enthusiasm, and even the Paladins and squires shouted "Yes" in unison and cheered as if they have been given chests of gold.

"Brawk!" Timbers said into my ear. "She does love her drama."

"Then here it is," the voice bellowed, "the Grand Pronouncement!"

We waited. And waited. The Oracle frowned. She squinted her eyes. She looked as if she might be dealing with an upset stomach. But still no Grand Pronouncement. She pressed her hands against her temples. I took another sip of my strawberry drink and was about to speak, but Timbers must have sensed it. He flexed his talons.

"Don't," he whispered as soft as a bird can. "She'll get it."

Finally, she looked at the servant beside her. "It's no good. Hit it again."

I saw watched the servant's foot again step on whatever she had on the floor, clearer now that I knew what to look for. I couldn't hear the release of the vapor, but I could smell it. The wind shifted at that moment, and I got a nose full of the scent. It overwhelmed the strawberry taste in my mouth and filled it with lemons and cinnamon. My vision cleared. The world became brighter, noises louder and sharper. I could have done without the last since the monoliths already made my teeth vibrate, but another effect presented itself. I had been able to read no thoughts or emotions from the Oracle or her servants. But now, the Oracle's Grand Pronouncement came to me half a moment before she said them. It created a strange audio and visual echo that made me nauseous.

The Oracle spoke, her musical voice echoing in my head. "You must go to the Outer Chaos, beyond the home of the gods, and enter the fifth door on the right. There you will fight the Hispit, Guardian of the East Hallway. From there, go to the third door on the left and battle the Eykantcey, Sentinel of the West Hallway. After that, you should pause for refreshments, then go to the end of the hallway, enter the Great Golden Door, and master the Slobbering Beast of Chaos. When you have done this, a portal will appear. Go through the portal. There you will find Ublek and Ubel. Ublek will likely be aware of you by then, so be ready. Defeat Ublek, and you can free Ubel. I'm tired."

The strange sensation of prescience disappeared, taking the nausea with it, but my throat felt dry. I drank more of my drink and heard a sharp slurping sound as I reached the end. "Could I get another one?" I asked Mathra.

"Four coppers," she said without hesitation.

Grumbling, I dug into my pockets and found some money. I handed it over, and she left to get my drink. I felt strangely calm about what the Oracle had just told me, considering I knew I should be scared spitless. Then again, maybe that's why my throat was so dry. My body already knew what my brain hadn't processed.

The Oracle obviously wasn't concerned at all. She had fallen asleep. Her head tilted daintily forward, chin resting between her...well, you get the idea.

"Ladies and gentlemen," the deep voice rumbled. "Thank you for attending. Go forth and spread the word that Briar, son of Ubel, is going on a grand quest to save us all from destruction by his insane half-brother. Should he fail, we will all perish at the whim of this mad deity, so care for your loved ones while you can. Take your leave now, get home safe, and have a great evening."

I'm not sure where the strange, disembodied voice pulled all that from, but the audience didn't seem to care. Fear and regret ran rampant through them, and they fled the bleachers like water when the plug is pulled. Quicker than I could have imagined, we were left alone, just us, the servants, and the sleeping Oracle. I could only imagine the widespread panic when these people reported what they had heard.

"I think this all could have been handled better," Elder said.

I looked at Elder, pointed at him, and put my finger on my nose.

"What do we do now, Holy Briar?"

We forget this ever happened and go home. That's what I wanted to say; I really did, but what came out was, "We find out how to get to the Outer Chaos and go rescue my father."

You could have caught a horde of flies with the open mouths that greeted that statement.

"Sounds great," Elder said after he recovered. "Lead the way. Chaos seems to be your forte."

I looked at Mathra. "I don't suppose you know how to get to the Outer Chaos."

"No, but the Oracle does."

I looked at the still sleeping girl, her face peaceful, her beauty unwavering, even with the runner of saliva that trailed to her dress. "Do we, uh…" I made a motion as if to shake her awake.

"No, no," Mathra said. "Come with me. I'll show you to the Green Room, and you can rest." She started to walk, her robe flowing behind her.

"How much will that cost us?"

That seemed to confuse her. She hesitated a moment, then said. "Nothing. It's where all the Oracle's guests wait after her pronouncements. She will recover and come to see you in a more intimate setting."

Something about the way Mathra said "intimate" made my body tingle, but I figured it was just all the sugar in my drink.

Mathra walked toward the back of the stage. As we followed, I considered the Oracle's words. I had to face Pimple, my half-brother, who also happened to be a demigod. Of course, I was a demigod, too, but Pimple had much more practice than I did. My enthusiasm for this endeavor suddenly took on the excitement of a condemned man heading for the gallows.

"We will have to make sure you are amply provisioned," Mathra said. "The Oracle has certain needs that must be attended to."

"The Oracle?" I asked.

"She has foretold it," Mathra said. "She is to accompany you for your confrontation."

"Brawk," Timbers said. "That's just wonderful."

I smiled. For the first time in this whole mad affair, things suddenly seemed brighter.

20

The Green Room turned out to be so named because it was, in fact, filled with greenery. I had no idea how large the room was because a jungle had exploded inside it. Plants filled the space, including trees that reached the ceiling at least fifty feet above us and vines that draped back down like octopus tentacles. I suddenly got a crushing sickness for Frostishak since this terrain looked so similar. The only things missing were the breath-clogging humidity and the rank perfume of rotting vegetation.

Mathra took us down a path toward the room's interior, and I couldn't see five feet to either side. It wouldn't surprise me if an alligator jumped out and attacked us.

As we drew closer to the center, pleasant aromas reached me. Ginger, honey, the succulent smell of roasted meat. My mouth watered, and I realized I was famished. After another few feet, the jungle broke away and created a square clearing. Laid out in the middle was the feast to end all feasts. Food and drink filled five tables, everything from a whole pig with an apple in his mouth, to roasted apples stuffed with duck liver. I saw pitchers filled with liquids of various colors and caught the scent of alcohol from at least half of them. There were fruits, vegetables, grains, and things unrecognizable. At least three farms must have been sacrificed to the bounty before us.

Across from the feast sat seven or eight trestle tables with dark wooden benches and silverware of actual silver, something I had never seen. At home, we were lucky to have tin forks and wooden spoons.

"Please enjoy some food," Mathra said, extending her robed arm toward the cornucopia, "while you wait for the Oracle."

"Is it free?" Elder asked.

"Of course."

She had to tell none of us twice. We rushed toward the food like half-starved boar hounds, but Lucifer was there before all of us, hand extended. We stopped, and the urge from several Paladins to knock Lucifer down and toss his unconscious body into the corner hit me. Not a knightly sentiment, but hunger can do that.

"Holy Briar may have first choice of the food."

I smiled. Maybe there were some perks to this demigod thing. I moved toward the food, ready to gorge myself silly. I noticed the empty drink cup still in my hand and realized two things: one, the servant had never brought the other one I paid for, and two, my squires had not only gotten me a drink but had purchased it with their certainly meager funds since squires make even less than scribes. I saw a way to ingratiate myself with not only them but the rest of my coterie.

Diverting myself from the delicacies before me and facing the group, as if that were my intention the whole time, I wiped the saliva from my mouth and said, "I decree all shall eat before me, in order of rank from lowest to highest. I shall eat last."

Lucifer looked like he wanted to argue. I saw the struggle in the quivering of his square jaw. I had just slapped the face of knightly tradition and spit in its eye for good measure.

Some of the other Paladins weren't so ambivalent in their facial expressions. They felt they had taken the brunt of the trials thrown at us and deserved to take their accustomed place in the pecking order. They seemed prepared to countermand me, and I'd get no support from the confused Lucifer.

I held up my right hand, fingers spread apart in as menacing a gesture as fingers spread apart can be, and said in a forceful voice, "Anybody got a problem with that?" I wished lightning would jump between my fingers to add gravity to my statement.

Lightning jumped between my fingers.

"Holy crap," I said, leaping back and dislodging Timbers. With a squawk, he flew away and landed on Raith's shoulder. I stared at everyone, who looked as shocked as I felt. Emotionally shocked, not physically, since the lightning had done nothing other than raise the fine hairs on my fingers.

I recovered quickly. "Holy zap," I said to cover my surprise. "If anyone has a problem, I'll give them a holy zap." I held up my hand again and thought about lightning. This time it arced from finger to finger and back. I smiled. *Is it that easy?* I thought.

For a child, a voice said in my brain. It wasn't my father's. That disconcerted me, and the lightning threatened to go out as my hand shook, but I held firm.

You and I need to have a long cha....

Oh, I'll be here when you arrive, Pimple thought. He offered a giggle I'm sure he considered evil sounding, but which made me think of a three-year-old laughing at dolls. *I'm sorry*, he continued, *if you arrive. But I don't think we'll be talking. Best practice while you can, brother.* I got the sensation of him flicking a finger, and a psychic thump between my eyes instantly became a headache.

OW, I thought. I looked at the others, who still waited to see what I would do. "So, squires first, priests and workers second, Paladins, Lucifer, then me. Let's line up and eat."

My little power display settled everything, and the groups fell in line in the order I gave. Soon the sound of food slopping onto plates filled the room, almost overpowered by the rumbling of stomachs. I was glad I chose to eat last. My appetite had diminished. I had hoped to get some surprise on Pimple, at least get halfway through the Oracle's convoluted instructions before he knew I was coming. I should have known better. He had been able to track me every step of the way, so what made me think I could lose him now?

Could I?

What was the extent of my powers? Ubel could tell me, but I suspected that pathway was currently closed. Pimple would be on him constantly, keeping him from me. How was he doing that? And could I return the favor, hiding our whereabouts from the little snit? What could—

A rustling in the jungle surrounding us interrupted my thoughts. I saw movement to my left, leafy fronds vibrating as something moved toward us. A tiger?

No, it was something much worse.

"I'm the Oracle's agent," the little man with the dark glasses who saved us from the Ticketmaster said as he broke through the foliage, stomping like a dyspeptic rhino. He regarded us through the smoky spectacles. "Who's in charge of this group?"

No one spoke, and the clattering of spoons scooping food from dishes stopped. I realized everyone was staring at me except the man in glasses, who looked at Lucifer.

"I am," I said, forcing the words out. I pointed at Lucifer and Elder. "And these are my able seamen." I suspected that wasn't the right word, but it was the only lower rank I could remember from my time on the ship. "What can we do for you?"

"We need to discuss the Oracle's contract."

My utter confusion must have shown. After a pause, he continued. "The Oracle is accompanying you as a guide, therefore, as required by the Oracle's Guild—"

"Guild?" I asked. "She's the only one; how can she have a guild?"

"It's a guild of one!" he snapped. Literally, he snapped his fingers in my face as he said it. "Now, let's discuss her fee."

"Fee?" I felt like I had entered a game of twenty questions. "First, I didn't realize she was coming with us." At the thought, my heart did a little pitter-pat dance of joy. "Second, if she does come with us, I assume she would do so for the good of the world, out of the kindness of her heart."

The agent gaped as if I told him she would run spikes through his eyes. "*She* might very well do that. That's why she has me. My heart was removed when I got my degree." He pulled a quill and piece of parchment from the sack on his side. The sound of clanking silverware returned. Apparently, the others decided we would handle this. No sense in delaying their dinner.

The agent licked the tip of the quill. "Now, since the accustomed tribute was 'lost'," he said it as if he suspected us of either lying about losing it or never having it to begin with, "I should think twenty percent of the treasure would be fair."

"Treasure?" I asked. "We're going to rescue a kidnapped god."

It was the agent's turn to look confused.

"Gods are above the need for treasure," Elder said.

The agent laughed. "Your god, maybe. But Parsimony is my god, and his only concern is treasure."

I felt rather than saw Lucifer come up behind me, menace roiling off him. The agent looked past my shoulder at the Paladin. "Wow, you're a big one. Of course, everyone's a big one to me."

"Are you a merchant?"

"Merchant? Pah! Merchants wish they could be me." He returned his attention to me. "No treasure, huh? Okay, then she gets first rights on writing any tomes based on your little adventure."

"I'm a scribe," I informed him. "I might want to write a tome based on it."

He lowered his glasses and peered over them. His eyes were black as a mineshaft at night. "You really think you'll survive going up against a god?"

I had, for once, been able to hold self-doubt at bay and did think I might survive, especially with the group of people I had around me. But this little snit pierced that like a pitchfork through hay.

"He's not a god," I said. "He's a demigod. And so am I." I could hear the petulance in my voice, but I didn't care. Until I realized I sounded like Pimple, and that scared me.

"I'm open to negotiation. We need to reach some sort of agreement. The Oracle has commitments, so either we make some arrangements, or she doesn't go. You could offer a buyout fee. Let's see." He wrote on his paper and muttered to himself. Words like "days away" and "gross lost revenue" came out. After a minute or so, his shielded eyes fell on me. "How about—"

Lucifer had had enough. His hand went to *Heathensmasher*. "How about we go without the Oracle? We have no need of your blasphemous witch. We will find our way with guidance from Ubel."

The agent laughed. "Ubel? You mean the one who got kidnapped? Good luck."

The sword came out. I jumped out of the way so I didn't get caught by the blade or blood spray. "I think someone needs their heathen merchant tongue cut out."

"There's no need for that, you big lunk."

I recognized the dulcet voice and smiled. I turned to see the Oracle standing in the clearing, beside a table of goblets, one of her servants behind her. A pair of squires stood at the table, pouring drinks. One of them stared at her, mouth agape, the wine overflowing the cup and dripping to the floor. I had an urge to run over and punch him for his lack of respect. The Oracle still wore her clingy pale lemon dress but had tied her hair back with a thin leather strap. My heart sped up as she walked toward us, the servant following.

The agent turned to watch them approach. His voice changed, and he suddenly sounded like the merchants Lucifer hated. "Hey, baby doll, there's no need for you to worry your pretty little head here. Me and the client here were just—"

"I know what you were doing," the Oracle said. She pointed at her temple. "Oracle, remember?"

"Well, then, you can just take it easy and—"

"You're fired."

That shocked him so much that he took off his dark glasses to reveal his pitch-black eyes. "What?"

"You can leave; I don't need you anymore. You're holding me back."

"I'm making you rich."

"I don't want to be rich; I want to be free. I want to see the world in something other than visions." She started pacing back and forth. "I want to travel, do things, make stuff happen, get dirty, find a boyfriend-"

My face heated up. I grew so distracted by the possibilities that I didn't hear anything else until she suddenly screamed, "I said GET OUT, and don't ever come back." This was followed by a flying goblet. It passed over the agent's head and struck me in the chest. The goblet shattered, and red liquid stained my tunic.

The Oracle looked at me. "That's what you get for being in the way." She picked up another goblet, raised it over her head, and glared at the agent. "This one won't miss."

"Fine, you ungrateful little wretch," the agent shouted back. He threw his glasses to the ground and stomped on them, shattering the lenses. "That's what I think of you, you brat." He looked at the group, his gaze somehow encompassing all of us. "I hope you all fall into a crevasse," he screamed, then focused on Lucifer. "And you're lucky I don't send a carrier pigeon to my cousin. He's a lawyer, you know. I could have you thrown in a dungeon for threatening me."

He started crying as he turned back to the Oracle. "You're tearing my heart out. Come on, we don't want it to end like this."

"Save it for someone who believes you." She made a motion to throw the goblet.

The agent's tears stopped as if he had turned a valve. "Fine. Have a great life." He stormed toward the foliage, turned, came back, and grabbed his broken glasses. "Damn things are expensive," he said to no one. He resumed his march toward the exit. "Women," he muttered as he disappeared into the greenery.

"Gnomes," the Oracle grumbled as she held out the goblet. The servant filled it with a purple liquid. The Oracle took a sip, smiled, and strolled over to us. When she saw us staring at her, she said, "Commission an artist to do a painting; it will last longer. Quit gawking at me and eat. I'm hungry."

I HAD no idea how a person could eat so much and not be the size of an aurochs. The Oracle piled her plate a foot high with roast beef, potatoes, green beans, at least two loaves worth of bread, a slice of lemon pie, and a strawberry tart. I had chosen much the same, only in more modest portions, and grabbed a glass of lemonade and a small plate of snicker-doodles.

"Pronouncements always make me famished," the Oracle said as the servant sat the plate before her while another poured her more grape juice. I still couldn't tell the servants apart.

"You realize if you go with us," Elder said, "you will actually have to do some things for yourself."

"Nonsense," the Oracle said as a napkin was unfolded and laid in her lap. "These two will accompany us."

"Impossible," Lucifer said. "We can't have servants bogging us down."

Her eyes narrowed at Lucifer, which had no effect on him. "I'm sorry, what are those?" she pointed at the squires, who ate with the ravenous-ness of starving mice given a wheel of cheese.

"They are squires," Lucifer said, his tone offering *silly little girl* as an addendum.

"Servants with a superiority complex," the Oracle said. "If yours can go, mine can go."

Lucifer prepared to offer a retort. This could last forever. The Paladin and the Oracle were used to things being done their way, and neither was going to give in. "They can go," I said. "This is my edict."

Lucifer nodded, clearly unhappy. "As Holy Briar wishes."

If it weren't for having to confront my psychopathic half-brother, I could get used to being a demigod.

The Oracle nodded at me and then stuffed a hunk of roast beef the size of my hand into her mouth. Even with gravy dripping on her chin and her cheeks stuffed with dead cow like a squirrel with acorns, she still radiated beauty. I glanced at Raith and saw him leaning on his hand and staring at her, ignoring the squires around him. He caught me eyeing him and grew interested in his food. He tried to stuff a piece of chicken into his mouth so fast that he jabbed his lip with the fork. I winced even as he did but was glad. That's what he deserved for looking at my girlfriend.

She was going to be my girlfriend. All I had to do was convince her.

I stabbed a slice of duck and put it in my mouth. I didn't know who cooked it, but the taste was exquisite.

The Oracle swallowed her food, took a drink, and looked at Timbers. "So, how have you been, dad?"

To my credit, I didn't spit the food or do a double take. But I choked as my intake of breath lodged the wad of meat in my esophagus.

After Lucifer dislodged the deadly gobbet with a hammer blow to my back that made my ears ring, I sucked in beautiful, life-giving air. "Thank you," I told Lucifer, my voice raspy. "I'm fine," I told everybody else before they could ask. I looked at Timbers. "Dad?"

"Brawk," Timbers said, and the squawk sounded embarrassed. "It's true."

"Okay." I stood up and addressed the room. "Anybody else here have any unusual parentage or deep secrets about their family tree they want to share? Let's get all the twisty surprises out of the way, so I don't stand any further chance of death by shocked asphyxiation."

After a pause, Rikan, in a timid voice, said, "I have two fathers." One of the squires giggled, and Rikan smacked him on the head.

"Oookkaaayy," I said. "Anybody else?"

No one else offered any revelations.

"Very well." I sat back down and looked at Timbers. "Please, continue your tearful reunion."

"I've been fine," Timbers said.

"Not feeling a bit flighty?" the Oracle said. I wanted to groan but refrained.

"You're the flighty one," Timbers said. "Remember, that's what started the whole thing."

"I remember—"

"Brawk. Perhaps we can discuss this in a more private setting." It was then I noticed no one had gone back to eating. Everyone listened, breath held, to the Oracle and Timbers. "Unlike you, I'm not comfortable on a stage," Timbers said.

The Oracle shrugged. "Your choice. Not that anything is going to change." She looked at me. "Tell me about this dream of yours."

I did.

She frowned, which created an adorable dimple in her round chin. "Although that sounds much like my grandmother, I didn't send you that vision. I can't do that."

"You can turn someone into a bird, but you can't send visions."

"Brawk! She had help."

"Leave Mom out of this," the Oracle said. She took my hand. A quiver of pleasure shot through me, bouncing from spine to head to groin. I thought I might pass out. "I will do some divination to see if I can find out where this dream came from." She looked at the two servants who stood behind her. "Mathra, prepare the chamber."

Both servants bowed and left.

"They're both named Mathra?"

She released my hand, to my dismay. "All my servants are named Mathra. I have too much else to worry about to remember servants' names."

I wondered at the mental capacity of someone who couldn't remember more than one name, but she was too beautiful, and dangerous, for me to bring it up. That did lead me to another thought. "What is your name? I assume it's not, 'The Oracle.'"

She smiled. "Oracle is good enough. Or 'Your Most Supreme Oracle.' We need to keep this on a purely professional level. I don't get involved with clients."

Her words crushed me so hard I could only pick at my food while my heart flopped, trying to recover from the mortal blow. Raith, who hadn't heard her, continued to stare at the Oracle like a cat regarding a slab of tuna. Disgusted and hurt, I threw a piece of bread at him and scowled until he turned away.

If the Oracle didn't like me, she couldn't like anybody.

I SPENT the rest of dinner moping and picking at the now unappetizing food. Afterward, we were taken to our guest rooms. There were so many of us we had to take the rooms in pairs. Which was fine since Raith and I were used to sharing a bed. Several Paladins grumbled about having to room with a squire until Lucifer reminded them that they could sleep on the stone benches if they preferred. Lucifer and Elder got a room together, and Timbers went with the Oracle, presumably to discuss their strife.

Despite having only one bed, the rooms were quite pleasant, with a dark wooden dresser, a marble table with two teak chairs, and something I had only heard rumors of: a tub with running water. Fresh clothing hung on the door, an olive-green tunic with a white undershirt, a pair of green pants, and a set of black leather boots. I tried everything on, and it all fit. One advantage to knowing who your guests are going to be.

"She's beautiful," Raith said.

"Who?" I asked, playing dumb.

"The Oracle. She's the most beautiful girl I've ever seen."

"That's not difficult," I said, "given the lack of them back home." Living in a swamp made for rugged work and rugged women. "I guess she's okay."

"Okay?" Raith's watery eyes had gone moon calf on me. "She's gorgeous. Her hair is like…and her skin is so…and her brea…"

"I get it," I said, resisting the urge to throttle him. "I don't think she likes you, though."

"Why?" His voice broke like his heart had snapped. "Could you…" he pointed his finger at his head.

I couldn't lie to him. Even without my vow, I would never lie to Raith. Not even to get him to keep his grubby eyes off my girl. "No, I couldn't read her thoughts, but it seemed like she paid much more attention to me. Makes sense, my being a demigod and all."

"So, is that how it's going to be?" Raith said. "After all I've done for you, you're going to use your semi-divine status to take the girl I'm interested in because you are too?"

On occasion, I wondered if Raith could read my mind, even though I couldn't read his. This was one of them. "Uh, when you put it that way, it makes me sound like a jerk."

"That's because you're being a jerk," Raith said. "You're my brother, a—

"

"Half-brother," I reminded him.

"*Brother*," Raith said, his eyes turning to limestone, which is about as hard as his eyes could ever get. "You're my brother, and I love you, but you can be a real dick sometimes. I've been beaten up more times than I like because of that, but I'll always be there for you. You're smart, you're a demigod, and you're better looking than me. You could probably get the Oracle to like you. But don't. I'm asking as a favor."

It was the most emotional I had ever seen Raith get. It made my eye twitch as if a tear might be forming somewhere inside me. I wanted to tell Raith yes. I wanted to say the gorgeous creature could be his if she wanted him. I wouldn't interfere, I wouldn't try to win her heart, I wouldn't be my most charming to win her affection. I wanted to say all of that.

What I said was, "Let's just see what happens."

Raith slowly nodded his head, sadness and anger having a fistfight across his round face. "Fine," he said and grabbed a towel.

He spent a long time in the tub that evening. When I asked him what he was doing, he said "nothing," his face ruby red, and quickly exited the tub, his back to me as he dried off and crawled into bed.

21

As it turned out, getting to the Outer Chaos wasn't that difficult; it mostly involved descending a lot of stairs.

The next morning, Raith had little to say to me. He offered a curt "good morning" and not another word as he dressed, packed, and ate the breakfast that somehow appeared in our room. I let it go. Not my fault he was mad at me. Okay, it was my fault, but I wouldn't feel guilty about it. The Oracle was fair game.

Mathra, the same one or different, I had no idea, led us to a small underground chamber. It held nothing but damp earthen walls, with the requisite muddy smell, and two wooden doors, one on the side opposite the one we came through.

Apparently, some negotiation had taken place while I ignored everyone the previous night. The only other people in the room were Lucifer, Elder, Timbers, the Oracle, and Rakin.

"Each person who wanted a servant got one," the Oracle explained. "That keeps things manageable. Where we're going, superior numbers aren't really an advantage. If this group can't handle it, an extra ten people are just in the way."

I supposed I should have been comforted by that, but I wasn't.

"Drew the short straw, did you?" I asked Rakin. I hadn't requested a servant, but I wasn't going to turn one down.

"No," he said. "Malian and I played three rounds of sword, jerkin, torso. I won."

He smiled at me, and my mood imitated a kite. The Oracle might not be my girlfriend yet, and my brother would fight me for her, but I had a friend unrelated to me, something I never had before. Things might turn out okay yet.

As soon as I had the thought, I waited for something to destroy my optimism, but all that happened was the Oracle opened the closed door and said, "Down we go to the Outer Chaos. Everyone, take a backpack."

"I shall lead," Lucifer said. True to his word, he grabbed a backpack and went first, Raith behind him, sparing a fawning glance for the Oracle and a dark squint for me. Elder went next. I followed. As I grabbed my pack, I noticed we were one short. Rakin grabbed one, and Mathra took the other, leaving the Oracle empty-handed. Guess I should have expected that.

Timbers left Elder's shoulder and settled on mine.

"We won't have a repeat of yesterday, will we?" I was wearing my new clothing.

"Brawk. As long as we don't learn any more exciting tidbits about you."

"Yeah, good thing I didn't react the same way about your little secret."

I stepped into the doorway and started down a flight of stairs. I expected darkness, but each step had a gem beside it, set in the wall and glowing bright yellow, giving us ample illumination. I noticed everyone had fresh clothing, and we all smelled like honeysuckle. The Oracle and Mathra had changed into more practical attire of pants and a loose tunic, which in the case of the Oracle was disappointing but less distracting.

"Did you get things worked out with your daughter?" I asked Timbers, keeping my voice low.

"Brawk! Am I a two-hundred-pound man?"

"Gotcha," I said. Obviously, he didn't want to talk about it, so I shut my mouth and we descended the stairs.

We walked down, and down, and down some more. We stopped on a landing with an alcove and some small benches for a quiet lunch of bread and sausage from our packs. Raith and I sat beside the Oracle. She ignored us and talked to Lucifer about whether she really was an affront to the gods. Raith and I spent the time glaring at each other.

We continued down.

Shortly after we ate, I spotted a golden glow that steadily grew

186

brighter. It soon grew so bright we had to squint. We eventually reached a large landing and found the glow came from five golden archways set in the left-hand wall, each at least thirty feet high and gleaming as if fairies polished them daily. Beneath each arch was a ten-foot-tall door made from a silvery metal with the luster of pearls. Each entry had a symbol carved into it, larger than my head. From left to right, they were a sun's rays, a stack of coins, a puppy, a schooner broken in half, and a penis.

"Is this what I think it is?" Elder asked with a sense of awe in his voice I had never heard.

"Yes, it's a penis," I confirmed.

"Not that," Elder said.

"Yeah, not that, stupid," Raith said. He stood near the Oracle.

And Lucifer stood behind him. He gave Raith a slap across the back of the head. "Don't call the Divine One stupid."

"Don't hit the Divine One's brother," I said. Raith and I might be having a fight, but that didn't mean I would let someone else abuse him.

"Shut up!" the Oracle said. "You're all acting like a bunch of spoiled children. Mathra, wipe my brow. It's moist."

I kept my mouth shut.

As Mathra took a linen cloth and dabbed at the Oracle's furrowed forehead, the Oracle looked at Elder. "To answer the question you asked before the Three Jesters opened their gobs," she eyed the three of us with her agate orbs, "this is indeed The Home of the Gods." Mathra stepped away, and the Oracle gazed from door to door.

"The Gods live in a pit underneath you?" I asked.

"That's blasphemous," Lucifer said.

The Oracle rolled her eyes. "It's symbolic. They live in a place beyond the physical world. This is only a portal to that plane. But something's wrong." She frowned.

Elder had walked over to the door with Ubel's symbol, his face like a child's on Giftfest Day. He stood before the door, reached up, hesitated, and then touched the glyph, standing on his tiptoes.

The door went dark. "I'm sorry," a gentle voice said in a tone that immediately made me want to rest in a field of daisies. "Ubel is not currently in residence. Please offer your supplication at a later day, or speak to your nearest priest, who will make sure Ubel receives your prayers. Have a benevolent day." The door lit up again.

"That makes sense," the Oracle said, mostly to herself, "but the rest doesn't."

"What's wrong?" Raith asked, putting a hand on her shoulder. I wanted to pull a Lucifer on him, but I was too far away.

"I'm not sure," she said, shaking off Raith's hand, which made me smile. She sounded frightened. When you're used to seeing things before they happen, not knowing something would be a splash of cold water. I felt similar those few times I found someone whose emotions I couldn't read.

"Perhaps we should move on," Lucifer said. "Ubel is our goal; we need not meddle with the other gods. I would not care to meet Parsimony."

Probably because you'd attack him, and he'd dip you in gold and keep you as a statue, I thought.

Despite Lucifer's suggestion, the Oracle went to the door with the gold coin symbol and touched it.

This portal also went dark. "What do you want?" a voice said, grating as a barnacle toothbrush. "Parsimony isn't here. If you want a loan, the interest rate is twenty-seven percent, compounded monthly, payments due on the tenth day of every month. Read the contract for full terms and conditions. See your local moneylender. If you want to make a payment, throw it at the door, and we'll suck it in. If you're a merchant with a dispute, handle it yourself. Your god has better things to do than deal with lowlifes like you."

The Oracle frowned. She walked over to the door with the puppy on it.

"I'm requesting that you stop," Lucifer said.

"Brawk! Good luck getting her to do anything against her wishes."

The Oracle touched the door with the puppy symbol. Again, the portal darkened. "Oh, hi there," the soft voice I recognized from my dream said. "Thanks so much for dropping by." Phoebe giggled. "I'm off making the world a better place for all living creatures. I hope your day is as gentle and pleasant as you want it to be. Here, have a puppy."

A puppy, white, fluffy, with brown eyes and a black button nose, appeared in front of the door. It barked, ran to me, and piddled on my leather boots.

The Oracle walked over to us. She appeared not exactly worried but concerned and uncertain. "This is strange. Someone should answer, either the gods or their retainers. Something other than a disembodied voice."

"What about the other two doors?" Raith asked.

"I'd get the same result, and I don't really want to hear Horn's greeting." She had avoided looking at the door with Horn's symbol. I avoided it, too, mainly because it gave me feelings of inferiority.

"What does it mean?" I asked.

"I'm not certain. But there's nothing we can do about it right now, so we should continue."

Lucifer sidled up to the Oracle. "Do you speak to the gods often?"

She regarded Lucifer as she might study a bowl of curdled milk. "Of course not. I'm just a blasphemous witch, remember?" She picked up the puppy and walked away, taking the lead.

"You might want to apologize to her," I said.

He went into his offended posture, back straight, jaw set like a brick in mortar. "Is that the Divine One's command?"

"Not at all," I said. "Just a suggestion. An apology made on command isn't sincere. It's your choice." Of Lucifer's many flaws, lack of sincerity had never been one. I wasn't going to make it one now.

Eventually, when I thought we had gone through the planet and prepared to come out the other side, we reached a landing with no more stairs. It was another room, twenty feet to a side, with nothing except a circle in the middle of the floor black as an inkblot.

We stood around the spot and looked at it. "What do we do?" I asked.

"Not my place to say," the Oracle answered. The puppy had fallen asleep with its head on her shoulder. It was the most adorable thing. I wanted to kiss her. The Oracle, that is. The puppy, I wished we had left upstairs with some food and water.

"I thought you came along to help us," I said.

She pointed at Lucifer and, apparently still mad at him, said, "According to Bright Eyes there, you don't need my help. Your god is going to take care of you. I just came to escape the slow suffocation my life was becoming."

"Brawk! You ran away from your responsibilities. What a surprise."

"If I want any beak out of you, Dad, I'll pull your tail. You're one to talk about running away."

Timbers flapped his wings in agitation, smacking me in the cheek. "Brawk! I...I..."

"Everyone, stop it," I said. "If you two are going to argue the whole way, you can leave now, and I'll figure this out myself. In fact, we all need to stop arguing." I stared at Raith, but he just returned my gaze with his watery eyes, giving no indication of agreement. "If we're going to do this, we must do it together. I haven't come this far to be stopped now. Pimple has to pay for what he's done, and I need your help to do it."

My speech had some effect on Raith. "Who are you, and what have you done with my brother?"

I tried to ignore him, but his words struck something in me. Who was I, indeed? I still wanted nothing more than to go home, but I knew that couldn't happen until I faced Pimple. I had no illusions about the outcome. I would try, and they would someday sing songs about my ineptitude. Songs I likely wouldn't be around to hear. But if I could distract the brat, maybe Lucifer, who was competent with a sword, could do something effective, like decapitate him or stab him in the gut. I knew demigods could feel pain. After all, I was one, and stubbing my toe made me cry like a baby.

But I couldn't confront my nemesis if I didn't reach him, and to do that, I needed everyone's help. I stared at the circle on the floor. Nothing gave itself away. No glowing vortices, no runes traced in silver, none of the things that trumpeted such magical devices.

After a minute with nothing coming to me, I looked at the others. "Anyone?"

They all shook their heads.

"You need my help, don't you?" the Oracle said.

I looked at her. Her hands rested on her cocked hips, and she had a smug smile, her default expression when she was right. I nodded.

"Step on the circle."

"And?"

"Step on the circle."

I stepped on the circle.

And found myself standing alone in another room. I stumbled, hands out to keep from falling, even though I hadn't felt a drop or any sense of motion.

After getting over my "what the hell" moment, I studied the room. It gave off dusky light, a faint orange hue tinged with pink, despite no visible source. It was the kind of color I tried with no success to duplicate in my paintings.

The walls, instead of being solid stone, roiled like bubbling tar, and the room had much the same smell. The walls rocked, or the floor swayed; I couldn't tell which, but it dizzied me. I closed my eyes, and the vertigo stopped. I hoped I didn't have to walk through this fiasco with my eyes closed. It would make it difficult to fight.

I heard a strange sound, like a dog coughing, followed by Elder saying, "Well, that was easy. Great Ubel, I think I'm going to be sick."

"Close your eyes," I said. "It helps."

After several more coughs and no one bringing up lunch, everyone stood in the room. I opened my eyes and focused on staring at people instead of the walls. It helped. "I could have figured that out," I told the Oracle.

"Yeah, but how long would it have taken you?" she smugged. She pointed at a door I hadn't noticed and added, "We go through there. Fifth door on the right."

"I think I can manage that."

She smiled, and my heart flopped. I could tell she was warming up to me.

"You taking bets?" she said.

I frowned. She was pretty, but it dawned on me that she might not be a particularly nice person. I pushed open the door and prepared to walk through.

The room was upside down. I could tell because the small chandeliers that lined the hall stood on chains and stuck up from the floor like stalagmites. Each held ten candles that rested in them upside down, but the flames burned as if natural law had taken a holiday. The doors were set closer to the top of the room than the bottom, and the whole thing screamed topsy-turvy.

I looked at the Oracle. "Has this room always been like this?"

"I don't know."

"Is that an 'I'm not going to tell you' I don't know, or an 'I really don't know' I don't know?"

"I'm the Oracle. What do you think?"

"That you're being a real b-" Timbers's talons gripped my shoulder, "beneficent person to help us as much as you have."

"That's what *I* thought, too," she said, thankfully missing what I intended to say. Or, more likely, choosing to ignore it. "But's it's kind of fun," she said. "Mathra, I need some water."

I had almost forgotten about the Oracle's caretaker. She dutifully poured water into a silver cup and handed it over.

"Have you ever considered doing things for yourself?" I asked.

"Absolutely not. Why would I?"

I didn't know how to react to such an attitude, so I decided to move on. After all, Pimple was waiting. And since he knew I was coming, he was doubtless getting impatient. I walked down the hall, followed by everyone else. The walls still had the boiling tar look to them, and as I walked, I glimpsed objects moving through the darkness, things that had the whiff of nightmare about them. I considered asking the Oracle but decided I didn't really want to know.

Raith was either more curious or wanted to hear the Oracle speak. "What are those?"

"You don't want to know," the Oracle said. "And don't think about them; that draws their attention."

"Great," Raith said. "How am I supposed to *not* think about them now."

Something significant bumped the wall, giving off the sound of a bird hitting a pane of glass. I'd heard that enough at the church back home to recognize it. But this was no bird, and despite my best efforts, I was far from home.

The Oracle sighed, a petite sound of frustration. "Think about this instead." She leaned over and kissed him for ten seconds, full on the lips.

That did the trick. I completely forgot about the hall, the things beyond it, and everything else. All I could envision was my brother...no, half-brother, being kissed by the most beautiful creature for five hundred miles. The stunned, flushed look on Raith's face made me want to punch him. It wasn't fair. I was the good-looking one. I was the smart one. I was the demigod.

Maybe I misjudged you. You might not be so bad after all, a voice said. Pimple, inside my head. I blinked. What happened? Had I been thinking about punching Raith, the only person who ever liked me until I met Rakin? The idea of physically assaulting Raith had never seriously entered my conscience in all the arguments we had ever had. Shame washed over me. Something about this place, this quest, was changing me. I didn't know what, but we needed to keep moving before it dug deeper and made me homicidal.

I marched down to the fifth door on the right and studied it. It looked like all the others, wooden with a round metal handle. Nothing to mark it as special. But it was the one the Oracle said. I reached out to open it, stretching to grab the knob.

I stopped and looked at the Oracle. "You said fifth door on the right?"

"Yes."

"Did you mean if the hall was right side up or upside down?"

She looked confused. "I didn't get it that clear. I only got a wooden sign that said, 'fifth door on the right.'"

A voice giggled in my head.

Shut up, I snarled. I studied both doors. Nothing different about them. A fifty-fifty chance. I reached for the knob again.

"And a second sign that said, 'dire consequences if the wrong door is chosen.'"

I stared at her again. I doubted she meant going through the wrong door would take us back to Captain Timbers's ship. "Gee, I'm glad you decided to share that little tidbit."

"Brawk! I told you she loves her drama."

"So which door do we go through?"

"I don't know," the Oracle said.

"You should consider having that embroidered into a tunic," I told her.

"I can help," she snapped, "but you must ask the right question."

"So, what's the right question?"

"I can't tell you."

I had heard the expression numerous times before and thought it hyperbole, but for the first time ever, I considered pulling out my own hair in frustration.

Elder stepped up. "I think I've got this one." He looked at the Oracle and smiled. He had gotten back some of his color and vigor since leaving the ship. The lack of burdensome confessions had done him good. He pointed to the door on the left, which would have been the right, or correct, door in a room that obeyed proper construction techniques. "What will happen to us if we go through that door?"

The Oracle stared at the door and put her hands on her temples. Her brow bunched in concentration as her eyes narrowed. Her beauty glowed. And Raith gazed upon her like Pony gazed upon Justice. Jealousy tweaked me, but not as bad as earlier. In a surprisingly short time, I realized that while the Oracle was *a* girl, she might not be *my* girl. She reminded me of the swamp salamanders back home. Beautiful and regal, but if you got too close, they spit poison in your eye.

After thirty seconds or so, the Oracle had offered nothing. She looked at Mathra. "I need help."

Mathra nodded, removed her backpack, and took a silver bottle topped with an odd round button. She put the bottle near the Oracle's face and pushed the button. It gave off a *psssttt* sound and a mist drifted across the Oracle. I caught a familiar smell.

"What is that?" I asked.

"Quiet," the Oracle said. Her pupils grew wide, and her hands floated as if air pockets held them aloft. "I'm divining." She held her hands to the door, and her voice took on the lilting tones she had before her audience, with a tad less pompousness. "Through that door lies death. The destruction of all in roaring fire, freezing wind, and slicing blades. Blood, guts, and utter annihilation lie but one foot through yon portal. Step in there, and you're screwed."

The Oracle's hands dropped, her pupils ceased imitating marbles, and she looked at me.

"Can't fault your specificity," I said. "The other door it is." I walked toward the door.

"I shall open it," Lucifer said. "It is my job to protect you."

It was indeed. I magnanimously waved toward the door, allowing him to do his duty.

Nodding, he twisted the knob and pushed open the door.

And came face to face with the Guardian of the East Hallway.

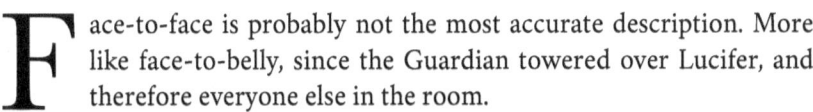

22

Face-to-face is probably not the most accurate description. More like face-to-belly, since the Guardian towered over Lucifer, and therefore everyone else in the room.

It was a snake of some sort, at least thirty feet long, its body as thick as two of me, with a head the size of a wagon. Iridescent red scales covered its bottom, gradating to black on its back. It had reared up and glared down on us with eyes of black that promised pain, death, and slow digestion inside its gut.

Looking back, I can relay all of this. At the time, my thought process was more like, *sn- wha-? Gah!* The last happened as the creature, in a blur, arched over Lucifer and aimed for me, mouth open, fangs dripping green ichor. I froze and knew this was it. Forget confronting Pimple; I wasn't going to make it past the first obstacle.

The world tilted as something slammed into my side, and the floor greeted me, followed by whoever had pushed me landing on me. I said *oof* or something similar as the ability to breath abandoned me.

I heard shouting, drawn weapons, loud squawks, and furious wing flapping. There was a *thump*, followed by an angry hiss, like a kettle long past boiling. Rakin rolled off my chest, and I could breathe even though it hurt. The creature, which I now recognized as the giant snake I described earlier, turned to me. The floor had cracked where its nose hit, leaving a splotch of blood. Dust-coated crimson covered its snout. It reared back for another strike. Rakin lay stunned, having taken the brunt of our collision. He couldn't save me a second time.

"Go away," I screamed, voice high-pitched enough to shatter goblets. Without conscious thought, I extended my arm, three fingers pointing toward the creature. A bolt of lightning forked from each finger and arced toward the snake. Two of them missed, obliterating pieces of the ceiling and creating a storm of dust. The third bolt hit the monster square in the throat, or what passed for a throat. It staggered back and hissed.

That's my boy, my father said.

"I don't think ssssoooo," Pimple said, his voice coming through the snake. Its yellow eyes had turned blue and glittered with malevolent, bratty intelligence.

"Oh, that's not fair," I said.

"Too bad." He flicked his two-foot-long forked tongue at me. "Time for you to d-urrghhh!" He whipped his head around to face Lucifer, who had stabbed the creature in the side with *Heathensmasher*. Thick blood poured from the wound. The thing's tail swung and caught the Paladin in the chest. He flew backward and slammed into the wall, his grip on his sword lost. Another hiss, and Pimple reared back.

"I don't think so," I threw back at my brother. This time, I pointed with only one finger.

Faster than I could blink, Pimple struck, mouth open, ready to engulf Lucifer in one bite. He moved so fast I would never hit his head.

Which was why I hadn't bothered to aim for it. I aimed at something more stationary, something a famous magician had proven decades ago allowed lightning to travel through it.

I aimed at *Heathensmasher*, an object made of forged metal.

Snakes are fast; lightning is faster. The bolt arced true and struck the sword. I winced as some of it washed back on me, standing my hair on end, but the blue crackled up the blade and into the snake's side. Its open mouth froze a foot from Lucifer who, to his credit, had his fists up, ready to fight even though he lay sprawled on the floor. The creature vibrated, the air sizzled, and the smell of burning meat filled the room. For ten seconds, no one moved, fascinated as smoke wisped from the reptile's side and leaked through its nostrils.

"Son of a bitch," Pimple said.

The snake exploded.

Gobbets of sizzled serpent flew in all directions. I ducked and covered my head but still got pelted by several chunks. Someone cried out in disgust, and I realized it was me.

When it was over, I stood and gaped at the destruction. The body lay in three separate pieces, the head and middle in the larger room, the tail in the hallway. Large sections of the creature lay in pieces spread throughout the room, blood coated the walls like an artist with a paintbrush and seizures paid a visit. It was the most disgusting thing I had ever witnessed.

"Remind me not to make you mad," Elder said. His hands shook, and he looked ready to let his lunch fly, but he held himself together. I didn't know which scared him more, the snake or me.

Most everyone avoided the worst of the monster's demise, only getting spattered by blood drops and perhaps a random gobbet of meat. Lucifer, however, took the full brunt and lay against the wall, unconscious and coated in more fluids than I cared to consider. Raith, his face the color of curdled milk and his eyes runny as egg yolks, knelt by his knight and wiped Lucifer's face with a cloth and water from the skin in his backpack.

"You might want to save that," the Oracle said. "I don't think there are any streams down here."

"Then I'll be thirsty," Raith said.

"Is everyone okay?" Considering the last time I used my powers, I would hate to think a rib bone punctured through someone, and I hadn't noticed. But a chorus of "yes" confirmed that, despite the sudden abattoir ambiance of the room, no one had been injured.

"Brawk! I shudder at what the next beast will be like." Either through luck or agility, Timbers had wholly avoided the gore storm.

"We'll be prepared for the next one," I said. I looked at Rakin, who stood near me. Blood speckled his white squire's uniform, giving him the air of a bizarre art experiment. "You saved my life. Thank you."

He shrugged. "That's what squires do."

I could have hugged him for his humility.

"I have slain the beast," said his polar opposite from across the room.

"Actually," the Oracle said, "Briar slew the creature. Quite well." Her sharp eyes bore on me. "You should have been less messy about it, though. It's going to take Mathra hours to get these stains out."

I couldn't even think of a comeback for that, so I turned to Lucifer, who stood and wiped chunky bits off his armor. Raith had grabbed

Heathensmasher and dragged it to his master, struggling the whole way. Lucifer saw me. "Is it true you destroyed the creature?"

I heard the hope in his tone that I hadn't. That he had been the one to bring the beast low. How he figured his one sword stroke had turned the snake into a vivisected triplet, I had no idea.

I couldn't lie to him. "It's true."

But I could make him feel good. "It was quite clever of you to jam your sword into its side so I could use it to send my electricity into him. I don't think I could have done it without you."

That last statement was entirely true. My first bolt had done little more than annoy the snake. And with Pimple possessing the creature, I wouldn't have had many more shots. Lucifer had distracted the monster and possibly saved us all.

My words had the desired effect. He puffed out his chest and held up his chin. "I'm pleased you saw the whole of my plan. But you are the Divine One; I shouldn't expect less."

I doubt he had considered strategy that far ahead, but if he wanted to believe it, I wouldn't stop him.

We finished cleaning up. We used the water as sparingly as possible, so we still looked like a traveling butcher troupe as we walked into the east hallway and continued our trek. Thankfully, the builders constructed this corridor in the proper orientation.

"How long will we be down here?" I asked the Oracle. We could start to stink if we had to wear these clothes too long.

"Until you confront Ublek and defeat him or lose."

"I know that but how long—forget it."

We walked down the hallway with the same type of walls as the previous corridor. Again, I caught glimpses of creatures only a madman could conjure, and I did my best to ignore them, thinking instead of painting pictures of the beach.

A shuddering thump against the wall made me squeak like a mouse. I saw rows upon rows of teeth, white and sharp, each long as my arm, grinning from a mouth below purple skin and red eyes. I didn't see any more before it moved away, leaving an imprint of its molars in the wall. "What *was* that?" I said.

"Who's thinking about them?"

"I'm sorry," Raith said. "I can't help it. I'm scared." He looked at the Oracle, his face full of enough hope to fill a treasure chest. "Maybe if you kiss me again?"

The Oracle walked up and puckered her lips. Raith leaned in to receive the kiss. She slapped him.

"Concentrate on the pain," she said.

"I liked the kiss better."

It occurred to me I could help. I could read their emotions. I could even do it with Raith, though I couldn't get his thoughts and wouldn't even if I could.

If I could sense people's thoughts, it stood to reason that I could control them. Actually, it made no logical sense, but some inner feeling told me I could do it anyway. "Everyone, look at me."

They did.

"I want you all to think about something other than the creatures just outside who could rend us to pieces."

Raith let out a squeal, and suddenly there were four sets of teeth, three yellow claws, and a mauve tentacle beating at the wall. I wasn't sure, but I think I heard chanting, too.

"Raith!"

His pale face focused on me.

"Think about your duties to Lucifer. Think about what you need to do once we get out of here."

He nodded. "The horses will need to be groomed."

"Among other things," Lucifer said.

"All of you, think about once we leave this place."

That's a big assumption.

Get out of my head, brat. I mentally slapped him and almost fell over when he fled with a squeal. I smiled. Maybe I stood a chance if we could get through without the creature's—

Something roared outside the hallway. Time to follow my own advice. "Think about what you will do when we are far away from here, and this is all something we're telling our grandchildren. Now, let's go."

I didn't have the luxury of dreaming about what I would do once this was over. I had to determine the best way to confront Pim—no, Ublek. I refused to fight someone with a stupid nickname—and remain intact and breathing.

Not knowing the extent of his powers or what he had at his disposal, I had no idea.

So, to occupy my mind, I counted footsteps. I reached a hundred and two before we arrived at the first door on the left. My mental push seemed to be working, since none of the Chaos creatures approached the walls again. I wondered how much I could do with my newly discovered ability. I pondered what other powers I had waiting to be unleashed. If only I had a father who explained all this to me before getting kidnapped. Or even a mother who had dropped a hint or two that I might have more going for me than the average peasant.

We went another hundred and two steps before we hit the second door on the left. Considering it was in the Outer Chaos, the hallway was amazingly consistent. We reached the third doorway after a hundred and four steps, but I suspected that was a miscount. The door looked the same as every other door we had seen. If it weren't for the wretched denizens clamoring to destroy all life, Chaos would be a boring place.

I looked at the Oracle. "Do I even dare ask?"

She smiled. "You want to know what's on the other side of the door."

"Yes. And don't you dare say the Eykantcey Sentinel of the West Hall-way. I know that part already."

"Then you know everything I know. I made the Grand Pronounce-ment, and that's all I get."

"But what about back there?" I pointed down the hallway. "You told us what to expect."

"I told you what to expect if you went through the wrong door. I can see things that I haven't already predicted." She looked across the hallway. "Sorry, no other door for me to tell you about."

"Because that's exactly what I want to know, what's behind a door I'm not planning to open."

"You two bicker like lovesick school children," Lucifer said. "Let us open the door and be done with it."

"Yeah, that worked so well last time," I said. "And we're not lovesick. Well," I pointed at Raith, "maybe he is."

"He's not lovesick," the Oracle said. "He's just hor—"

"I think my master is right," Raith said, his face the color of a ripe cherry. "We should go through the door. In fact, I'll take the lead." He placed his hand on the doorknob.

"Wait," I said as I ran and pulled Raith's hand away. Epiphany had bounced on my brain and grabbed it with sharp claws. I lowered my voice. "The Sentinel inside is blind, so if we can be quiet, we may get by him."

"How do you know he's blind?" Elder asked.

I looked at the Oracle. "You were naming the creatures in the tongue of Ancient Obveus, weren't you?"

"Aren't you the clever one, figuring that out after only a whole day."

Elder nodded, the lantern suddenly shining on him too. "Of course."

Raith smiled, and I knew he had it too.

"Perhaps," Lucifer said, "you should explain it to these others here who are not versed in the Obveus tongue."

I looked at Rakin, perhaps the only other person in the room who might not be familiar with the language. "Hispit is the Ancient Obveus word for snake, and our first challenge was a giant snake."

"Yeah, I know," Rakin said. "And Eykantcey translates to 'blind.'"

"Exactly." I turned at Lucifer.

It took him thirty seconds, but he finally nodded. "I see."

"But the creature doesn't," Rakin said with a snicker.

"So maybe we can sneak by him," I said.

"If he is blind, we don't have to sneak," Lucifer said. "We will just force our way past him."

"I wouldn't do that," I said.

"Of course, you wouldn't."

"No, he's right," Raith told his master. "I read about the creature in the church library. It can't see, but it can still fight."

"How?" Lucifer asked.

Raith shrugged. "The book wasn't specific, but in the story it killed four men who tried to steal a goat."

Lucifer gave a martyr's sigh. "As you wish, Divine One, we shall try and *sneak*." He almost spit the word. I would have thought he would want a reprieve after the last butt-kicking, but paladins aren't known for their ability to accept defeat.

"You can open it," I told Lucifer, pointing at the door. "In case something goes wrong."

That made him happy. He gripped the handle, and cracked the door an inch.

A bell sounded through the hallway, loud as if it sat on top of my head. Once again, I amazed myself with my bladder control.

"Who's there?" a voice on the other side said. It was a deep, loud voice. A voice that promised a thick black beard and muscles able to wring necks. None of us spoke, and the voice continued. "There's no sense in trying to pretend you're not there. I can hear you breathing. And the smell is enough to knock me off my chair. Did you bathe in snake blood?"

"Sort of," I said, bending to his logic. He knew we were here. Now it was either fight or talk our way out of it. "Open the door," I said.

Lucifer obeyed without question, either because I was the Divine One or because he wanted to fight a blind foe, which seemed rude, but what did I know?

The room extended fifty feet to a side, larger than the last one. The walls here were solid stone, a pleasant surprise. They were bare, which made sense, and they didn't bubble and boil. Again, I saw no light source, but I could see in the room as if lanterns lit it. Pondering this paradox distracted me, so I put it aside, realizing I could use it when we inevitably returned to the Roiling Hall of Impending Chaotic Death.

A large bed sat in one corner, a round hole cored the floor in another, and in the third corner, the one farthest from us, a pen constructed of wood held ten of the most beautiful goats I'd ever seen.

I realize "beautiful goats" is not an expression one usually hears. It's one I never considered until that day. They were average size, with the things you expect goats to have, like horns and hooves, but their coats gleamed like sunshine and summer had been woven into them. Their eyes radiated friendliness, and they made soft bleats so adorable the mews of kittens sounded like a donkey's bray in comparison.

They weren't your average ungulates.

On the other hand, their owner could have destroyed crocodiles in an ugly competition. He was short, maybe four feet tall, with a hunched back, hair the color of dead grass, and a bulbous nose resting under two eyes that bulged out like marbles stuck in the mud. His skin, what little I could see through the spotted tan robe he wore, was a mottled brown with coarse greenish hair. His eyes had once been black, but a spiderweb coat of gray covered them. He sat in a crude wooden rocking chair near the pen. A doorway rested behind him.

As we walked in, he lifted his head and gave several loud sniffs, like a dog with a sinus problem. "Eight of you. That's a lucky number."

"It's a manageable number," I said, thankful we had left behind the rest. We would have looked like a parade moving down the halls, and while they might have been handy dealing with the snake, they could just as easily have gotten in their own way.

"Why are you here? My goats are not for sale."

"How do you feed them?" Raith asked. I'm not sure why that question popped into his head.

The creature smiled and walked to the pen, leisurely as if he could see. He extended his arm into the pen, and one of the goats took dainty nibbles from the hair on his arms, which I now realized resembled blades of grass. In fact, the Sentinel looked like a lawn come to life. "You've come to ask me feeding tips?"

"No," I said. "We need to find Ubel, who has been kidnapped."

"Ubel has been kidnapped? That's horrible," the lawn man said. "By all means, you must go and save him."

"Thank you," I said and walked toward the man.

He stood up. "Unfortunately, I can't let you through this door."

I stopped. "Why not?"

"I'm the Sentinel of the West Hallway. It's my job to stop you."

"I figured it was your job to tend these beautiful goats."

"No, that's more of a hobby. Something to pass the time while I wait. People don't come down here often. In fact, it's only happened once before. Four nice fellows showed up, but I had to explain that my goats weren't for sale. I had to explain quite firmly."

I guess the church book Raith read got something right. Although I didn't know how anyone found out if all the men were dead. I looked at the Oracle, who gave me a smile she probably thought was enigmatic, but which I read as, "one of my ancestors passed the story along to keep people away."

"Good sir," Lucifer said, "we needs must pass through the door. In what way may we achieve this goal? I do not wish to fight you."

"No, you don't," the Sentinel said. He grinned wide, revealing teeth that looked like sharpened tree branches. "You may pass if you purchase one of my goats."

"You said your goats aren't for sale," I said.

"They aren't. Quite a conundrum, isn't it?"

Lucifer took a step toward the man. "While I admire your anti-merchant philosophy, we must go through that door. Step aside, good sir."

"Not going to happen."

"Very well." Lucifer drew *Heathensmasher*.

Before I could pull another breath, one of the goats, with a melodious bellow, leaped the pen and smashed headlong into Lucifer. Its horns and the Paladin's skull collided with the sound of boulders crashing. Lucifer dropped, his sword sliding from his hand. The goat landed, walked up to the unconscious Paladin, licked his face once, and then laid down next to him.

"Awww," the Oracle said.

I wheeled on her. "Feel free to offer up any Oracular wisdom."

"It would be wise for you to not talk to me in that tone. How's that?"

I growled in frustration and looked at Raith. "She's all yours."

He tilted his head in confusion, and I didn't blame him. I turned to everyone else. "I'm open to suggestions."

"We could turn back," Rakin said. Three days ago, those words would have been music, and I would have run through the door before Rakin could finish the sentence. But I couldn't do that now. I had come this far, despite my best efforts. Fate wanted this, so I had to accept it.

Of course, Fate could feel free to lend a hand.

Another goat jumped the pen. I flinched, fearful it was about to take me out. Instead, it walked up to me. Its coat glimmered white and brown, and it walked with a grace courtesans could only dream about. It sniffed my hand, licked it, made a sharp bleat, and fell over dead.

"Billy," the Sentinel cried.

"I didn't do anything," I shouted, cringing back. Rather than charging me or sending the other goats to pummel me, the Sentinel's ugly face turned thoughtful.

"Who are you?" he asked.

"Briar."

"What is your father's name?"

"That's a tricky one," I said. "You want the guy who raised me or the guy who cuckolded the guy who raised me?"

The Sentinel stomped a foot. "What is your surname?"

"Patch."

The Sentinel looked at—well, not looked at, but turned his head toward—the Oracle. "He is Briar Patch, the killer of goats, just as you foretold?"

"He is," the Oracle said.

"Wait a minute," I said. "You knew I was going to kill this goat? And how did I kill it anyway?" I certainly hadn't meant to kill it.

"I knew you had the potential. The divine power running through you is too much for mortal animals to withstand. Unless you will it to not happen, any animal that has contact with you will suffer a heart attack from awe."

"What about my horse?"

"Saddle and gloves."

I thought about it. She was right. I had never touched the horse. Raith groomed him, and anytime I rode him, I had riding gloves—or wet socks—on my hands. I had never bothered to pet the horse since I had no reason to do so. I recalled an incident when I was much younger and tried to pet one of the village cats. It had died when I touched it. I cried and ran away, horrified and confused. No one saw it happen, and I never told anyone. But every cat in the village hissed at me from that day forward. Cats are smart. Smarter than goats, apparently. "Why didn't you warn me this might happen?"

The Oracle stared at me as if I didn't have the capacity to count. "I can only predict; I can't interfere."

I clenched my fists and shook a second, letting out a shrill of irritation. "Gods and Oracles have some of the stupidest rules. If I ran the cosmos, things would be so much different."

"Funny you should say that."

"What?" I asked, taken aback.

"What?" the Oracle repeated, all innocence and pigtails.

"You may pass," the Sentinel said. "Please just don't kill any more of my goats." He skulked over to the door and threw it open. Tears dabbed his cheeks. "They're innocent creatures."

I felt bad for him and for the goat.

"It had to happen," the Oracle whispered into my ear as if she could read my thoughts. For all I knew, she could, which sent a chill up my spine, and not the good kind like her breath in my ear gave me. It was a very confusing moment. "It was the goat or us."

"I could have just threatened him," I said, looking at the poor dead goat.

She shook her head. "He wouldn't have believed it. Some people have to have Fate slap them in the face before they listen."

I could relate.

"We should go," she continued, "before he changes his mind and decides to take revenge."

I nodded, although the Sentinel wept like a baby and seemed to have forgotten we were there.

The Oracle walked over to him with the puppy, who had slept through everything, and sat it in the man's lap. "This can't replace Billy, but hopefully, it helps."

So, she could be a caring person. Who would have guessed?

Lucifer was still unconscious, and it took four of us to pick him up and carry his armored form through the doorway. Mathra threw *Heathensmasher* over her shoulder like she might a bundle of cotton and followed the Oracle.

"I have to do more strength work," Raith muttered when he saw Mathra.

"I'm sorry," I said to the Sentinel as we left, but he didn't acknowledge me.

Mathra closed the door, and we spotted an open room fifty feet down the chaos corridor.

"Is that where the Slobbering Beast of Chaos is?" I asked, huffing under Lucifer's weight. "I'm sure we'll need Lucifer to face that."

The Oracle said nothing.

"It can't be," Elder said. "There's no Great Golden Door."

"Glad to see someone paid attention," the Oracle said.

I've never wanted to kick a girl until then.

We struggled to the hallway and tried to set Lucifer down gently. It would have worked better had he not slipped out of Elder's grasp and landed on his head before crashing down with a clang of metal. He groaned, and his eyes fluttered open.

"It's happened before," I assured everybody. "I don't think there can be much more damage done."

"I could use that refreshment," Raith said, sweat coursing down his rosy face.

"What refreshment?" I asked as Elder helped Lucifer sit up.

"Did you even listen to my pronouncement?" the Oracle asked. "Mathra, refreshments, please."

"Yes, Prescient One." She opened her backpack and pulled out a flask long and thick as my arm, followed by eight large goblets, then a variety of finger sandwiches and a pudding. I had no idea where she kept it all.

Drinks were poured and sandwiches handed out. I took a sip. It was the strawberry concoction I had drank earlier. That first sip was delicious.

"Enjoy this," the Oracle said. "After this is the Slobbering Beast of Chaos. You're going to need your strength."

And the rest soured as soon as it hit my stomach.

23

You sure you're okay?" I asked Lucifer. We stood before the Great Golden Door, so named because it was large and coated in gold...paint. Not real gold, which would have eventually earned it the name the Door With Great Gouges In It. Even though it was only paint, it must have fooled someone since the dull brown wood showed through at various spots. The door lived up to the "Great" part of its name, standing twelve feet high and six wide.

"I'm fine," Lucifer said, even as he shook his head to uncross his eyes. "It takes more than a goat to knock the sense from me."

"I wonder if a whole herd could knock some *into* you," Elder said. "Not every problem needs to be solved with a sword."

"I was doing what I felt necessary to protect Holy Briar."

"And I appreciate it," I said, "but Brother Elder has a point. I feel we could have talked our way out of that one."

"Or you could have just killed some more goats," the Oracle said with a smirk.

"You're not helping," I said.

"I might need to sit a few more moments," Lucifer said as he leaned against the door and slid to the floor.

After our refreshment break, Lucifer had recovered with nothing more than a headache. But as we walked down the hall searching for the last door, he had begun weaving like a sailor departing a tavern. We stopped and let him rest, then continued.

We did that five times in the thousand feet it took to reach the door.

Timbers leapt off my shoulder and landed on Lucifer's knee. "Brawk! Look at me."

"Which one of you?" Lucifer said.

"This isn't good," Timbers said. "Follow my movements."

The parrot jumped from the Paladin's right knee to his left, then back. He did it four more times. Lucifer's head followed about a second behind each movement. On the fifth time, Lucifer said, "Please stop. I'm going to be ill."

"Brawk! Close your eyes and rest." With a violent flap of wings, Timbers took off and landed on my shoulder. "I fear he may have a concussion."

"Become a doctor in your spare time, did you?" the Oracle asked.

"Brawk! I've seen enough men get hit by debris to know a concussion when I see it."

"What does that mean?" I asked.

"It means he needs to rest. And he shouldn't fight."

I started laughing. I couldn't help it. "Fate has a wicked sense of humor," I said between fits of giggles. "We're about to face the Slobbering Beast of Chaos, a name that practically screams 'make sure you have swords,' and our main fighter has a headache with delusions of grandeur."

"I can fight," Lucifer said, struggling to stand back up. "Ubel will give me strength." He slid back down.

"Ubel isn't in a position to give a fish water," I said. I kicked at the ground. "We have to turn back. We have to wait until Lucifer is better."

Elder looked at the Oracle. "What will happen if we wait past today?"

Without being asked, Mathra took the metallic cylinder from her backpack and sprayed the strange but delicious smelling liquid into the Oracle's face. The Oracle closed her eyes.

"I see a pockmarked face rising in glory. I see the world split asunder. I see the gods reveling in unfettered debauchery and the people crying in despair. I see a bad moon rising; I see trouble on the way." She opened her eyes. "There'll be some earthquakes and lightning too. It won't be good."

"So I gathered," I said. "What are we going to do?"

"I can fight," Raith said.

"What are you talking about?" I asked. "You can't even lift the sword."

"No," Raith said, his cheeks red as he stared at the floor. "But I have this." He pulled out his dagger, five inches of fine-tempered steel. Every squire had one. For cutting meat and rope, there was no equal. Against an unarmored opponent, it stood a reasonable chance in the right hands. Against something called the Slobbering Beast of Chaos, I expected it to be as helpful as a toothpick.

"Look, you can't—"

Raith cut his eyes toward the Oracle and then back at me. Good grief, life and death are on the line, and he wanted to impress a girl. Well, I *had* told him he could have her.

"—do better than a fine weapon like that. That will certainly help." I didn't offer my full thought, which was *help get us killed.*

"I have one, too," Rakin said as he pulled out his dagger.

"That's all well and good," Elder said, walking up to me. "But I think it's going to be you who has to fight."

"Yeah, because I did so well against the sailor." I winced as I remembered that thrashing. And that was just fists. I pictured the Beast with gnashing fangs, talons long as my arm, and a slimy tongue. "I'm not a fighter."

Elder grabbed my arm and held my hand in front of my face. "I think this says different. Lucifer is a great fighter, but he can't conjure sparks. He can't destroy ships. You are fated to meet your half-brother in single combat. You will beat the Slobbering Beast of Chaos. You have to, or the world is screwed."

"Wow, if that's your idea of a rousing pre-battle speech, you suck," I said. "But you have a point. I can shoot lightning." I looked at the Oracle. "Earthquakes and lightning?"

"Bad times today," she confirmed.

I sighed at the inevitability. "Okay. Lucifer, can you stand?"

"Yes."

He could, with Raith and Rakin helping him.

"I will fight for you," the Paladin insisted.

"You will guard the rear," I said. "You will not attack; you will only defend. You will protect the lady and the Oracle. That is my Holy Command."

"As say you," Lucifer said. "I am command … to yours… or something."

I patted him on the shoulder, and he wobbled. "Good man."

I stood in front of the door, Raith on one side, Rakin on the other, both with their shiny but pitiful blades ready. I glanced back at Elder, and something occurred to me.

"How come you don't have a staff?"

"What?"

"Don't priests usually carry a quarterstaff?"

"That's monks," he said. "Monks carry a quarterstaff. They also carry vows of chastity and poverty, neither of which appealed much to me, nice as a quarterstaff would be now."

I nodded.

"Briar," Elder said.

"Yes."

"I know you can do this. I have faith in you. I always have."

It was a nice sentiment, somewhat undercut when he walked back ten feet to stand behind Lucifer.

With a wry grin that hopefully hid the fact my nerves were tight as an over-tuned lute, I turned to the door and thought about lightning. Sparks crackled in my fingers. I put my hand on the doorknob. "Here we go."

I turned the knob and pushed the door open.

Awwoooffffff.

The howl of the beast echoed through the room, This time my bladder control held. I'd like to think it was because I was getting braver, but more likely, I was just empty. Before I could do much of anything else, I heard the thud of something running hard. A four-legged shadow, large and black as death's coal chute, launched toward me. I tried to backpedal, but it came too fast. It hit me full force, and I fell on my back. Its hot breath washed across my face, redolent with the odor of beef, and I felt my death in the rasping of its gritty tongue. It licked me, no doubt softening my skin.

It continued to lick me, and I felt something thump back and forth between my raised knees.

"Stop it; that tickles," I said.

"It's just a dog," Raith said.

I opened my eyes, which had closed against my will, and saw Raith was right. Black, wooly, and scary large, it was nothing more than a dog. An incredibly friendly one, judging by its attempt to spit-shine my face and its hairy, wagging tail.

"Don't lick me, you stupid dog; you'll die." I refrained from pushing at him, not wanting to kill him like I did the poor goat.

"I think if he was going to die, he would have already," the Oracle said.

"I'm betting something called the Slobbering Beast of Chaos isn't a normal dog," Elder added. "Nothing else here has been normal."

My face felt like I had been caught in a rainstorm. "Okay, boy, that's enough, get off." I just assumed it was a boy since I hadn't seen the evidence either way.

The dog rolled off me, sat on its haunches, and stared at me, tail dusting the floor and tongue hanging. Saliva dripped from its mouth and puddled on the floor.

"You got the slobbering part right," I told the Oracle as I wiped my face, soaking the sleeve of my tunic. "But I'm not seeing the whole Beast of Chaos thing."

I stood up. "It certainly doesn't look like anything we've seen battering the walls." I checked to make sure the room's walls remained solid. I would hate the irony of avoiding thinking about the creatures all the way here only to have them swarm me because I talked about them.

"My prophecies are never wrong, just open to various interpretations. Have you mastered him yet?"

I looked down at the dog. It wasn't much of a look down since his head came to my chest. His big eyes stared at me. They slowly changed colors, from green to brown to blue and back to green. It was hypnotizing and disturbing.

"Chaos, boy. Is your name Chaos?"

He thumped his tail on the floor, then reached up and scratched his ear with his back leg. I took that for a yes.

"Stand up, boy."

He did. By this point, a little lake of doggie spit had collected below his mouth.

"That's disgusting," the Oracle said.

I shrugged. "Roll over," I told Chaos. He dropped down, rolled one way, paused, and then rolled back. He gazed at me and cocked his head as if to say, *that the toughest you got?*

"Walk on your back legs."

He did, moving with the grace of a furry dancer.

"Play dead."

He instantly fell, hitting the floor so hard I feared he hurt himself and flopped onto his back, legs sticking straight in the air. He turned his head to the side, and his tongue flopped out, touching the floor. It was such a bravura performance Raith and Rakin clapped.

"Come sit next to me."

He jumped up, alive again, and dropped to his haunches to my left and slightly behind me. I looked at the Oracle. "Looks like I control him pretty well."

"Perhaps," the Oracle said, clearly indicating she didn't believe it.

I ignored her. "Let's see if we can find a way out of here and get to the Blazing Pits." I looked at Lucifer. "Feeling any better?"

"I'M FINE," he shouted. "BUT I WISH THAT BELL WOULD STOP RINGING. THAT'S A NICE DOG YOU HAVE."

That answered my question. I had no idea how we would make it past the Pits without his ability. I suspected they wouldn't be quite as easy as the "beast."

"Let's go," I said. As soon as I took a step, Chaos walked in front of me. He caught me at calf height. I flipped over him and landed hard, coming within a red camel hair of busting my head on the floor. My backpack flap opened, and everything spilled out.

"Oh yeah, complete control," the Oracle said.

I stood back up, grumbling, while Rakin and Raith helped gather my spilled supplies. Chaos offered a stupid doggie grin like he had done the most helpful thing ever. "Do that to the enemies, not me. Understand? The enemies."

He shook his head, sending a spray of spittle in every conceivable direction. I ducked to avoid getting soaked. My two helpers weren't quite so lucky.

"Yuck," Rakin said.

"I'll second that," Raith said.

Once we gathered everything, I slung my backpack and walked into the room. We hadn't gone ten feet when I heard, "Whoa," followed by a thud and "ooof." I turned to see Raith on the ground, one leg resting against Chaos.

"This isn't going to work," Raith said.

He was right. We—and by we, I mean I—had to figure out what to do. I couldn't have the dog tripping someone every ten feet. And I had no idea if he would get in someone's way at a crucial moment during a fight. We could leave him behind, but I suspected that wouldn't go well. I was beginning to understand how these things worked. There was a reason he was called the Slobbering Beast of Chaos and not Spot. It was his job to cause problems. It was my job to make him cause problems for me. No, that wasn't quite right. I had to figure out how to make him cause problems *to others* for me.

He sat down beside me again. He obviously understood some of what

I said. He followed my commands well enough. I only needed to get him to follow my intent since I doubted "don't trip us" would stick in his canine brain for long.

Thinking about his brain chimed something in mine. Could I read his thoughts? Could I control them? I had never tried getting an animal's thoughts before. Until recently, I had never tried getting anybody's thoughts. They always came unbidden, but never from an animal. Except for the village cats, who made their feelings well-known.

It was worth a try. The worst that could happen was nothing. I looked at his whirling eyes and tried to see beyond. Mainly to determine if I could reach the thoughts behind them, but also because they made me dizzy.

Can you hear me? I thought. I had no idea how to speak dog, so I had to hope the concepts somehow translated across. *Hello? Anything in there?*

Food?

The thought didn't come to me as a word so much as an image, a bowl overflowing with brown chunks of meat slathered with gravy, but I picked up the meaning.

You want some food?

His floppy ears perked up. *Food?*

I opened my backpack and gave him some links of the summer sausage. He gobbled them down as if the answer to life would be revealed in their consumption.

More food?

Not right now, I thought to him. *In a minute. Do you understand?*

A minute? Yes, it is a measure of time equal to sixty seconds. More food?

That threw me for a moment. This was not a dumb dog. *Do you want to go with us?*

Do you have food?

Yes?

Do you have belly rubs?

I think we could manage that.

Will you throw the ball?

What ball?

He ran across the room, giving us a moment to walk in and see where we stood. It was a plain stone room, not much different than the others we had encountered. The Chaos Planes needed an interior decorator. A stack of blankets with a dog-shaped indention took up one corner. A ten-foot square of grass grew in the middle, with ample evidence it served as a place for Chaos to relieve himself. Another corner had a water dish and an empty food bowl that showed signs of being gnawed upon. Chaos ran to a spot between the bed and bowls and took a sizeable yellow ball into his mouth. He bounded back and dropped the ball, where it bounced twice before resting against my foot.

I picked it up. It was leather, and the outside swam in slobber. *Who is your master?*

He did a funny hop-step thing, like an apoplectic rabbit. *If you will throw the ball and feed me and take me walkies, you are my master.*

Don't you already have a master?

He stopped bouncing, and his tail went between his legs. *Yes, but he does not throw the ball. I do not like the food he brings, and the walkies are non-existent. He is not what I would call a good master. I would, in fact, call him a bad master.*

The dog's sadness engulfed my brain. He only wanted someone to care for him. *Will you be loyal and do what I command?*

I will be loyal to whoever throws the ball and takes—

Yeah, I got all that. I had never owned a pet before. Considering what their fate would have been soon as I touched them, that was a good thing. But Chaos was immune to my awesomeness, which made him just like everyone who knew me, so it would work out fine. *I will do the things you wish. I will be your master.*

He bounded at least two feet off the air. *Oh boy, oh boy, oh boy. Seal the deal. Seal the deal.*

I wasn't sure what he meant, but his deep brown eyes darted from the ball to the other side of the room. I threw the ball.

Yippppeeeeeee! He dashed after it as if it had kidnapped his mother. It bounced once, and he leaped up, snagged it out of the air, and shook it, slinging saliva everywhere. I would seriously have to consider getting him a muzzle with a bucket.

Satisfied he had shaken the life from it, Chaos trotted back over, almost prancing, his head held high. I looked at the Oracle. "There, now I have mastered the Slobbering Beast of Chaos."

"So, it appears you have," she said, but she looked frightened for some reason.

"What's the—"

I stopped when the sound of a thousand cracking bones echoed through the room. Chaos howled and ran behind me. We all flinched at the noise, which sounded like the planet was breaking.

Fissures appeared in the wall opposite us, running in zig-zag patterns from floor to ceiling. Red light broke though.

"This is really happening, right?" Lucifer shouted. I thought it was a stupid question until I realized he wanted to make sure it wasn't a hallucination because of his concussion.

"Yes," I shouted back, "but I really wish it wasn't."

"That makes...all of us," Elder said.

We edged back toward the door, ready to run if chunks of the wall started flying at us. I tripped over Chaos and landed on my butt, but only because he had glued himself to my legs, and I hadn't realized it.

The splintering stopped, and for a few seconds, nothing happened. Nobody moved or spoke. I'm not even sure anyone breathed. I know I didn't.

Then the wall evaporated. That's the only description. Solid stone turned to powder in a blink, like a brick hit by the world's largest hammer. Another blink later, the powder disappeared. It was as if the wall never existed.

The wall's disappearance revealed red and black, flame and rock, sulfur and saltpeter. A cragged landscape of stalagmites, steam, and gouts of fire stood before us, stretching beyond the edge of sight.

"This isn't good," Lucifer said. Master of the self-evident, our Paladin.

So, this was the Blazing Pits the Oracle had mentioned. After meeting the Slobbering Beast, I had hoped the Pits would be two craters with a campfire between them, but this obstacle won the truth in advertising award. "Any idea how far across it is," I asked the Oracle, although I didn't expect her to know.

"About two miles," she said. When I looked askance at her, she said, "I did my own divination. I like being informed."

"So, it's just the information-sharing part you have a problem with," I said. I hoisted my backpack. "Two miles. Thirty, forty-five minutes." I smiled at everyone. "Shouldn't be too bad."

You'd think by now I would know better.

24

The trek across the Pits started well enough if you consider walking through a furnace a good time. Within a hundred feet, the uncomfortably warm air had everyone drenched in sweat. The Oracle still looked beautiful, and her wet clothing clung in distracting ways that I ignored by remembering her personality.

I expected Lucifer to take the worst of it. His metal armor made him a lobster in a pot of boiling water. But it seemed to invigorate him; his eyes looked clearer than when we started. On the other hand, Timbers squawked in misery at the unrelenting heat.

Pant pant pant pant pant.

I had never realized dogs thought of panting as they did it, but you learn something new every day.

After probably three hundred feet, I felt the journey, while wretchedly uncomfortable, was still manageable.

Then the demons attacked.

I call them demons only because they had horns and black skin and breathed fire. Down here, that probably qualified them as someone's pets. They stood three feet tall., with wicked claws splayed at the end of spindly hands. Every part of their bodies was thin, like they had been assembled from burnt twigs.

They sprang upon us, more than I could quickly count, from within the pits, bouncing up like someone had poked them with a pitchfork like the ones they held in their hands. They landed, surrounding us.

Chew toys, Chaos thought as he launched at one, snatched it up in his slobbery jaws, and shook it like a doll that offended his masculinity. His saliva turned to steam and floated up in wispy trails.

"Their skin is hot," I screamed.

"To arms," Lucifer cried as he unsheathed *Heathensmasher*. Habit, I guess, because there were no other Paladins to bear arms. Raith and Rakin drew their daggers. Raith had gone the color of watery milk, and his hand trembled as if the idea of fighting flame demons terrified him.

I should have been terrified, but serenity wafted over me like a spring breeze. I had made it this far; I would make it the rest of the way. Once I reached Pimple, who knew? But I had nothing to fear from these puny creatures.

This bliss lasted until one of them sprang from nowhere and latched on to my leg.

"Gahhh," I shouted in a very not calm fashion. The thing sank its teeth into my leg, making any previous pain, from my drunken headache to the pounding by the sailor, feel like a sting from an anemic mosquito. "Excruciating" comes close but throw in "agonizing" on top of "torturous," and you're getting closer.

Suffice it to say, it hurt like hell.

It also angered me. I was destined to confront Pimple, and this small, toothy creature stood in my way.

"Get off me," I shouted, thrusting my hand at it. A wave of force charged from my brain like a maddened bull and stormed down my arm. It struck the creature, who flew off me, shredding my leg along the way, and slammed into a giant stalagmite. Rock beats flesh every time. I heard several cracks as the creature tried to bend around the rock in ways never intended. It bounced back, landed on the ground, and didn't move.

I stared at my hand, impressed. Unfortunately, no one else saw it, engaged with keeping themselves alive. Chaos joyfully lived up to his namesake, snatching and tossing the creatures around like the sticks they resembled. I could hear *so many chew toys* deliriously repeating in the back of my mind. He was having fun.

He was the only one. Elder, the Oracle, and Mathra had formed a back-to-back triangle, backpacks in front of them serving as the worst shields ever. Lucifer laid to and fro, like Paladins do, cleaving the creatures in half and lopping off heads. Raith and Rakin had his back, but their daggers were nearly as useless as the backpacks. I turned to see a creature rake its claws across Raith's forearm, digging deep, blistering furrows that made him drop the dagger.

"Leave him alone." I threw another bolt of force that flung the creature into the air. It flew twenty feet and splashed into one of the lovely fire lakes that dotted the Pits. It laughed and crawled back out. Uh-oh.

The force also caught Raith, but only at the edge. It stumbled him sideways, where he tripped over the frolicking Chaos and hit his head against a rock, stunning him. Double uh-oh.

"Protect Elder," I yelled to Rakin. He nodded and ran toward the trio. He wouldn't offer much protection, but it got him out of my line of fire. The creatures had rightfully determined Lucifer to be the main threat and converged on him. A pile of ugly black-horned corpses lay at his feet, but the demons would overwhelm him eventually. They couldn't break through his armor, but they could drag him to the ground and get to his unprotected areas. He already had two on his pack, yanking at his back-plate and threatening to throw him off balance. Another thirty, at least, advanced on him.

I held out my hands and sent out force, trying to imagine the creatures tossed like autumn leaves while Lucifer remained immobile like the rock of holy goodness he represented.

This poetic sentiment failed miserably. Everything got caught in my blast. The creatures, Lucifer, loose rocks, and a salamander I hadn't even seen. The monsters went far, letting out howls of rage followed by splats of death as they hit boulders, stalagmites, and the ceiling. Lucifer, being heavier, didn't fly so much as slide across the ground, arms flailing. He refused to let go of his sword and almost sliced off his own head. Twice.

His path took him toward a lava pit. He was going to tumble into it. My hands still out, I tried to stop him, sending out a mental image of a rope. Before I even got the first strand formed, Chaos, chasing one of the creatures—

Fast chew toy

—ran behind Lucifer and clipped his legs. The Paladin stumbled forward and fell to his knees. He extended his hands to stop his fall and crushed two more of the creatures that pursued Chaos.

If nothing else, someone had named the dog well.

I ran up to Lucifer as he stood and put a hand on his head. "Are you okay?" The irony of my asking this was not lost on me.

"I shall reinspect the barracks, your Grace, to ensure my men are not continuing to hide whiskey."

"That's a good idea." I pointed to Raith. "Go speak to the commander there, and he will assist you."

"As you command." Lucifer walked toward Raith. I didn't know how he fought so well with his head messed up, but I suspected it was so ingrained he could have fought with his head *missing*. I didn't want to test that theory, so he could sit this one out. Chaos and I would deal with the rest. I hoped.

I first needed to keep the demons from bothering my huddled cohorts, with Lucifer reporting to a confused-looking Raith. I had no idea if Rakin could fight, but unless my half-brother had trained in secret, he possessed the combat acumen of a weak-kneed rabbit. I'm not sure whose bright compromise it was to leave the other Paladins behind, but if I ever found out, I might well slap them.

I needed to become the main threat. Chaos was the most significant threat—

Chewy chew toys

—and several of the demons chased after him, but he moved too quickly. Any he did let catch him quickly ended up as steaming piles of goo and leathery skin. So, I had to content myself with being the second threat. I could accept that.

"Right here, you little bastards," I shouted, lifting my hands. Lightning sparkled between them, and I felt invincible. A lovely sensation that everyone should get a chance to try. Several more demons turned their red eyes and sharp teeth my way. They advanced, claws held out, marching toward me like demented children. Or pages.

I smiled, picturing the beast in the lead as Crow, with his spiky hair and superiority complex. I would never kill the little twit, but these monsters made great proxies.

Twenty feet away, several of them bounded at me. I launched a bolt at the lead one. Lightning struck it, and it burst apart, splattering ichor everywhere and leaving behind a smell of tar and sulfur. The lightning arced to the next one with the same result. Ten of them blossomed like popping corn before the energy grounded into a stalagmite.

I laughed. This was easy. Five more launched toward me and met the same goopy fate.

I don't know how long this went on, but by the time the creatures stopped assaulting me, black blood spattered my clothes, face, and arms, and chunks of demons littered the ground. Chaos ran back to me, his tongue lolling and drooling, making a trail through the muck.

Let's do that again.

"Maybe later," I said. By later, I meant never, but he seemed so happy I didn't want to disappoint him. And for all I knew, another legion waited further in to oblige him. I turned to join the others. That's when my ankle reminded me it had been bitten.

"Gahhh," I said for the second time as I collapsed to the ground. I rolled up my pants to find a bloody and puffy ball of flesh with my ankle hidden somewhere beneath it. Dizziness hit me.

"Brawk, that looks bad," Timbers said as he landed next to me.

"Let's leave the obvious statements to Lucifer, can we?" I retorted. "I can't take it from more than one person."

Timbers bobbed his head, nodding.

The others walked up, awe written across their faces and emotions. Even the Oracle seemed impressed.

"That was incredible," Raith said. "You really are a demigod."

"I don't know about that," I said. I did know because ordinary people couldn't do what I just did. Still, I thought divinity should come with certain benefits, like being impervious to injury.

The Oracle knelt beside me and studied my swollen foot. She nodded as if secretly satisfied, and held out a hand. "Comfrey salve."

Mathra reached into her backpack and pulled out a squat, round pink jar. She handed it to the Oracle, who removed the lid. With three fingers, she scooped out a purple paste that gave off a scent of flowers and camphor. "This might hurt," she said, smiling.

She was right. As she rubbed the paste over the swollen skin, I gritted my teeth, refusing to say "gah" a third time. It hurt, but after the pain of the initial bite, it almost tickled. I pounded my fists on the ground and waited. The pain eventually subsided and I looked to find the swelling gone, leaving nothing but four jagged teeth marks.

"Bloodwort," the Oracle said, and another jar, this one bright red, appeared from the backpack. She applied the ointment, which for some reason smelled like buttermilk, and the wounds all but disappeared. "You *are* a demigod," the Oracle said, pointing at my healed leg. "That wouldn't have worked on a normal person."

Okay, that was a plus. I would rather not get hurt at all, but quick healing made it more bearable. "So, you always carry around jars of pastes to cure demigods, do you?"

"Of course not," she said. "This is the first time I've been anywhere in ten years." Here she glared at Timbers, who stared back with his impassive expression.

"So, you knew this was going to happen?" I asked.

"Of course."

"And you know everything else that's going to happen? How this is going to end?"

"Of course."

"So, you're going to tell me?"

She gave a wicked little smile. "Of course not."

"Right," I said. "Cosmic loophole."

She stood up. "No, that's not it."

I stood up too, then sat back down as the room spun. Apparently, my lightning spree had taken something out of me. "Oh, that's right. I have to ask the proper question, and you have to have cinnamon-lemon dust sprayed in your face."

"That's not it either. I just don't feel like telling you. It wouldn't be fair."

"Fair to who?" I asked, but she had already turned to Raith and checked his injured arm. As she tended to the blisters, Raith's eyes almost fell out of his head with adoration.

"Has she always been this infuriating?" I asked Timbers in a soft voice so she couldn't hear me. Then I realized that was stupid; she probably already knew what I was saying.

"Brawk! You have no idea."

I stood back up, slower this time. My head still wanted to float away, but the room didn't spin. I tested my ankle. No more pain. I could get used to this divinity thing, although I'd prefer it without the whole "having to rescue gods" part.

"We better get moving," I said. "We only have—" I looked back and was reminded we had gone only a hundred yards "—another eternity and a half to go." It wasn't a measurement, but it felt accurate.

As it turned out, the Pits only held one more surprise for us, but it was a doozy. Either we had killed all the demons, or my electrical display had scared them away. We suffered no more attacks. The heat was still oppressive, the fire still blazing, and the landscape as gloomy as a depressed monk, but after a mile, I began to cautiously let optimism slip into my thoughts again. I didn't say anything out loud, having learned how much Fate enjoyed spitting in my eyes, but I did allow hope to creep into my secret dreams.

Turns out Fate is a mind reader too.

"Is that the portal?" Raith asked, pointing to a speck of blue glowing against the black and orange. I never had figured out how he saw so well with such watery eyes, but he had always been more observant than me.

"I don't know," I said. I looked at the Oracle. "Will you deign to tell us, or do we have to go over there and hope it's not a will o'wisp with a bad attitude?"

She smirked at me. "That's the portal. Your destiny is through there."

"My destiny is sitting back home pretending none of this ever happened," I said. "But I guess I have to go through there before that happens."

We trudged toward the speck, which quickly grew larger until it looked like a door, if doors were oblong and glowed cyan.

We were a hundred feet away when the ground rumbled and split. Before anyone could say, "look at that giant hole," something large, black, and blazing burst from the ground. It looked like the other creatures that attacked us, only five times larger. Obviously, the daddy.

With a roar that shook my brain, it swung a hand as large as my body at us, making a wicked *whoosh* through the thick air. Everyone ducked except Chaos and the Oracle. The hand passed over the dog and smacked into the Oracle. She, in turn, slammed into a boulder with a squeal of pain and collapsed.

"Brawk!" Timbers said and flew toward her.

Lucifer reacted first, jumping up and whipping his sword out. He charged the beast, which made a backswing that would have sent the Paladin airborne like a bolt from a ballista.

It didn't connect. Blade met arm, and a gong sound rattled my teeth while a flash of light shut my eyes. I opened them when the demon roared, and I saw its arm lying on the ground, bouncing around, apparently unaware it was no longer useful. Lucifer stood before the monster. It towered twice his height and width, with eyes that promised death and teeth that offered pain.

I spread my hands and thought about the lightning. Nothing happened. I thought about it harder. Nothing continued to happen. Had I broken myself fighting all the demons? Or did I just need time I didn't have to regain power? I had no idea. I decided to try the force bolts again.

I didn't need to bother. Lucifer raised his sword, vengeance incarnate as the firelight reflected off his armor. "Ubel guides me," he shouted. Ubel was preoccupied, so Lucifer guided himself, but I wasn't inclined to tell him that. "You will not have the Divine One."

The creature roared and launched toward me, leaping right over the Paladin. Lucifer ducked, brought his hilt down to his waist, then thrust the sword up, jumping as he did so. *Heathensmasher* caught the demon in the chest and pierced the skin, again with searing light and gonging toll. The demon's speed carried it forward and down, the sword slicing it open like a cheese rind. By the time the monster landed five feet away from me, three-quarters of it lay split open, and unidentifiable but nasty bits of stuff splattered on the ground. The smell of...well, let's call it offal, swished around me, a mist of nasty. The creature stared at me for a moment, its red eyes dimming. It let out a feeble groan of fetid breath, and its eyes stopped glowing. It was dead.

Another groan sounded, this one soft and feminine. The Oracle. I ran over to find everyone gathered around her. Timbers sat on her chest, which moved slowly up and down. Mathra knelt beside her, a wet cloth pressed to the Oracle's head.

"Brawk! What do you mean 'who am I?' I'm your father."

The Oracle offered a weak smile. "That's silly. You're a bird. A bird can't be my father." She sounded younger, more innocent than she ever had.

"You transformed me into this after we argued."

She made a delicate *pfftt* sound with her lips. "I couldn't do that. I'm not a magician. I'm just a normal person."

"You're the Oracle," I said.

She looked at me. "You're very handsome. What's an Oracle?"

"Here," Mathra said, the first word had spoken since this trek began. She held out a pewter cup. "Drink this. You'll feel better."

The Oracle, or whoever she was now, drank the green liquid, which smelled like bananas. She smiled. "That tastes good. I think—"

We didn't know what she thought because she fell straight into sleep.

Mathra regarded us. "She is not the Oracle anymore. She is just a young lady, like everyone else." Here she gave a Medusa gaze to Timbers. "Just like she always wanted to be."

Timbers hopped from foot to foot, and a few feathers popped out and floated in the air. "We decided together."

"No, you coerced her and made her think it was her decision. She eventually figured that out, or don't you remember?"

"Then how come my wife isn't a bird too?"

"Because she apologized, something you never managed because you decided it was better to leave than own up to what you did."

Timbers flapped his wings, and another shower of feathers drifted out. Much more of this, and he would be bald. "She knew this was going to happen. She wanted it to happen. Why didn't she tell me how to change back?"

The smile Mathra offered Timbers should have turned the Pits into a glacier. "I guess she didn't want you to know."

She put her arms under the ex-Oracle and, proving far stronger than she appeared, picked up the girl. Her blue eyes fell on me. "You seem nice enough. Good luck."

"Thanks."

She turned and walked back across the pits.

"Brawk! I can't believe she would do that to me."

"I'm sorry," I said, although I couldn't help but feel Timbers had brought his fate upon himself. That thought made me feel bad because I liked the captain. "If we survive this, I'll help you find a cure."

"Brawk! Thank you," he said, though he didn't sound encouraged.

"Shouldn't we follow her?" Raith said, watching his chance at a girl-friend disappear. "Make sure she's okay."

"No. I imagine the Oracle looked far enough ahead to know they would get out safely." I turned and stared at the portal, its dark blue glow inviting and terrifying me. With courage I really didn't feel, I said, "Let's go. I've got a half-brother's ass to kick."

25

I stepped through the portal and found myself in another room of stone walls and felt glad for something familiar after the Blazing Pits. Chaos followed on my heels, almost bowling me over in his eagerness. I waited for the others to come through.

And waited.

After what felt like a minute, I grew concerned. Had something happened after I left?

"They're not coming," a familiar voice said. I turned and found Pimp—Ublek, my half-brother, standing twenty feet away. Having built him up in my mind, he was a disappointment in person. His face was as pockmarked as my visions, but he didn't loom over me, floating in empty air. He stood on the floor, like me, and rather than large and towering, as I expected, he was short and thin. He wore a black tunic and pants, naturally, with a skull embroidered on the breast in silver thread. A skull buckle fastened his leather belt around his waist, and tiny bones hung from chains wrapped around his high leather boots. A gold skull gleamed from his left ear.

I thought he was rather overdoing the whole skull motif.

"If you've hurt them—"

"Oh, shut up," he said. "They're fine. I don't care anything about them." He saw the dog sitting next to me. "Chaos, come here."

Bad master.

Yeah, I kind of figured that one out already. "He's my dog, now. Actually, he's his own dog, and he can do what he wants."

"Isn't that sweet?" Pimple said, disgust thick as the oil on his skin. "Fine, you can have him. I can just get another one from Phoebe. Let's fight."

"No, we can talk first," I offered. He didn't appear impressive, but he was a demigod, and I saw what he did when he put his mind to it. I impressed myself with what I managed after only a day. I suspect having several years of practice gave him an advantage.

He shrugged. "If you want." He smiled, and I recalled how the Archbishop had looked at me so long ago when this began. I shivered.

"I'm going to kill you," he said in the same way he might say *I'm going to eat a piece of cake*. "You know that, don't you?"

"I know you're going to try," I said. *And most likely succeed*, I thought, but he didn't need that sort of encouragement.

He waved his hand, and a pair of wooden stools appeared. I jumped as if a snake had popped up beside me and Ublek laughed. So much for a brave front. Ublek took a seat; I remained standing. He might be trying to catch me off guard.

He smiled again as if he knew what I thought. "You could have avoided this. All you had to do was turn back and never come here."

Despite my fear, I laughed. "I've been trying since this fiasco started. All I've wanted to do this whole time is turn back."

"But you didn't," Ublek said, agitated. "Despite all my warnings, and my clever omens, and my welcoming committee—"

"Welcoming committee? You mean the people who called themselves Scions of Ublek."

"Catchy name, don't you think?"

"They killed my Paladin friends and almost killed my brother. They were fanatical psychopaths."

He shrugged again and pushed a lock of blond hair off his greasy forehead. "I say welcoming committee; you say fanatical psychopaths. And you shouldn't interrupt; that's very rude."

"That doesn't sting as much coming from you as other people."

He ignored me. "Despite giving you every opportunity to back out, you kept coming. You whined and moaned about it, and believe me, I got tired of hearing *that*, but *you kept coming*. Why is that?"

I stood there gobsmacked. He was right. I could have turned back. All this time, I thought things conspired against me to prevent it. Lucifer and Elder forced me to go at the insistence of the Archbishop, who knew all along what I was. Then they dragged me with them on the quest to find the Oracle. But all it would have taken to end it was me sticking to my refusal to go forward. To say no and mean it. I kept going because I didn't have the will to not go.

I ended up here because I couldn't stick to my own convictions. It was a disturbing realization, but not one I was about to reveal to Pimple. "I came to free my father."

"I would have let him go if you had turned back." He shrugged again. "I only kidnapped him to get you to start on the journey. I didn't expect you to finish it." He shrugged once more. I began to suspect it was a nervous habit. "I guess we have to fight."

"I could still go away," I said. "Let Ubel go, and I'll leave, and everything will be good."

He shook his head, and regret tinged his speckled face. "Too late now. You're in the Chaos, so your power will manifest. If you had turned away, I would be the only one to inherit father's power, and turning away would have been a refusal of your gift."

"How could I refuse a gift I didn't know I was getting?"

"You couldn't know, or your power would manifest whether you refused or not. Only by you unknowingly refusing would you lose your power."

"The power I didn't know I had?"

Pimple nodded.

"And I thought the Cosmic Loophole was a goofy concept," I said. "So, if I had refused, then—"

"Then all the power would have come to me," Pimple said. He stood up, and the chair flew across the room, despite him not touching it. "It *should* have come to me. I'm not what you'd call a sharing person."

"You're not what I'd call a sane person."

He offered a chilling smile. "That may be. What I *am*, however, is the firstborn, and you're in the way of my inheritance. Time to change that." Thunder rumbled through the room and Ublek's eyes turned red. "Teatime is over. Prepare to choke on your own entrails."

I gulped. That didn't sound like a particularly pleasant fate.

I brought my hands up, ready to bring on lightning and force. They were my only tricks.

The thunder grew louder, the floor shook, and the walls suddenly split apart, raining dust upon us. I had no idea what was happening. I looked at Ublek, and he appeared as confused as I felt.

"What's going on?" he said.

"It's your plane," I shouted back. "You tell me."

The walls disappeared, and we both stood on fine brown sand. I heard the noise of a crowd chanting and thought I was back at the Oracle's, but a glance around showed we were somewhere far larger than the Oracle's stadium. The floor where we stood could have swallowed five of her arenas. We were in the center of a round, open building that rose at least a hundred feet into the air. People filled the building, sitting on stone bleachers, looking down at us and cheering. It was random noise, rising and falling like a wave. All the people had colored triangle flags, many red, far fewer yellow, and they waved them back and forth.

"What is this?" Ublek screamed at the air.

A shimmering yellow light appeared in a special seating area on the lowest level of the arena, soon replaced by the gods, all except Ubel. They sat there, dressed in fine togas, each a different color. Phoebe wore bright yellow, and her blonde hair curled in ringlets to her waist. A puppy and a kitten sat on her lap, wrestling playfully.

"We've come to watch," she said, and her voice echoed across the arena, silencing the crowd, although they kept waving their strange banners. "There hasn't been a game like this in a long time."

"This is between me and Briar."

"Briar and me," I said.

"Shut up," he yelled at me, his eyes glowing. He looked back at the gods. "This is a personal matter. We don't need an audience."

"Don't need or don't want?" Titanicus asked in his rumbling, oceanic voice. "Want to keep it to yourself? What a greedy little snit you are."

"Greedy?" Ublek stormed up toward the seats. The gods towered over him physically and metaphorically, but they didn't cowl him. I admired his bravery even as I wondered at his idiocy. He and Lucifer had a lot in common. "What's greedy about wanting your birthright?"

Titanicus made a sound like a tidal wave crashing to shore. I think it was his version of *harrumph.* "It's greedy when you kidnap your father and want to kill your brother to claim something that was already yours. But I think I speak for all of us when I say 'thank you.'"

"For what?"

All the gods grinned. "You'll see," Phoebe said.

This is not good, a kind voice said in my head.

Ubel, I thought. *Are you okay?* You've never done strange until you've asked after the health of a god.

Yes, but—

"You two stop talking to each other," Ublek shouted at me. I felt his mental slap, but either it was weak, or I was getting stronger. I could still feel Ubel in my head. "Enough delays. Let's end this."

"Not yet," Parsimony said from his spot next to Titanicus. He watched us, his eyes glittering like the gold that lay on a pile in front of him. He wore a dark green toga embroidered with mystical symbols in gold thread.

"Arrgghh. What now?" Ublek stamped his foot. Who knew evil was prone to tantrums?

"Ladies and gentlemen," Parsimony said, sounding much like the disembodied voice from the Oracle's. "In this corner," a misnomer since we were in a round arena, "standing five foot six inches and weighing a hundred and twenty pounds, the Petulant Pounder, the Greedy Grinder, and the Pockmarked Terror. The one, the only, Ublek, son of Ubel."

The crowd took up their screaming chants again, most cheering, some booing. The red flags waved as if a gale-force wind had seized them. The yellow flags stilled.

This went on for fifteen seconds while Ublek fidgeted, obviously ready to tear into me.

"And in this corner," Parsimony said. "Standing five foot seven inches and weighing a hundred and twenty-five pounds—" Hah, I was taller and heavier than my divine brother, "the Whining Wonder, the Sarcastic Snot, Mister I Wanna Go Home. The one, the only, Briar of Frostishak, son of Ubel and some mortal woman."

"Her name is Stella," I shouted, but no one heard me over the cheers and boos. The red flags stopped, and the yellow ones entered their frenzied wave. Seeing my flags outnumbered at least two to one hurt, but I was on Ublek's home turf. I assumed. At this point, I wasn't certain *where* I was.

"And now," Parsimony continued. "No more betting. The main event begins. Gentlemen, and I use the term with great irony, fight."

"Finally," Ublek said. He flung his hands out, and a glob of glowing greenish-yellow light flew toward me, the world's biggest divine loogie. Before I could react, it slammed into my chest, lifted me in the air, and dropped me to the ground. I couldn't breathe. I knew every rib had been cracked like a stale breadstick. Ublek would come over and finish me off now. At least it had ended quickly.

Old master chew toy.

I stared at the space above me. It didn't look like sky so much as nothing. I heard Chaos run away from me. Then I heard Ublek say, "stupid dog," followed by a sizzle and a canine yelp.

That wouldn't stand. Ublek could hurt me, but I wouldn't have him harming a defenseless, or at least out-powered, dog. I took a breath, which felt like sucking sand through a reed, but I did it. I sat up. My ribs weren't broken, but I suspected a snotball-shaped bruise in my future.

Chaos lay unmoving in the sand, twenty feet away from Ublek. "Leave him alone," I screamed and flung my hand out. Force shot toward Ublek. He waved his hand like chasing away a gnat, and my bolt ricocheted away from him, came back at me, and slapped me like a courtier challenging me to a duel. I fell backward, my head ringing. The crowd cheered, and Ublek took a bow. My already low spirits sank past the depths of despair to chart their own territory. I was doomed. Anyone, most especially me, who thought I could be any sort of savior had to be insane.

Ubel chose that moment to speak up again. *You can't beat him alone. You need the others to help you.*

Great plan, but they seem to have been left behind.

You don't need them, Ubel said. *You just need their strengths.*

How do I get that?

Think about it. He left.

Great. I teetered on the precipice of death, hanging by my fingers, and Ubel would let me plummet with a riddle on my mind. How could I get the strength of my companions without them here? *Think about it,* Ubel said. Think about what, how much I wish I could teleport them, and maybe an army, to help me?

It hit me much like Ublek's snot bolt had, only with less pain and more enlightenment. I could read my companions' thoughts and emotions, and I could control their emotions, so perhaps I could absorb them. I might not be able to physically teleport them to me, but if I could figure out what gave each person their power, I could borrow it for myself. I was a demigod; it should be as easy as wearing someone else's clothes.

It better be, or I was a *dead* demigod.

"Get up," Ublek said. "I won't have it said I killed an opponent on his back."

"Then I'll just lie here a second if that's okay," I shouted back.

"It's not." I felt something under me. A giant hand. It lifted me off the ground and stood me like I was a poppet owned by a deranged child. The hand began to squeeze.

"It's going to be fun to watch your head pop like a zit," Ublek laughed.

"Something you know all about," I wheezed out.

He stopped laughing. "That was mean."

As opposed to crushing me like a python, which was all fun and games. I had to think quickly, which is not easy to do with an invisible hand treating you like a bellows. I needed to break the grasp.

I needed Lucifer. His strength was strength. And fanatical devotion, but I didn't see that aiding right now. I thought about him, his incredible power, and asked him to lend it to me.

As the Divine One wishes, I heard in my head. A rush of energy followed, running up from my toes, filling my legs, coursing through my abdomen, and stuffing my arms. I didn't appear any bigger, but I felt immense. I also felt bruising pressure in my head and lungs that had nothing to do with strength and everything to do with imminent death by compression.

I flexed, pushing out with my arms. The hand gave a little, and I could breathe again. I pushed again, putting everything into it. The hand burst apart, energy shattering at my effort. Ublek reeled from the backlash, stumbling. Cheers from my fans, or at least those who bet on me, exploded from the stands.

Sucking in deep breaths, I smiled. I had always known how strong Lucifer was, but this was the first time I had ever really *known* it. No wonder he had so much self-confidence.

Confidence was something else I needed. Mentally I might be a challenge for Ublek, but it was apparent we weren't going to suddenly break out into a game of chess. He could still destroy me, and I needed to believe I could beat him. I needed someone who believed in me more than I did. That was pretty much everyone, but Elder perhaps the most. He was the one who forced me to continue even when—especially when—I didn't want to. He was a pain in the rear, but for a good reason. I reached out to him. *Believe in me.*

I do. We all do.

Another flood of energy hit me, different but no less effective. I could win this. I had to win this.

"So, the little demigod wants to play," Ublek said. He pulled his arm back and flung it forward, like throwing a ball for a dog to fetch. Another glob of glowing mucus appeared and hurtled toward me.

I spread my arms and thought of Raith, the half-brother who had always protected me. Who had almost given his life for me. He was my shield. Without even asking for it, his energy plunged into my brain. A wall of shimmering blue appeared before me. Ublek's missile splattered against it, smashing into a gloppy green mess. "That's disgusting," I said.

"Then try this," Ublek shouted. He spread his hands, and sizzling blue lightning danced between them. I knew this trick. It would go right through the shield.

Can I fly? I asked Timbers.

Brawk!

As Ublek fired, I jumped into the air. I soared ten feet as the blue bolt struck where I once stood and turned the sand into a three-foot sheet of glass. I aimed myself and flew toward Ublek. I almost flapped my arms before I realized I didn't have to. I was glad; that would have looked ridiculous.

The look of surprise on my half-brother's face was almost worth everything I had gone through.

It felt even better when I landed before him and smashed my fist into his face. Alone, it would have had the impact of being accidentally bumped by a bee. With the strength of my friends behind me, it knocked Ublek flat, and blood poured from his nose. That was a surprise since you don't expect gods to bleed.

I didn't waste my advantage. I straddled him, my hand inches above his face, and brought up a ball of lightning.

"Please don't," he said. And then he started crying.

But he was evil, so I immediately suspected a trick. He was trying to get me to feel sorry for him. And dammit, I did. But I played tough. "Give me one reason I shouldn't kill you."

"We're...we're brothers," he blubbered.

"Yeah, I've felt all that brotherly love since we first met."

"I'm sorry," he said. "I was...I was," he swallowed. "I was..."

"A stutterer?"

"Jealous."

That rocked me back. Literally, I fell backward on my butt, landing at Ublek's feet. The lightning disappeared from my hand. If my half-brother was playing a trick, now was his chance to act. But he just laid there. Sobbing.

"Jealous? Of what? You're a god, and I'm a scribe in a nowhere town on a nowhere island. I wouldn't expect a one-eyed swamp rat to be jealous of me."

He moved. I got ready to strike, but he just sat up and wiped a black sleeve across his nose. "You existed. I was jealous because you existed. And because you were all father could talk about. How proud he was of you. How smart you were, and how he couldn't wait until you were of an age to come into your power. I got sick of it. I wanted all the power for myself, so I decided to do something about it."

"Decided..." I stopped for a whole ten seconds, trying to absorb the information. "So, you kidnapped our father, got several people pulled from their homes to go on a quest, and got a score or more people killed. All because you were jealous?"

"I may have overreacted."

"You think?"

He frowned. "It's all your fault, really. If you had turned away—"

"Yes, we've gone through that already. You know what Raith and I do when we have a disagreement? We talk about it. That's what non-psychotic people do."

While we spoke, the crowd had been growing restless. They booed, and goblets flew from the stands to land at our feet.

"Finish fighting," Parsimony said, and the other gods murmured their agreement. "Someone has to win, so I can collect."

I stared at Ublek. He had stopped crying. He no longer looked like a bastion of evil, only a confused kid who wasn't sure about his future and where he fit in. Or maybe that was just me. In any case, I didn't want to fight him anymore. I just wanted to go home. "It's up to you. I have the power now. We can fight and end this nastily, or you can let Ubel go, and I'll go home, and we never have to see each other anymore."

"You won't use the power to create your own cult of worshipers and try to take over the world and usurp the power of the gods?"

"Interesting idea, but it hadn't even crossed my mind. I'm not much into having people fawn over me. Just ask Lucifer."

Ublek smiled. He looked to the gods. "We're not going to fight. I've changed my mind."

The crowd disappeared in a blink, bringing a vacuum of silence that almost hurt my ears. The gods didn't seem happy, and I wondered if they would turn on us. But then they glanced from one to the other, brows furrowing in concentration. A strange, almost painful buzzing went through my head. Images nearly formed but wouldn't come into focus. I got a headache.

Then the gods turned toward us, and the headache went away. Titanicus spoke this time, and I could almost smell the ocean's salt as he spoke. "Thank you for the distraction. You've done well. We can finish the rest." With that, he clapped his hands, and the sand swirled around us, obscuring everything. I shielded my eyes until it died down after a few seconds. I spit grit out of my teeth.

"What did that mean?" I asked.

"I don't know," Ublek said, but I felt he wasn't being sincere.

"I'm glad we ended this without anyone dying. You going to release father now?"

Ublek snapped his fingers. Nothing happened. "He's free."

"I'm just supposed to believe you."

I'm free, Ubel said. He appeared in my mind's eye, looking better than he had before.

We need to talk, I said.

Yes, we do. About many things. But it needs to wait. First, I must deal with my wayward son.

I could tell from Ublek's expression he heard it too. I imagine it would involve more than a spanking and time standing in a corner. "But I really—"

We'll talk soon.

Before I could say anything else, I found Chaos and myself standing in the stone room with everyone else. The portal was gone, and everyone except Rakin was unconscious. I looked at the ceiling. "We better talk."

Nobody answered.

I shook my head. "That's just rude."

26

A god's idea of "soon" is not the same as a normal person's.

Rakin and I woke everyone. They all recounted the experience of hearing me talk to them and then passing out. They had no memory of exactly what I asked them, which was probably just as well. I did tell them they were instrumental in helping me win the day, and they seemed to accept that.

The return trip was nowhere near as difficult. Amazing how easy traveling is when you don't have a psychopathic deity dogging your every move. We stopped by the Oracle's, but it had been abandoned. A note lay on a table addressed to Timbers. I opened it for him and, although I shouldn't have, I read behind him as he bobbed left and right, taking it in with his one good eye. I could hear the Oracle's musical voice speaking the words as I read them:

Father, if you are reading this, everything I predicted has come to pass. Briar, congratulations on peacefully resolving your problems with your half-brother. Too bad it's only the beginning. Dad, I never wanted to be an Oracle, and I can't really forgive you for forcing me into it, no more than mom can. However, you've probably suffered enough, so I'll tell you how you can change back.

Just kidding. You need to stick to crackers and perches for a while longer. But there will come a day when you'll see me again. I won't know you and will be able to help you then. Don't expect an explanation right now. It's too difficult, and I've got to finish directing Mathra on what to pack so we all survive the coming ordeal. And yes, I could have avoided getting hit, but I chose not to. You've probably figured that out already.

Take care of yourself. You too, Raith. And Briar, you shouldn't read other people's letters. That's as rude as interrupting them.

TIMBERS TURNED and glared at me. I looked away, heat in my cheeks. He muttered and waddled away. I kept my mouth shut.

Timbers gave us a ride back on his ship, and we regaled the crew with tales of our adventures. I don't know that they believed half of what we told them, but I was no longer Pukeboy. I kept everyone except Lucifer from calling me Holy Briar or Divine Briar. To most of them, I was just Briar, which was fine. They were much kinder to me, and I didn't mind that.

We came home to zero fanfare. No one actually expected us to make it back, but once they realized we had, the Church decreed a celebration. They took down our funeral wreaths and black tapestries and replaced them with more festive, but equally gaudy, decorations. Our parents had to put the furniture back in our bedroom, which my mother turned into a sewing room after a suitable period of mourning, which apparently was soon after our body heat left the bed. She was pleased to see us alive and well. My "father" was pleased to see Raith alive and well. Raith and I kept silent on my actual parentage, but I'm sure my father still knew something wasn't right.

I considered confronting my mother about her indiscretion but couldn't work up the nerve. She seemed so happy to have us back that I saw no sense in ruining it. I would wait and speak to Ubel about it. Hopefully, he could explain it all to my satisfaction.

But the months came and went with no contact from my father. I tried speaking to him. I tried speaking to Ublek. No response.

Otherwise, things returned pretty much to normal. The swamp I had missed so much on my journey quickly reminded me why such feelings were misplaced. It was as hot and wet and miserable as ever, something I had conveniently forgotten in my time away.

In recognition of my service to the Church, I was made head scribe, which got me a wage I could almost live on. It also got me the services of a personal page. With a wicked glee, I chose Crow for the duty. Rakin showed a propensity for letters and became an apprentice scribe and my best friend. Well, he was my only friend, but that was enough.

A YEAR PASSED before I heard anything from my divine relatives. Raith and I were standing in the training yard watching Crow clean up the melons Lucifer had recently hacked to bits. He threatened to tell the Archbishop I was abusing my power, but a low growl from Chaos put a stop to that.

"Trust me," I told the page, "you wouldn't want me abusing my real power."

Raith picked up his sword and swung it at a leftover melon, splattering Crow with it. Puberty had attacked Raith with a vengeance. He had sprung up to just shy of six feet. His muscles had filled out so he was almost a quarter of Lucifer's size, his voice had dropped so low he sang bass in the church choir, and he had to visit the town barber for a shave twice a week. Annoyingly, he had dreams of going to find the Oracle someday. "She's my soulmate," he would swoon, "and we are meant for each other."

"Soul*sucker*," I would mutter, but never where he could hear me. It was a harmless enough dream, and I knew eventually, one of the village girls would catch his eye and make the Oracle a distant memory. I had such plans myself, but so far, none of the girls would even look at me, much less talk to me. Some things never change.

"What do you want to do today?" I asked Rakin and Raith since we had a free day.

I never found out their plans. Before they could say anything, Ublek appeared in a bright light and a pop sound. Crow saw it, his eyes rolled up in his head, and he fell into a pile of melons.

"What—" I started.

"No time for that," Ublek said. "Father's been kidnapped. I mean really kidnapped."

"Who—"

"The other gods have taken him."

"Why—"

"Stop with the twenty questions. I'll explain on the way. Short version —the gods are going to remake the world in their image, which will destroy every living thing on it. We have to stop them."

I fainted, landing right next to Crow.

THE END

ABOUT THE AUTHORS

Steve Murphy has spent much of his life in uniform, starting with four years in the Navy, then a stint in the Army National Guard, followed by 23 years as a police officer, 9 of those as a SWAT sniper.

So naturally, he writes science fiction, fantasy, and space opera. This is his third novel, with several more in the works with Paul. In addition to writing, Steve has also worked as a consultant and set decorator for the film industry. Steve is an outdoor enthusiast who enjoys camping, back-packing, whitewater, sailing and motorcycle riding. The father of two boys, now grown men, Steve lives somewhere in North Carolina with his wife and two dogs.

Paul Barrett has had multiple careers, including rock and roll roadie, theater stage manager, mortgage banker, and support specialist for Microsoft Excel.

This eclectic mix allowed him to go into his true love: motion picture production. He has produced two feature films and two documentaries. When not producing films, he works as a script supervisor or props assistant. Amidst all this, Paul worked on his writing. This is his fifth novel, with more on the way. Paul is an avid board gamer, miniatures painter, movie enthusiast, and all-around nerd.

Paul lives in North Carolina with his graphic designer husband and three furry overlords.

Paul and Steve have been friends since 1980, enduring the rough and tumble of life through thick and thin.ince 1980,

MORE FROM THESE AUTHORS

Paul Barrett & Steve Murphy

Knights of the Flaming Star

Knight Errant

Knight Ascendant

Paul Barrett

The Malaise Falchion

The Saga of the Necromancer

A Whisper of Death

A Cry of Decay

FRIENDS OF FALSTAFF

Thank You to All our Falstaff Books Patrons, who get extra digital content each month! To be featured here and see what other great rewards we offer, go to www.patreon.com/falstaffbooks.

PATRONS

Dino Hicks
John Hooks
John Kilgallon
Larissa Lichty
Travis & Casey Schilling
Staci-Leigh Santore
Sheryl R. Hayes
Scott Norris
Samuel Montgomery-Blinn
Junkle

www.ingramcontent.com/pod-product-compliance
Lightning Source LLC
Chambersburg PA
CBHW050202120726
47903CB00002B/724